About the editor

Maxim Jakubowski was born in Barnet but brought up in Paris. He followed a career in publishing by opening the Murder One bookshop in London in 1988. He writes, edits and publishes in many areas of genre fiction, including SF and fastasy, mystery and erotica. He is an official adviser to several international film festivals, writes for a variety of publications including the *Observer*, the *Daily Telegraph* and the *Guardian*, and reviews crime in a monthly column in *Time Out*. He is also contributing editor to *Mystery Scene* and a winner of the the Anthony Award.

CHRONICLES OF CRIME

The Second Ellis Peters Memorial Anthology of Historical Crime

Edited by Maxim Jakubowski

HEADLINE

First published in 1999 by
HEADLINE BOOK PUBLISHING

10 9 8 7 6 5 4 3 2 1

ISBN 0 7472 7548 3

Typeset by Palimpsest Book Production Limited,
Polmont, Stirlingshire
Printed and bound in Great Britain by
Clays Ltd, St Ives plc

HEADLINE BOOK PUBLISHING
A division of the Hodder Headline Group
338 Euston Road
London NW1 3BH
www.headline.co.uk
www.hodderheadline.com

TABLE OF CONTENTS

Introduction

A few years have now passed, all too quickly, since the death of Ellis Peters. Crime writers and readers throughout the world still mourn her and sigh sadly at the prospect of no further adventures for that most beloved of Benedictine monks, Brother Cadfael. But the influence of her writing keeps on spreading, and at the cusp of the Millennium, the historical mystery genre stands stronger than ever as more and more writers embrace the field for its capacity to tell wondrous, gripping stories, to educate and entertain.

In 1999, recognition of Edith Pargeter's achievements as Ellis Peters was highlighted by the publication of *Past Poisons*, the first volume of this anthology, in which many leading British and American mystery writers paid homage to her influence. This was followed by the Crime Writers' Association decision to create a new annual Dagger award for excellence in the field of historical crime. The first, popular winner was Lindsey Davis, for her Falco novels set in the bustling world of ancient Rome. Lindsey was, of course, present in *Past Poisons*, and was in fact instrumental in inspiring me to launch this series in memory of Ellis Peters.

Once again, I have asked some of my favourite writers in the crime and mystery genre to contribute new stories with an historical setting, and the sheer time span and breadth of geographical locations conjured up by their imaginations is astounding, ranging from Ancient Egypt and Rome to suffragette times, with a nod in passing to gothic horror, westerns and amazing variations on known themes and dastardly deeds.

I am quietly confident that Edith, had she still been alive, would have relished these colourful tales of puzzlement and adventure. I'm sure you will. Enjoy.

Maxim Jakubowski

The following tale of blood and murder is set in the West Country. True, this is not the Shrewsbury of Ellis Peters, with its wood-filled valleys haunted by the ghost of Cadfael. Nevertheless, I hope the great author would have enjoyed this tale of mystery set in a medieval tavern in those heady, busy days in Gloucester towards the close of the eighteenth century. When touring Cadfael country recently I stopped at many of the old 'taverns' along the Welsh border; they inspired this story.

Paul C. Doherty

The Musket Ball

Paul C. Doherty

Squire Trelawney was murdered just as the bells of Gloucester Cathedral tolled out over the city, a sign to its inhabitants that the 18th October 1768 had at last dawned. Both God and Mammon demanded their return to work. Squire Henry Trelawney, however, was not intent on work. He had lodged at the spacious White Hart tavern which stood on the corner of an alleyway just off the cathedral square. According to all the witnesses available, Trelawney was intent on coming downstairs to fill his large paunch with bacon, kidneys, crumpets, the finest sausages and a plate of eggs. A fleshly man, Squire Trelawney; his dark, curly wig framed a fat, rubicund face; he left his chamber at the usual time, came to the top of the stairs and coughed. A maid cleaning the passageway beneath, glimpsed his black, shiny buckle shoes, snow-white stockings and blue woollen cloak. She then moved away. The customers in the taproom were busy on their own affairs, either ordering breakfast or finishing it. A coach had pulled up outside and more guests were arriving. A busy, friendly scene; not the place, nor the time, Squire Henry Trelawney expected to be called to make his final account.

Whenever he came to Gloucester, Henry Trelawney hired the Lion Chamber on the first gallery with its large four-poster bed, chest of drawers, paintings on the clean-washed walls and the finest turkey carpets on its shining floor-boards. A man of property, Squire Trelawney: he owned a fine house just outside Cheltenham with fertile fields and well-stocked barns, whilst he invested money in the East India Company and in even riskier ventures. Some termed them piracy, others, 'merchant venturing' in South America and the Carolinas. A bachelor born and bred, Squire Trelawney did like the ladies, however. A young courtesan had dined with him the previous evening then left in the early hours: she was the best measure of Squire Trelawney's view of womankind.

'Like horses,' he would trumpet. 'They are to be ridden and whipped!'

Few dared disagree. Trelawney was a vicious man with all the arrogance of Lucifer; he would take a wrong look as the gravest insult. He had powerful friends, both at court and amongst the Whig party in the Commons. People whispered how, twenty-three years earlier as a colonel in a regiment of Hessians, Squire Trelawney had done good service against the Jacobites of Scotland. He had not only taken part in the massacre at Culloden but swam most vigorously in the sea of blood which ensued. Indeed, in some parts of the highlands, they still talked about the 'Terrors of Trelawney', his blue-coated, white-fronted Hessians, who seemed to have no fear of either God or man. Trelawney had hunted down rebels with bayonet, sword, fire and noose. He'd shown no mercy to man nor beast: wherever he went, devastation and death trailed close behind. Trelawney had turned his hand to bloody deeds which other English officers had refused to countenance. In doing so he had amassed a small fortune: treasure looted from Jacobite lords, whose corpses had been buried in Scottish bogs, or who had been hanged near the cross in some market town or who, if they were more fortunate, had followed Charles Stuart back to France.

After there were no more Jacobites to kill, Trelawney had moved to Cheltenham, buying up an old estate and refurbishing it for his own pleasure. A local justice of the peace, God help any poacher, highwayman or other malefactors who appeared before Trelawney. A hanging judge, the squire would eat and drink, slurping from his large-bowled wine cup as he sentenced the guilty to their fate.

Every autumn Squire Trelawney spent a month in Gloucester, attending different balls and functions before travelling south to Bath and then on to meet old cronies in London. Squire Trelawney was always on good form. The landlord of the White Hart, Thomas Neville, was terrified out of his wits of him and spent all his waking hours worrying about Squire Trelawney and his various needs. Nevertheless, Trelawney always paid well and, when he left, tipped most generously.

On that particular morning he must have left his chamber as usual, his black tricorne hat keeping his heavy wig firmly in place. A travelling preacher, Samuel Butler, not to mention Lady Georgina Fitzherbert, an old lady also on her travels, declared they had heard the click of his cane as he marched along the gallery to the top of the stairs. Trelawney had started to make his way ponderously down the stairs. No one could precisely describe what happened next. They heard a crash: Trelawney, joined by his hat, wig and cane, came tumbling down the long narrow staircase, landing with a bone-jarring crash on the paving stones below.

At first there was an eerie silence. Customers stared gaped-mouthed. Neville and two of the tap boys ran across to him. Trelawney was a tough old cock. He was not the first to fall downstairs. However, the

4

pool of blood seeping out of the hole in the centre of his forehead and a similar trickle running down the slack jaw, clearly informed them that Squire Trelawney had, at last, gone to meet his Maker.

By chance, a physician, Matthew Dudley, was staying in the tavern. A ship's surgeon, Dudley had had plenty of experience with wounds on His Majesty's frigate *Redoubtable*. He had the corpse lifted and, together with the wig, hat and cane, taken into a small, white-washed chamber off the taproom. Neville used to rent this out to local businessmen for their meetings, now it served as a death house. The long, black polished table was cleared and the squire's corpse laid out. Dudley immediately told Neville that the room had to be guarded, and sent one of the tap boys running for the local coroner and city magistrate, Sir Peter Philsby. Philsby arrived a short while later, a number of city bailiffs in tow. He quickly interrogated Neville and summoned all the guests into the huge taproom.

'I am afraid, whatever your business, you must stay here for at least another day. Squire Trelawney has been murdered. A musket ball through his forehead and the culprit must be found.'

Now, that's where the mystery began. Matthew Dudley immediately took off his waistcoat, rolled up his sleeves, borrowed an apron from Mine Host and began the grisly work of extracting the musket ball from Squire Trelawney's head. A gruesome task. One of the chamber maids, bringing in a flagon of wine and some bread for the doctor's refreshment, took one look at the bloody, mangled corpse, Dudley's red-smeared hands, gave a small scream and promptly fainted. The rest of the customers seated in the taproom took this as a welcome relief from the tedium of the long wait. They protested and complained but Philsby informed them in no uncertain terms what an important personage Squire Trelawney had been; even ministers in London would demand answers about his death.

Shortly after ten, Dudley finished his grim task and met Sir Peter Philsby in an adjoining chamber. He handed a small bowl with its solitary content to the coroner.

'That's the musket ball,' Dudley declared, sitting down on a chair and mopping his brow with the edge of his apron.

Philsby picked it up and studied it curiously. 'This is old. A little larger than what we use now.'

He took the musket ball to the window and, holding it in the palm of his hand, examined it more closely. Philsby could see that it had been shot from a musket, slightly jagged and scored, then he noticed the strange markings.

'Dudley!' he declared. 'Damn me, if this ain't curious. Get Mine Host to send for Atherton, he's a gunsmith in Cathedral Lane. I want him to look at this.'

Until the gunsmith arrived a short while later, Philsby refused to comment any further. Huffing and puffing, Atherton was led into the chamber, a small leather bag clutched in one hand.

'I know what's happened,' he announced as Philsby handed him the musket ball. 'It's all over the city. Old Trelawney's been murdered so there's bound to be a hanging.'

'If there's to be a hanging we need the murderer,' Philsby retorted. 'Atherton, what do you make of this?'

The gunsmith took the musket ball, stared at it curiously, muttered to himself then fished in his leather bag. He took out a powerful eye-glass and once again closely examined the killing shot.

'It's a musket ball.'

'Most perceptive,' Philsby remarked drily.

'It's an old musket ball,' Atherton continued. 'It's definitely been fired. There are grains of powder in it, slightly scored and burnt. You see?' He lifted his head. 'When the ball's pushed down the barrel it has to be rammed in, don't care what it's made of it, always leaves a mark and carries grains of powder.'

'So?' Philsby sat on the edge of the bed and glared at this most lugubrious of gunsmiths. 'We know it's a musket ball, we know it's been fired from a pistol and we know it killed Squire Trelawney. What else, Atherton?'

'It's old,' Atherton repeated. 'Musket balls today are much smaller and the pistol or musket which fired it would also have been old.' He wagged a finger at the coroner. 'I'll tell you a bald fact: the musket which fired this, in a tavern such as the White Hart, well, it would thunder like a cannon shot!'

'Yes, yes,' The coroner replied testily. 'There have already been whispers about that yet no one heard a sound. But go on man, look at the musket ball, those markings?'

Atherton again stared at the offending object. 'It's not English. I've seen musket balls like this. It's German, used by some of His Majesty's regiments: Hanoverians and Hessians. There used to be some quartered in the area, though that was years ago.'

The coroner looked at Physician Dudley, who sat slouched, refreshing himself with a cup of canary.

'Wouldn't a musket ball like this go straight through a man's head?'

'Not necessarily,' Atherton replied briskly, 'particularly if it was an old pistol or musket. It would do its damage being lodged in the brain. Death would be fairly instant. I wager there would be blood trickling out of his nose and mouth.'

'Yes, quite,' Philsby snapped. 'Physician, are you sure this is the musket ball which killed our good squire?'

Dudley sighed and put the cup down. 'Let me show you myself.'

He took them to the death room and unlocked the door. Trelawney didn't look quite so pompous or fearsome. The plump red face had turned a ghoulish white. Little effort had been made to close the popping eyes or strap up the jaw. His fat cadaver sprawled on the table like meat on a butcher's stall, his quilted waistcoat and shirt soaked in blood. Some attempt had been made to clean the gore at the top of the table, whilst the squire's hat, wig and cane lay forlornly in a corner. The doctor grasped the dead man's head between his hands: in the centre of the forehead was a black, oozing hole.

'The musket ball penetrated fairly deep.' Dudley picked up a pair of pincers and pointed to the jagged skin and bone around the wound. 'Some of that's my work but the rest's the musket ball. He was definitely shot.'

Philsby took out his pince-nez and perched them on the end of his nose. He drew a deep breath and leaned over, following the physician's stubby finger around the yellowing scraps of skin fringing the wound.

Atherton, who'd left to be sick, now returned and leaned white-faced against the door. Dudley, however, was enjoying himself. 'After this I'm going to have a good steak and kidney pie,' he whispered.

'For God's sake man!' Philsby moaned. 'Tell us what you have to.'

'As our honourable gunsmith will inform us,' Dudley replied, picking at a small shard of skin, no longer or thicker than a fingernail. 'When a musket ball is fired, it is hot; nothing is more sensitive to burning than human skin. Now our good squire here received the ball in the centre of his forehead. The ball, as you have seen, is sharp and jagged in places and, propelled by the force of the powder, entered deep into the brain. So there you have your cause of death, Master Coroner.'

'Murder,' Sir Peter concluded.

'Very well, murder by a musket ball, fired from the top of the stairs, killing Squire Trelawney instantly.'

The coroner snatched his handkerchief from the cuff of his expensive shirt and dabbed at his lips. 'S'truth!' he whispered, walking to the door. 'I have had enough of the corpse. My good physician, we know the effect of the musket ball, but who shot it, how, where and why? Let me show you a real mystery!'

Philsby took Dudley and the gunsmith past the taproom to the bottom of the stairs.

'Look now!' He gestured. 'These stairs are steep and narrow, yes?'

Dudley agreed. Philsby patted the wooden balustrade fastened to the walls on each side by iron clasps.

'These stairs,' he continued, 'are like a shaft going down through the house.' He tapped at the walls on either side. 'Whoever goes down is protected to the left and right by sheer wall.' He then gestured at the ceiling. 'This, too, provides covering until you are almost at the top. Come!'

They reached the top of the stairs and stared back down. Dudley was the first to realise what the coroner was saying. The gunsmith looked puzzled.

'Let me explain.' The coroner smiled. He placed one hand on the newel of the staircase and went down a step. 'We know that Squire Trelawney reached at least this step: his shoes and stockings were glimpsed by a maid below. Others in the tavern distinctly heard the sound of his footsteps and the rattle of his cane.'

Philsby walked back up into the gallery and over to an iron milk-pail standing next to the door of the Lion Chamber. He took out the horse pistol which he'd asked to be placed there and sardonically bowed to the physician.

'My good doctor, pretend you are Squire Trelawney going down-stairs.'

Dudley obliged. Philsby told him to stop when he reached the second step.

'I will pretend to be the murderer.'

'Saints and sinners!' the gunsmith breathed. 'Sir Peter, I see the problem.'

'Do you now?' The coroner sighed. 'I see it too but not the solution. Squire Trelawney took the musket ball in his forehead. For that to happen the assassin must have been in front of him on the stairs. However, if that was the case, the maid would have seen the murderer, and more importantly, so would Squire Trelawney. Now, I assure you sirs, if I was going down to break my fast and I saw someone coming up the stairs towards me with a musket pointed at my head, I would raise the alarm. I would shout, scream, try to defend myself. Trelawney did none of these. The maid saw him at the top of the stairs. A few seconds later Trelawney's corpse came tumbling down. The assassin could not have stood at either side of this staircase; there's a brick wall on each side.'

'What if the murderer followed our squire to the top of the stairs, crouched down and softly called his name?' Atherton asked. 'The squire turned round, the assassin fired and our good squire fell dead.'

'We'll try that,' Philsby declared. 'If our noble physician could oblige?'

Dudley once again descended the stairs. Atherton, pretending to be the murderer, crouched down and called out. Dudley half turned. Atherton snorted in exasperation.

'There's the problem,' Philsby said, coming alongside. 'If you are going downstairs carrying a cane and you hear your name called, you stop, you look over your shoulder. If Trelawney did that, the ball would have entered his left or right temple. However, to take him where it did, Trelawney would have to turn round fully, a hard task: the stairs are narrow and very steep, Trelawney was an old man carrying a cane.

Have you ever seen anyone on a staircase turn completely round to face someone standing at the top?'

Atherton shook his head. Dudley rejoined them.

'And even if that did happen—' the physician started.

'—We come to the real problem,' Philsby interrupted. 'I have examined the top of the stairs most closely. I can detect no powder from a musket, whilst nobody in this tavern heard the crack of a shot. Listen to this!'

He went across to the iron milk-pail and took up the pistol, gesturing at Atherton and Dudley to draw closer.

'Listen now!'

Philsby pulled back the cumbersome hammer of the pistol and aimed into the thick, wet sand packed hard in the iron bucket. There was a crack like a small explosion, the smell of gunpowder and a billowing haze of greyish-blue smoke. The door to the Lion Chamber was flung open and one of the bailiffs came out, startled. A similar consternation rose from below stairs.

'It's all right! It's all right!' Philsby shouted. He went to the top of the stairs and peered down. 'Master Neville, Mine Host, tell our customers not to be frightened, I am only experimenting.'

The bailiff returned to the Lion Chamber and the customers in the taproom went back to their conversations. Sir Peter put the pistol down, leaned against the wall, crossed his arms and stared bleakly at his two companions.

'Here we have our good squire going downstairs to break his fast. We know there was no one on the staircase in front of Trelawney. Anyone who shot him from the foot of the stairs would have been seen by the host of customers and servants in the taproom. We know the good squire was shot in the forehead whilst he was on that staircase, though how is a complete mystery. If a musket was fired, then it was as if by magic! As you can hear, a pistol crack echoes like a cannon shot in this place.'

'Is it possible?' Dudley asked walking across to the Lion Chamber, 'that Squire Trelawney was shot elsewhere and his body tossed down the stairs?'

'We have the same problem,' Philsby replied. 'Squire Trelawney was an old soldier.' He tapped the door to the chamber. 'This was always securely locked. If Trelawney had an unexpected guest why didn't he object? Scream before the hammer was pulled? Moreover, if he was shot in his chamber or anywhere in this tavern, the noise would have woken the dead. Finally, the only blood I've found is on the stairs and, naturally, the corpse.'

'And Squire Trelawney was definitely alive this morning?' Atherton asked.

'Oh yes.' Philsby sniffed, coughing at the smoke which still swirled around the gallery. 'Half an hour before he made his fatal descent down the stairs, a maid brought up a hot cup of chocolate. She tapped on the door and Squire Trelawney answered it. The maid entered the room; there was no one else present, she was sure of that. The bed curtains were pulled back. Squire Trelawney took the cup of chocolate, squeezed one of the maid's tits, smacked her on the bottom and said that he would soon be down in the taproom and that his food, like his women, had better be hot.'

'Very well! Very well!' Dudley raised his hands in exasperation. 'I accept that Squire Trelawney was in the best of health when he left his chamber. The testimony of witnesses indicate there was no one on the staircase below him. The construction of that staircase means that our squire was protected on his right and left by bricks and plaster. Yet he must have been killed by a musket ball from the front though no one heard a sound. So,' Dudley raised a finger, 'the assassin must have been on this gallery, surely?' He walked down the narrow passageway and counted four other rooms. 'There is only one entrance to this gallery, isn't there?'

'That's correct.' Philsby confirmed. 'The tavern is built in a square: each side of it is served by a staircase like the one we have inspected. I accept your conclusion, Master Dudley: if the murderer was not in the taproom or on the staircase, he or she must have been somewhere up here.' He pointed to the Lion Chamber. 'When Trelawney was killed, four other guests were preparing to dress to go down to breakfast: an old lady, Georgina Fitzherbert; a merchant, Josiah Woodville; a pretty young thing, Lady Mary Castell, travelling to rejoin her family in Bristol; and one of those itinerant preachers, the Reverend Samuel Butler. They saw or heard nothing amiss. Lady Georgina Fitzherbert stoutly declared she heard the old rogue, for that's what she calls Squire Trelawney, leave his room; his heavy footfall and the rattle of his cane echoed along the gallery. I have asked all four to be detained separately from the rest.' He pushed open the door of the Lion Chamber. 'They are within.'

'Do you still need us?' Atherton whined.

'Yes I do!' Philsby snapped. 'Physician Dudley will be my witness and you can provide expert testimony. This will not take long.'

The four guests were waiting in the Lion Chamber, a spacious room with a window seat, a large four-poster bed, a gleaming oak wash-stand and fine, quilt-padded furniture. Philsby quickly made the introductions. Lady Georgina Fitzherbert was a small, stout, grey-haired woman with a podgy, stern face, black gleaming eyes and puckered lips. She was wrapped in a voluminous bath robe, and her resentment at being detained was obvious. Josiah Woodville was tall, with grey hair, parted neatly down the middle, falling to his shoulders. The merchant was dressed soberly in grey trousers, spotlessly clean

10

stockings and a maroon, three-quarter length jacket; his shirt and stock collar were a crisp white. He sat in the window seat neatly balancing a walking cane across his knee.

On a small couch was Lady Mary Castell. Physician Dudley admitted she was a beauty. She was apparently preparing to leave and was covered from neck to toe in a dark-blue riding coat, edged at the collar and cuffs with ermine. Her raven-black hair was piled high, held in place by jewelled pins and covered by a gauze veil. Light-blue eyes stared wistfully out: her high cheek bones, perfectly formed face and soft sweet mouth reminded the physician of a porcelain doll that one of his daughters owned.

The Reverend Samuel Butler was dressed in black from head to toe, the only contrast being his white stock collar neatly buttoned round his neck. He had riding boots on, spurs attached, and his cloak lay draped across his lap. In one hand he held a well-thumbed copy of a bible. A scholar's face, Physician Dudley thought, the dark hair neatly parted but cut short below the ears, brooding eyes and a slightly hooked nose above a harsh mouth and chin. He was clean-shaven; a composed, self-assured man. He regarded Philsby from head to toe and returned to the passage he was reading. None of the guests stood when Philsby entered the chamber, except for the bailiff sitting on a stool just within the doorway.

'I heard a pistol shot.' Woodville demanded. 'The bailiff says you are carrying out an experiment. Why is that, sir?'

'And why are we detained?' Lady Georgina trumpeted. 'I have yet to change and break fast.'

'Will we miss the coach?' Lady Mary Castell asked quietly. 'My family will be waiting.'

'Will they now?' Philsby smiled back. 'And pray, Madam, what family is that?'

'If you send a courier to Bristol,' the lady answered, 'my husband will assure you of our status and standing in the city.'

Philsby swallowed hard and quietly cursed. Now he recognised the name. Sir Reginald Castell was a well-known merchant and alderman of Bristol, with powerful connections in the Whig party, both in the south-west and London. Philsby gave her the most elegant bow.

'Madam.' He apologised. 'I regret the delay but, I promise you, the coach will be detained and I will personally assure your safe arrival in Bristol.'

'And what about me?' Woodville the merchant asked sardonically. 'I am to meet certain merchants at the Guildhall.'

'In which case, sir, you can take my personal apologies. I will ensure that any meeting you have missed will be rearranged at your convenience.'

Woodville bowed his acceptance.

'And I suppose I don't matter?' Lady Georgina got to her feet. 'I'm not to leave till Thursday to take the waters at Bath.'

Philsby walked across, took her hand and lightly kissed the tips of her fingers.

'Madam,' he soothed. 'Your assistance in this matter is vital. Before I leave, I shall ask Mine Host to see to your every comfort.'

Lady Georgina simpered and retook her seat.

'You seem in no hurry, sir.'

Philsby walked over to the preacher who sniffed and put his Bible down on a cushion beside him.

'My life and my time, sir, are in the hands of God.'

Philsby stared down at him. 'Are you a Quaker?' he asked.

'You can call me that, sir: I am a Christian spreading God's word.'

'Are you now?'

The preacher fished inside the pocket of his jerkin and brought out a neatly folded, yellowing piece of parchment.

'That's my licence to preach from the sheriffs of London.'

Philsby carefully unfolded the licence. He recognised the seal at the bottom and the flowery hand which gave permission to one Samuel Butler to preach in the shires both north and south of the Trent.

'I have other testimonials,' the preacher offered.

Philsby shook his head and handed the parchment back.

'You are, all of you,' he smiled around, 'what you claim to be. I am Sir Peter Philsby, coroner of this city. Early this morning, at around seven of the clock, Squire Trelawney was viciously murdered by a musket ball to his forehead. Death was instantaneous. We have established that Squire Trelawney came to the top of the stairs, intending to break his fast in the taproom below. A maid cleaning at the foot of the stairs glanced up and saw his shoes and stockings as well as the hem of his cloak.' Philsby lifted the tails of his coat, sat down on a chair and crossed his legs. He sighed like a justice coming to judgement.

'You have seen the staircase,' he continued. 'It's more of a shaft, brick walls on either side, each with a handrail, narrow steps and a roof which slopes high at the top, low at the bottom. We know Trelawney would not have turned on the stairs, yet his assassin was able to shoot him in the forehead.'

Philsby beat his hand against his knee in exasperation.

'The assassin was not on the stairs or below in the hallway whilst the staircase provides no angle for anyone to shoot. All we can deduce is that, somehow or other, the assassin got in front of Squire Trelawney and put a musket ball in his brain.'

'But . . .' Woodville the merchant held up his hand.

'I know, I know.' Philsby gestured for him to be silent. 'No one in this tavern heard a musket shot yet the ball was certainly fired, singeing the skin of poor Trelawney. My bailiffs have found no powder in the gallery, in fact no trace of any musket or pistol being fired. Now Trelawney was alive at least half an hour before he left this chamber to break his fast. I can only conclude—' He smiled sheepishly at Dudley. '—We can only conclude that the assassin was someone on this gallery.'

'Couldn't the murderer have climbed through a window?' Lady Georgina spoke up. 'Walked along the gallery, killed Trelawney and left by the same route?'

'The gallery has two windows at either end,' Philsby explained. 'Both look out on to very busy lanes. My chief bailiff has examined both.' He looked at his official who nodded solemnly. 'He has also made careful enquiries. First, those windows have not been opened for weeks. Secondly, there is no sign of anyone entering or leaving by that route. Thirdly, there are small markets in both lanes: no stall-owner, or those who loiter there, saw anything untoward.' He drummed his fingers on his knee. 'The assassin—' Philsby paused.

'Must be one of us.' The preacher spoke up.

'I am glad you said that.' Philsby coughed, clearing his throat.

'Couldn't the murderer have come behind Trelawney when the squire was at the top of the stairs, called his name, killed him when he turned, then fled?' Woodville suggested.

Philsby shook his head. 'First, Trelawney was at the top of the stairs facing down, the maid is sure of that. We have some evidence that he may have even reached the second step, in which case he was in the stair shaft protected on all sides by brick walls. Secondly, Trelawney would have surely heard someone coming behind him; if he turned he would have protested, and that would have taken more time yet the maid is sure the squire fell very shortly after she glimpsed him. Thirdly, even if that was the case, why didn't anyone hear the musket crack, or find traces of smoke or powder?' Philsby smiled coldly. 'But I take your point. The assassin must have been somewhere on that gallery. So I must ask, did any of you know Squire Trelawney? He was, how can I put it, a peculiar man, though a landowner with powerful friends in London—'

'As have I,' Lady Mary Castell interrupted.

'Quite so. Quite so.' Philsby ran a finger round his neck cloth and scratched the sweat. 'But my question still stands.'

All four stared back.

'Well, did you?' Philsby insisted.

'I knew him by sight.' Lady Georgina spoke up. 'When I stayed here, sometimes he did. I avoided him.'

'Lady Mary? Master Woodville? Our good preacher?' Philsby glanced at the other three.

They all shook their heads.

'We have another problem,' the coroner continued, wishing he was elsewhere. 'Not only did no one hear a musket being fired but the ball which killed Trelawney is of German origin. It's probably quite old and may have been used by His Majesty's forces in Scotland during the repression of the Jacobite rebellion. Squire Trelawney played, er, an important role in those troubled affairs. Do any of you have business in Scotland?'

'I preach the length and breadth of this kingdom,' Butler offered. 'But the furthest north I've been is Berwick.'

'Master Woodville?'

'I have no business in Scotland,' the merchant replied.

'Ladies?'

Both women denied this. Lady Mary seemed more concerned with noise from the streets below.

'Very well.' Philsby was about to continue when there was a knock on the door. A bailiff entered and whispered in his ear.

'The windows of all your chambers look out over the stable yard,' Philsby explained. 'My men have searched it thoroughly and closely questioned the grooms and ostlers. They saw nothing suspicious.'

'Such as what?' Woodville snapped.

'Oh,' Philsby blew his cheeks out and looked beseechingly at the physician.

'We are looking for a musket or a pistol,' Dudley explained. 'Perhaps it was thrown out of a window?'

'Good Lord, man!' Lady Mary Castell exclaimed. She held out her hand. 'Do you think I'm strong enough to hold a musket?'

'Are any of you armed?' Philsby asked, dismissing the bailiff.

'I have a sword,' Woodville replied. 'But it's with the rest of my belongings in my chamber.'

'Ah, I'd like to come to that.' Philsby rubbed his hands together. 'I am a law officer of this city. I am also a magistrate. I can, if I wish, have warrants sworn out to search you, your chambers, all your possessions.' He paused and stared at one of the bed posts. 'If you have nothing to hide,' he added, 'you have nothing to fear. I believe that will be the next appropriate step.'

Lady Georgina sprang to her feet, huffing and puffing.

'If it means this silly business will be ended sooner rather than later . . .' the preacher almost drawled, spreading his hands, '. . . my luggage is in my chamber.'

'Thank you.' Philsby smiled at him. 'And, of course, I must search your persons.'

'If you lay a hand on me!' Lady Georgina pouted.

'No, no,' Philsby reasoned. 'I suggest the two ladies go into an adjoining chamber where Mine Host's wife and a maid perhaps . . . ?'

Lady Georgina was about to protest but Lady Mary rose elegantly to her feet.

14

'Our good preacher is correct,' she soothed, grasping the old lady's hand. 'The sooner we do this the sooner we are gone. Sir Peter?'

'Yes, my lady?'

'Why should any of us here wish to kill a fat old squire who may have been obnoxious to everyone else?'

'I don't know; that's what I'm trying to find out.'

The two ladies left and Philsby and the physician, helped by the bailiff, searched Woodville and Reverend Butler, patting at their clothing. A short while later the ladies rejoined them. Lady Mary was as cool as ever but her older companion looked red-faced and flustered. Philsby ordered wine and platters of bread, cheese and ham to be served with a dish of onions. His four 'guests', as he called them, sat with napkins over their laps, eating, drinking, talking amongst themselves, whilst Sir Peter, who left the door open, went back along the gallery to search their chambers.

He came back, his face twisted into a wry apology. 'Nothing,' he murmured. 'Not a musket or a flask of powder.'

He stared at the gunsmith Atherton, seated grim-faced on a chair in the corner, cradling a pewter jug of ale. Dudley looked deeply exasperated and kept pulling at the fob watch in his waistcoat.

'Sir Peter, it's almost noon,' he pointed out. We have been at this now for over four hours.'

The coroner sat, elbows resting on the arms of his chair, fingers to his mouth, staring up at the ceiling.

What have we here? he thought. First, Squire Trelawney was alive at least half an hour before he took his fatal fall down the stairs. Second, a maid sees him there, standing by himself, ready to come down. He glanced at Lady Georgina. Third, the old lady heard Trelawney leaving his chamber. Fourth, how on earth could anyone get in front of him without raising the alarm or being seen by the maid or Trelawney himself? Fifth, why was there no trace of the musket? No powder stains on the floor, no odour and, above all, no reverberating crack which would have roused this tavern? Finally, why was a musket ball of German origin, and of quite considerable age, used in the murder? Yes, that was interesting: as if someone from Trelawney's dark past, particularly his bloody work in Scotland, had caught up with him. So what could he ask himself? Had the musket ball been fired? It had to have been. Atherton had confirmed this whilst Dudley had pointed out how the skin had been burnt and scored, it certainly needed some force to penetrate Trelawney's thick skull. Could he have been killed somewhere else, taken to the top of the stairs and thrown down? But how could he account for Trelawney's cane being heard, whilst the maid definitely saw the squire's stockinged legs at the top of the stairs?

The coroner stared around the chamber. There was no sign of any

15

violence here. Moreover, even if he could prove that Trelawney was not killed where people thought he was, the mystery still remained: how could that damned musket ball be fired so silently, and yet so effectively?

Woodville coughed.

Sir Peter shook himself from his reverie and apologised to his 'guests'. 'Let me take another tack. The good squire arrived here three days ago, yes? Lady Georgina, you were already here?'

The old woman nodded.

'I believe the rest of you arrived yesterday afternoon?'

'That's correct,' the preacher declared. 'But I hired my chamber, oh, at least a week ago.'

'Did you now?' Sir Peter sensed he had discovered a loose thread. 'And you asked for that particular chamber?'

'Of course! This is the most salubrious part of the tavern. I have stayed here before in my peregrinations. Check with Mine Host.'

'And Lady Mary?'

'I often stay here on my journeys to and from Bristol,' she replied. 'Master Neville knows my needs and wants. I always have the same chamber.'

'And you, Master Woodville?'

'I could say the same,' the merchant drawled, 'but I took pot luck. Sir Peter, what are you getting at? People travel the same roads, visit the same city, use the same tavern. We all know Master Neville, the landlord. We have all seen each other before. I recognised Squire Trelawney by sight and knew something of his reputation.' Woodville rapped his cane on the floor. 'But that doesn't mean I killed the man. It certainly doesn't provide enough evidence to send any, or all of us, to the scaffold.'

Lady Georgina gave a low moan.

'That's what we are talking about, aren't we, Sir Peter?' The merchant pressed his point. 'A horrible murder, by person or persons unknown, of Squire Trelawney. Now, I arrived here yesterday afternoon. I took dinner in the taproom below before retiring to my chamber—'

'Whom did you dine with?' Philsby interrupted.

'I shared a jug of claret with our good preacher.' The merchant smiled. 'We took our cups up to our chambers and wished each other good night. I slept soundly, much later than I thought. In fact, it was the pandemonium which broke out after Squire Trelawney was killed which woke me.'

'And you, Lady Georgina?' Philsby asked.

'I don't eat in the taproom.' She sniffed. 'I dine in my own chamber. I did so last night as I always did. I was busy about my toilette' – she emphasized the word – 'when this dreadful event occurred.

People running up and down stairs, all along the gallery. One of your bailiffs told me to stay where I was, then dragged me in here to be questioned.'

'And did you speak to Squire Trelawney?'

'Good Lord no! I don't speak to people like him!'

'What do you mean, people like him?'

'He was sottish in his ways. I always objected to Mine Host about the squire bringing trollops up into his chamber.'

'Master Woodville?'

'What would I have to do with Trelawney?' he murmured. 'A gentleman has to be careful of the company he keeps.'

'And does that include you, Reverend?'

'We are all God's children,' Butler replied. 'Trelawney was a sinner. I have, on different occasions, tried to draw him into conversation to show him the path of repentance. But, as the Book of Proverbs says: "The sinner returns to his crime like a dog to his vomit".'

'More specifically,' Philsby asked, 'did you approach him yesterday or this morning?'

The preacher lifted his hand and raised his eyebrows. 'I did knock on his door last night and asked if he wished to join me in prayer.'

Philsby ignored Physician Dudley's muffled laughter.

'And I suppose,' Philsby said, 'the squire was pleased to see you?'

'No sir, he was not. He damned me for my insolence and slammed the door in my face.'

'And that was it?'

'No sir, I knocked again a short while later. I said I objected to his bad manners. Once again he told me to go hang and slammed the door shut. It's a pity.' The preacher pursed his lips. 'Repentance was offered, repentance refused.'

'And you, Lady Mary, would have little to do with a man like Trelawney?'

'I did last night: I ate in my own chamber, but I spoke to him this morning, shortly after six o'clock.'

'I beg your pardon?'

'You heard me, sir,' Lady Mary replied. 'My chamber is next to his.' She coloured slightly. 'I heard his drunken revelry last night and what Lady Georgina calls his trollop leave in the early hours. Sir Peter, I stay at this tavern to rest and pay good money to do so. I did not pay,' she continued through gritted teeth, 'to listen to the lustful revelries of a fat old squire!'

'What happened?' Philsby asked curiously.

Lady Mary took a fan from her small reticule, flicked it open and waved it vigorously in front of her face.

'Sir, I had a perfectly wretched night's sleep. In the usual course of events I would ignore a man like Trelawney, however I knocked on

17

his door and gave him a piece of my mind. He merely jeered. I assure you, he was very much alive then. If you check with Mine Host, the serving wench came up later.'

The preacher got to his feet. 'Sir Peter, I appreciate that you are a city coroner and have a task to do. I and my companions also have tasks. We have answered all your questions. We have allowed you to search our persons, our baggage and our rooms. You have no proof.' He snapped his fingers. 'No sir, not even a shred to link any, or all of us, with Squire Trelawney's death, and that's the truth of the matter.'

Philsby looked at the physician. Dudley hunched his shoulders and shook his head. Atherton, still sitting in the corner half-asleep, looked solemn and disgruntled. Philsby stared down at the floor. The preacher was correct. He did not have a shred of evidence against anyone in this tavern. If he continued much longer, Woodville, and certainly the two ladies, would start talking about *habeas corpus* and their rights under the law.

'I beg your patience a little longer.'

Sir Peter gestured at his two companions, left the chamber and paused at the top of the dark cavernous stairs. The noise echoed from the taproom below; the front door was open and market traders and costermongers were coming in for their mid-day meal and tankards of ale. The stairs were still guarded by his bailiffs. Sir Peter looked despairingly once more at the walls on either side and the dark plaster ceiling which turned the staircase into a hollow passageway. He stood, feet apart, and once again asked Dudley to walk down the stairs.

The physician made a rude sound with his lips but obeyed.

'Stop!' Philsby called out. 'Turn!'

Dudley half turned.

'No, right round!'

The physician did so but had to hold on to the rails.

'My heels jut out over the step,' Dudley called back. 'What is more, Sir Peter, if you had to shoot me in the head, you'd have to crouch down. We know this did not happen with Trelawney. It's all too cumbersome!'

'Go to the bottom!' Philsby commanded. 'Near the front door where the maid stood.'

The physician clattered down, his annoyance apparent in his heavy footfalls. He reached the doorway and looked back. 'Before you ask, Sir Peter, all I can see are your boots, nothing else.'

Philsby looked at Atherton. 'You are sure that musket ball was fired?'

'Sir Peter, I have already told you what I know. That ball was fired from a musket. It was of German origin, slightly larger than our present type and possibly used in muskets carried by mercenaries whom His Majesty employed, both here and in Scotland.'

18

Muttering curses, the physician made his way back up the stairs.

'You are the new city law officer,' the physician exclaimed. 'I am your witness and so is Atherton. You've done what you can. There is no solution to this mystery. Trelawney is dead and only the good Lord knows who murdered him, how and why.' He gestured at the Lion Chamber. 'You have no choice but to let those people go.'

The coroner stared at the heavy oaken door. In his heart of hearts he believed that one, two or all of those people in the Lion Chamber were somehow involved in Trelawney's death, but the truth and the law were two different things. He licked dry lips.

'Master Physician, tell them they are free to go. I am going to wet my throat on Mine Host's finest ale.' He shook the hands of Dudley and Atherton. 'You are my official witnesses: there is nothing more we can do.'

'And so, my brothers.' Reverend Butler looked down the dusty hall attached to the small chapel on the outskirts of Bristol. 'And so, my brothers.' He paused once again to stare at the soberly dressed traders with their wives, his usual congregation at these meetings. 'Live righteous lives before the Lord! Seek his will! Use the talents God has given you, and He will bless you both now and for ever!'

'Amen!' came the low chorused reply.

Butler bowed his head and, in a powerful voice, led the closing hymn. He raised his head slightly and stared from under heavy-lidded eyes at the female figure shrouded in a cloak, seated at the back. When they had finished, Reverend Butler gave his final blessing and watched the small congregation file out into the gathering dusk. He left his makeshift chapel and walked into the small shabby room at the rear which the minister had provided as a place of rest and refreshment. He took his tinder, lit the six candles in their brass holders and turned the chair to face the door. Cradling a Bible in his hands, he waited for his visitor to arrive. She slipped into the room like a ghost, closing and locking the door behind her.

The cloak Lady Mary wore was not fashionable: a thick serge blanket-like cloak favoured by His Majesty's soldiers. Nevertheless, it served as a good disguise and kept her warm. She pulled back the hood. Butler could see she was nervous, her eyes bright with excitement. Without saying a word, she opened the small reticule and placed the heavy leather bag of clinking coins into the preacher's outstretched hands.

'You are rightly named,' she said. 'The Vengeance of God!'

'I am a rod in the hands of the Almighty,' Butler intoned. 'Dispensing justice, bringing retribution to sinners.'

'My husband has served as a sheriff in Bristol.' Lady Mary whispered, her eyes studying that dark saturnine face. 'I have heard him and his colleagues talk about an assassin whom no one knows, of mysterious deaths which cannot be solved.' She leaned forward, hands clasped. 'I prayed you know. I prayed that I could meet such a man. I never realised how that prayer would be answered!'

'The mills of God grind exceedingly slow, Madam,' the preacher replied, 'but they do grind exceedingly small.'

'I never guessed when I attended one of your meetings, more as a diversion than anything else, that Reverend Butler and the Vengeance of God were one and the same person.' She smiled. 'Your words about retribution moved me: no crime goes unpunished in the eyes of God. You invited your congregation to open their hearts . . .'

'And you opened your heart to me.' The preacher looked over the pretty young thing from head to toe and licked his lips. 'And you told me your story. Your real name is MacGregor? Your father a minor Scottish laird who supported the Jacobite cause?'

The young woman's eyes brimmed with tears.

'I was six at the time,' she murmured. 'We owned a small castle, really nothing more than a peel tower and outlying buildings next to a shiny lake in wild countryside.' She breathed in sharply. 'Trelawney came with his troopers. He raped my mother and made my father watch before he shot him with the same musket ball you used. Trelawney was a demon from hell. He laughed all the time. He plundered our house, burnt it then left me, my mother and my father's corpse out in the heather.' Lady Mary closed her eyes. 'We stayed for days until neighbours came. My mother had the musket ball dug out. She survived a few months but she kept that musket ball smooth in her hands. She never let it go.' Lady Mary blinked away the tears. 'Mother faded away, just like a flower but, before she died, she pressed that musket ball into my hands. "Vengeance," she whispered. "Vengeance for me and your father!" I took that musket ball and hid it away. I was passed from family to family till I was adopted by the Swynnertons of Staffordshire. I took their name, the rest of my life was that of any young English country lady.'

'Except for that musket ball?'

'Yes, except for that musket ball. I held it so often, noticing how round and smooth it was. I learnt it could be fired again. I met you, The Vengeance of God, and I knew my father's and mother's blood would be avenged.' She narrowed her eyes. 'How did you do it?'

The preacher stretched across the table and filled two small cups with red wine. He gave one to her then sipped from his.

'Have you ever been to the Americas, Lady Mary?'

She shook her head.

'A place of magic,' the preacher explained. 'Dark green forests, tribes of natives called the Iroquois, expert hunters, fierce fighters. When they hunt they plan, when they kill they plot the most cunning ambush. I learnt from the Iroquois: never be hasty, measure your time, choose your place and seize your opportunity.'

'I thought you had forgotten.' Lady Mary declared. 'It is at least four months since I first met you.'

'It was easy to plan.' The preacher pulled at his lower lip. 'Trelawney always went to the White Hart in Cheltenham. He always stayed in the Lion Chamber. I noticed that Lady Georgina, God bless her sharp tongue, rented the second chamber which left two. It was the only weakness in my plot but Sir Peter Philsby could not use that as evidence against me. I hired the third chamber and, of course, Lady Mary Castell could easily hire the fourth, as I instructed you. Josiah Woodville lived the fifth and I took care of him.' He sipped again at the wine. 'It was the stairs which fascinated me, like a shaft down into the ground. I also studied the routine of the tavern. Winter or spring, Christmas or Easter, the routine of those places rarely varies. If anything, Squire Trelawney was also a creature of habit. The serving maid would come up at six-thirty, our good squire always left at seven. Mine Host, his legion of scullions, maids and tap boys were always busy in the kitchens and elsewhere. No one came up those stairs. Why should they? Breakfast had to be served, the stairs are steep, customers are coming down, and it is only later in the morning that the chambers are cleaned. I chose that as my ambush. True, true, something might have gone wrong, in which case I would have changed the place or the time.'

'And so?' Lady Mary asked.

The preacher smiled. 'I asked you to do one task: knock on the door before the maid came and ask Squire Trelawney would he accompany you down to breakfast? The old lecher wouldn't refuse an invitation like that.'

'So when he opened the door to you he was expecting me?'

'Yes, he'd been primed and surprise was essential.'

'But why did you knock on his door the previous evening?'

'I wanted to see how he opened that chamber door, where he stood, the angle of his body, the tilt of his head. I knocked a second time, just to make sure.'

'And the musket ball?'

'Well, I studied it closely. It had been fired once and I fired it again some days earlier so, to Atherton, it was ingrained with powder, recently discharged by a pistol or musket.' The preacher put his cup down. 'I had a wife like you once; the Iroquois killed her. I was also a carpenter and hunter, a very good one. You've seen a crossbow or arbalest?'

'Yes, there are old fashioned ones hanging on the walls of my husband's hall . . .'

'Aye.' The preacher interrupted. 'And there are smaller ones, no

21

bigger than a handspan or so across. A crossbow is, truly, quite a primitive affair: a very taut cord which is pulled back by a trigger over a tab, a small piece of strengthened leather in the middle. When the trigger is released, the tab goes down and the cord lunges forward sending the bolt, placed in the groove, directly towards the target. Only this time I tapered the groove specially to take your musket ball.'

'But would that kill?'

'Have you ever seen a shepherd with a sling shot? Or a boy with a catapult? They can bring down birds or kill a dog.' He lifted the Bible up. 'Did not David kill Goliath with a simple pebble?'

'But Sir Peter said that the skin round the wound had been tinged and burnt?'

The preacher pulled the candle stick closer.

'I did that. I took the musket ball in a small set of pincers and held it above a candle flame. It became hot.' He pushed the candle stick away. 'But not hot enough, so I placed it on a steel tray and shoved it amongst the embers of the fire in my chamber. At last it was fiery to the touch, spluttering on the powder ingrained. I heard the maid leave. I knew you had knocked on Squire Trelawney's door so I left my chamber and tip-toed across the gallery. I glanced quickly down the stairs. The maid was beginning her work. I went back to my room, put the musket ball in a piece of cloth, primed the arbalest and knocked on Squire Trelawney's door.'

Lady Mary sipped from her wine and stared at this skilful assassin.

'Trelawney opened the door softly, expecting you. He would have protested but I shoved the arbalest against his forehead and pushed him back into the room..He was speechless. He thought the arbalest was already primed and was only too willing to keep his mouth shut as I gently closed the door. It was over in a matter of seconds. I kept the arbalest to his forehead, the groove running dead centre above his eyes. I loosened the cloth with my gloved finger, put the ball into the groove, nestling where it should. I released the trigger and Trelawney died. From the moment I entered his room to when the musket ball entered his brains, much less than a minute's span. He slumped to the floor, I worked quickly. I put the arbalest on a hook on my belt. With a cloth, I made sure there was no stain of blood on the floor. I went back on to the gallery, it was still deserted. The maid was working at the foot of the stairs. I quickly rearranged Trelawney's wig and hat and picked up his cane. Holding it under the armpits, I took Trelawney's corpse along the gallery, the short distance to the top of the stairs. Keeping his head tilted back so no blood splattered on the floor, his walking cane, which I had slipped through my sword belt, beat its usual tattoo. At the top of the stairs I paused for a few seconds and coughed. The maid looked up and moved away. I let the corpse fall and walked back to my own chamber.'

22

'But the maid said she saw only Squire Trelawney's stockinged legs, buckled shoes and cloak?'

'That's what she expected to see. His cloak was draped over his shoulders and fell down to his heels. It served as a curtain for me, hiding my legs and feet.'

The preacher drained his cup and refilled it.

'Whilst the body fell, I quickly retraced my steps. Nothing in the gallery, nothing in the Lion Chamber, I was safe. When I returned to my own room, I put the cloth which held the musket ball, as well as that which had mopped up any blood, together with the arbalest, fashioned out of simple wood and cord, on the fire. All were burning merrily before Sir Peter ever arrived at the White Hart. I washed my hands and face, the rest you know.'

'Someone could have seen you?'

'Who? I've told you, I know the doings of that tavern: when the maid would go up, when Squire Trelawney would go down.'

'But Lady Georgina, the merchant Woodville?'

'Lady Georgina never comes out of her chamber before nine, and only when her toilette is complete. Woodville and I,' the preacher toasted her silently with his cup, 'we'd shared a jug of wine together the previous evening. The cup Woodville took back to his chamber had a sleeping draught which would provide him with a good night's rest. Before I struck, I listened at Woodville's door. All was quiet.'

'And Squire Trelawney's walking cane?'

'I slipped it into his hand just before he fell.'

'But when you struck him on the head with the ball, his clothing would have been stained.'

'Well, Squire Trelawney had been murdered and taken a dreadful fall down steep, sharp steps. You'd expect to find blood, and Dudley of course made it worse. Sir Peter Philsby may be a good law officer, a conscientious coroner, but there is a limit to what he could deduce.'

Lady Mary got to her feet. 'You planned well. You truly wanted his death?' The preacher quietly toasted her again.

'I didn't want it.' He replied. 'God did.'

The difficulty about writing medieval stories lies in finding that thin line between historical accuracy and telling a tale present-day readers can understand.

Take language as an example. I make no apologies for writing in a twentieth-century style; my protagonists all speak as we do today, with few lapses into 'olde English'. There's a simple reason for this: the English spoken in the early fourteenth century was not like our modern tongue. It's a foreign language, with words stolen from French, Celtic, German, Latin, even Arabic. To make life still more confusing, certain words which one assumes to be fairly new, can be very ancient, for example 'posse'. It may bring to mind a group of grubby extras riding across a cinema screen, but in fact the concept of the armed force raised by the local sheriff was medieval, mentioned as far back as 1285 in the Statute of Winchester.

The writer must also try to explain how people thought and behaved. Although many of Chaucer's humanitarian views would be accepted by many of us today, other facts of medieval life we would find repellent: butchers voiding the bowels of dead oxen in the Thames upriver from the brewers; officers leaving bodies hanging from gibbets or spikes on London Bridge *pour encourager les autres*; watching men and women fighting with swords as entertainment. Trying to put oneself in the mind of someone who lived at this time is not always easy, but I do believe that bringing history to life is useful. However, that's not why I sit here day after day staring out of the window and daydreaming about how things used to be. I just happen to enjoy making a living from crime – from medieval murders – and I can only hope that you enjoy reading this example as much as I enjoyed writing it!

Michael Jecks

The Coroner's Tale

Michael Jecks

I'll always remember Sir Baldwin de Furnshill as he was in that dingy alley near the inn in Crediton. He was in his element, studying that corpse. Mind you, I prefer not to recall the scene in too much detail. I can still smell the sharp, rank tang of urine, the sweetness of putrefying fruit, the soft mustiness of the decaying dog's corpse. Next to them, the faint whiff of perfume from the slight body was like a breath of fresh air.

She was young – not yet out of her teens – and living I would have found her greatly attractive. Her body was still coltish, but her well-rounded figure was that of a mature woman, while her face had the same high brow and delicately arched eyebrows as my own good wife, partly covered by the long tresses of yellow-blond hair which had jerked from under her wimple in her final throes.

I shook my head. It wasn't difficult to infer what had happened. Like so many girls before her, and no doubt countless others who would follow, she had, probably unknowingly, fired a man's lust. 'It's easy to see how it occurred, Sir Baldwin,' I said. 'She was accosted here in the alley, and when she refused him, he tried to force himself on her. She tried to escape; he killed her.'

Sir Baldwin nodded, but I could see I wasn't holding his interest. His lean face with its neatly trimmed beard was focused on the body. 'Murder, certainly,' he said heavily as he squatted, thoughtfully studying her hands. 'No rings, although this, her wedding finger, shows an indentation as if she wore one very recently. No purse either; both must have been stolen. She hasn't cut her hands, so she put up no fight. Perhaps he came upon her from behind and she didn't realise he was there.' He glanced up at me. 'Do you object to . . . ?'

'Carry on,' I said, waving a hand dismissively.

Under my gaze he and his servant removed her tunic, wimple, undershirt and skirts, and left the girl naked under the sky. Slim and pale as marble where the moonlight caught her, she appeared almost to shine. For me, Sir Eustace of Hatherleigh, Coroner to King

27

Edward II, in this the fourteenth glorious year of his reign, the sight was nothing new, and yet it made me shake my head with sadness to see such beauty destroyed, ready only to be set kneeling in her grave, bowing to her God as she awaited the resurrection. I loathe to see waste of human life, but this in particular was painful. I couldn't help thinking of my own sweet Lucy, lying quietly at home in her bed at this moment, her little face so serene and peaceful in sleep. Lucy is twelve, almost old enough for her own husband, and surely only six or seven years younger than this child.

As I sighed and considered the sadness of the life ended for so little reason, the knight rolled the small form over and exposed her back. He pointed to the stab wound, and I nodded again while the priest at my side crossed himself.

'Stabbed after being raped – or perhaps before,' the knight concluded as he stood, wiping his hands free of her blood on a piece of her clothing. 'And with a blade one inch wide at the thickest. It really is most difficult to find a murderer when we don't even know his victim's name,' he continued, frowning.

I nodded, but not without a slight sense of disappointment. It sounded as if he was not going to trouble himself over the case, and yet why should he? He'd been dragged here with me away from the great church hall where we had been feasting with the Dean to celebrate St Boniface's day. I was uncomfortably aware that the best of the food would already have gone while we stood there studying her small form. And yet he managed to learn a little from her.

'She was no servant or villein. Her hands are unmarked, and if she had been used to menial work they would have been calloused.'

'I, Sir Eustace of Hatherleigh, Coroner, declare that this young woman was stabbed to death here on this evening, June the fifth in the year of our Lord 1321,' I intoned solemnly. I always find that making the formal statement helps the locals to come to terms with the discovery of a body, not that it mattered in this case. No one could possibly know her.

The people in this area were thin, hungry-looking tatterdemalions. This part of the town was inhabited by the poor, who eked out a living by helping farmers during the summer months and fighting for menial work through the rest of the year. Their money would go on ale, while they would beat their children if they complained for lack of food. For the most part they were of the lowest class imaginable. If they'd possessed any pride or common dignity they would have gone to a manor and served a lord rather than live in such squalor. Surely the status of a villein would suit them better than filthy poverty. Yet some folk will always assume that freedom is better than serving a lord. They forget that freedom to live is often the same as freedom to die.

I think Sir Baldwin saw my look, for he gave a wry little smile. It made his face move oddly, twisting the side where a long scar ploughed the line of an old wound, running from temple to jaw. I've heard it was won in Acre many years ago where he fought to save that last Christian city in the Holy Land from the Moorish hordes, but I never dared ask him. Sir Baldwin gave the impression that he had an aversion to revealing his past, and such an enquiry would have been impertinent.

In any case, for all his vaunted understanding of human nature, he completely misunderstood my feelings about the citizens haunting the alley. They were all of them hanging around to see the body. It was right that the jury of fourteen should witness the body's inspection, but it was obvious that most of the men there that night were only satisfying a prurient interest; they inspired my contempt.

He waved a languid hand towards them. 'This child does not look as if she came from the same stock as these poor fellows, does she? They are all emaciated and worn down from their work, but look at her: well-fed and an easy life, if I am any judge,' he said softly in his quiet, contemplative voice. Then, casting an eye over the audience, 'Ralph, have you seen her before?'

The man he called to was one of a small crowd of townspeople. I had them waiting so I could get their names, for these men lived nearest the alley. That was the nice thing about my business in towns: it was always easy to find out who lived closest so that the fines could be imposed for breaking the King's Peace. Out of town things were often more difficult, especially when the locals refused to pay my fees, the ignorant cretins. One vill towards Tedburn refused to pay my fee, so I refused to view the body. By the time they agreed, the corpse was rotted, and to protect it they'd had to go to the bother of setting a hedge about it. I fined the lot of them double for wasting my time. You can't let these people get away with such wilfulness.

Looking at these folks again, I must say I wasn't impressed. Ralph was a sallow, gaunt-looking man in his early twenties, with fair hair that seemed to have dirt ingrained in it. The other neighbours were no better looking, all being wan, stooped, bandy-legged fellows.

Nearby was another huddle of locals, some of whom I recognised, like the tall and melancholy John, who owned a small alehouse on the Exeter road. At his side was the innkeeper, Paul, greying and harassed, avoiding my gaze, nervously lifting his hand as if trying to conceal himself behind it. Standing behind them I could see the tranter, Edward. Usually a cheerful, confident little man, he kept his eyes fixed firmly on the body, his lips pursed in a thin line of anger. These churls are all the same; no doubt they all had their minds fixed on the fine they must pay.

Ralph shuffled forward, his head down. He mumbled for a moment, and I snapped at him to speak up. The trouble one has with these people!

29

'Sir Baldwin, I saw her here this afternoon going past my place, but never before that, I swear.'

'You were the first finder of the body, weren't you?' I demanded. It helps to keep a stern tone with his sort. 'You'll have to be amerced to make sure you come to the court. Give your details to my secretary here.'

He shuffled a bit more at that. I could see Sir Baldwin wanted to question him further, but to tell the truth I was more interested in getting back to the Dean's feast than staying out there in that dank and noisome alleyway. While Ralph muttered to the priest at my side, the townspeople gradually drifted away until we were almost alone. The innkeeper and his friends were all gone before Ralph had finished. Once he had, the knight spoke again.

'Ralph, tell me, which direction was she going in?'

'First time I saw her she was walking towards Paul's place, the inn. She looked exhausted, like she'd only just arrived; her clothes were covered in the red dust you get on the roads around here, and she was stumbling a bit, as if she'd covered a lot of miles since daybreak. Later I saw her leaving Paul's and go down to the alehouse at the bottom of the hill. I reckoned she was looking for a place to stay the night.' He looked down at her sadly. 'Poor lass! She must have come here for the market, and this was her reward.'

'When was this, when you saw her?'

'A little before dark, because I had to go out to get rid of some rubbish, and it was while I was there by the gutter that I saw her the second time.'

'Was she alone?'

'Yes, sir. Paul came out and watched her, but so did I: she was such a pretty young thing, and yet seemed so sad. I watched her until she entered the alehouse.'

'That was the last time you saw her until you found her here?'

Ralph scuffed his shoes in the dirt, and Baldwin had to repeat his question before the man would answer, giving me an odd little sidelong glance. 'No, sir. I saw her again a while later, walking quickly up the hill to this alley. I was clearing up, and when I realised she hadn't come back again, I just thought I should make sure she was all right.'

'Did you see anyone else going in there?'

He shook his head, avoiding our gazes. 'Sorry, but no. No one else that I saw.'

'When she came into town, did she carry anything? A basket? Did she have a bag of goods to sell?'

'Nothing much, Sir Baldwin, only a small pack like a traveller would carry.'

'Then why did you think she was here for the market? Surely she would have brought something to sell? Even if she came here to buy, she would have brought something to carry off her purchases: a basket or sack at least.'

'Why else would she be here?' I interrupted reasonably.

'Perhaps when we know that, we'll know why she died.'

'Oh, Sir Baldwin!' I protested. 'She was obviously murdered by some drunk who met her in the alley, or maybe in the street itself, and who dragged her in here to molest her.'

'It is rare for a man to hurt, far less kill, a woman he has never met before,' said Baldwin confidently. 'I would think it far more likely that she was followed here to Crediton by a man she was trying to evade. He stabbed her in the alley because she wouldn't do what he wanted. Or perhaps that is the wrong way around, and in reality she was herself searching for a man, and when she found him, he struck her down.'

'I'm afraid I deal in facts, Sir Baldwin,' I said, a trifle brusquely I fear. 'If you want to invent a story, that's fine, but in the meantime I have to find out what I can for the inquest.'

'Shall we go and question the other men now, then?' he asked, and I thought I saw a gleam of amusement in his eye.

'We should wait until the morning for that,' I snapped. If we didn't get back there wouldn't be anything left to eat or drink.

The next morning I awoke with a head like a lead ball and a belly that roiled and bubbled as strongly as a witch's cauldron on a hot fire. There was a constant flavour of bile in my throat until I slaked my thirst with a pint of good strong wine and ducked my head into the horse trough at the back of the Dean's stable. Then, dried and cleaned, I went to the hall to break my fast. There was cold meat in profusion, and I ate my fill of bread with thick slices of pork before heeding the request of the knight's servant that I should meet him near the alley. I confess I didn't see the need to hurry, and I drank off another pint of wine before making my way to see Sir Baldwin.

It was interesting for me to see how the knight worked. Of course, he didn't have the same position as me, for he was only a Keeper of the King's Peace, not a Coroner, with all the powers that the title confers, but still his reputation was quite daunting. It was always said that criminals avoided his eye because he was so keen-witted and shrewd that he could see through a wall to a man's guilt, but rumours like that abound in a desolate little backwater like Crediton, so far from the bright life of court, so remote from civilisation.

'A good morning to you, Sir Baldwin. I hope I find you well?'

He uttered the usual courtesies, but I could see his mind was concentrated on the dead girl. Soon we were discussing her.

'I can only assume she was looking for a means of earning money, if you are right and she didn't come here to buy or sell.'

31

He shot me a glance at that. 'You mean she was prepared to sell her body?'

'She may well have hoped that she wouldn't have to,' I said. I always like to give a young girl the benefit of the doubt, and it was only fair. 'But on arriving in the town and seeing how busy and bustling it was, no doubt the poor chit realised that any jobs would be filled by those who have always lived here. Who would wish to employ a stranger? And after that realisation, what else could she do, I ask you? She needed money for food, for board, and to travel on to somewhere else. Maybe to Exeter. What else could she do but try to sell her body? And I fear that her first client saw her and stabbed her.'

We were almost at the door of the alehouse as I spoke, and I looked up at the small uprooted bush that dangled above the door. 'You want to go in here?'

He grinned at my distaste. 'I have drunk good ale in here many times before, Coroner. We have to try to discover what happened to the girl when she came in here.' And so saying he ducked his head beneath the lintel and went inside.

I need hardly say that I was not used to frequenting such low, mean dwellings, and would have protested at the thought of going in, but with Sir Baldwin's servant behind me, I felt I had little choice. With a sense of chagrin I followed him.

Inside there was already quite a collection of rough, brutish men sitting on benches and supping their first whet of the day. All stared as I stood there, my eyes becoming accustomed to the dim light, which wasn't easy. The room had a small fire, but this early the air was still so chill that the smoke hung heavily above the hearth, and there was only one window in the opposite wall to permit a tiny shaft of sunlight. I heard a scrape of metal, as of a knife easing in its scabbard, but before I could move my hand to my dagger's hilt, Sir Baldwin's servant moved past me, his own blade spinning in the air. He caught it and held it by the tip, ready to throw. When I glanced at his face there was an utter deadness to his eyes. They were as cold and unfeeling as a fish's. The room was quiet for an instant, and then the men at their tables began to murmur quietly to each other, studiously ignoring we three strangers.

Sir Baldwin appeared entirely unaffected by the brief tension. He was leaning at the doorway in the far wall, talking to a tall, grave and lugubrious man.

'Sir Eustace, this is John, who owns this place.'

The innkeeper barely acknowledged me beyond a short nod. His attention was fixed on the knight, with, or so I felt, a degree of nervousness as well as respect. 'She did come here, sir, yes, quite early in the evening. A right pretty little wench, not much older than my own. Came here asking for a room. Said she'd already been to the inn, but that they charged too much for a room. I said to her, "This is no place for a gentlewoman", but she insisted. Had tears in her eyes, she did. Almost thought she'd go down on her knees to me. Said she couldn't afford another place to stay, and begged me to let her have a room.'

'You'll pardon my agreeing that your house is hardly the sort I would expect a girl to beg to stay in,' Baldwin noted.

The dour face cracked into a grin. 'Sir, it's not the sort of place I'd expect a girl to *look* into, let alone walk in!'

'How can you be sure she was a gentlewoman and not merely some hussy?' I asked, and I must admit that I scoffed. His conviction about her status was ludicrous. As far as he was concerned she might have been a whore touting for trade in a new tavern.

He kept his eyes on Sir Baldwin as though I hadn't even spoken, the bastard. 'Her dress was worn and showed some hard use, but I think that was recent. It was good cloth, and her face and hands were clean. Dust from the road had marked her apron and wimple, but her figure was good and full, not skinny from poor food, and her voice was confident enough. Yes, I'm sure she was well-born. As for her being a slut, well . . . I saw the way she walked in here, like it took all her remaining courage just to enter. She daren't even shoot the merest look at the men in here, for fear of bursting into tears, just strode up to me and kept her eyes on me, poor thing. There was nothing brazen about her.'

'Did she wear a purse?'

'No, not that I saw, Sir Baldwin. That was why she came here, I think, because she had no money on her to take a room in a better house. I took pity on her and said she could use one, and a meal for the sake of St Boniface.'

'Did she take a room?'

'Yes, a small one behind the hall. It's near my own room, and I thought I could protect her if anyone got amorous overnight. But she left before anything happened.'

'When was this?'

'Just as night fell. Before the church bell for the last service of the evening.'

Sir Baldwin nodded and thanked him, then stood abruptly and walked out. I found him with his hands hooked in his belt, leaning against a hitching post and glowering at the view.

'I know how you feel, Sir Baldwin. It's awful if she truly was a respectable woman, having to beg for a room in a place like that.'

'Hmm?' He gazed at me for a moment as if he didn't recognise me at all. Then a slow smile began to spread over his features. 'Oh, I see. No, I was just thinking that she must have come from that direction, from the east; if Ralph was right and she came past him, she must have been coming from that way.'

'So what? Does it really matter?'

'Perhaps not, Sir Eustace. But it means she was walking in the wrong direction for Exeter. If she was some girl who had been running away from home, or, to take your example, if she was a whore looking for a new patch to work, she'd surely have been going the other way. No, she came here for a specific reason.'

'We're unlikely to discover what it might have been, though.' To be honest, I was finding his continual inferencing to be more than a little irritating. I was a Coroner, and had better things to do than stand in the street getting hot and dust-blown by passing traffic while my companion guessed at a range of different motives and explanations for how someone he had never known might behave.

'There is one thing that surprises me,' he muttered, this time peering over his shoulder westwards, towards the inn. 'Why should she come to town without money? Is it possible she was robbed on her way here? Or did she have some other reason to come here instead of staying in a decent, clean inn?'

'Who knows?'

'Let's go to the inn and ask Paul.'

If possible the innkeeper looked even more fretful and anxious than he had the night before. He had few enough customers this early, only a small number of tranters and hawkers and a couple of my own men, but insisted on calling his servants and ordering them about for some time as if demonstrating that he had much to do and couldn't spare a few minutes in idle chatter. Of course, that is often the way of men who are confronted by their Coroner. Our post is so important that it can cause the foolish to lose their tongues, so I didn't look upon his behaviour as suspicious. I merely waited, casting an interested eye over the women he had in there.

One was a real beauty, fair-haired, well-built under her tunic from the look of her swelling chest, with a bawdy, excitable look in her bright green eyes. I made a mental note to return to see her when this silly affair was over.

When I cast a sidelong glance at Sir Baldwin, I was surprised to see him lounging and gazing up at the ceiling. If I had to guess, I'd say he hadn't noticed the aproned idiot's play-acting. Sir Baldwin sat patiently until the innkeeper was ready, and then the stupid serf stood in front of us, asking in his whining, troubled voice whether we wanted a drink.

By this time I was hungry, and demanded a fresh meat pie. Baldwin seemed surprised at my desire for food, but he shrugged, merely asking for a quart of weak ale. The innkeeper scuttled away happily. It was so like a man of his class to hurry off when given an order by men of a higher standing. They need instruction, folk of his type, or they feel at a loss.

When he was back, and had hesitantly obeyed Sir Baldwin's next order and seated himself, the knight began his interrogation.

'The girl in the alley. I understand she was here yesterday afternoon?'

Paul licked his lips and glanced at both of us before studying his hands, clasped in his lap. 'Yes, sir, but only for a short time.'

'What did she do?'

'She came in late in the afternoon and asked for a room, Sir Baldwin. I saw her myself, and I was sure she was a real gentlewoman.'

'You were? Yet she came here alone, without a horse or companion. What made you think she was anything more than a common vagrant?'

'Oh, she had a real presence about her, Sir Baldwin,' he said, looking up at last. 'And her purse was filled with good money. I asked her whether she had coin on her, and she showed me – it was full.'

'When we found her body, there was no purse,' Baldwin commented.

The publican glanced at me and nodded. 'It must have been stolen,' he said miserably.

I stirred. 'All too often these people will steal after they have killed, you know, Sir Baldwin. You and I don't suffer from want, but common villeins in a neighbourhood like this would slit the throats of their own mothers to win an extra penny.'

He ignored me, which I have to say was insulting. His attention was fixed on the man opposite. 'She showed you her purse; then what?'

Paul's gaze returned to his hands. 'Sir, she came in exhausted, demanding a pint of watered wine, pleading a parched throat. I wanted to see her money before I went to fetch it, but when I saw how much she had, I brought her a jug . . .'

'And how did she appear? Happy, sad, anxious . . . ?'

'Oh, tired from her journey, but happy enough, I think. Later she got a bit nervy-looking. It was when Edward the tranter came over and spoke to her. She got all flushed, like she was worried about something.'

'When was this?'

'Late afternoon, I suppose.'

'Did you overhear what Edward said?'

'No, sir. He spoke too quietly, and just after that she dropped some coins on the table and left with him, leaving her small pack on her stool. Later she came back for it, but by then she had this sort of lost look to her. I felt so sorry for her, I offered her a bed over the stables, but she just shook her head – didn't say a word, just shook her head, staring at me with her eyes scared and sad, and her mouth all quivering like she was going to burst out in tears.' The innkeeper shook his own head as if in sympathy, studying the rushes at his feet, then looked up at Sir

Baldwin. 'She saw or heard something that devastated her, sir. She thought her life was ended.'

His story struck a cold chill in my bowels and I felt the anger colouring my face. 'Do you think this Edward tried to force himself on her?' I demanded. 'If he did, by God, he'll answer to me!'

'Oh, no, sir. I'm sure he'd not have done that. Edward's been coming here for donkey's years.'

'Was he drunk?' Sir Baldwin asked quietly. I couldn't help but feel he thought my outburst was excessive, but then I must admit I was finding his coolness annoying.

The innkeeper gave a faint grin. 'You know Ed, Sir Baldwin! It'd be a rare day he wasn't a bit drunk. Still, he wasn't bitter or angry, just a little, well, thoughtful, I suppose.'

'Did you see where they went?'

'Yes, sir. I thought . . . Well, she was an attractive girl, and I couldn't help watching her. They went down the street a short way and into the alley near Ralph's place. The one where she was found last night. They went inside, but then I had to go to serve a customer. A while later she returned, took up her pack and went off. Ed came in a few minutes after her, and he went to his seat at the back. He stayed there for a good bit, before taking a game of dice.'

'Who were the other players?' Baldwin asked.

'The Coroner's men-at-arms, Sir Baldwin. I'm sure they'll remember him, he played with them for quite some time.'

'When did he leave?'

'Early evening, I suppose. One of the girls tried to tempt him, but he told her to piss off, and went out.'

'So by now he was bitter and angry in his cups?'

'I suppose so, Sir Baldwin. But like I say, he left here long after her.'

Sir Baldwin led the way to the street. There he paused and motioned to his servant, spoke to him quietly, and sent him off on some errand. Sir Baldwin and I began to make our way back to the Dean's house, but to my surprise he turned off and instead headed towards that damned alley. By now Sir Baldwin's attitude was making me quite warm. The man was deliberately taking over my inquest, and wouldn't even explain what he was up to. I tried to control my growing annoyance, but I think a little of my feeling must have come across from the way he stopped and stared at me.

'Is there something the matter, Sir Eustace?' he asked.

'Yes, there is,' I declared hotly. 'God's blood! What in the name of hell are we going down here for?'

He began to walk again. 'I have an inclination that we might see something in daylight which we missed before. Clearly the girl had her purse stolen or she mislaid it between leaving the inn and going to the alehouse. I merely wonder whether she might have lost it here.'

I kicked a pebble from my path, but there was little to say. His decision was logical, and the purse had to be somewhere. Like him, I knew that most thieves would drop a purse once they had emptied it. There was no point keeping hold of something which could prove guilt.

It was only a short way from the inn, and soon we were in the gloomy corridor. The place where her body had lain was scuffed and muddy from all the feet which had come to see where she had died, and I was confident the knight was wasting his time. I leaned against the wall while he probed and searched. He gave a short exclamation, and sprang towards me, snatching something from the ground at my feet.

'What is it?' I asked, and in answer the grinning knight held out a small circle of yellow metal, crusted with mud.

'So the thief dropped her ring as he fled?' I suggested. His look sent a shiver of expectation trickling down my spine.

He ignored me and peered at the wall. It was of cob and had probably been the outer wall of a house, but now it simply enclosed a garden. Baldwin turned and returned to the street, going to the front door and asking the bemused owner if he could go into the garden. As we walked through the little house, he gave me a dry little smile. 'If someone stole her purse, he may well have taken out all the coins and thrown it, empty, over the nearest wall. That would be sensible, wouldn't it?'

I grunted. As far as I was concerned the man was a fool, wasting my time as well as his own. I saw no reason to alter my opinion when we arrived in the yard. Sir Baldwin crouched and scrabbled among the weeds near the wall. And then, to my astonishment, he lifted up her purse. I couldn't mistake it.

He hefted it in his hand, head on one side as he surveyed me. 'It's still full, Coroner,' he said softly, and there was a coldness to his voice and manner which I didn't like. But I felt it would be better not to take umbrage. Saying no more, he turned away and stalked from the place.

We had only gone a short way down the street when it happened. I should have expected it, of course, but when the tranter shouted and pointed at me, it was still a shock.

'Murderer! Bigamist!'

The blood turned to ice in my veins, my bowels felt as if they had turned to water, and I swallowed and retreated before the accusing finger Edward pointed at me. He had been waiting with Sir Baldwin's servant; obviously the knight had sent his man to fetch the tranter so that he could accuse me in this way. In the middle of the street, mark you!

'What do you mean by pointing at me? Do you dare to suggest . . .' I blustered, but the man leaned forward and spat at me.

'Look at him, Sir Baldwin, a *noble* knight he'd have you believe, but he's a murderer of women! He has his wife at home, but he desired this young girl, so he swore his vows to her and enjoyed her nuptial bed, and then deserted her. And now he's murdered her to stop her spreading word of his faithlessness and deceit!'

The Dean was kind. He refused to allow the inquest to continue until I had drunk a full pint of wine, and I gratefully swallowed the jug in two draughts. I hadn't expected my secret to be so speedily discovered. When I had drunk, the Dean sat on a bench and Baldwin motioned to his servant, who walked from the room, I thought to fetch more wine, before speaking.

'Now, Edward, perhaps you could tell us why you made your accusation?' Sir Baldwin was seated in the Dean's own chair across the table from me, the purse and ring before him, and I could almost feel his look, as if his eyes could shoot flames.

'I knew the girl. Her name was Emily, daughter of Reginald, a merchant in Tiverton. I used to have dealings with her father, and met her at the inn yesterday afternoon. She was tired, but thrilled to be here in Crediton, and I asked her if her father was with her. She went quiet at that, and said he wasn't. I pressed her, but she wouldn't say much, only soon she admitted she'd married a man by exchanging vows, but her father wanted her to wed someone of his choosing, and she'd left home rather than tell him what she'd done.'

The Dean nodded. 'If the two exchanged vows the marriage was legal and valid, even if they didn't have the banns read or have a priest witness their nuptials.'

'Yes, it was valid, sir, except she confessed that her lover was the Coroner, and this Coroner of ours is married, with a daughter. I realised immediately what had happened. Emily was a beautiful girl, Sir Baldwin, any man would be proud to possess her, and this one wanted her all the more because she wouldn't satisfy his lust without a legal marriage. So he swore to her, and took her, and left her. And yesterday I had to tell poor Emily that he was married. She was desolate. Can you imagine it? Her lover had lied; she had lost her maidenhead to a man who couldn't ever be hers. For him she had forsaken her father and her family.'

'What do you say to this, Coroner?' Sir Baldwin demanded.

'It's rubbish. How can you trust to the word of a man like this? I . . .'

The blasted tranter cut me short. 'Sir, another thing is, this Coroner met her while he was in Tiverton performing the inquest on a girl who'd been stabbed in the market.'

'You can't suggest that I had anything to do with that,' I cried. 'Christ's blood! It was two days after the murder that I arrived in town!'

'You were there all the time,' he countered, 'staying with the Courtenay family at the castle.'

It was true, and there was no way I could deny it with conviction, but I still appealed to Sir Baldwin. 'Sir, you must believe me when I say that I had nothing to do with this murder! I couldn't have killed the poor girl. I loved her.'

That brought a chilly comment from the Dean. 'And what of your wife, Coroner? What of her whom you should have loved before you ever perjured yourself to this poor girl?'

'Dean, I loved her! My wife and I have been married for years . . . You can't understand, your vow of chastity has emasculated you, but a man like me can love many women and . . .'

'Enough!' Sir Baldwin snapped. 'There is no need for you to say more, it is clear you accept your bigamy.' He turned to Edward again. 'You have done well to bring all this to my attention, yet I would like to hear why you are so convinced that he killed her as well.'

The tranter took a deep breath. 'After I spoke to her, she was devastated. She said she would speak to the Coroner. I told her it would be foolish, but she begged me to intervene on her behalf, to speak to one of the Coroner's men at the inn and demand a meeting between them. When she went to fetch her stuff from the inn, I sat back and thought about it long and hard, but finally did as she asked. Back at the inn I got into a game of dice with some of the Coroner's men, and explained what had happened. The fellow gave me to believe it wasn't the first time something like this had happened, and agreed to ask the Coroner to meet her near the alley where you found her body.'

'That's true enough,' I said, trying to show my innocence by assisting, but all I got was a chilly stare from Sir Baldwin, and I subsided.

'He promised that the Coroner would be there late in the afternoon, and I saw her as she left the inn and told her where to go. She thanked me, and went down to the alehouse, fearful of meeting someone she might know if she stayed at the inn, and she concealed her purse when I suggested it. An alehouse is not the place to take lots of coin. She laughed then, sort of bitter. Said it wasn't hers now anyway. I . . . I also decided to go to the alley and see that she was all right. I was worried, I thought he might harm her.'

'What did you see?' Sir Baldwin asked quietly.

'Sir, I found them right where her body was later. She accused him, and he confessed, sneering . . .' I felt the priest's cold, angry eyes fix themselves upon me '. . . and said he would pay her to go away. Said she should go back to her father and not waste the Coroner's time. She dropped to her knees and begged his help, and he laughed. Said he'd already paid her a small fortune. She said she'd thought he'd given her the purse of money to let her set up their home, and he laughed, saying it was the price of her virginity. Then she stood and threw something at him, calling him names. He seemed touched by her rage and misery, and apologised. I heard him promising her more money if she'd stop crying. They were walking towards me by now, so I ducked into a dark corner until they'd passed, then left. I needed a drink to wash away his deceit.'

I must confess to a vague sense of disinterest in the matter now. Maybe it was the wine, but it was as if all rationality had left me, and I was merely the shell of a man observing the destruction of another. I found myself biting my nails, bleakly watching the knight and priest with bland unawareness. It was as if all my reasoning abilities had flown.

Sir Baldwin nodded, drumming his fingers on the table before him. Shielding his eyes, he said, 'You went back to the inn, I suppose?'

'No, the alehouse owned by John and his wife.'

'And you did not see her again until you saw her body?'

'That's right.'

Now Sir Baldwin frowned at the table top before him. 'Is there anything you want to add, Sir Eustace?'

'It's a lie,' I spat. 'The man's jealous of me because she wanted me, and he's prepared to lie to have me hanged. He hates authority! Look at him, you can see it in his eyes, for God's sake! I met her, it's true, but she had her purse on her, and she held it to me and told me to take it back because she couldn't keep it, not now, and that was when I left her. Her tears were painful to witness, so I left her and came back here to the church for the feast. I wouldn't have killed her! Why should I? What would have been the bloody point?'

There was plenty more I could have said, damning him, the miserable tranter, even the Dean, but I held my tongue and dumbly shook my head. The truth is, I was too appalled by my position to be able to think clearly at all, and seeing the loathing in the Dean's eyes, where the night before they had been full of respect and friendship, left me feeling shrivelled and withdrawn.

Sir Baldwin sat silently and stared, yes, stared at me, for a good long while. All the time the room was quiet, as if everyone there was waiting for him to decide on my sentence. I wanted to scream out, 'It's not true, it's all a lie!' but I knew there was no point. Even the brilliant Sir Baldwin wouldn't be able to prove my innocence, and to be fair, it looked as if he had already made up his own mind about my guilt.

He finally pulled his eyes from me as if with a real effort of will, and drew them down to the table. He pulled the little purse towards him and untied the strings.

40

'I believe you are innocent, Coroner,' he said, and with those words I felt a charge like a blast of gunpowder thrill my whole body. I staggered as if physically struck, and couldn't help but let out a gasp.

'*No*!' The tranter shook his head in disbelief and gazed wildly from the knight to me, his mouth working in rage. 'You can't let him go! I told you he was there, and I saw her with him. Who else could have killed her?'

'You,' said Sir Baldwin equably without looking up. He up-ended the purse and tipped out a bright stream of copper coins. 'And this money is why.'

Well, I confess I began to wonder about his reasoning then. He sat there, sadly studying the small pile of cash before him, like a seneschal who has just been told a serf can't pay more towards his rent. When he spoke, his voice came from far away, as if he was relating a story long rehearsed.

'The Coroner had no reason to kill the girl. Why should he? She could have embarrassed him, but what of it? From all I have heard of Sir Eustace, he is quite used to conducting affairs of the heart, and I expect his wife knows all about them. One more could hardly cause him or her any concern. So I can see no logical reason why he should murder the girl. Yet if he *had* killed her, he is not the sort of man to leave all this money with her. You, Edward, say that they walked away together. Yet they didn't: she died there on the ground.'

'Because he killed her!'

Sir Baldwin held up a handful of coins. 'The Coroner would not have left this behind.'

'He must have thrown it over the wall!'

'No, *she* did. Shortly after throwing her ring in his face. Just after he left her, in a fit of anger and fear.'

The tranter stared while Sir Baldwin allowed the coins to dribble through his fingers. 'No, if the Coroner had killed her it could only have put him at risk. He was used to paying for his women, and he expected her to take the money and start a new life. But she threw the ring at him. She was honourable and wanted nothing of his once she realised how he had dishonoured her. That was why she threw away the money. Every coin was a reminder of his faithlessness. But you didn't know it had gone, did you, Edward? You saw the Coroner leaving and hid until he had passed, but you had one thought on your mind: the money! You had seen how much she had at the inn, and you thought it would be easy to slip your blade between her shoulders and take the lot for yourself. Especially since you could incriminate the Coroner at the same time. And perhaps enjoy her body as well.'

'No! *He* killed her, just like Susan in Tiverton . . .'

'But as soon as the Coroner left her, she chucked the purse over the nearest wall. You were hiding and did not see. You thought she still had her purse on her. But when she was dead, you found nothing on her. Not even her ring.'

'I never looked for her . . .' He stopped himself suddenly while Sir Baldwin nodded slowly.

'And you were in Tiverton, too, weren't you?' he said.

As he spoke, his servant returned. In his hand he held a loose bundle which he untied before his master. There inside was my spare knife, and the man pulled it free from its sheath and held it to Sir Baldwin. The knight took it and studied it closely, then set it aside and picked up a second knife.

'That's mine, what are you doing with it?' The panic in the tranter's voice was a warm, soothing balm to me. I could have sagged with relief as I saw the knight frown and pick at the hilt. He wiped his thumbnail over the base of the blade, and looked up coldly. 'Edward, I accuse you of murder. You will be taken from here to the gaol to wait for your trial when the judge is next here. And God help you!'

Later I went to the Dean's buttery and poured myself some of his best Bordeaux wine. It sank down wonderfully, and when I heard the knight's footsteps, I immediately rose and waved to him to offer him some so that he could drink to my wonderful success and freedom. I called out about the blond girl at the inn, and said I'd give him the first opportunity to assault her defences, all in good jest, you understand, although I admit I had been thinking about her, and about her wayward-looking eye.

And that's the other thing I remember about the man: his intolerable rudeness. He must have heard me, but while I stood there holding the jug high, he walked straight past me without a word, hardly even looking at me.

I mean to say, it's not as if I'd done anything wrong, the arrogant bastard.

Imagine the full horror Safeway's on a Saturday morning – kids screaming, trolleys barging, old ladies wielding sticks – and there, standing on a shelf with a cover that immediately caught my eye, *The Leper of St Giles* by Ellis Peters. It is said that there is a moment in everyone's life when things change irrevocably, and from that inauspicious beginning everything changed for me.

Completely hooked, I went to the local bookshop and started to work my way through the Brother Cadfael novels, my admiration growing with every book I read. Quite honestly, I had never heard of history/mystery, as the Americans call it, and what a door was opened for me. Having exhausted Cadfael I turned to Lindsey Davis and Edward Marston and rejoiced that such a genre had come into being. Then came a grave moment in my career. I had been writing historical novels with a moderate amount of success, and couldn't understand why one of my best had failed to do well. Then somebody pointed out to me that historical novels were 'dead in the water' – oh, chilling phrase – but that historical crime was doing well. Thus my entire career changed direction and the John Rawlings series of detective novels was born.

I had researched the lively apothecary some years earlier for Canada Dry, who wanted to find out who was the originator of their Rawlings tonic and soda waters. I had a few clues, and at the end of two weeks' fascinating work, the young man himself came popping up, bright as a bubble in one of his carbonated brews. To me, he was the obvious choice for my detective. I had joined the ranks of the history/mystery writers.

I owe it all to Ellis Peters and Brother Cadfael. Firmly taking me by the hand they led me down a fresh and enjoyable path, introduced me to a new genre and a lot of new and exciting friends, fellow members of the Crime Writers' Association. John Rawlings and I are deeply grateful to them both.

Deryn Lake

Death at Strawberry Hill

Deryn Lake

It had once been a beautiful face, there was no doubt about that. Through the thick enamel make-up, worn to try and disguise time's cruel devastations, the fine lines of the woman's face were clearly and somehow touchingly visible. Lying semi-conscious in his arms, into which he had lifted her after she had collapsed on the floor by his chair, John Rawlings, concerned for her health as he was, still could not help but appreciate the exquisitely chiselled nose, the passionate lower lip, and the curve of the lids above the lustrous, frantic eyes.

'Help me.'

The woman's voice was a rasp and John raised her even closer to his ear to hear what she was saying. 'Where is your pain?' he asked urgently.

'All over. Every muscle aches. And I feel so nauseated. Oh God help me, I believe I am going to die.'

'Nonsense, Madam,' the Apothecary answered briskly, and reached in his pocket for the salts which he carried with him at all times.

He had been sitting in a coffee house situated in Church Street, Twickenham, that village on the Thames described by Horace Walpole, the cultivated and eccentric son of Robert the former prime minister, as 'a seaport in miniature', when the incident had taken place. At one moment the Apothecary, far from his shop in Shug Lane, Piccadilly, had been reading the newspaper, minding his business, and enjoying the sharp autumn air blowing in from across the river, the next the woman had fallen to the floor at his buckle-shoed feet.

John's reaction had been instantaneous. Trained to prescribe for and attend the sick, he had dropped to his knees beside her and felt the woman's racing pulse. Then he had raised her in his arms.

Now she spoke again, very faintly. 'Those salts, Sir, are too strong for me. I feel as if I might vomit at any moment.'

Acutely aware that he was wearing rather select clothes that day, fashion being the Apothecary's principal weakness and most of his

45

spare money going to his tailor, John carefully shifted the position of his patient's head.

'Madam, I think it might be better if I helped you outside. This is hardly the place, I believe.'

And indeed it was not, the coffee house containing such elegantly dressed company, so dazzling an array of delicacies, so tempting a show of iced buns and mouth-watering cakes, as to rule it a temple of refinement.

Therefore, much to the relief of everyone present, particularly a beau with his hat pulled so far forward he could scarcely see and who accordingly had been forced to stand on a chair to get a better view, the Apothecary contrived to get his patient into the fresh air. There, sorry for her though he was, John Rawlings stood back a little while the wretched woman was violently sick.

'Oh God help me!' she exclaimed once more as the spasm ended.

Hampered indeed by the lack of his medical bag which he had left behind at his lodging, John answered, 'Madam, let me escort you home, then call upon you there later to attend you.'

She glanced at him in surprise. 'Attend me, Sir?'

'I am an apothecary by profession and feel that I may be of some assistance to you.'

The gorgeous features concealed by their mask of white looked incredibly sad. 'I believe that I am beyond help. There is some malignancy eating away at me that drains all my strength. There is a canker within, Sir. A canker within.'

'Have you seen a physician?'

The woman sighed. 'Several, but none has been able to cure me.'

'Then let me try,' said John, attracted to her despite the fact that she was clearly older than he was by many years, and far from looking her best at that somewhat desperate moment.

She smiled suddenly and the Apothecary saw again just how lovely she must once have been. 'Very well.' She held out her hand. 'My carriage is waiting for me at the end of the street.'

'Would you permit me to ride with you, then return to my lodging house to fetch my physicks and pills?'

'How very kind of you. I would be most grateful.'

As they crossed the cobbles and the equipage came into view, John was amazed by its splendour. He had put the woman down as a creature of fashion, a member of the *beau monde*, a person of means, but the conveyance that awaited her far exceeded what he would have considered such a being to have owned. Indeed, its style was almost royal, from the elaborate paintings on the doors to the excellence of its cushioned interior and elaborate gilt ornamentation. Unwittingly, John's eyes widened.

46

Seeing her approach, one of the postilions, joking with his companions, hurried to open the door and pull the step down.

'We were not expecting you quite so soon, Madam.'

The woman shook her head. 'Alas I was taken ill again, Chivers. Horribly so.' She turned to John. 'Sir, I am staying at Strawberry Hill with my friend Horace Walpole. Do you know him at all?'

The Apothecary bowed low. 'No, I have never had the honour, though I once treated one of his servants for gout.' He produced a business card which read "John Rawlings, Apothecary, at the Sign of the Cherry Tree, Shug Lane, Piccadilly, and also of 2, Nassau Street, Soho." 'I hope I can help you as I helped him.'

The woman gave another of her haunted smiles, then glanced at John's card. Once again her hand was extended. 'I am Georgiana Ashley, Mr Rawlings.'

John kissed her fingers, noticing, rather to his astonishment, that her nails were coarser than he would have imagined those befitting a woman of her station. Surprised, he glanced at them, but Georgiana snatched her hand away as if she were aware of what he was thinking.

'Now, let us get back. I feel another wave of faintness coming over me.'

'As soon as you get to Strawberry Hill you must go straight to bed and rest. Such an attack as you have suffered will have drained your strength.'

She did not reply, merely casting her glistening eyes over him, dark in her pallid features, as the coachman cracked his whip and they set off for Walpole's gothic castle, standing amongst its gardens of shady bowers, nodding groves and amaranthine shadows.

Sitting beside her on the coach's padded seat was an extraordinary sensation. For there could be no doubt that Georgiana Ashley, ill though she might be, exerted a deadly attraction for men. Knowing that she was probably twice his twenty-nine years of age did not detract from the powerful feelings that she aroused in the Apothecary, an admirer of the fair sex who suffered from an alarming tendency to take to bed ladies under suspicion in the murder enquiries in which John had sometimes assisted Mr John Fielding, Principal Magistrate of the lawless town of London. Unable to help himself, he took Mrs Ashley's elbow lightly in his hand, and was still holding it when the carriage drew up outside the pillared entrance to Strawberry Hill.

'May I beg a further moment of your time?' asked Georgiana, turning her painted face towards him.

'Certainly,' John answered, his smile just a fraction foolish.

'Would you explain to my host exactly what took place in the coffee house?'

'By all means,' said the Apothecary, glad of an opportunity to see the fabled interior of the amazing gothic castle, remodelled by Horace Walpole from a simple country cottage. Yet what he had not expected as he followed Georgiana into the famous Round Room was to find the place full of people. It seemed that the master of Strawberry Hill was not only entertaining Mrs Ashley that day.

Sprawled on the curving window seat of the turret was a young man of about eighteen years, his long, lank sparrow-brown hair tied back in a bow. He stretched and yawned indolently as the newcomers entered, dislodging the pair of rimless spectacles which perched on the end of his nose. The face of this somewhat unappetising individual, peppered with pimples, was as thin as his lanky body. Yet despite his generally unprepossessing appearance, John sensed that there was an arrogance about the fellow which he personally found irritating. Somewhat reluctantly, the youth stood up in order to make a bow.

Also getting to his feet was a very different type of individual, his only similarity to the other the fact that he, too, was tall and slim. But there any resemblance ended, for this man had black hair, deep brown eyes, and handsome looks fit to make a maiden swoon.

There were also two females in the room, a mother and daughter John presumed, for there was a certain superficial similarity between them, both the women having auburn hair and tilting cat-like eyes. But there the likeness ceased, for where the mother's look was bold and taunting, the girl seemed half dead with shyness, unable to give John even the most timid of glances, a fact quite at odds with her feline appearance.

In the middle of them all, contentedly ramming a long stemmed pipe with tobacco from a jar, sat Walpole himself, pale of face, excessively thin, yet with the most wonderful dark, lively eyes, very bright and penetrating. He got up and hurried forward as he caught sight of his guest.

'My dear Georgiana, what is the trouble? I see you are trembling from head to foot. Has your illness returned?'

Mrs Ashley touched his arm, then leant on it more heavily than she had intended. 'It has never gone away. I fear that the fresh air of Twickenham has not cured me as we had hoped. Oh Horace, I fell to the floor in pain today. Had it not been for the good offices of this young man, Mr Rawlings, an apothecary from London, I fear I would have disgraced myself in public.'

John spoke up. 'Mr Walpole, it is a pleasure to meet you. Allow me to present my card.' He waited a second while Walpole perused it, then said, 'I was able to render some assistance to Mrs Ashley today, but feel I could do more if I were to fetch my medical bag.'

'Which is in his lodging,' Georgiana continued. 'Horace, with your consent I have asked Mr Rawlings to attend me here later.'

'Certainly, my dear,' answered Walpole, his dark and lively eyes full of sympathy. 'Allow me to ring for your maid to help you to bed. You look quite wretched.'

Mrs Ashley nodded wanly. 'How very kind of you.'

Once more she leaned on her host and Walpole put a thin arm round her shoulders, supporting her against his own slender frame until, a moment or two later, a round-bodied, round-eyed, white-haired servant hurried into the room and led her charge away as if she were a sickly child.

The pimply young man addressed himself to John, his voice lowered to an undertone. 'You seem to have made a great impression, Sir. Allow me to introduce myself. Mrs Ashley's cousin, Robert Clements. But however clever you are you'll never cure Cousin Georgiana, you know.'

John, having bowed, looked at him in surprise. 'Why do you say that?'

'Because her illnesses lie in her head.'

'So do many other people's. But that does not mean their maladies cannot be taken away.'

Robert smiled nastily. 'I think you misunderstand me, Mr Rawlings. Georgiana *enjoys* the attention that her condition brings. I mean to say, what else would she have had to talk about after wee Georgie was sent to the Colonies.'

The apothecary stared at him blankly. 'Wee Georgie?'

But before the young man could say another word, there was a rustle at his side and the mother and daughter appeared, the older woman shooting a challenging glance in John's direction.

'Did I hear Georgiana say you were an apothecary?'

John bowed deeply, very aware of the slanting eyes assessing him. 'I am indeed, Madam.'

She inclined her head graciously. 'Lady Fairbury. And this is my daughter, Millicent. I am an old friend of Mrs Ashley's. Now, what has that reprobate Robert been saying to you?'

'Nothing that would not deserve a whipping for answer,' said the dark young man with an extremely pleasant smile which he directed straight at the discomfited Clements. 'Carter Grey, Sir.' He bowed with far more elaboration than befitted a meeting with an unknown apothecary.

John replied with a simple salute. 'John Rawlings, of Shug Lane, Piccadilly.' With a look of complete innocence he turned to Robert. 'You were saying about wee Georgie, Sir?'

There was a stunned silence during which Lady Fairbury hissed a breath and Millicent turned even paler than she was naturally.

Carter Grey's dark eyes grew molten. 'You are a bloody fool, Robert. 'Zounds, but you should be thrashed for this.'

The apothecary, who had long since developed the art of assuming differing expressions to suit particular occasions, now put on his contrite look.

'Forgive me, ladies. I had no wish to be tactless. To tell the truth I was merely making conversation.'

Lady Fairbury recovered herself. 'Do not blame yourself, Sir. It is another who seems to take perverse delight in discussing his family's past.'

Robert chimed in, his spots glowing red as he blazed defiance. 'The truth, whether they like to admit it or not, is that Cousin Georgiana had an indiscretion in her youth, an indiscretion which was bundled off to Virginia so that it wouldn't cause any embarrassment.'

'How dare you!' spat Lady Fairbury, cracking her fan across Robert's cheek. 'You little beast! You ought to be ashamed of yourself.'

'I've a good mind to take you outside,' snarled Grey.

And it was at that moment, in the manner of high comedy, that Horace Walpole, totally unaware of the scene unfolding within his walls, turned from the window through which he had been gazing lovingly at the rich colours of his autumnal gardens, and said, 'Will you join us for dinner Mr Rawlings, once you have attended Mrs Ashley? I have not been in town these last few weeks and would so love to hear a fresh view on the start of the new reign. Is there a good deal of gossip in the capital?'

John put on his young, eager face. 'Oh indeed there is, Sir. And, yes, I would be honoured to dine with you. At what hour will dinner be served?'

'Four o'clock.'

'Then I shall return straight away to get my physicks.'

But John did more than that, making time to change into his midnight blue silk with the heavy embroidery, thinking it to be far more suitable for an evening in the elegant surroundings of Strawberry Hill. Always practical, however, he put his long apothecary's apron into his bag before he got into Mrs Ashley's waiting carriage.

Visions of her lovely haggard face came to haunt him on the short journey between Montpelier Row and Strawberry Hill, and once again that odd wave of attraction flared in his blood. Indeed, there was something very sensual about Georgiana, and the news that she had borne a bastard was of little surprise to him. What was so odd though, John thought, was the extraordinary way in which the others had reacted to Robert Clements' indiscreet remarks. Illegitimate births were commonplace at all social levels, and wee Georgie would not be the first to be sent to the Colonies to make his way in the world. So why, he wondered, were Georgiana's friends so angry on her behalf?

Still turning these ideas over in his mind, John climbed a staircase and entered a large bedchamber in the north wing, then stopped short in the doorway. Georgiana Ashley lay in a vast canopied bed, looking as small and frail as a wraith beneath its overpowering drapes. Leaning over her was the servant who had fetched her from the Round Room, sponging her brow and holding a bowl into which Georgiana had recently been sick. There was the terrible stench of vomit and loose bowel movements everywhere, together with something which frightened the Apothecary. In that huge room there was also the unmistakable odour of death.

Without thought, John threw his beautiful evening coat on to a chair and donned his great apron, then hurried forward to the bedside.

'What has happened?' he asked abruptly.

The servant jumped to her feet and gave a bob of a curtsy. 'She's been ill again, Sir. In fact she's very poorly. Heaven preserve her is all I can say.'

'Has there been any further muscular pain, do you know?'

'She's been complaining of what she calls cramps.' The woman burst into sudden and rather shocking tears. 'Oh Sir, is she going from us?'

'Not if I can find the cause of this wretched illness,' John answered grimly. 'Now, stay close. I'm going to have to examine her body, and no use opening your mouth in protest. It's a question of necessity.'

And with that he drew back the bed covers and delicately started to unbutton Georgiana's shift.

'She wouldn't like it, Sir. Not you a stranger and all,' the servant protested.

''Zounds, woman, would you have her die rather than confound her modesty?'

'No, Sir.'

'Then hold your peace.'

He had undone Mrs Ashley's shift to the waist and was already raising a candle to help him see any signs of a rash that might be there. Yet despite the fact that he was now in the role of medical examiner, John could not help but notice that the breasts he was looking at were wonderful, as firm and splendid as those of a woman half Georgiana's age. Angry with himself for straying a moment, the Apothecary firmly closed down that part of his brain and continued his search. And there, sure enough, faintly visible but definitely confirmed by his fingertips, were the weals of an abdominal rash.

The Apothecary sat upright, memories of old lessons with his Master pounding through his head. Then, after a moment or two, he looked for signs of the outbreak elsewhere on her body, collecting his thoughts all the while. Rather as he had suspected, there were none.

He turned to the servant. 'May I know your name?'

'Emily, Sir.'

'Thank you. I am John Rawlings, an apothecary. I want to remove your mistress's face enamel. I need to look at the condition of her skin beneath.'

51

'Oh, she won't like that, Sir. Mrs Ashley never allows anyone to see her without her paint.'

'The situation is too critical for such niceties. Fetch soap and water and I'll do it myself.'

Emily's round countenance seemed to swell to half its size again. 'No, that you will not, Sir. I have helped my lady dress for the last fifteen years and no other being will lay a finger on her.'

John paused and looked at her sharply. 'Twenty years, you say?'

'Yes, Sir.'

'Then can you tell me how long she has been exhibiting these symptoms?' Emily looked blank. 'How long has Mrs Ashley been ill like this?'

'Oh, a while, Sir.'

'How long exactly?'

Emily burst into another attack of sudden tears. 'Oh don't be so fierce. What have I done wrong?'

'I don't know yet,' John muttered under his breath. In his usual tone, he said, 'Well?'

'She's been down in spirits for the last four years or thereabouts, but in the past month her condition has become chronic.'

'And does the start of her illness coincide with the time when wee Georgie was sent to Virginia?'

'What do you know of that?' Emily asked suspiciously.

'Enough. Now tell me exactly everything you can remember. It might be very important.'

The servant hesitated, then launched into her tale. 'Well, Georgie went off three-and-a-half years ago. The spring of 1757 it was. I can recall that because it was shortly after his twelfth birthday, when he was considered old enough to fend for himself. As soon as he was gone Mrs Ashley took to her room with a fit of the vapours and wept herself dry.'

'Quite understandable. Did she vomit at all at that time?'

'A little. But nothing like she does now. Oh Sir, is my lady dying?'

Suddenly sorry for her, John threw his arm round the servant's shoulders. 'I've told you already, not if I can help it. Now get that enamel cleaned off fast. It's vital that I examine Mrs Ashley's skin.'

While Emily worked with soap and water, the Apothecary delicately picked up strands of Georgiana's hair, at which she moaned and opened her eyes. She stared at John in consternation.

'Who are you?' came the thread of a voice.

'The apothecary you met today. I'm trying to help you get better. Just lie quietly.'

But the whispering words went on. 'Emily, what are you doing? Why are you removing my enamel?'

'Because the gentleman wants to look at your skin.'

The lustrous eyes rolled in John's direction. 'Why are you doing this?'

'Because it is vital for your well-being that I see you as nature intended. If you fear that I will think you old without your *maquillage*, rest easy. You are a beauty and always will be. Believe me, Mrs Ashley, you are one of the most striking women I have ever met.'

Georgiana smiled wanly. 'Once, long ago, perhaps.'

'No, still. Let me assure you.'

She produced a thin hand from beneath the bed coverings and took the Apothecary's in a cold grasp. Her nails were as coarse and dry as autumn leaves, yet he raised her fingers to his lips and kissed them one after the other. But even while he did so the memory of something he had seen while he had been apprenticed and called out with his Master to attend a dying man, grew more and more frighteningly intense. And the locks of hair that he now stroked so gently, endorsed all that he was beginning to suspect. Shiny though they might be, they were thin, sparse even.

Georgiana closed her eyes. 'Oh Georgie,' she said, so quietly that John could barely hear the words.

'Do you still hear news of him?' he asked, equally softly.

A tear ran down the cheek that Emily was cleansing of its make-up.

'Georgie is dead,' Mrs Ashley answered with a sob. 'He died all alone in the Colonies, my poor boy, with no mother to comfort and hold him. I should never have let him go but they put much pressure on me to do so. I saw him sail away, waving his little hat till he was just a dot in the distance. Oh Georgie, Georgie.'

She turned her face into the pillow and wept, but not before the Apothecary had seen what lay beneath her usual mask of enamel. Astonishingly, the skin was as white and clear as if it were still in place. John thought that he had not come across such a lovely pale complexion in years, and felt his heart lurch as this final fact confirmed his diagnosis. Hardly able to believe it himself, he drew Emily to one side.

'I am going downstairs to speak to Mr Walpole. Meanwhile, you are to give your mistress nothing to eat or drink, nor are you to allow anyone to visit her. Do you understand?'

She looked at him in consternation. 'But Lady Fairbury . . .'

'Not even she is to cross this threshold. Is that clear?'

'But how do I keep her out?'

'Repeat my instructions. Bar the way. If you cannot cope I'll send a footman to assist you.'

Emily nodded her head. 'I think you should, Sir. They are very persuasive, this particular bunch of people.'

'So I would imagine,' John answered harshly.

He found Horace Walpole, who had changed for dinner, standing

53

before the fire in the library, holding his hands out to the blaze. The two women were presumably still at their toilette but at the ends of the room, as far away from one another as they could get, sat Robert Clements and Carter Grey, each staring into a book they were not reading.

John, who had forgotten to remove his apothecary's apron, gave a bow and stepped up to Walpole with a most serious expression on his face.

'Sir, may I have a word with you in private?'

The older man looked somewhat surprised. 'By all means. If you would care to come outside.'

He opened a door and the Apothecary went through, finding himself on a dimly lit staircase, sinister shields and arms and a mighty suit of armour guarding the stairs like the ghosts of long-dead knights.

'Is it about Mrs Ashley?' Walpole asked, his voice ringing down the stairwell.

'Yes. I have to inform you – and there is no easy way to say this – that she is being slowly poisoned with arsenic. I have absolutely no doubt about my diagnosis. I saw such a case some years ago and the similarities cannot be denied.'

The older man gaped open-mouthed. 'You are absolutely positive?'

'Absolutely. Further—' John dropped his voice. '—The fact that her symptoms have worsened in the last few days suggests to me that her poisoner is here, in this very house.'

Horace Walpole gave an almighty shudder and clutched the Apothecary for support, his long frail body swaying as if he were going to faint. 'This cannot be true,' he whispered. 'Everyone staying here is known either to me personally or to Mrs Ashley. Not one of them would be capable of murder.'

Naturally pale of complexion, Walpole now looked like death itself, and his words came in a terrible rush as if they were being squeezed out of him.

'I think you had better sit down, Sir,' said John anxiously. 'Let me get you a brandy.'

He turned as if to go back into the library, but Walpole raised a hand. 'No, I must collect my thoughts before I face those two. Take me to the Round Room where I can sit quietly.'

Declining to join him, anxious to look in again on his patient, John was just about to descend the staircase, having seen Walpole comfortably settled, when voices from above, from the Tower Room, the door of which stood half open, caught his attention. Flattening himself against the wall, the Apothecary listened.

'. . . if she finds out that it is me, not herself . . .' said a female voice, the beginning and the end of her sentence totally inaudible.

A man answered much more clearly. 'To the devil with her, she's a spent force.'

'You didn't think so at one time. It was her that you fell in love with remember?'

'Until I saw you, sweetheart. Now, have you memorised all that must be done in two days' time?'

'Of course I have.' The female laughed lightly and then John heard one of them walk across to the door and close it, after which the voices became an indistinct murmur. Deep in thought, he continued down the stairs then out into the garden to breathe the fresh night air before returning to the sick room.

It was cold now, a true November dusk, the sky lavender tinged by a deep and misty pink. In Strawberry Hill all the candles had been lit and their combined light threw a glow on the lawn where John stood, looking around. Ahead of him lay an open grove, through which he could see a field and a winding wood made up of trees and flowering shrubs; to his left, by contrast, stretched a fine view of the town and church of Twickenham. Standing on a small hill as it did, its delightful meadows sweeping down to the river, Walpole's gothic castle commanded a stunning vista which, on a summer's night, one could have stood and enjoyed for hours. However, at this time of year, with the night closing in and the temperature growing sharper by the minute, John felt that he must return inside, and would have done so had it not been for the strange sight of Robert Clements, spectacles awry and clothes somewhat disordered, scrambling out of the wood and hurrying up the hill towards the villa.

So that young man, unless he moved very fast indeed, could not have been in the Tower Room a few minutes earlier. Thoughts of people skulking furtively round Strawberry Hill brought Mrs Ashley to the forefront of John's mind and he turned on his heel and hurried within, making his way straight to the North Bedroom.

His orders had been flouted. Sitting on the bed and leaning right over an unconscious Georgiana, whispering to her, was Lady Fairbury, while Emily stood cowering in a corner, her hands over her face.

'You must leave at once, Madam,' called John in a voice that rattled with ice.

Startled, Lady Fairbury rose to her feet and whirled round. 'How dare you give orders to me!'

'I dare, Madam, because I am in charge of this patient and, as there is no physician present, her welfare lies entirely in my hands. I left instructions that she was not to be disturbed in any way. Tell me, have you given her anything to eat or drink?'

But the question was in no need of answer. Standing on a table close to the bed stood a glass of water. Without a word, the Apothecary strode into the room and picked it up, sniffing it suspiciously, then cautiously dipping in a finger and tasting it.

Lady Fairbury stared incredulously, her feline face set in a haughty expression, her dark curls tossing. 'What are you doing, you impudent rogue?'

'I am looking for traces of arsenic, Madam.'

'Are you implying . . . ?'

'I imply nothing. I state facts. Mrs Ashley is dying of slow poisoning.'

Lady Fairbury whirled on him like a vicious virago. 'Watch your tongue, young man. You'll not make accusations of that nature and emerge unscathed. A physician shall be sent for forthwith. I'll not trust the charge of my dearest friend to an unknown from the streets one second longer. Leave this house, do you hear me. Leave this house.'

The cowering Emily spoke up. 'No, m'Lady. That would be evil. I shan't allow Mrs Ashley to be without help at her extreme hour.'

'You? Allow?' answered Lady Fairbury scornfully, and actually laughed.

A voice spoke from the doorway. 'Mind your tongue, Harriet. There may be a lot at stake here. Send for a physician by all means, but do not be seen to leave Georgiana without medical assistance at the mercy of amateurs.'

It was Carter Grey who had spoken, and now he came into the room smouldering with anger, his handsome features contorted into a glare. Instantly, Lady Fairbury softened, going to him and laying her hands on his shoulders. Certain ideas that had been half formed in John's mind crystallised.

'But this man has been making imputations, my dear.'

Grey turned his dark eyes in John's direction. 'And what might they be?'

'Simply, that someone is making an attempt on Mrs Ashley's life, Sir. Arsenic has been administered to her. I'd stake my reputation on it.'

'Those are strong words, Sir.'

'Murder is a strong act, Mr Grey.'

They stared at one another in the candlelight and then Carter wheeled round to go, taking Harriet Fairbury with him. He looked back at the Apothecary over his shoulder. 'You had better be right in what you say, Sir. By God, you had.'

Harriet turned a mocking head, flicking it in Emily's direction. 'You're a fool to put your trust in her. Why, the woman's as corrupt as they come. I caught her out years ago, though I've kept my mouth closed till now.' She stared at the servant menacingly. 'Why don't you tell this clever young creature what you are really doing in Mrs Ashley's household. Go on! Traitor!' The door closed behind them.

'Well?' said John.

But Emily was saved by her mistress who gave a great groan of agony and opened eyes which glowed like gemstones in her ashen face. 'Oh, come to me someone. It is getting so dark.'

Instantly the Apothecary was at her side, raising her in his arms, just as he had done at their first meeting. In a convulsion of weeping, Emily took Mrs Ashley's hand. 'I grew to love you, truly I did,' she said.

'I know, I know,' whispered Georgiana, giving a ghost of a smile. Then she fixed her brilliant gaze on a far corner of the room, murmured 'Georgie?', and died without another word.

Unaware that she had gone, the servant continued to sob and talk to her, until John, very gently, patted her hand and shook his head. Then he laid Georgiana back on the bed, drew down her eyelids, and kissed her gently on her rapidly cooling forehead.

He stood up and looked at Emily, well aware that he would get no sense out of her at this point.

'Mr Walpole must be informed,' he said quietly.

'Yes, Sir.'

'And you must do so, Emily. I shall stay here with Mrs Ashley. She is not to be moved or touched until the physician has seen her.'

'Very good, Sir.'

She made to go. 'I'll talk to you later,' John added. 'And I shall require the truth.'

The servant cast down her swollen eyes. 'Yes, Sir.'

In the sudden silence of the empty room John stood perplexed, gazing about him as if for inspiration. That Mrs Ashley had been murdered was abundantly clear to him, but exactly how it had been done was still a mystery, just as was the motive. With a sigh he turned back to the body and mentally prepared himself for explaining to the physician exactly how he had come to his conclusions.

The Apothecary did not have long to wait. About ten minutes later footsteps sounded in the corridor and the door opened to reveal a little fat man, almost as broad as he was long, puffing crossly at the exertion of having to climb the stairs. He had obviously been told by Lady Fairbury that he was about to deal with a charlatan and a quack, for he glared at John angrily.

'And who might you be, Sir?'

John put on the most serious and solemn face in his entire collection of expressions. 'John Rawlings, Yeoman of the Worshipful Society of Apothecaries,' he answered calmly. 'And you, Sir?'

'Dr Eastwood of Twickenham, Sir. I have been called to this most unfortunate case by Mr Walpole.'

'You have been informed that the patient died within the last thirty minutes?'

'I most certainly have. And I have also been told that you believe her death to be by foul play. Poisoning by arsenic no less.' He gave a snigger which developed into an attack of coughing, which unfortunately for the doctor's dignity ended in a robustly rounded fart.

John contrived to look more solemn than ever. 'You know the symptoms of that?' he asked politely.

Dr Eastwood blew up like a fighting cock bantam. 'Of course I do. I am a physician, Sir. Death in such circumstances may not be a commonplace but I am well aware of the evidences.'

'Then be so kind, my good Sir, to examine the hair, the skin, the abdominal rash and coarse fingernails of the dead woman. These, together with the vomiting, liquid bowels, muscular aches and pains, and general nausea that she suffered, led me to form my opinion.'

The physician appeared very slightly startled by this concise diagnosis, but John continued to regard him gravely, pulling back the bed coverings to reveal the form of Georgiana Ashley, looking small and vulnerable in the grip of death.

Dr Eastwood grunted. 'Bring all the candles close, young man. Nobody could be expected to make an examination in this light.' He bent over the body, then looked up. 'What did you say your name was?'

'John Rawlings, Sir.'

'Um. Well, you're right about the hair. It's very thin yet very shiny. Did you know that in the past, giddy girls took arsenic to improve their complexions?'

'Yes, I did.'

The physician bent over the dead woman's abdomen. 'I suppose there could be no case of that here?'

John shook his head. 'Highly unlikely. Mrs Ashley always wore the full enamel. In fact she did not like to be seen without it.'

Dr Eastwood gave a small smile, his first friendly gesture. 'Vanity, vanity, all is vanity.'

'Indeed.'

The ice was broken and they talked as two professional men, examining the remains together and comparing notes. Eventually, both straightened up.

John put on his most eager face. 'Well, Sir? Was I too bold in my assumption?'

Dr Eastwood shook his head. 'Not at all, not at all. I'm afraid the parish constable will have to be sent for.'

Inwardly, John groaned. Compared with the Beak Runners of Bow Street, this form of law enforcement was primitive to say the least. The role of constable was not only an unpaid post but also compulsory. Each parish kept within its boundaries and every parishioner within that boundary was liable for service as a constable for a period of one year, continuing with his own employment the meanwhile and supposedly carrying out his constabulary duties in his private time.

Wealthy parishioners unwilling to take on such a task frequently paid deputies to act on their behalf, a custom which had given rise to a band of men who were professional deputy constables. Only in London, where the brothers Henry and John Fielding had organised the system, was there any form of proper policing at all.

He sighed. 'Yes, you're right, of course.'

Dr Eastwood smiled without amusement. 'We'll never get him out at this hour of the day. He's the landlord of the Red Lyon, not far from here, down near Cross Deep.'

'Then we'd best lock this room until he has seen it. Though I doubt there is much he can learn from it. The poison must have been administered in the poor woman's food or drink.'

'I quite agree with you,' said Dr Eastwood as he turned the key in the bedroom lock, then pocketed it. 'So need we look much further than the servant?'

The Apothecary frowned. 'That seems a little glib to me.'

'Yet the poison would have to have been taken daily, which rules out the casual visitor, does it not?'

'In that sense, yes it does.'

Dr Eastwood emitted a gusty groan. 'Well, we must face Mr Walpole and tell him what has transpired.'

'Which is not going to be easy,' said John grimly.

They found that everyone had forgathered in the Blue Breakfast Room, Walpole's favourite den. On the window seat, sitting in rather an uncomfortable row, were Millicent Fairbury and her mother, together with Carter Grey, the older woman's hand resting very lightly on the young man's thigh. She removed it as soon as she saw John's eyes flick in that direction, giving the Apothecary a deep dark scowl in return. Millicent, by contrast, had her usual shy look, eyes cast downward and not a word to say for herself, but there was a pinkness in her cheeks that had not been visible previously. Carter, for one so handsome and debonair, looked decidedly ill-at-ease, apparently not wishing to converse with either of the ladies.

Robert, who had tidied himself up since his excursion into the woods, had removed his spectacles and consequently squinted at the world small-eyed. Indeed, the redness round his puffy lids suggested to John that the young man had been crying, and he instantly wondered if Cousin Georgiana had meant more to him than he cared to admit.

Walpole sat in an armchair in the midst of them, very much the worse for liquor, a surprising fact considering that normally he was a most abstemious man, drinking little wine and relying on iced water for his usual beverage. Of Emily there was no sign, and John presumed that she had been banished to the servants' hall to weep in peace.

Every head turned as he and Dr Eastwood entered the room, and Harriet jumped to her feet.

59

'Oh my dear doctor, tell us the truth. Is darling Georgiana really dead or has that fool Emily got everything wrong as usual?' She turned another furious gaze in John's direction. 'I see that the so-called apothecary is still with you. I am surprised that you suffered his presence long enough even to speak to him.'

Fat and dumpy though he was, Dr Eastwood contrived to look immensely stern. 'Madam, I have to inform you that Mr Rawlings is a man of medicine just as I am. His diagnosis of the way in which Mrs Ashley died is the correct one.' There was a general in-drawing of breath. 'She was killed by slow arsenical poisoning and the parish constable must be sent for as soon as it is light.'

'Oh my God,' Robert Clements shouted into the stunned silence, and burst into choking tears, made all the more terrible by the fact he was unsuccessfully trying to control them.

The effect on the others was equally profound and dramatic. Lady Fairbury, her face the colour of chalk, helped herself to brandy from a decanter that stood on a tray nearby. Then she turned and pointed directly at John. 'Look no further than Emily, you interfering busybody. She was put in place to watch Georgiana as long ago as 1740, when the King was in high fig after the defeat of the Jacobites . . .'

'Speak not one word more,' thundered Carter Grey, whose face had grown so dark with emotion that he looked more Spanish than English.

She turned on him. 'It's over, isn't it? Say it, you devil. You could not treat me the way you have done over the last few weeks unless your feelings towards me had changed.' She flounced to the door. 'I am going to my room. Millicent, attend me.'

'No,' said her daughter. And John saw to his astonishment that the meek-and-mild Miss, though pale with shock, had raised her chin and was radiating defiance, and looking most attractive in the process.

'What?' thundered Lady Fairbury.

'I said no, Mother. There are more important things at stake here. Georgiana has been murdered. This is no time to dwell on one of your tedious little love affairs with a wet-eared cove straight from school.'

She glared at Carter as she said this, who, most unexpectedly, exploded into genuine laughter and tickled her under the chin.

John stood aghast at so much revelation, thinking that a great deal of wine must have been consumed in the last hour or so, a notion which a quick glance round the room at all the empty bottles confirmed.

Harriet shimmered in the doorway. 'You wretched little minx, you haven't heard the last of this.'

'And neither,' Millicent answered with amazing bravado, 'have you heard the last of me.'

There was silence as Lady Fairbury practically threw herself into the corridor and vanished in an explosive rustle of satin.

'Oh dear!' said Walpole, and smiled owlishly.

'I rather imagine,' remarked John into the somewhat strained atmosphere that followed this extraordinary exit, 'that dinner is waiting to be served. I should advise you to go and eat something, Sir.'

'Damme, but that's a good notion,' said Dr Eastwood, rubbing his hands together. 'I'll escort you, Horace. I'm famished myself.'

They left the Blue Room together, the tall thin man leaning on the shoulder of the short stout one, a somewhat poignant sight in view of Walpole's usual self-sufficiency.

'Now,' said the Apothecary, looking round the room as the older couple disappeared out of earshot, 'I think it would be better for us all if the immediate truths came out.'

'What do you mean?' asked Robert, who had finished weeping and was staring open-mouthed at the high drama taking place.

John sat down and poured himself a glass of wine. 'We are all of an age, us four, and I've seen something of the world, in one way and another. Might it not be wiser for you to tell me what you have all been up to so that we can find out who poisoned Mrs Ashley?'

'Why should we?' asked Carter, his usual insolence returning.

'Because,' the Apothecary answered levelly, 'I overheard you and a female, presumably Miss Millicent, planning something, something that might just conceivably have been a murder, while you thought you were alone in the Tower Room.'

'You eavesdropping dog . . .' Carter started, giving a fine display of teeth.

'Oh don't be so foolish,' Millicent snapped crossly. 'It's perfectly obvious that we must clear our name before the constable gets here. Simply put, Mr Rawlings . . .'

'John, please.'

'John . . . we were planning to elope. Carter was my mother's lover – she has had a succession of them, each progressively younger, ever since my father died – but he transferred his affections to me, an old enough tale I'm sure you'll agree. However, we were not going to risk her wrath and intended to leave Strawberry Hill at some ungodly hour on Tuesday morning and head straight for London where we were to be married in secret.'

'And what do you know of the late Georgiana?'

'Other than the fact that she had been a life-long friend of my mother's and the mistress of the late King, very little.'

'I would agree with all of that,' said Carter Grey, looking positively amiable and clearly under her thumb.

'The late King,' John replied reflectively. 'I see.' And he thought he did.

'It's true enough,' put in Robert. 'He was the father of little Georgie, of course. That's why the wretched child had to be sent to the Colonies.

61

It was too dangerous to have George II's bastard so close to home. That particular monarch had had enough of a fright when the Young Pretender marched south. He didn't want any more claimants to the throne coming out of the bushes.'

John smiled, his mouth curving up at one corner, an odd characteristic of his. 'Talking of bushes, what were you doing earlier this evening scrambling out of the wood below the house?'

Robert went puce. 'I was meeting a young female from the village whom I happened to chance on the other day when walking.'

Carter Grey chortled. 'Studying nature, eh?'

Poor Robert looked even more discomfited. 'You could put it that way, yes.'

Before the Apothecary's eyes all three of them were evolving and changing character. It was now quite clear that Millicent's shyness had been a mere pose and that she was a powerful and organised young woman, whilst Carter Grey's apparent lack of moderation was caused by the difficulties with which his love affairs presented him. Whereas Robert, for all his spitefulness about Georgiana, was not arrogant at all, merely a plain young man looking for fulfilment.

John turned to him. 'You must have known Mrs Ashley well, as you were related to her. Did she have any enemies that you are aware of?'

Robert took out his handkerchief and cleaned his spectacles before placing them back on his nose. 'The same enemy that Georgie had, in my belief.'

'What do you mean exactly?'

'I told you, the child had to go because he was too near the throne. Apparently he died in Virginia in most mysterious circumstances. A drowning accident it was reported to Georgiana. How very easy to arrange is what I thought at the time. And I maintain it still.'

'Do you mean . . . ?'

'That Georgie was killed? Yes, I do. And now, with George II dead but a month and his grandson the new monarch, it was thought the time was right to get rid of the dead boy's mother as well. Does it not all make a terrible sense to you?'

John nodded slowly. 'Yes, it does.'

'Are you saying,' asked Carter slowly, 'that Georgiana was killed by an agent of the state?'

Robert shrugged and spread his hands. 'To me, it is all too clear.'

'It must have been someone with access to her home,' John interposed. 'The poison had to have been introduced into her food or drink.'

'Then Emily is clearly the person to speak to.'

'Or me,' said Robert quietly. He cleared his throat. 'I stand much to gain from Georgiana's death. As her closest living relative the bulk of her fortune will come to me. Further, as an orphan, she had control of my affairs and we quarrelled constantly about the size of my allowance. That's why I was feeling so bitter today and said to you what I did about Georgie. But I swear to you, John, I did not kill her. In fact her death has upset me far more than I would have thought possible.'

He looked so sad with his silly spectacles, reddened spots and obvious blazing sincerity.

'I believe you,' said the Apothecary. He stood up. 'Thank you all for being so honest with me. I had no right to pry into your private lives like that.'

'You've done this before, haven't you,' Carter Grey stated shrewdly. 'You're used to handling people. Surely that's not just through your training as an apothecary?'

John shook his head. 'No, you're right. I have worked from time to time with Mr John Fielding of Bow Street.'

'The Blind Beak himself. Something of an honour I would say.'

'Something of an education, more likely,' John answered, and laughed. He turned to go. 'Well, I'd better see what further light Emily can throw on the matter. I'll bid you all good evening.' And with that he bowed and left the room.

He found her in the servants' hall, sitting alone and staring into a bowl of soup which some kindly soul had been good enough to provide. Emily looked up as John came in and he saw that her eyes were practically closed with weeping. Drawing up a chair, he sat down opposite her and came straight to the point.

'Emily, Lady Fairbury said that you were put in place to watch Mrs Ashley as long ago as 1740. What did she mean by that?' There was an agonising pause during which the servant stared at him dumbly, her expression full of fear. Eventually John went on, 'Were you being paid by the Secret Office to observe her because she was the King's mistress? Come on now, out with it.'

A distressed whisper finally murmured a reply. 'To my eternal shame it's true, Sir. I was told to write down anything of interest that she might say or do and report back to my overseer.'

'And who was he?'

'A gentleman, Sir. He never told me his name nor even showed me his face. He was directly answerable to the Secretary of State, that is all I can tell you.'

'And did you poison Mrs Ashley on behalf of the Secret Office?'

'No, Sir. I swear it. Yet I feared that was what might be happening. For I had grown to care for her, you see. I broke the rules and cherished my victim, and her baby son. In fact I felt so much love for her that recently I had begun to taste everything she ate and drank before it was taken to her.'

A finger of ice laid itself along John's spine. 'What did you say?'

63

'That for the last month I have clandestinely been acting as her food taster.'

'Lord God almighty!' the Apothecary exclaimed, slapping his hand against his forehead. 'Then the poison was given to her by some other means. But how?' He rose to his feet, moving swiftly as a hare. 'I must go back to that bedroom. Where are Mr Walpole and Dr Eastwood now?'

Emily stared at him in bewilderment. 'Still dining as far as I know.'

'Don't worry, I'll find them.' He patted the servant on the hand. 'You have given me an even greater puzzle – but for all that you've answered a vital question.' And with that he was gone.

He found the two gentlemen in the Round Drawing Room, Walpole asleep in an armchair, snoring brandy fumes, Dr Eastwood partaking of a little port. He looked up in surprise as John bounded in. 'Mr Rawlings, what is it?'

'I've got to have another look in the North Bedchamber. I feel there is something vital in there that we have overlooked.'

The little fat man stood up at once. 'Then I'll come with you. I think one would need nerves of rock to enter that place alone.'

And how right he was. The room, still lit by guttering candles, was by now full of pools of darkness where their illumination did not reach. And out of one such pool rose the great bed, the corpse, its face covered by a cloth, like a broken doll in its depths. Unwittingly both men of medicine stared in Georgiana's direction and, strangely, both had the same illusion that she moved.

'Christ's blood,' swore the doctor, grabbing John's arm.

'I know. But it's only the candlelight. She's dead for sure.'

But to reassure himself, the Apothecary strode to the bed and raised the linen that protected Georgiana's features.

The face was as white and still as if it once again wore the full enamel, the eyes closed peacefully just as John had left them.

'Look at her,' he said, almost to himself. 'Still beautiful, even at the end.'

'Why did she have to wear all that wretched stuff?' asked Dr Eastwood, coming to stand beside him. 'Don't see none of it round Twickenham.'

'It's a town woman's ploy and considered very *bon ton*,' John answered thoughtlessly – and then he stopped. 'Of course,' he said. 'Of course, of course!'

'What is it?' asked the physician breathlessly.

But John didn't answer, instead hurrying to the elegant dressing table covered with its crystal jars, glass bottles and silver-backed brushes. With one sweep of his long fingers he picked up Mrs Ashley's powder bowl, and beckoning to Dr Eastwood to follow him almost flew down the stairs, then ran through the house to the Round Tower, in the base of which stood the kitchen.

Pushing aside a startled scullery boy, John seized a piece of muslin, used for covering milk, and drained the powder through it into a brass saucepan which he held below.

Dr Eastwood, who had been puffing in his wake, now caught up with him and said, 'Are you . . . ?'

'Yes. Normally I would use an alembic but this will have to do.'

To the powder that had escaped through the muslin, the Apothecary now added a cup of water, then placed the saucepan on the range, at the point where the heat was lowest. Both he and the doctor stood in silence as the steam began to rise and the water began to evaporate.

'I have never witnessed this before,' said Dr Eastwood, a certain awe in his voice.

'I am only copying what I once saw my Master do. It is not the sort of experiment one usually conducts,' John answered, a bitter note in his voice.

Eventually all was finished. The water had completely boiled away, taking the remnants of powder with it. But at the bottom of the saucepan lay five tiny white grains. John put out his finger and touched one, then gingerly licked it. He looked the physician straight in the eye and shook his head sorrowfully. 'Arsenic,' he said.

Dr Eastwood raised his eyebrows till they almost touched the line of his wig. 'Absorbed through the skin! Who would have thought it?'

'A woman,' John answered sombrely. 'Only a woman would think of that.'

It was dark going down the Great Cloister towards the Beauty Room, that pretty bedchamber furnished in yellow, so-called because it contained many portraits of ladies of the Court. Approaching the door, John, who had taken the precaution of borrowing Mr Walpole's pistol, felt his heart thud with fear at the thought of what might lie waiting beyond. In fact it was no surprise to him to see that it stood slightly ajar and needed only the merest push to open it.

Lady Fairbury, dressed for riding, stood with her back to him, surveying herself in a mirror. Looking over her shoulder, the Apothecary saw himself reflected as the door swung fully open. And so did she, for their eyes met in the glass. Harriet whirled round.

'I've been expecting you, you wretched little know-all.'

John made a cynical bow. 'How easy it must have been for you to tamper with her powder bowl, always in and out of her boudoir, chatting as only old friends do. And what a clever way of killing someone. Were you told how to do it or did you have the specialist knowledge yourself, looked up in some book perhaps?'

She sneered. 'That's something you'll never know.'

John smiled. 'Perhaps not. But my guess is that you worked for the

65

Secret Office as did the wretched Emily. They are very powerful, are they not, these unknown men behind the scenes? Even those connected with royalty are not beyond their grasp should they become dangerous for some reason. And now, with George III newly ascended to the throne, Georgiana had become just that. Thus she had to go.'

Harriet shot him a challenging look. 'Stand aside, young man. I've heard enough.'

'I warn you, I'm armed.'

'You'll never shoot me. Nor will you ever be able to prove a thing against me. Let your blundering constable raise a hue and cry, you will find that any charges will be dropped at a far higher level if ever I were brought to book.'

'I don't doubt it. The power of the faceless men stretches wide indeed.'

'It's a pity you are so honest,' Harriet answered with a laugh. 'For you're a handsome fellow when all's said and done.' And with that she pushed him so hard that John lost his balance and fell against the door jamb.

He heard her feet, brisk in their riding boots, run down the Cloister and disappear into the night.

''Zounds,' said Dr Eastwood, stepping out of the shadows. 'She passed so close to me I could have shot her, but somehow I couldn't bring myself to do it.'

'I felt the same,' answered the Apothecary.

'Will she get away, do you think?'

'She might well.'

'I could sink a deep brandy,' said the fat man, mopping his brow.

'And so could I,' John answered.

At which they laughed, though without a great deal of humour, thinking of poor Georgiana Ashley, and went out of the cold November night into the welcoming warmth of Mr Horace Walpole's gothic castle.

I came to the genre of historical mystery by accident. I'd been thinking of doing one of those heavy introspective novels which rarely get beyond the planning stage. Mine was to be based on the life of Pharaoh Akhenaten, the philosopher-king who invented monotheism around 1360 BC; but no sooner had I completed the research than a revised standard biography of the Pharaoh appeared, as well as a volume of brilliantly rogue scholarship by Ahmet Osman which sought to prove that Akhenaten and Moses were one and the same man. I felt I couldn't outshoot these big guns, but I still loved the period and wanted to do something with the material. I knew and admired Ellis Peters' work, but didn't think I'd ever dare emulate it. Nevertheless, the challenge of recreating a remote period of history and the ways of thinking of its inhabitants was too great to resist and, inspired indirectly by Brother Cadfael, my own 'problem solver', the former scribe Huy, was born.

Huy, an official at the court of Akhenaten, is no longer allowed to practise his profession in the wake of the Pharaoh's disgrace, and has to find other employment. Reluctantly and by accident he becomes a private detective, a job he loathes but which he is good at. By a stroke of historical luck, the most important of the gaggle of minor pharaohs who succeeded Akhenaten was the one everybody knows: Tutankhamun. With such a familiar name to kick off with, it wasn't such a struggle to introduce an unfamiliar setting to readers. And although the period of history is remote, human nature hasn't changed much. What's fun is trying to recreate human nature informed by a very different set of beliefs from our own.

Anton Gill

Author's Note on
Huy's Egypt

Most of the references to ancient Egypt in the story which follows are clear enough, or can be looked up easily. The reader may find it helpful, however, to know that the ancient Egyptians believed that the human being was divided into eight parts which joined at birth and parted at death: the Khat (body), the Ba (soul), Khou (intelligence), Ren (name), Ka (double), Ab (heart), Khaibit (shadow) and Sahu (husk). The ancient Egyptians also believed that people thought with their hearts. The brain's function was to keep the sinuses clear.

Lord of Storms

Anton Gill

R a blasted down on the red desert but beneath their canopies the King and his priests were tranquil. Before them a sea of human backs, red as the sand, bent in obeisance across the court of the new Temple to Ptah, god of the Southern Capital. Horemheb, who had waited so patiently and so long to sit on the Golden Throne, was consecrating this first great edifice of his reign to mark the end of his first year as Pharaoh.

It should have been a happy occasion, but the King was irritable and uneasy. His hard eyes took in the people bowed before him. Hand-picked administrator-priests and scribes; no threats there. He had enjoyed a good first year: the seasons had been kind to him; the river, which glittered sullenly beyond the outer walls of the temple, had brought a good flood soon after he had taken power, and the Black Land had darkened and been fertile in the season of Peret which followed. Now it was the dry season again. Time to take the men off the land and set them to building. Horemheb would build more mightily than any of his predecessors. He would make sure that his Name was never lost, so that his Ka would never wander abandoned and forgotten like so many that he had sent to the Fields of Aarru.

He watched the ceremony draw to its close with impatience: what good was it if at last he felt safe from any menace from within his frontiers, when the power he had fought and schemed for so long to obtain might now be threatened from outside? Things had gone wrong and Horemheb knew he would have to act fast. A lot hung on the meeting which would follow this ceremony.

It was a relief to be able to stand and follow the Chief Priest down to the inner sanctum of the Temple, through the cavernous central hall with its two hundred pillars, each bearing Horemheb's name. Here, the harsh sunlight could not reach: there was a smell of damp stone.

They reached the serdab, the holy of holies, where the most sacred statue of the god was about to be sealed behind its stone door for no layman's eye ever again to rest on. Horemheb paid scant attention to

71

the short ceremony. He watched the woman seal-setter, in her black ceremonial wig and turquoise robe, place the Book at the feet of the god and step back for the two shaven white-kilted assistant-priests to swing the stone door shut. She fumbled with the three seals, taking too much time, it seemed to the King, who was eager for the business to end.

But at last it was over; the bronze trumpets blew and the thousand men and women in the blazing courtyard rose. Horemheb's procession drove a furrow through their ranks and beyond the gate the King mounted his chariot and took the reins himself: he was old, but he was still a general, and he believed that the strength of his body showed the people the power of his heart. He cracked his whip over the heads of his four brown horses. The chariots of his attendants found it hard to keep up.

Neferhotep had summoned Huy to the Palace of the Southern Quarter from the State Archive, where Huy had been working for two years now following his reinstatement as a scribe during the reign of the Pharaoh Ay. Never a friend of Horemheb, Huy had not expected to keep his job when the old pharaoh died, but he had kept his head down and looked for nothing more, now that he had witnessed more than forty cycles of the seasons and could therefore be looked upon as old, than to pass the rest of his days quietly and modestly.

Neferhotep was secretary to the Black Medjays, Horemheb's special guard. He was no friend of Huy's either, resenting the problem-solving training which the King had made Huy give the ambitious policeman. An inept student, Neferhotep ended up as an administrator, which was certainly the fate his Khou would have damned him to from the first. Power without talent. There were many now with such position and such disability. But Horemheb loved them. He could swim among them as a fish swims among the reeds. As for Huy, Horemheb recognised his gifts but kept him in a backwater. The king knew the scribe was no threat, though he had the Khou to be one. In any case, it was worth the risk to keep him alive, for the times when he could be useful.

Now Huy waited in the third hall of audience. Others might have cared about this insult to their status, but Huy had already lost too much in his life to care. He was merely jaded, with nothing to read and nothing to do, having watched Ra's chariot make its slow progress through the arched body of Nut for two hours as he waited.

At last he heard footsteps: many urgent, important footsteps in the lobby outside. He stood up and tidied himself, noticing an inkstain on the front of his kilt. Well, it was too late to do anything about that now.

The four house servants who had shared his wait wordlessly, beyond the formal offering of bread and beer when he arrived (as this was the Palace, Huy had been offered figs and Dakhla wine instead), and who

72

stood on either side of the cedar doors, now swung them open to admit the Pharaoh, dressed in his preferred black robe and gold arm and ankle bands. Behind him were a cup-bearer, and two scribes whom Huy recognised. These squatted down and unslung their palettes, moistened their brushes in their mouths, and prepared to write on fresh papyrus which they uncurled on top of their portable desks. New papyrus? This was an important meeting.

'Huy.'

'Lord.'

'Get up.'

Huy, who had dutifully prostrated himself, rose painfully, noting as he always did nowadays the ache in both knees and ankles which would not go away. He also noted – who could fail to? – the Pharaoh's ominous tone.

'You need not start writing yet,' Horemheb told the scribes. They laid down their pens but continued to look at him.

'Huy. You did not train Neferhotep well.'

'I did what was possible.'

'I know what you want to say: you cannot make a good ship without cedar.'

Huy was silent.

'It may be that I will ask you to train other men for me. Your Khou is too valuable for its influence not to be felt by the ones who come after us.'

'It may be that it is something I cannot pass on. I stumble on truths; I rarely detect them.' Huy had no desire to spend the rest of his life teaching people how to pry into the affairs of others. Especially not the King's police.

'You uncover them.'

'It has been said of me.'

Horemheb spread his hands impatiently. 'How you do it does not matter. Look. I cannot talk long. There is an important document. A copy of it has disappeared. I want you to find it.'

'What is it?'

'I cannot tell you.'

'Then how can I look for it?'

'One scroll. A cubit long. On new paper. And with my seal, if the seal is still on it.'

'When did you lose it?'

'It was in the Military Library three days ago.'

Huy was silent.

'It cannot have gone far. The alarm was raised immediately.'

'If it has gone, in what direction is it likely to have gone?'

Horemheb hesitated. 'North.'

'Downriver?'

'Yes.'

'Towards the Great Green?'

'Yes.'

'As there are no rebels left inside the Black Land, it is bound out of the country. What does the paper tell of?'

'I cannot tell you.'

'How many copies were made?'

'One.'

'Then it is important.'

Horemheb clapped his hands at the scribes. 'See,' he dictated, 'that I appoint the chief archivist Huy to locate an army document, and that I empower him to ask whatever help he may need from whatever source he may seek it, without notice of rank.' He turned to Huy again, his body slumping as he returned to his private self: 'Find it fast, Huy.'

'And if I cannot?'

Horemheb spread his hands. 'What real good would it do me to punish you? You are a man who no longer minds what happens. But I know that you cannot help but practise your art. Otherwise, why would you live?' The King paused. 'If you succeed, I will give you two deben of silver. If you fail, I will take your home away.'

'Where shall I start?'

'Talk to Neferhotep. You have two days.'

Horemheb turned on his heel and left. Behind him, the scribes hastened to gather up their desks and palettes and follow him with the cup-bearer, who had been dozing on his feet during the interview. It had been a long day.

The scarab, pushing backwards, its hind legs raised high above its head, urged the dungball full of its eggs over the ridges of the sand. It was the hottest time of day, when Ra was at his zenith. The beetle cast no shadow. Its dungball, like the sun, was round and burdened with life. Its carapace protected it and at this time of day no bird or mammal would harm it. It alone was lord of mid-day. It knew the desert through its legs and feet; the grains of sand were familiar stones and pebbles.

But now the dungball stopped, impeded by something. The beetle pushed and scrabbled, but its efforts came to nothing. Its time-rooted memory told it there should be no obstacle here, so it went on pushing, clambering over the ball, falling on to its back and righting itself several times before it rolled its burden off confusedly in another direction.

The body spreadeagled in the sand and pinioned at wrists and ankles to wooden stakes had felt the tiny pressure on its lower calf.

'I am still alive, and I can still sense. I even know what that must have been. The carrion-eaters will not appear until Ra is passed into the Seqtet Boat and they will not eat me until I am dead although they may peck at me. My main fear is for my eyes. I will not be able to use my arms and hands to keep their beaks away from my eyes. But I am alive.'

There had been such pain that now all feeling was reduced to dullness, like a deaf man's listening, like the slow shift of the silt on the bed of the river.

Other sensations came to the body which its heart would not analyse. The heart did not realise how well it could lie to itself. The seethings, the itchings, the warm tickling that it registered coming from the armpits, the groin, the ears, anus, nose and mouth, were caused by ants and flies. The same sensations came from the breast, too, and a smell came from there. There was a crawling and delving about the eyes too, and the precious eyes, closed against the sun to protect them not only from its light but from the sticky legs and jaws of insects, sent frantic messages to the heart. But the heart did not respond. It could only cling to the thought of life, which the insects recognised had long since been abandoned. Death begets life. Flies were already laying their eggs in the red chaos that had been the body's chest and the body's genitals. Ants sucked up the honey that had been smeared there, and in all the body's portals, and probed and crept.

'But I have kept the secret. They did not take the secret from me. I may not have succeeded, but I have not entirely failed.'

Hope is vain. Hope's only function is to lead us pleasantly towards death. But hope is always there, a pernicious friend. The heart in the body refused to accept the truth of the insects, and prayed for rescue.

The hours passed, and the body became used to the insects' activity. Soon the Khat would give ground to the Sahu, and the bird of the soul would be released from its cage. But still the heart sat at the centre of things, and the ears listened, straining for any sound other than the dull wind chafing the sand, and the eyes, as the heat left the burnt lids, dared open a slit, for with the cooling of the air, the insects withdrew. They knew that the feast would still be here tomorrow.

Night falls fast in the desert, and the eyes saw nothing but the cobalt sky with a smattering of early stars above. The head would not, or could not move. By looking downwards as far as possible, the dull unfocused mound of the chest came into view. To right and left, little; upwards, nothing. The movement of orbits in sockets hurt.

And then there was a sound. It had become colder and it was easier to hear. The noise was familiar: a deliberate gait, a plodding in the sand, the rustling of a saddlepack and the faint tinkle of a bell. A donkey. And a laden donkey would not be alone. In confirmation, the ears heard the sound of a blow from a switch across the animal's back, and a man's voice cursing.

Animal and man drew nearer.

Had they come back to inflict more pain? Or was it somebody else?

75

Someone who might take pity. The mouth tried to open, to make a sound.

Meryre's donkey was old. It would not live much longer and he did not know what he would do when it died, for although the harvest had been good, Meryre's rent had swallowed up most of the profit. If only the donkey would last another year, and the flood be kind next season, life might improve. The donkey was slowing down, and it was growing dark. Had he laden the beast too heavily? He struck its back again with his rod, and the animal stumbled into a trot. Meryre looked about him fearfully. He wanted to be home before dark.

He had seen the mound, its outline indistinct in the dusk, some time before, and taken it to be sand blown around a rock. The reason he decided to skirt it was that he did not remember seeing it before, and this route across the desert to the east of the Southern Capital was very familiar to him, though few others used it. Meryre's farm was isolated, on the edge of the irrigated land.

As he watched the mound he thought he could see it move, which frightened him more, but he could not make the donkey go any faster and the animal would not leave the track it was used to. Meryre was not too far away to hear the groaning the mound made as he approached. The groans formed themselves into words, just recognisable, pleading for help.

Meryre was not a complete coward; he had served as a young man in the army under Horemheb when the Pharaoh had been commander-in-chief to Akhenaten, the king whose name had been blotted out for crimes against the state. Though his throat was dry, Meryre approached the body.

He'd been upwind of it, but now the wind veered to the east and the stench caught the back of his mouth and nose so violently that he retched. Behind him, his donkey, which had come to a halt, stamped nervously. There was still enough light to see by. Holding his shawl across his face, he moved closer; curiosity had got the better of fear.

What he saw as he stooped over the body made his stomach rebel again. The body was naked, and what skin was left had been burnt by the sun. Where the chest should have been was an enormous open wound, black and shining, in which Meryre could see the glint of insects as they moved – not all had left with the setting sun. The genitals were gone; there was nothing but a bloody mess where they should have been. The wrists and ankles were torn by the leather ropes which bound them tightly.

Eyes looked at him, and below them the mouth moved, beseeching. The face was burnt red, freckled. There was enough light for Meryre to see that the hair framing the face was red too. He drew back in revulsion: this was the face of Seth, the Lord of Storms, the enemy of Horus and of the light. Meryre didn't hesitate. He drew his bronze knife and slit the creature's throat: this may have been a dying demon, but it was better to make sure that it was dead. He did not look at the eyes again. The eyes might have had the power to kill him yet.

Meryre stood up and made his way back to the track. The donkey, smelling blood, balked at his approach.

'The officials at the ibu house didn't want to take the body in at all. As it is, they've insisted in placing it in an outer hall, and none of them wants to go near it. It's in the shade, but it's falling apart very fast,' said Cheruif.

'We'd better hurry,' said Huy.

Meryre had reported the body the next morning, saying that he had discovered it on his way across the fields after waking. It was, just, within the perimeter of his land. The state of decay it was in meant that it had to be buried quickly, but Cheruif, the police official landed with dealing with the case had ordered that it be sent to the embalming house for examination first. Then he had gone straight to Huy.

'It's good of you to look at it,' said Cheruif. 'I do not think we will find a killer. If the heart was not still in the body, I would say that whoever it was had fallen victim to an Undead.'

'The Undead take the Ab,' said Huy. 'They do not destroy the rest of the Khat.'

They arrived at the ibu house to be greeted by an ill-tempered assistant. 'Just follow your noses and get the thing out of here by nightfall,' he said, gesturing down a corridor which ran along the south side of the embalming complex.

He had not been exaggerating. The smell, though someone had attempted to disguise it by dousing in vinegar the linen wrappings surrounding the corpse, caught at their throats before they had entered the side-chamber in which it lay.

'Whoever it was had red hair,' said Cheruif.

'That wouldn't have made them popular.' Huy looked at the head. The eyes had been closed, but the expression sealed on the face was one of pain and betrayal. He looked carefully at the hair, which was long enough to frame the face, but very fine. There was no trace of hair on the cheeks, but it was a young face and perhaps no beard had yet begun to grow. The freckles would have been hard to disguise, though there was no reason to suppose that in life the person would not have worn make-up; and a wig would have taken care of the hair. Nevertheless, it was a mark of extreme misfortune to be redheaded in the Black Land. Seth, the bringer of storms and of death and damage through water, was redheaded.

'Do we know anything about who this might have been?' Huy asked.

77

Cheruif and he went back many years, and though they were not friends, a friendly respect existed between them.

'Nothing.' Both men had wrapped their shawls around their mouths and noses. Cheruif pulled back the linen covering the body. It stuck on the blood and he had to tug at it. 'Look what they did to it. We cannot tell anything of it.'

Huy forced himself to breathe deeply and evenly. He said his Name to himself, to reassure and protect himself from evil. This was not just torture, surely. He looked at the weals on the ankles and the wrists. The feet and hands were slim and well-formed. The feet, though naked, were not calloused, nor was the skin of the sole thick and ridged. This was somebody who had been used to wearing sandals. The hands too were not the hands of a worker. Huy looked at the fingers. They could have been the hands of a scribe. There were small spots on the fingers which might have been inkstains. And there was something else. Huy looked more closely. Then he stood up, spreading his hands.

'Anything?' asked Cheruif.

'No.'

'I thought something attracted your attention.'

Huy smiled. 'I was mistaken.'

'Do you think this might have been a foreigner?'

'It is possible. But not a sailor or a quarry-worker.'

'Someone from the Land of the Two Rivers?'

'It is possible. I have heard that there are people in the lands to the north of the Great Green who have skins far paler than ours, which the sun burns red.'

'A race of demons?'

Huy spread his hands.

'There are enemies to the north. Their strength is growing,' said Cheruif.

'So I have heard.'

'There may be war again.'

'Not if we can hold our frontiers.'

'But you have heard the rumours.'

'Yes.'

Huy spat for luck. He had never freed himself from superstition, but it was dangerous to profess scepticism under Horemheb's rule. Anyway, this would not be the first time Huy had played dumb; nor had he the slightest intention of telling Cheruif what he had noticed on the body.

'I don't think we can learn anything more here,' Cheruif said. 'I suppose the body had better be buried while it can still be moved in one piece.'

'Yes,' said Huy, reluctantly. 'Unless someone claims it.'

'Is that likely?'

'Is it possible to put pressure on the people here to keep the body, even if only for two more days? It may be that someone will come forward. This was a person who lived indoors, not under the sky. Someone will have noticed the disappearance.'

'I will do what I can.'

But the next day a body-servant of Cheruif, not an official messenger, came to Huy with a note from the policeman to say that the body had been destroyed the previous night on orders which it had been beyond his power to countermand.

Huy knew what that meant, and was grateful to Cheruif for letting him know. Well, perhaps it was not that important after all, though he said a prayer for the departed Ba of the corpse, hoping that whatever gods looked after it would accept the petition of a Black Lander. Even enemies deserved a better fate than this poor creature had suffered.

The scribe ordered his litter, and had himself carried from the State Archive along the narrow paved thoroughfare that divided the city from west to east until he reached a market square. Here he descended and dismissed his littermen. There was perhaps no reason why Horemheb should have him shadowed, but Huy knew that Horemheb trusted no one and therefore could not himself be trusted. It was easy to lose himself in the crowded market, and once he had made two or three more or less aimless circuits of the stalls and satisfied himself that anyone following him must by now be separated from him by at least twenty people and three stalls, each guarded by nervous, snapping watch-apes, he slipped down one of the alleyways that led off the square into the labyrinth of narrow streets that made up the central part of the city. Huy knew them intimately, and made his way fast towards another, much smaller square. One side of this square was dominated by a tall building whose small windows were placed high in its wall. Glancing swiftly round the otherwise deserted square, Huy entered the building through a narrow door.

This was the Office of the Sealers – the home of the women who were entrusted with locking all important documents, archives and statues of the gods under seal so that no one without the permission of the Sealer could gain access to them.

It was many years since Huy had seen Abana, and he saw now a stouter woman with a face full of wrinkles – as she no doubt saw a similar man. But her hair was black, her skin dark, and her eyes humorous still. Abana had been a minor scribe when Huy and she had for a hopeful moment tried to leap the abyss of love together. Now she was assistant chief of the Sealers; married to District Administrator Anen, with seven children and three grandchildren.

'Yes, not long ago,' she said in response to his question. 'She was a senior and had been here for three cycles of the seasons.'

'What did she look like?'

Abana was surprised. 'Like the rest of us. But look, we all have dark hair which is a wig, and we all have dark skin, but we cover the true colour of our skin with make-up.'

'I see.'

Abana looked at Huy. 'I am telling you no more. You are working for someone?'

'Yes.'

'Whom?'

'The King.'

'Have you proof?'

'No.'

'I know you are telling me the truth, but without a document I will tell you no more.'

'You have told me much.'

'I know.'

Huy looked at the face he had loved once. It was turned in on itself now, as a stranger's would be. We can become intimates and strangers again overnight, and do. But we are primitive creatures, he thought. In any case, he had learnt what he needed to.

He turned to go, but she called him back.

'You will need these,' she said.

In her hand were three seals.

She smiled. 'Has life been kind to you, Huy?'

'No. But it has not got the better of me, either.'

'Nor me.'

In the shadowless noon, nothing stirred. The priests of the Temple of Ptah had already eaten their second breakfast, and had lain down for the Sleep of Mid-day. Huy, his shawl soaked in the river and wrapped round his head, scuttled from pillar to pillar, white as a ghost, covered in white linen, invisible.

He passed through the first three halls of the temple without meeting anybody. The guard at the first gate was asleep and there had been no one beyond him. Now he passed out of the sun into the dark hall which was the antechamber to the serdab. Before him through the gloom he saw the tall granite door of the holy of holies. His heart beat faster and to soothe it he spoke the Magic Words of Power to himself, aware of his superstition. Then a voice cried out angrily behind him. He braced himself against one of the columns supporting the roof of the hall and froze to it, hoping to blend with the white limestone. He heard the sound of running feet and dogs barking, but the noise passed twenty or thirty cubits to the west in the hall, and the wind was in his face. If there had been a patrol, it had missed him.

It was cold in the dark inner hall and he shivered, waiting for his eyes to become accustomed to the gloom. During this time he listened for any further sounds of people, but he had chosen his time well, and the pursuit, if there had been one at all, showed no sign of returning. His breathing returned to normal, and his head stopped pounding.

He could see the grey door of the inner sanctum rising in the gloom before him, its top lost in darkness, but he knew that it was designed to swing open and closed effortlessly despite its size, for the annual cleaning and reclothing ceremony of the god within.

He moved forward and found the seals placed on the door. As he had suspected, they were not pressed together but only gave that impression. The cords were simply tied, not very tightly at that, behind the seals. Whoever had done this had intended to return and reopen the door with the minimum of effort, taking as little time as possible. Huy was scared. There was a god behind the door, and one whom he was supposed to believe in. Ptah was a god who had the power to summon Shesmu, headsman of Osiris, who would come in anger and hurl Huy into the lakes of fire forever. But reason told his heart that a mortal had falsified the sealing, and that mortal can have had no fear of the god within. Saying his Name to himself for protection, and deciding that if he did not act now he never would, Huy quickly loosened the cords, and, finding the indentations carved into the door for the purpose, gripped with his fingers and pulled with all his strength.

Soundlessly, the door swung wide, so effortlessly propelled by its own weight that he had to prevent it from opening farther than he needed. Inside, there was room only for the statue, which loomed above him, but did not move, nor give any sign of life. The box containing the Book was at Ptah's feet. Huy bent down and slid the lid back. There was just enough light for him to see the great scroll of the Book of the Dead within. He removed it and tilted it. A smaller scroll on new papyrus which had been rolled up within it slid out.

Huy quickly replaced the Book and closed the lid. Now, his ears straining for any sound of temple priests, Huy unrolled enough of the papyrus to see if it was what he was looking for. Had Horemheb not thought that he would read it? And if he knew its contents, what would Horemheb do to him then? Huy strained his eyes to read in the dim light. The first few lines confirmed that he was right – he even recognised the hand of Wennekhu, a scribe in the Secret Archive – but after the first sentences the writing broke up into a code which he could not read. Rolling the scroll up again, Huy stowed it in the belt of his kilt and swiftly closed the great door, replacing the false seals with the true ones which Abana had given him. As part of his training as a scribe he had learned the correct method of placing them.

He reached home, sure that no one had been aware of his movements, and congratulated himself on having had the foresight to keep so many of his hard-won secrets from Neferhotep when he was in charge of the man's training. If the Black Medjays were watching his house, at

81

least they would not be sure where he had been during his absence. Of course, Horemheb could have Huy brought in at any time, but he would not act until he was sure that the scribe had either failed completely, or got something for him.

He closed his front door behind him and pegged it shut before going through the narrow hall to the cluttered living-room, where he kicked off his sandals and sat cross-legged before his writing-table, sweeping it clear of papers and unrolling the papyrus from the Temple of Ptah. He was not familiar with codes, but he had no intention of handing this one over until he knew what it was about, and he had one last night before Horemheb's patience reached its end.

It was quiet in the room, and yet so absorbed was Huy in the task before him that it must have been several minutes before he realised he was not alone. Not that anyone spoke or moved. He simply became aware of another person's breathing.

He didn't move. There was nothing urgent or tense about the breathing. It was calm, relaxed, even companionable. But that made it seem all the more dangerous. Whoever it was felt that they were in control, must be supremely confident.

'You've noticed me,' said a quiet voice behind him at last. 'It's all right. You can turn round. I'm not about to cut your throat.'

Huy looked behind him in the direction of the voice, but the rear of the room was in shadow and he could only see the feet and the lower part of the legs. He knew the voice and felt more astonishment than fear.

'Are you going to break the code?'

'I was going to try.'

'It is a dangerous thing to do. You should not meddle, Huy. That was always your greatest weakness.'

'It is true.'

'But of course in this case it may be helpful. Come and sit by me so that we can talk more comfortably.'

Huy moved across the room and sat on the clay bench built into the wall under the high window.

'I must offer you bread and beer.'

His visitor laughed. 'One of the things I have always liked about you is that even at the most critical moment you do not forget your manners.'

Huy spread his hands. 'It helps me when I am taken aback.' Then he became serious. 'What are you doing, Abana? You accuse me of meddling dangerously, but you are sailing in much deeper water.'

Abana leant forward so that the light fell on her face and Huy could see that she was no longer laughing. 'I have helped you, Huy. Now I expect some help in return. Give me the scroll.'

'You helped me because you could not have got the scroll otherwise.

82

It was subtle of you to confirm my suspicions. I had not the slightest idea you were using me.'

Abana looked at him. 'You can help me or you can refuse to help me. But I will still have the scroll.'

Huy returned her gaze. 'Who was your friend?'

'The rulers of the Black Land have become its destruction. For the people of this land to have true justice again there must be a flood through the house of the Pharaoh to wash it clean. That flood will come from the north, from the land of King Suppiluliumas that lies beyond the Great Green and beyond the Land of the Two Rivers. But Horemheb, the worst and last of a putrid harvest, knows of the preparations and has plans to stop it. Those plans are within that scroll. My friend comes from the land to the north. For years before she came here we wrote to one another. I protected her when she arrived and trained her in the work she needed to know for our purpose.'

'She took the scroll and hid it.'

'Yes. Until we could organise her journey downriver. She hid it in the safest place – under the nose of Horemheb, as he sat in the fullness of his pride.'

Huy nodded. 'You have dug deep. Your marriage, your work, and the work of your friend. What preparation.'

'For years we have been watching and waiting. It was a matter of inevitability that Horemheb would become King.'

'Could you not simply have killed him?'

'He is well protected.'

'Yes. And the power of the north was not strong.'

'But now it is.'

'Horemheb will change his plans.'

'No. The code has to be broken here and then the scroll must be rescued. I have known you long, Huy. We thought perhaps Neferhotep would be put in charge of the investigation but you are so much better. You have discovered the scroll. Now you must help if you wish to live.'

Huy did not think his chances of survival were high now that he was so deeply involved, nor did he have much confidence that playing dumb would dupe Abana: she had known him too long.

'You are a Black Lander. Why are you helping an enemy?'

'The old Hyksos kings came from the north, beyond the Black Land, but they were good rulers. When farmland becomes foul, it needs new farmers.'

There was a light in Abana's eyes which Huy did not like. He thought of the body Cheruif had shown him. He had suspected that it was a woman, and had known where she worked from the moment he had seen the traces of hardened sealing paste under her fingernails. And redheads were rare in the Black Land.

'What happened to your friend, Abana?'

Her face darkened. 'At the last, your protégé, Neferhotep, showed that he had learned something from you. My friend was at the South Quay. There was another agent of Suppiluliumas she was supposed to meet to arrange passage to Kizzuwatna. But Neferhotep sent Black Medjays to take her. He didn't know anything of course for sure but Horemheb told him to have her taken out into the desert for strong questioning. She had red hair so the men had no qualms about what they did to her. They destroyed her sex but it is clear that they did not discover her secret. Shebat and Shaushka held their hands over her and gave her strength.'

'Have you abandoned our gods for theirs?'

'You abandoned all gods long ago, Huy. You cannot deny the brutality of your king.'

'All those who lead are brutal.'

'They are a force we can channel. Help us, Huy. This country has done so little for you. You could stand by the side of a new king.'

The blow on the main door of the house was so violent that the whole place shook. And a hammering followed when the door did not give; Huy had had deep-socketed bronze door-pegs made which would bend a little but never snap.

'Huy!' It was Neferhotep's voice, high and strangled in excited authority.

Abana and Huy looked at each other like nervous lovers. It was a desperate moment and yet it was also almost comical.

'How did he trace me?' said Huy. 'I took such care.'

'Perhaps he traced me,' said Abana. 'He had a good teacher.'

The hammering resumed. They had a wooden ram out there and were swinging it against the door. The cedar planks – Huy spared no expense where his security was concerned – buckled but did not split.

'Run,' Huy said. 'I will keep them here as long as I can.'

Abana looked at him. The light in her eyes had gone out. 'No,' she said. 'I cannot run now. It is too hard. There is nowhere for me to run to.'

'Why?'

She spread her hands. 'I cannot go to Kizzuwatna. Even if I got there, if I arrived empty-handed after all this time Suppiluliumas would have me killed. And you will not let me take the scroll.'

'I cannot. I do not believe what you believe.'

'You believe in nothing.'

The noise and the yelling continued. Neferhotep had many Black Medjays with him. If kings were brutes, they were the dogs of brutes, recruited from the quays and from army rejects, and trained out of any humanity they might once have had.

'If they take me,' said Abana, 'they will do to me what they did to my friend.'

'Then you *must* run.'

The door lurched and the central panel splintered.

'Now.' Huy stood to place a stool on the clay bench so that she could reach the window. 'There is a way. We will both go. I will lead you.'

'We are no longer so active. Look! We are old.'

'We still have life.'

She took his face in her hands. 'No, Huy. There is no time to talk any more. Do not let them take me. You must kill me.'

'No.'

'They know. Someone close has denounced me. I have been careful and Neferhotep is not that clever.'

The wood splintered. Suddenly the voices became far clearer, and they rang triumphantly. The warm air poured in, spoiling the coolness of the room.

'Kill me, Huy. At least you will gain some honour. And think what you will spare me.'

'I will protect you.'

'How?'

Through the hall Huy could see a thick brown arm forcing its way through the hole smashed in the wood, the hand feeling for the peg, and failing to reach it. Outside, Neferhotep shouted obscenities at Huy and at his men. He was scared that the scribe had gone.

Abana drew Huy's old bronze knife from his belt and slashed him across the chest. The blood was warm and it shocked him to see how much spread out, like a greedy flood.

'Kill me.' She held the knife out to him.

He was angry at the blood. Beyond him they were kicking away enough space to climb through.

'Kill me. It is only a few years that I lose. Where are you sending me but to the Fields of Aarru, and there is no pain there.'

He struck her twice. He knew how to kill. She fell instantly into the Boat of Night.

The door of the house collapsed. Neferhotep's men crashed into the hall. Neferhotep stood over Huy. There was so much blood that the official thought the scribe was dying. There were flies in the room already.

'She held a knife to me,' said Huy. 'And there was a struggle.'

He gave the scroll to Neferhotep. It was soaked in blood.

Neferhotep looked at him. The scribe was bleeding hard. Neferhotep picked up Huy's knife and considered his next move.

H enry Ford once famously declared, 'History is bunk!' He may have been right in some respects; many historians have twisted the facts to fit their own pet theories regarding events which occurred long ago, but there is no doubt that history comes vividly alive in the best fiction devoted to that genre.

From an early age I was gripped by Conan Doyle's historical novels, notably *Sir Nigel* and *The White Company* and, of course, his Sherlock Holmes tales. Mary Shelley's *Frankenstein* and such Gothic novels as *The Monk* and *The Castle of Otranto* certainly influenced my own work, both in my Gothic novels, *The Black Death*, *Necropolis* and *The House of the Wolf*, and my Sherlockian pastiches, the Solar Pons series. These works were set in my favourite periods for fictional recreations of the past, the late nineteenth century and the 1920s. These periods embraced most of my fictional favourites in the criminal genre; Sheridan Le Fanu, H.G. Wells – whose horrific short stories are often overlooked today – Robert Louis Stevenson, Poe, M.R. James and E.F. Benson, particularly. The fog-bound streets of London once haunted by Jack the Ripper, bleak moorlands and old houses whose very stones breathe the stuff of history, enchant the reader safely ensconced in an armchair in the security of a modern well-lit room.

My present tale, though bringing history up to date in that it is set in the present, borrows all those historical aspects of the Gothic tale while remaining firmly within the parameters of the genteel criminal genre, the very ordinariness of which, in real life, adds to the horror. Or at least, one hopes so.

Basil Copper

Line Engaged

Basil Copper

It was a bright April day with pale sunshine and scudding clouds when Edward Marsh was laid to rest. The great writer, full of honours and in his 87th year, had had a morbid fear of death, but the funeral was almost a festive occasion according to newspaper reports.

He had lived in a handsome Georgian mansion in Sussex and the funeral was private, within the grounds of the estate, though several hundred people, representing all strata of the arts, media and government had been invited, such was his status in the world of literature.

He had left no less than ninety major works in his long life, as well as thousands of articles and essays. A great eccentric in many ways, he must have been a difficult man to live with, and both friends and the general public were startled when, at the age of seventy, he married a beautiful and vivacious woman of thirty.

She was apparently an old family friend and had later volunteered to become his secretary. There were whispers at the time as Marsh was immensely wealthy and it was well known that she had no means of her own. All this came to me much later, when I was engaged by the widow to write the official biography, but at the time I read with great interest the details of the funeral, which was all of a piece with the great writer's lifestyle. The interment took place in a handsome mausoleum in the grounds, which he had had constructed as his final resting place when he was only in his early fifties.

This was extraordinary in itself, but as I began to delve among his papers and the vast detritus of a glittering career in the literary world some years later, I also began to discern disturbing aspects of the morbid nature of the man and realised that my task was to be a long and complex one; but this is to run ahead.

According to newspaper reports at the time of the funeral and what I later gleaned from the widow, the then Minister of Culture had made a long and tedious speech outlining the distinguished writer's career. Fortunately this was in the Great Hall of the mansion, where the casket, on its stand in the centre, was the focus of all eyes. But from what I could gather, there was also a lavish buffet consisting of many delicacies, washed down with a liberal supply of champagne and other rare wines during the funeral oration. This was bizarre in the extreme but all in accordance with Marsh's own wishes, as he had ordained that the occasion should be a happy affair, with the men wearing light clothing and the ladies' dresses of bright colours.

The eulogies, both spoken and written, continued to pour in for some months, both on radio and in newspapers and magazines, and there was also a special, hour-long tribute on television in which I was interested to see the widow, Deirdre Marsh, speaking of her fond recollections of their life together. Later, Marsh and his affairs had faded into the background, as such things go, though I had taken the opportunity to read several of his finest novels and again marvelled at the man's insight into the quirks and foibles of human nature.

But then, when I had almost forgotten Marsh as I pursued my own busy life, I saw an intriguing piece about him in one of the major Sunday supplements, which again ignited my interest. It was headed: FAMOUS WRITER'S BIZARRE LIFESTYLE with the sub-head: A Voice From the Grave? I was fascinated by what I read and only then did I realise what a morbid turn of mind Edward Marsh must have developed in his declining years. Apparently he was much absorbed with his own impending death, though he remained in extremely good health for a man of his years.

His thoughts had been turning to the problems associated with cata-lepsy or coma and he had a great fear of being interred alive. As I read on I became convinced that Marsh had been reading too much Edgar Allen Poe, for his imaginings strongly resembled events described in that magnificent writer's *Fall of the House of Usher* and *The Premature Burial*. I then realised why Marsh had had the mausoleum constructed and that he must have had such morbid thoughts even as a relatively young man.

The facts as outlined in the article were indeed bizarre, as the newspaper heading indicated. Not only had he insisted that the lid of his casket – which he had himself designed – must be left unsecured, but that air-holes should be bored in the lid and sides. The weirdest aspect was yet to come; he had actually installed a telephone, which was to be placed by his right hand within the coffin and connected to the main circuit in the house, so that all the extensions would ring at once, summoning help in case he awoke in the tomb. Not only that but throughout the remaining years of his life, when he was in residence at his Sussex home he would get one of his gardeners to visit the vault and pick up the telephone, which had been left on a marble plinth intended for the ultimate resting place of his coffin, and the man would have to ring the house so that he could check that the instrument was in full working order.

I should imagine that there would have been a brisk turnover in the gardening staff involved in such a weird routine. This article, and an accompanying photograph of the vault, with an inset of Marsh himself, must have set in motion a faint desire in me not only to find out more about the writer, but eventually to write his biography. Nothing other than infrequent articles had yet appeared on his life, and I began re-reading his earlier novels and gathering together such cuttings and memorabilia regarding the author that came my way.

By a strange coincidence, Marsh's widow herself telephoned me a few months later, to my great surprise. She had read one of my major biographies and thought I would be the right person to write the official life of her husband. Though enormously flattered, I was cautious in my response and said I would think the matter over and contact her again. She gave me her ex-directory number and that was the way things remained for the next few weeks, as I was much engaged at the time in lecturing both in Britain and on the Continent, and was also putting the finishing touches to my first work of fiction.

A month or more must have elapsed when I again received a call from the widow. Naturally, I apologised for the delay and explained the reasons. Then, quite unexpectedly, I agreed to take on the commission and said I would arrange to go down to Sussex to see her and discuss the matter within the next fortnight. She was delighted and said she would send me a list of primary sources on her husband's life; a tentative bibliography of both his prose and fictional works, and a summary of other material that might be useful.

The library and archives at Beaufort Place, his Sussex mansion, would be open to me and I would be free to interview and discuss his work with relatives, friends, fellow authors and critics. She stressed that it was to be a critical biography, warts and all, and I was not to write a sanitised life story of a man who had become almost an idol to millions of people the world over. That was the only stipulation she made. I would be free to come to Sussex and stay at Beaufort Place as long as I wished in order to research and work in the library and archive. The terms of the contract would be worked out amicably and would be of a generous nature, she added.

Few writers could have resisted such a tempting offer and I was not immune to her persuasive charms. I had seen photographs of her in the newspapers and she was still a very beautiful woman, now married to a scholar, I believed; she still insisted on being called Deirdre Marsh because of, I should imagine, the cachet attached to it. I thought long and hard about the offer, discussed it with my wife and agent and then, a week later, accepted her invitation to visit her Sussex home. I packed a few things in a holdall, for she had asked me to stay the weekend so that I could 'soak in the atmosphere', as she put it, discuss the contract, and browse in the library to make a few preliminary notes.

*　　*　　*

It was a brilliant, warm day in early May and it was an exhilarating drive as I steered the car through narrow, leafy lanes. I arrived soon after four in the afternoon, with the scent of new-mown hay permeating the air. If I had expected something unusual, I was not disappointed. The huge mass of the house was slowly revealed through the interlaced trees that fringed the long, winding drive and at last I drove on to a gravelled concourse, amazed, not only at the size of the place but at the sight of a huge circular edifice, resembling a Martello tower that had been grafted on to one end of the structure. Or, to correct myself, the house had been grafted on to the tower, as I later learned that it dated from the early eighteenth century. I naturally assumed it would have been Edward Marsh's ivory tower – or ivy tower as it was smothered with the stuff – but it transpired that it was merely the repository for all the author's old proof copies, covering over sixty-five years of his writing life. I was relieved to hear from Mrs Marsh when she telephoned, however, that everything relevant to his literary activities, which included correspondence, was held either in the study or the library, as I would not have relished climbing all those stairs every day.

Deirdre Marsh was waiting on the front steps to greet me. She was a beautiful woman in her late forties, with ash-blonde hair clipped fairly short, clear skin and an unlined face. She wore a grey tailored suit, which set off her fine figure to perfection, and when she smiled revealed a perfect set of teeth which owed little to dental surgeons. In short I was immediately captivated and I could only conjecture what a sensational impact she must have had on the late Edward Marsh.

She led me across a great beamed hall with a tesselated floor, to a handsome drawing room where a loaded tea trolley awaited. While we ate the thinly sliced sandwiches and drank the delicately perfumed tea, she outlined her ideas on what shape the biography should take. She spoke easily and sat back on the silk cushions of the divan facing me, in a relaxed manner. As the minutes passed her animated conversation and her alert and intelligent mind impressed me greatly. Here was a woman with whom I could empathise and I was sure she would be a willing helper in what promised to be a long and arduous task. I estimated that it would be all of two years before the book would be ready for publication, but she quite understood the problems.

When we had finished tea we adjourned to the library, a large room flanked on all sides by massive pine bookcases. A gallery ran above and here were the hundreds of editions of all of Marsh's works, in no less than twenty-five different languages. In the narrow spaces not occupied by the ranked leather-bound volumes, there were framed portraits

92

and photographs of the great and famous with whom the writer had consorted in his lifetime.

But I had little opportunity to take all this in for Deirdre Marsh had produced a series of leather-bound photograph albums, and I was told to feel free to select any which I felt would be suitable for illustrating the book. Then she handed me a typed contract which her lawyer had drawn up and I was staggered at the size of the advance she was prepared to give me. My mind was quite made up at this point, no doubt swayed by the beauty of my hostess, the generous terms of the contract, and the prospect of a free hand to write a critical biography of a man whose works were read by the million world-wide. I signed on the spot, much to her delight.

When she had counter-signed, she said with a light laugh, 'Now you can't get out of it!'

I replied in the same jocular manner that I had no wish to do so, and she then took me on a guided tour of the mansion, which was extremely impressive, as might be imagined. I was introduced to a discreet dark-haired girl, whom I understood was her private secretary, and a grey-haired butler called Simmonds, who had been in Marsh's employ for some forty years, but there was no sign of any other servants. Then I remembered that Marsh guarded his privacy fiercely, and would have only those people he greatly trusted around him and, as though divining my thoughts, Mrs Marsh explained that domestic help and gardeners came in daily from the village.

When we had once again returned to the drawing room I suggested one alteration to the contract, which was that she and I must share the book's profits fifty-fifty. She demurred at first. I knew she was immensely wealthy, of course, but the advance she had proposed and the monthly payments for research, travel and my other out-of-pocket expenses were so generous that I insisted, as a matter of principle. I think she was impressed with this for she agreed with a light laugh and we inked this clause into the two contracts and signed them, and she said that her lawyer would include them in a revised document in due course.

There was no sign of her new husband, but the secretary, Miss Marshall, told me that he was often abroad attending conferences or giving lectures, and was not due back in Sussex for some months, though the couple kept in close touch by telephone. I was tremendously busy all the weekend, meeting my hostess and Miss Marshall only for meals, which were sumptuous – there is no other word for it – served with rare wines both at lunch-time and at dinner. There must have been a first-class chef and kitchen staff on hand, but I was never invited to visit those quarters and saw no sign of them during my stay, the food coming up via a dumb waiter in the annexe adjoining the panelled dining room and served by the grave-voiced butler.

I had made a promising start on the work; sifting through meticu-
lously labelled file-cases in the archive room, where all the correspondence Marsh had carried on with the famous of the world was marked
with red-inked asterisks. I made copious notes as the hours slipped
by. If I was looking for sensational material – and I must emphasise
emphatically that I was not, for I don't write that sort of biography –
there did not appear to be any in my two-day trawl among the archives; if
there were any I should imagine they would either have been destroyed
by the widow or kept safely under lock and key.

My main research during the weekend was in the library, and this was
probably the most enjoyable part of the two days I spent at Beaufort
Place, along with my examination of the study, a small chamber off the
main library. It was obvious that all my research must be conducted in
the three places around which Edward Marsh's literary life had been
built: the archive room, the library and the study. It would be an
immense task to draw all the strands of his career together, but I knew I
could do it and work it all up into a vivid narrative. I had offered to show
Mrs Marsh the rough drafts of the chapters as they were completed, but
she had brushed aside my suggestion as being unnecessary. She gave
me a free hand, she said, and I could write what I liked. She did not
even want to see the final typescript and would read the volume when
it appeared from the publishers, such was my reputation as a biographer.
This was extremely flattering but it caused me some misgiving, for I was
not sure what I might turn up during my research.

There was a gold-coloured telephone at one side of Marsh's enormous desk in the library and I was at some pains to make out its function,
as there were already two phones on the right-hand side: one for internal
communication with various parts of the mansion and the other for
outside calls. The phones rang several times during my labours at the
desk but obviously I never picked them up, as the calls would not be
for me. Then, with a faint shock I remembered the newspaper reports
and realised that the gold-coloured instrument must be connected to
the dead writer's vault in the Grounds of the estate. I felt a faint frisson
of apprehension, and as I sat at the desk after dinner on the Friday
evening, the dying sun staining the window bars, I reached out my hand
and picked it up. It was ridiculous, of course, and I wondered why it
had not been disconnected and taken away. A sentimental gesture to
the dead writer's memory, perhaps?

I listened with strained nerves but there was only an eerie silence. I use
the word advisedly, though it was probably only my vivid imagination
that made me picture the darkened vault, the unlocked coffin lid and
the matching instrument lying by the dead man's hand. I put the phone
down hastily and the library resumed its normal aspect.

The next morning Deirdre Marsh took me on a guided tour of the grounds, where numerous gardeners were at work. There was an arboretum, several rustic follies, and a large lake, where, on a small promontory stood the famous mausoleum where the remains of her former husband were interred. It was a massive stone structure, already showing signs of the actions of wind and weather, with minute cracks in the portico. We skirted it slowly, without speaking, and I noted that it bore a simple inscription on a marble plaque over the entrance, which merely gave Marsh's name, dates of birth and death, and the one word: Author.

The entrance itself was barred by a huge iron grille, now somewhat rusted, and there was a stout iron-studded door beyond. The widow said nothing as we circled the forbidding structure, and the thing seemed so incongruous and sombre in that beautiful setting that the very day appeared overshadowed, the sunlight on the water drained of all luminescence, so powerful was the impression it exerted on my mind. It was not until we were sitting on a broad terrace at the far side of the lake, in front of a small pavilion, another of her husband's Gothic follies, that the widow spoke.

'I wish you to see everything, including my late husband's extreme eccentricities.'

I nodded, but said nothing in reply and presently we resumed our walk. By the time of my departure I had a thick wad of typescript, setting out my ideas for the book, with rough chapter indications and a host of notes on salient points that I must emphasise if I was to write a definitive biography of Marsh's life. It was a good start, and when I had put the material in order at my London home, I promised to return to stay in Sussex for a week of intensive research, and would then return on a daily basis as the work continued, for the house was only an hour and a half drive from London.

I would also need to interview the author's surviving relatives, friends and associates, and I had to make out a proper itinerary for all these multifarious aspects of the task Deirdre Marsh had set me. Like all the biographies I had undertaken, the work involved seemed formidable, but I had previously found that one settled into a routine and then, after some time, the material flowed into shape; it almost seemed to write itself. I had promised myself that two years would be the limit; I had to bring it in in that time for I had promised my wife an extensive tour of Europe for a forthcoming wedding anniversary.

As soon as I began the commission my wife and I settled into a routine for the first six months or so. I spent weekdays in Sussex and then went home on Friday nights for the weekend. This worked very well, and during that period I amassed a great deal of material and started roughing out the preliminary chapters of the book. True to her word, Deirdre Marsh evinced not the slightest interest in the results of my labours, and I marvelled at her self-control, though she was unfailingly courteous and charming and put herself out to cater for my every need, both during my working day and at meal times.

It was almost two months before I met her husband, who had just returned from a lecture tour in South America. He was a handsome, pleasant man in his early forties, and I gathered he was a doctor of philosophy and I know not what else. But he was just as unobtrusive as his wife and had his own study and library elsewhere in the vast mansion.

Things continued in this way for a long time, and as I interviewed elderly relatives, friends and former colleagues in the literary and publishing worlds in London, Paris and the north of England, a rounded picture of Edward Marsh emerged. Twice married – his first wife had died many years before he met Deirdre – he was somewhat reclusive and my study of him, though fair and unbiased, presented him as a man obsessed both with his own image and with his work, the latter to an excessive extent. For he more or less lived only for literary matters, and though he could be gregarious in company and was a generous host on occasion, he was obviously happiest when at his desk, pounding away on his ancient standard typewriter.

The machine was still there, and I had tried it once or twice, though the occasions gave me a slight uneasiness, as though the ghostly echoes the machine aroused against the panelled walls evinced the spirit of the long-dead author. I could not get on with the electric model Mrs Marsh had supplied, as I preferred my own portable machine, which I had brought to Sussex with me and which I left in situ, as I had another in my own study at home.

Most of the people I spoke to, even his intimate friends, were guarded in their remarks, as though in deference to the widow, but I managed to obtain what I felt was an in-depth study of the man, with nothing omitted. There were no deep secrets or great scandals; there was not even the slightest breath of the latter in my conversations with the author's distant relatives or closest friends. Not that I wished to go burrowing into sordid detail if there had been; I had no doubt there were literary jackals who might turn up unsavoury things in future years, but my work was the first and I wanted it to be both comprehensive and definitive. And in any case, many of the illustrations were unique, most of them from Deirdre Marsh's private archive.

I was somewhat hesitant about broaching the matter of the bizarre funeral and the telephone installed in the mausoleum, as I felt sure the subject would be distasteful to Mrs Marsh. But I was, however, spared that task as the reports in *The Times* and my interviews with old friends who had been present, provided me with all the information I needed.

I had already seen the exterior of the tomb and had no wish to see inside, and since my first visit, when we had toured the gardens and inspected the mausoleum, Deirdre had never said a word on the matter.

I respected her silence and had left that aspect of Marsh's strange career and obsessive lifestyle without going too deeply into his morbid habits.

To my surprise, and to my wife's relief, my labours finally came to an end, and after my secretary had immaculately typed the top copy and photocopied several more for safe-keeping, I duly delivered the completed book, together with some thirty photographs I had selected, to my publisher.

In only two days there came an enthusiastic letter from the managing director and the publication date was set for three months' time. They had prepared a big poster dampaign and press releases and the launch was fixed for a prestigious London hall, with signing sessions and a cocktail party for the press and invited guests. To my surprise Deirdre Marsh declined to attend any of the functions. She put this in the most polite way in both a telephone call and a tactful letter; her life with Marsh, she hinted, had been replete with such events, and she was heartily sick and tired of such junketings, though she did, at my behest, agree to give a few private interviews with respected writers from several literary journals, always at her own home and at a time and date to suit herself and her husband.

As expected, sales were phenomenal, thanks to the efforts of my own publisher and a good PR firm he had engaged, but in the end the book more or less sold itself, and there was a steady stream of reprints for the next two or three years, until the public interest in Marsh and his career was exhausted. Long before that, however, I detected strange undercurrents in the outwardly placid life of Marsh which I had so assiduously chronicled. They were very subtle and understated and one came from a prestigious literary journalist who had declined to be interviewed for publication. I was having a drink with him at the Savoy about six months after the book had appeared and while congratulating me on my labours, he dropped a hint, indicating that I had not delved deeply enough into Marsh's secret life and the circumstances of his death. He declined to be drawn further but hinted that there were many things about Marsh's lifestyle yet to be uncovered and that I should have given more attention to his extraordinary means of burial and certain indications in his will.

He said no more and I could not persuade him to enlarge on his cryptic remarks, but they remained with me for some time and I developed a certain uneasiness about my book, as though I should have concentrated more closely on certain aspects of Marsh's career and perhaps questioned Mrs Marsh more vigorously; the generosity as outlined in the terms of the contract and the lavish hospitality she and her husband had extended over the years had perhaps made me more discreet in my questioning than I otherwise might have been.

Then, years after publication, there came a bombshell. There had been a week of rain and violent storms, with much flooding and damage both in London and the West Country, and when I opened my morning newspaper I was arrested by a large four-column heading on an inside page: GREAT AUTHOR'S SHOCKING DEATH, with the sub-head: Bizarre Find in Vault. I knew the story was about Marsh even before I read the first paragraph

The report was even more horrific than I had imagined. A few days earlier, with the storms at their height, lightning had struck the Marsh tomb in the estate grounds. The roof was partially destroyed and there were great gaping holes with rain pouring through. Deirdre Marsh had immediately engaged specialist builders to repair the damage. Obviously they had had to open up the main vault doors and then the inner doors because the roof of the burial chamber had also been breached.

What they found had caused one of the younger workmen to faint. The coffin had been opened and the emaciated and desiccated corpse of Marsh had been found sprawled in agony at the vault door which was, of course, locked from the outside. The telephone, which was to have been his lifeline to the outer world in case of premature burial, which he had so feared, was still clutched in one claw-like hand. The police had been called, of course, and a coroner's inquest had been fixed for a week's time.

To say that I was shattered by this news was an understatement, and my wife was also deeply shocked. The telephone began ringing a few hours later as other newspapers were alerted to the story, with the callers asking for my comments. I dealt with these the best way I could and at last the flood of inquiries died away. At the first convenient moment I rang Deirdre Marsh, but was told by the butler that she and her husband had gone away for a few days. I was not surprised at this and said I would ring again to express my sympathy after the inquest.

This I duly did after reading a further newspaper report that a verdict of death by misadventure had been returned by the inquest jury, under the direction of the coroner. This was not surprising, though the exact cause of death had not been ascertained, due to the fact that certain organs had been badly decayed after so many years in the vault. It was also hinted that the depredations of rats had been mainly responsible for the condition of the body. It was a gruesome story, all in all, but I was surprised, when I eventually contacted the widow, that she seemed relatively nonchalant about the whole affair and brushed aside my expressions of sympathy with the offhand comment, 'These things happen, unfortunately.'

Then, to my surprise, she invited me down the following weekend, for a further accounting of royalties as she had just received the latest statement from her lawyers; in addition I had apparently left behind a great number of working papers and other documents in the study, which I might like to have. I immediately accepted her invitation, as

I was curious to hear at first hand all the circumstances relating to the bizarre find in the vault, though I realised I would have to be enormously tactful.

I arrived at Beaufort Place on the Friday evening and received a warm welcome from Deirdre Marsh and her husband, a somewhat shy but handsome man who had always hovered smiling in the background when I had visited in past years. In her customary brisk manner Mrs Marsh said business matters could wait until the Saturday, and we discussed merely trivial things during the course of the excellent dinner that was served. Before seeking my bedroom I again visited Marsh's study. I was in quite a nostalgic mood and opened a number of drawers, sifting through the papers I had left behind and putting them in neat piles on the desk top.

At one stage I dropped one of my old notebooks and bent to the floor to retrieve it, and in so doing I must have brushed against a projecting piece of carving or pressed it with my disengaged hand, for a hidden drawer opened silently before my eyes. Within it was contained just one object: a thick morocco-bound volume. A secret drawer! With some anticipation I gently pulled out the book, which was about four inches by six. Gold lettering glinted as I brought it up to the full light of the lamp. Stamped on the cover were the letters E.M. and beneath DIARY. It was with a somewhat quickened heartbeat that I quietly slid the drawer to and heard the smooth click as it relocked itself. I put the diary in my inner jacket pocket, extinguished the lights and made my way quickly to my bedroom, but not to sleep.

That night I stayed up late, reading Marsh's diary entries with mounting consternation. There were sexual revelations of which I had never dreamed when I began my researches – not that I would have included them in my work, of course. There were three-week debauches in Paris with very young girls, even into Marsh's old age, conquests of titled women in London and group sex in grand houses in Mayfair. I read on with increasing loathing and disgust. How, I wondered, could Deirdre Marsh have put up with all this? For it was surely impossible that she could not have known, or at least suspected such liaisons.

Yet this man, world-famous and honoured, had kept these vile secrets from the world for decades. During his lifetime there had not been the slightest breath of scandal attached to his name, but many of his closest friends must have known of his true nature. Perhaps he was simply too rich and too powerful. Hints might have been dropped in newspapers, but possibly their editors too did not wish to destroy the image of England's most distinguished novelist. It was an enigma and I read on with incredulity and distaste. Then, in later years, the tenor of this man's tortured and anguished soul took another turn.

There were the vaguest hints regarding his hitherto perfect health.

Suspicion was at first directed towards his wife, though this could have been paranoia. Then his venom was directed against his medical adviser. Though I had, of course, detailed the manner of Marsh's death in general terms, I had not been able to interview the local doctor who had originally treated him, as he had died some years before. My thoughts grew darker and more sombre as I read on. Then one scribbled sentence jumped out at me. 'I fear the doctor is poisoning me!'

He went on to describe stomach cramps and other types of pain, but they could have been mere imaginings or the usual breakdown in health that old age sometimes brings. The last entries in the diary referred to disposition of property and other details if he should die prematurely or lapse into a coma. He spoke of increasing lethargy and of long periods spent sleeping, though only a few months before he had risen promptly at 6 a.m. and gone to his desk to begin his day's work with renewed zest. The last words on a single page, in an almost incomprehensible scrawl, read, 'I am fading . . . God help me.'

I replaced the book among clothing at the bottom of my suitcase, my head filled with whirling thoughts. If he suspected his doctor was attempting to murder him why had the diary remained hidden where no one would find it? It was obvious that no one in the household had any inkling of the secret drawer or the diary would have been removed or destroyed in order to avoid any scandal or something worse: that Marsh had died insane.

That was quite a possibility. But if he were sane and had suspected his medical adviser, that would explain the elaborate precautions he had taken in having a telephone connected to the vault. I was at an impasse. The doctor was dead and that was the conclusion of the story. I had no wish to dig up ancient scandals. Best to let the great man rest with his reputation untarnished. And I could hardly mention the matter to Mrs Marsh and her husband. It was after 2 a.m. before I went to bed but it was a long time before I could get to sleep.

At breakfast next morning, Mrs Marsh, with the sensitive antennae that all women seem to possess, obviously realised from my demeanour that something was wrong. Her husband was nowhere to be seen, but he had work of his own to do and I understood he had breakfasted very early. She paused while pouring me a second cup from the silver-plated coffee pot.

'You seem disturbed. You have perhaps discovered something in Edward's papers that you had not come across before?'

I tried to hide my surprise, but from her expression I realised she knew she had hit the mark. My continued silence seemed to amuse her.

'Something scandalous?' she said in a mocking voice.

'There was just a hint . . .' I mumbled, avoiding her eyes.

I realised that I had to go on now that she had guessed so much. 'He was concerned about his health . . . The doctor . . .'

100

She interrupted quickly. 'Such fears are quite natural in very old men. I do understand that. My husband is a medical doctor in addition to his other qualifications and treated Edward in his last days. He also conducted the post mortem examination and death from natural causes was recorded.'

She bit her lip as though she had said too much. I stared at her for a long moment. I saw everything clearly then. It all came together in my mind in a flash. The eyes of Deirdre Marsh met mine and I knew she realised that I fully understood and that nothing could be done about it at this moment in time.

'I had many years of hell,' she said. 'There were perversions I cannot speak about, kept completely secret from the public. But I wished the world to think him a paragon, instead of a monster. You were the perfect choice.'

There was a look of defiance on her face. 'You don't know what a horrible man he was. I thought he would never die. But you white-washed his memory. You are puzzled about his awakening in the vault; a rare drug that induces catalepsy. I know nothing of these matters but my husband will explain.'

She gave me a brilliant smile. 'I cut the telephone wire. I expect he thought the line was engaged.'

She burst out laughing.

'Come and have a drink! You look as if you need one!'

Homage to Ellis Peters? The Cadfael book I liked most was the first, *A Morbid Taste for Bones*. Edith herself I liked very much, and I also liked her series of books set in India (and pinched little bits from them as well!). The later Cadfaels I found, sad to say, too historical, studded with too many facts interesting enough in themselves but getting in the way of the story, and I was glad that I ceased reviewing before she had written many of them, sparing myself a dilemma.

So, you may ask, what am I doing writing an historical short story myself? The answer, as I just remember, was that I was invited by the *Illustrated London News* in 1981 to contribute a story set in the past. And, when I had lowered my seine-net, what should float into it but a Victorian governess from the lowest depths of society, who by sheer intellect and determination had climbed up to that curious height between being 'a lady' and being a servant. Soon I had a name for her. If she had been born, illegitimate, in the workhouse, she would have been given her name by that fat tyrant with the big stick, Mr Bumble. And it was the beadle's habit in bestowing forenames of the poor nameless creatures that came under him to go through the alphabet. So after Twist, Oliver, it had to be Unwin and Harriet. And I liked her, and admired her. So over the years three books have followed and one or two short stories of which *The Fatal Step* is the latest.

H.R.F. Keating

The Fatal Step

H.R.F. Keating

If there are birthdays, there are also death days. In the home of the Reverend Theophrastus Mountjoy, Rector of Finchley, that leafy village some few miles north of London, the two were to become all too closely linked, and that link was to make Miss Harriet Unwin, governess, deeply regret that some six months ago she had accepted her post, well remunerated though it was.

Mr Mountjoy had had a family of ten children, all but two of whom had died in infancy, leaving only Ernest, his first-born, and Catherine, with whose birth his wife had sighed her last. It was because Catherine had no mother that Mr Mountjoy had employed Harriet Unwin. However, even before her worst trouble descended she had begun to feel her stay at Finchley Rectory would not be as agreeable as she had thought. This was not at all little Catherine's fault. She was a sweet and biddable child. Nor was it precisely the fault of Catherine's brother Ernest, though it was certainly Ernest's return from Harrow for the long vacation that first made her life distinctly less pleasant, and finally brought about her terrible time of trial.

The root cause of it all was that Mr Mountjoy had high expectations for his son and heir. He had decided Ernest was to follow his own footsteps into the Church. The lad was to gain a place at the same Cambridge college, one of the lesser ones, of which he himself had eventually become a Fellow, an achievement that had secured him in turn a pleasant curacy and before too long the Rectory at Finchley. All this he had told Miss Unwin while Ernest was still at school wrestling with the complexities of Latin. He had even indicated that, though he himself no longer hoped for preferment, he would die happy were Ernest one day to be consecrated a bishop, even a colonial one.

But Ernest, Miss Unwin realised soon after she had met him, though a pleasant lad and particularly delightful with his little sister – something not given to all fifteen-year-old boys – was not at all academic. His chief skill, as she found one day when she set out to investigate a curious hammering coming from the supposedly empty Rectory attic, was

105

with his hands. He was, she discovered, making a doll's house for his sister's birthday. It was a beautifully constructed piece, too, especially praiseworthy since the only tools the boy had were a blunt saw, an old claw-hammer and his penknife.

His talent was, however, something that Mr Mountjoy appeared to be altogether incapable of appreciating. He wished his son to be clever, and, if he had to, would himself thrust cleverness into him. So when other young Harrovians were enjoying the freedom of the summer vacation, Ernest was made to study. And to show results from that study. More, when they were not forthcoming, Mr Mountjoy's by no means well-controlled temper burst time and again into furious life.

Ernest, of course, was not the only victim in the household of that temper. In the short time Miss Unwin had been at the Rectory, Bennings, the butler, a fat and hopeless, wheezing fellow hardly capable of stooping enough to pick up a dropped spoon or fork, had twice been discharged for failing to bring, opened, to the dining room the bottle of wine Mr Mountjoy had personally placed on the cellar table earlier in the day. Of course twice, eventually, Bennings had been allowed to understand he was still in the Rector's employ. Then there had been the evening when Miss Unwin, sitting quietly at her work while Mr Mountjoy was snoozing over a book, had accidentally let fall her scissors. The slight clang had galvanised her employer's wrath. But the steady look in her eyes under the first wave of his onslaught had ensured it was never to be repeated.

Ernest, however, roused that formidable wrath two, three or more times a week. And when he did so, almost invariably he became the victim of a father's right and a father's strong arm. Barely muffled yelps of pain gave Miss Unwin, unable on occasion to avoid hearing them, some decidedly unpleasant moments. The moderate and careful use of corporal punishment she did not disapprove of. With other pupils at other houses it had been her duty to bring a ruler sharply down on to an extended palm. But it was plain to her that the Reverend Mr Mountjoy was attempting to secure his own will in a way that said more perhaps about himself than it did about Ernest's academic deficiencies.

Eventually she brought herself to speak to Ernest. She hardly knew what she could say, but she felt that to pretend not to be aware of how often and how vigorously – no, brutally – he was being punished was carrying a polite convention to a ridiculous point.

So she tackled him. At what might have been either a very good moment or a very bad one. Not five minutes earlier she had heard coming from Mr Mountjoy's study a good many of those by now familiar half-suppressed yelps of pain.

'Ernest,' she said, 'you've been punished again, haven't you? Is there nothing you can do to please your father better?'

He gave her a look of mingled surprise and relief.

106

'Oh, Miss Unwin, I'm afraid there isn't anything. Papa believes I'm a fellow with brains. And I just am not.'

'Well, could I perhaps help you with your studies?'

He grinned then.

'With Hebrew, Miss Unwin? Biblical Hebrew? That's what the Pater wants me to get the hang of. He says it'll stand me in good stead when I get to Cambridge. But the truth of it is, I don't think I'll even get the hang of enough Latin for that.'

'I see.' She thought for a moment, regretting her total ignorance of Hebrew. 'Well, Ernest, would you like me just to speak to your father, to try and convince him you have other talents than the acquisition of Biblical Hebrew?'

'But what other talents have I got when you come down to it?'

'Oh, Ernest, don't say that. You have a great gift for making things. I was astonished when I came up to the attic that day to see how clever, you had been with Catherine's doll's house.'

'Oh, but for heaven's sake, don't tell Papa about that. I mean, when I asked him the other day for some money just to buy a pair of pliers he went up in smoke. No son of his, he said, was going to practise a tradesman's work, not when he's paid hundreds and hundreds to send me to beastly Harrow.'

'But I could say something at least.'

'No, honestly, Miss Unwin. I mean, Papa thinks it's all for my own good, punishing me. And I suppose it must be. I don't really mind it. Well, not after a bit.'

And with this simple assurance that the boy bore his father no resentment Miss Unwin felt she had to be content.

The days went by until, towards the end of the vacation, there came the time of the Mountjoy children's birthdays, both of which fell within a short time of each other. Miss Unwin contrived well in advance that Catherine should purchase for her brother, whose anniversary came second, a particularly fine fretsaw and accompanying bundle of differing blades. But, while Ernest had succeeded in keeping his gift secret from his sister, and perhaps more importantly from his father, little Catherine was not so patient.

'Ernest, Ernest,' she blurted out on her return from the shopping expedition, 'you'll never guess what I'm going to give you for your birthday. A threat saw. A real threat saw to cut up wood with.'

However, on Catherine's birthday morning Ernest's handing-over of his still unrevealed surprise proved not to be a complete success. After Mrs Hopewell, the housekeeper, and fat wheezing Bennings had led the servants out of the dining room at the end of Morning Prayers, Catherine's father presented her with an embroidered purse containing a gold sovereign. He then explained at length its precise value, adding that it was not to be subject to 'any immediate disbursement. For your prompt enjoyment I dare say Miss Unwin is about to give you a little box of bon-bons or something of that sort' – she was not – 'but this is to be your first step towards accumulating savings which will give you some independence when in the course of time you come to be married.'

Little Catherine, much in awe of her seldom-seen father, took it all well enough. Miss Unwin, who had been concealing a small packet containing a pretty bead necklace, rapidly resolved to ring, earlier than planned, for Mrs Hopewell, whom she knew to be ready with a basket of peppermint creams of her own making. She counted, correctly as it turned out, that these would constitute enough of a diversion for her employer's notion about the 'little box of bon-bons' to be forgotten.

All seemed to go well. Mrs Hopewell was prettily, and spontaneously, thanked. One of the peppermints was, by permission, consumed on the spot. Next, Miss Unwin's packet was handed over, eagerly unwrapped and the necklace nestling within at once put on and inspected in an improvised mirror formed by a glass-fronted etching of one of Sassaferrato's Madonnas, of which Miss Unwin had been given an account by her employer on the very day she had taken up her post.

But then, when Ernest had slipped out and returned with his large parcel, events took a sharp turn for the worse. Miss Unwin was still congratulating herself on getting over the inspection of the necklace in the Sassaferrato before her employer had raised the spectre of sacrilege, when Catherine tore away enough of the wrappings of her brother's parcel for the doll's house to be revealed. Her exclamations of delight were immediately cut short, however.

'Do I understand, Ernest,' thundered Mr Mountjoy, 'that this – this object was made with your own hands?'

'Yes . . . Yes, Pater, it is. It was.'

'Then, my boy, it is my duty to tell you that wasting your time in such a manner is a perfect disgrace.'

He might have gone further, but Miss Unwin decided it was time she intervened. She said nothing to Mr Mountjoy himself, but giving him a single firm look suggested to Ernest that he had better carry the doll's house up to the nursery before breakfast was served.

She thought she had averted any worse rage, and certainly when Ernest returned the meal proceeded quietly enough. In fact, it was not until towards the end of the day that, entirely unexpectedly, real disaster struck. At precisely five o'clock Mr Mountjoy had, according to his invariable custom, gone to select from the cellar what wine he would take at his dinner. Ernest had finished his hour of tuition, succeeding for once in pattering off correctly whatever Hebrew verbs it had been his task to learn, and had made his way, stealthily, to his attic hideout. Miss Unwin, in the nursery, was supervising Catherine's birthday-cake tea.

And then from the very bowels of the Rectory there had come an appalling long-drawn, echoing howl, suddenly stopped.

'Stay here,' Miss Unwin shouted to Mary, the nursery maid. And down she went, heels tapping their tattoo on the carpeted stairs, kept securely in place at each tread with a daily-polished brass rod. At the bottom she paused for a moment. Silence. The unearthly howl as if it had never been.

But Miss Unwin understood now where it must have come from.

In seconds she was at the door to the wine cellar. It was ajar. She heaved it wide, peered in. Nothing. Blackness. Yet deeper silence.

Behind her she sensed rather than saw that three or four of the servants, headed by pale-faced, plump Bennings, had arrived to stand in a huddle, gaping.

'A candle,' she snapped. 'Quick as you can.'

It was the kitchenmaid who was alert enough to bring one, alight and dangerously guttering. Miss Unwin took it from her shaking hand, directed its now steadier beam downwards into the cellar. And saw at the foot of the flight of bare wooden steps the body of her employer, the Reverend Theophrastus Mountjoy, his head a pulpy, bloody mess.

But she saw something else, too.

The fifth step down from where she was standing was no longer there. In a moment she had discovered it, lying at the foot of the steep stairway next to Mr Mountjoy's extinguished candle. A single heavy plank. And even at a distance she could see that there were no signs of it having been torn away accidentally from where it had been securely in place for years.

She turned to the servants behind her.

'Bennings,' she said. 'Send the boot-boy to the police station, fast as he can run. Tell him to say that the Inspector must come at once to the Rectory.'

'Yes, Miss Unwin. Yes. But— But why?'

'Because I very much fear there has been murder done.'

When the police trap, its horse snorting, had arrived at the Rectory, Inspector McDiver proved to be not as easily convinced that murder was to be investigated.

'But, Madam,' he said to Miss Unwin at the cellar door, realising that it was she who was now in charge of the household, 'this is plainly only some mishap, appalling in its consequences of course, but no more than that.'

He stroked the ponderous moustache that decorated his upper lip.

'Inspector,' Miss Unwin said, 'get your constable to light his bull's-eye and direct its beam on to where that step is missing.'

The constable succeeded at last in casting a bright enough light on to the spot.

'Now, look closely,' Miss Unwin said with firmness. 'Can you not see there are no traces of split wood? It is plain that the step was prised clean away from—'

She came to a total halt in mid-sentence.

Something she had not had time to consider amid all the hubbub arising from the sudden death – the immediate arrangements, the confining of the Rector's orphaned children to their rooms, the quieting of two hysterical housemaids – had now abruptly come into her mind. Who, among all the people of the household, was most likely to possess the necessary skill to neatly heave away the fatal step?

The answer came to her simultaneously with the question.

Ernest. Even the pathetic carpentry equipment in his attic hideaway included the one tool necessary for prising that step from its place, the old claw-hammer. And if ever a boy might bear his father a grudge it was much-thrashed Ernest.

But . . . But could the pleasant boy she knew, the lad whom it was such a delight to see playing with his small sister, could he really have planned this terrible trap for his own father? Could the boy who had so modestly declared he was not 'a fellow with brains' have contrived such a deadly scheme?

But, she guessed, the young carpenter could indeed have planned the trap. After all, she thought bemusedly, how well do I really know Ernest? I have seen him for only a few weeks. Yes, in all that time he has done nothing to make me think he is anything but a particularly pleasant boy. But beneath. What may have been lying beneath all along? There is no telling.

Surely he is a nice good-hearted lad, she told herself. He is. Despite what he has done. *If* he has done it. The daring, disquieting thought came to her – should I cease at once my attempt to put into this asinine inspector's head the meaning of the evidence he has so far failed to grasp? Should I, eventually, let him stand up in the Coroner's court and state that a thorough investigation had shown the death of the Reverend Theophrastus Mountjoy to be accidental?

But almost at once she knew that she could not let that happen. Truth had to prevail. *Fiat justitia, Ruat coelum.* The words from her scanty store of gentleman's-preserve Latin came booming into her head. *Let justice be done, Though the heavens fall.*

'Inspector,' she said. 'Perhaps you should go down the steps as far as that missing one and give the place it came from a closer examination?'

Inspector McDiver looked at the perilous, ill-lit, steep flight down.

'Madam,' he said after a long moment, 'I see no necessity for that. It is as obvious to me, as you claim it may have been to you, that the length of wood forming the fifth step has been removed on purpose. I have to inform you that I consider that I am investigating a murder.'

Suggest to him next where his investigation will inevitably lead? To the Rectory attic, young Ernest's secret place, and the claw-hammer, perhaps still to be found there? To, in fact, the murderer? No. No. No, no, no. That is too much to ask of myself. No, let Inspector McDiver work his way round to that in his own good time.

And in the meanwhile? Find an opportunity of telling Ernest what I know must be the truth? Give him a chance to confess his guilt and find perhaps some mercy in court? Or . . . but this would be wrong. Surely wrong. Give him a chance to make away with that hammer and to flee before Inspector McDiver reaches the only possible conclusion? Before he works his way, looking for someone capable of prising away that fatal step, through every member of the household, from Mrs Hopewell, down through the ranks of the maids to Jack, the eight-year-old bootboy, then back up to Bennings, so plumply well-fed it is laughable to think of him at such work?

But, no. No, I cannot cheat justice so blatantly. It would haunt me all my life. So, not a word, not even a look, to warn Ernest. But, on the other hand, no word to Inspector McDiver either. Let events take their course. Do what I can to shield little Catherine from them, and try to not think about what must be happening.

It took Inspector McDiver three whole days, painstakingly questioning everybody who had been inside the locked doors of the Rectory that afternoon, before he made his arrest. Of fat, wan-faced, wheezy Bennings.

Miss Unwin, still in charge of the household while she waited to receive a letter from the bereaved children's sole remaining relation, heard the news from Inspector McDiver's own moustache-protected lips. She was for a moment deprived of speech.

It was a moment that gave her a chance to think. What should she say? What should she do? Tell the fool how wrong he must be? And then tell him, since he seemed incapable of ferreting it out for himself, what the true answer was?

An unbearably hard decision.

So let him take poor fat Bennings away to a cell until some defence counsel pointed out in court how ridiculously unlikely it was that a man of such a feeble physique could have managed to uproot that step. But did Bennings, most foolish of men, deserve even a few weeks of unjust imprisonment? Yet, if he did not, could she possibly now point out to Inspector McDiver where in all likelihood the instrument was that had been used to lay the trap? In the lair of the boy who – the servants must have talked about those frequent, savage beatings – possessed what must seem to be an overwhelming motive?

Ruat coelum.

'Inspector—' she began.

111

And then, just then, she realised something. Ernest did not have that overwhelming motive for murder. He did not. She recalled distinctly what the lad had said to her, with boyish candour, when she had offered to intercede with his father. 'I don't really mind it. Well, not after a bit.' Yes, Ernest had believed, without a doubt, that those beatings, cruelly painful though they must have been, were for his own good. She had conjectured herself – perhaps this had affected her customary clarity of mind – that there had been in the Rector's punishments something more than particularly stern justice. She had suspected there had been a savagery about them which might well have left their victim harbouring black revengeful thoughts. But, no. Surely Ernest, attributing to his father his own simple goodness, had believed nothing of that. So, despite the fact that he possessed the means necessary to uproot the missing step, it must be quite unlikely he had done so.

Then could Bennings after all . . . ? Well, it might just be possible. He had certainly shown no signs of grief at his employer's death. No, let others decide. Let a jury and a judge decide in due course.

'Well, Inspector, I must congratulate you on your work.'

She was not proud of the words, but they seemed to be the only ones she could utter in the circumstances.

Before long Miss Unwin found the responsibility that had so unexpectedly descended on her was to come to an end. The children's distant cousin had agreed that, straitened though his circumstances were, he and his wife would take charge of the two orphans. But before the day of their arrival, Ernest's birthday was celebrated, if mutedly. The 'threat saw' was handed over and received as enthusiastically as if Ernest had never had any notion what it was he was to be given.

Or, Miss Unwin thought, of the true *threat* that had hovered over him.

'Do you think, Miss Unwin,' the boy said, turning his present over and over in his hands, 'if our new guardian really cannot afford to keep me at Harrow, that he would feel it was not a disgrace if I was to be apprenticed to a cabinet-maker?'

For some moments Miss Unwin considered the proposal.

'I do not see why not,' she said at last. 'Would you like me to tell your Uncle Frederick, as you are to call him, that this is what you would most like?'

'Oh, yes, Miss Unwin. Yes, yes. And perhaps the toy cupboard in the nursery could be opened again, now that Papa has been dead as long as he has, and I could show the doll's house to Uncle Frederick when he comes. It was my best thing, and it could be a sort of sample of what I can do.'

'Well, yes, I suppose we might do that. However sad the tragedy of your father's death, Catherine's toys cannot be locked away for ever.'

112

'Oh, jolly good. I say, can we get it out as soon as Catherine has gone for her nap? I haven't seen it at all, you know, ever since you said it would be best if the toy cupboard was locked up.'

'Yes, I don't see why we should not do that.'

But when they went to the nursery and opened the cupboard, Miss Unwin suddenly saw why she should not have agreed to bring the doll's house to the light of day again. Because it brought into the light something she had altogether failed to take into account.

The very moment she held in her hands the ingeniously made little house, there came into her mind once more the words the Reverend Theophrastus Mountjoy had spoken when the gift had been unwrapped on the day of Catherine's birthday. 'Then, my boy, it is my duty to tell you that wasting your time in such a manner is a perfect disgrace.'

And at once she saw that, after all, Ernest had had reason to murder his father. Surely those few words, so much less harsh than any the Rector had spoken when badly learnt Hebrew lessons had led to his savage punishments, had by so calmly and loftily disparaging the sole accomplishment in which Ernest took pride, gone one fatal step too far.

All the doubts and fears she thought had been banished came rushing back in. She fought them away. In half an hour Catherine would wake from her nap, and it would be time for her afternoon walk; the time when, in happier days, she had been accustomed to draw the little girl out, showing her the different birds in the hedges and trees, the squirrels, the wayside flowers, teaching her their names, encouraging her to talk well and clearly. Yes, though her task as governess was soon to end, until it had it was still her duty to enlighten the child's growing mind. It must be done. No time for speculation about other things, no matter how pressing, no matter how grim.

But sooner or later, she knew, she would have to make up her mind what to do. Or rather, as she admitted to herself almost at once, she would have to put into effect what she knew she must do. With Catherine at last in bed for the night, she must go down to the police station and tell Inspector McDiver what she now saw to be the truth.

A momentary mental glimpse of Ernest, seemingly so innocent, opening and closing the doors of his doll's house, talking excitedly about what he could make as furniture when his sister had it in her hands again.

Could it be that beneath he was really . . . ?

Yes, however smiling and serene the surface, it could be. It was.

She had reckoned without the impenetrable stupidity of Inspector McDiver, however. He listened to her across his desk in the police station. He stroked his heavy moustache, with gravity. He spoke.

'My dear Miss Unwin, you really must let matters of this sort remain the province of those who are trained to deal with them. A boy of Master Ernest Mountjoy's sort, a murderer? No, no, no. You have let some wild idea take possession of your mind. Hear the words of an experienced police officer. There is nothing in this idea of yours, nothing at all.'

A further ponderous, fatherly stroking of that heavy moustache.

'Now, won't you listen to some advice from a man very much older – and I dare say wiser – than yourself. Forget about all this nonsense. And in ten years' time, when young Master Ernest is, very like, a clergyman as his poor dead father was before him, you'll wonder how you could ever have entertained such a thought in your head for one moment. Believe me, you will.'

But Miss Unwin did not believe him. He had given her nothing to shake her conviction about what she had seen with her own eyes, heard with her own ears. And so she resolved to take that conviction to where it was most likely to be heard by a police officer of intelligence. To the newly established Detective Department at Scotland Yard in London.

For the rest of that day she forced herself to harden her heart. Ernest, however young he was, however much in everything but this he was an innocent, had contrived to remove that step five rungs down the cellar stair. It was indeed one fatal step of his own he had taken when his father had humiliated him in that way. Justice must be done. *Ruat coelum*.

All next morning, as she sat at breakfast with Catherine and the cheerfully prattling young murderer, she dinned and drummed into her own head that this was what Ernest was. A murderer.

And yet . . .

As she was leaving the house for London, little Catherine asked her wistfully where she was going.

'To Scotland Yard,' she answered, knowing this would mean nothing to her charge.

'To Scotland, Miss Unwin? But you told me Scotland was far, far away.'

And it was with this small misunderstanding that a last idea came into Miss Unwin's mind. She did not stop to think whether it was good or bad. She simply added one thing more.

'Yes, Scotland. I shall be back for luncheon, though. But my having to go there is a great secret. So don't tell anyone, will you, not even Ernest. It will be a surprise for him. A big surprise.'

She left.

Would Catherine, no more able to keep a secret now than she had been when she had blurted out that she was giving Ernest a 'threat saw', tell her brother that her governess was going to Scotland this morning? And if she did, would he guess that this meant she was about to visit the Detective Department at Scotland Yard? And if he then realised what it must be she would have to say there, would he act on that knowledge? And how would he act? Would he succeed in causing all traces of that hammer to disappear? And, if he did, would that be enough to keep him from the clutches of the law? And was that what should happen to him? Arrest and trial. Or might he, once warned, simply flee? Attempt to disappear from view? To sink into the anonymity of some London rookery? Or get himself aboard a ship bound for America? For anywhere?

But would little Catherine blurt out the secret? Would Ernest, were she to do so, understand its true meaning? How would he act, if he did?

And what did she herself truly want? Did she want justice, though the heavens fall? Or had she, in tossing into the air that saving scrap, taken a fatal step of her own?

Let time tell.

S ince our own era provides a fertile environment for innumerable crimes, why set a murder mystery in the past?

Perhaps ancient landscapes lend a patina of the exotic to what are really sordid affairs. Certainly, different societies offer possibilites for problems and motivations less familiar than those we can read today in the newspaper. Poison, for instance, was more easily hidden when people were dying every day from eating pork that had been left in the sun too long. There were no police labs, no DNA testing, no fingerprinting, not even photographs of the crime scene or yellow tape to string around it. The investigator had to depend on his wits and the contest with the criminal was more finely balanced.

Another bonus for writers is that aspects of society taken for granted by the people of the time have become so alien to us that they can quite fairly be used to temporarily bamboozle the reader. Besides, how can any writer resist the endless possibilities provided by history? For example, a few lines in Virgil's *Aenid* inspired *A Lock of Hair for Proserpine*. The adventures of John the Eunuch continue in *One for Sorrow*.

Mary Reed and Eric Mayer

A Lock of Hair for Proserpine

Mary Reed and Eric Mayer

As Leontia bent down over the body of her brother, the newly widowed girl kneeling beside him, Neferet, lashed out, knocking the shears from the older woman's hand. They skittered across the floor and clattered into a corner of the small, octagonal room where the departed Krateros lay.

Leontia straightened, pulling the train of her embroidered robe over her arm. She drew back only a step. Her face was long and plain and her masculine jaw was set. 'All I ask is a lock of hair. Have some respect for the dead.'

Neferet cradled her husband's head, her dark slim fingers entwined in his sparse silver hair. Her own ebony hair fell across his open eyes, which in death had the misty look of fog over the Sea of Marmara.

Standing with his back to a window, the old merchant's servant, Castinus, considered the situation. The gale rattling the window-frame was nothing compared to the one now sweeping the elegant but soft-looking man's hitherto comfortable world. Krateros had been a fool to marry the little whore, any person of refinement would agree. Still, as between his deceased master's lawful wife and the master's sister, Castinus supposed he owed his services to the wife, at least until she saw fit to arrange otherwise.

'May I suggest, Mistress, that perhaps we should wait and discuss this matter when Hippoklides arrives?' he ventured, referring to the old merchant's partner.

'What about Isis?' Neferet spoke without taking her gaze from her dead husband.

'She has also been sent for, as you requested.'

Leontia compressed reddened lips. 'Isis?'

'A woman of substance, Ladyship,' Castinus assured her.

'She might seem so to a slave, but I've never heard her mentioned at court.'

Castinus's expression did not change. 'My apologies, Ladyship. I

119

thought at court they would naturally have mentioned the name of the wealthiest brothel owner in Constantinople.'

Less than a mile outside the walls of Constantinople, Madam Isis ordered her six litter-bearers to stop. John, Lord Chamberlain to the Emperor Justinian, sighed. He was a man who would have far preferred to be riding a horse, despite the miserable weather. Leaning forward, he pulled back the litter's sodden curtain to make inquiries.

The peasant John summoned was in the process of hitching his oxen to a poplar which had been blown partly across the Via Egnatia, evidently preparing to drag the tree aside and reopen the road.

'Krateros? Take the turning just ahead,' he informed John. 'But I don't suppose you'll be doing business with him today.'

'Yes,' confirmed John, 'I understand he died during the night.'

'Died, or was carried off. They say the wind was so fierce it drove crows into the church. This wasn't one of God's storms. This was evil come to claim its own.'

'Nonsense!' Madam Isis leaned her ample figure across John to scold the peasant. 'Krateros was a respectable merchant. I'd never have allowed him to purchase Neferet otherwise.'

'Meaning no disrespect to a lady such as yourself, but the people who live here say he practised the black arts. I myself have seen lightning leaping at the windows when there was never a cloud in the sky. Shadows stalking the fields when the moon was down. This winter, now he's gone, we'll all sleep more soundly.'

'Nothing but superstitious talk, as the Lord Chamberlain will surely prove!'

The Lord Chamberlain, following the peasant's gaze across the muddy field, joined the ranks of the superstitious for a second when he was startled by the sight of the Great Lighthouse of Alexandria. Had he been magically transported back to his time in Egypt, a time Isis often reminisced about, almost forgetting they had not known each other in those days? Then his eyes adjusted and he realised he was seeing a smaller replica, a truncated version of the octagonal second tier and cylindrical apex, which, in the case of the real Pharos, housed the fire basket and mirror. A clever work of architecture. Not magick.

Madam Isis sank to the mosaic floor to embrace Neferet in clouds of silk and perfume. 'My condolences.' An Egyptian herself, she spoke to the young widow in her native tongue. 'Such a terrible shock. How are you feeling, my dear?'

Neferet pressed herself closer to her husband's corpse. 'Make her go away,' she nodded towards Leontia. 'She insists we cut a lock of hair for Proserpine. But they are waiting for that. Can't you feel them here? The judges of the dead. Waiting to carry him off.'

120

'Don't worry, I'm sure Krateros need not fear the judges of the dead,' Isis comforted her.

Leontia, standing near the doorway beside John, eyed Madam Isis with disapproval. 'Must they speak that heathen language?' she muttered. 'Nobody knows what they are saying. Very sinister.'

She gave John a highly opinionated and in the circumstances, John thought, tactless history of the marriage of her wealthy older brother to a girl of low morals, young enough to be his granddaughter. Evidently she was a woman with some grievances. John wondered if she had knowledge of her brother's will. John was stiff from cramming his lanky frame into the litter, and the elaborate official robes Isis had suggested he wear, to lend weight to his visit, felt even heavier than usual.

'Of course, a man in your position, Lord Chamberlain, can understand my distress,' Leontia finally noted.

John had heard another version of the story from Isis when she turned up unexpectedly at his door late in the morning, insistent that he come out into the raging storm.

'The girl's mother was a dear friend and associate,' she had said. 'When she died I raised Neferet in my house – as a daughter, not an employee, though she worked for her keep. A wonderful cook, she was. No doubt still is. Her messenger just arrived and apparently the poor girl wants my help urgently. But I know of the family. Rich and haughty. Not to mention pagans, though they do not say it too loudly at court. You will know how to deal with them. All I know is that it's something to do with the funeral.'

Now Leontia was railing about the cost of the odd building in which her brother had died. 'An office – mind you, a simple office – in the shape of a lighthouse! And as if the lighthouse was not folly enough, what does he do but fill the villa with cat idols from her heathen homeland! And some very peculiar wall paintings.'

Isis broke in. 'A kind heart trying to make someone he loved feel at home.'

The Madam had persuaded Neferet to climb wearily to her feet. The widow looked like a forlorn child, clothed only in a thin, green tunic, the kohl around her eyes streaked and patchy from crying.

'Lord Chamberlain,' Neferet said, now speaking in Greek. 'Madam Isis tells me you lived in Alexandria for a time.'

John confirmed that this was so.

'Then it is possible that you, at least, will not be quick to dismiss a dream that I had last night. Krateros sent it to me, I am sure of it. And it told me that I was not to allow Proserpine's lock of hair to be cut. It is an old belief, my dear husband explained to me, that only after a lock of hair is sacrificed can the soul be released to go on to . . . whatever awaits.'

Leontia sniffed. 'What does this little Egyptian care about our beliefs?' she muttered to Isis.

'Look at her eyes,' snapped Isis. 'Do you think every young widow cries at the death of her aged husband?'

Ignoring the women, John gently prompted Neferet. 'Did your husband appear in this dream?'

'No. What happened was, I dreamed that I was in a sandstorm, such as we sometimes have in Egypt. But then it changed, and what began falling, in a sort of curtain, a veil almost, was not fine sand, but rather down, as soft as a caress. And the down fell faster and faster, and thicker and thicker, and I woke up afraid.

'Krateros hadn't come to bed. The door of his office was bolted from the inside and he didn't answer my knock. When the servants broke in they found him . . .'

'You believe your husband was telling you he had passed on?' asked John.

'More than that, Lord Chamberlain. I know what's been said about my husband's business profiting because he trafficks in the black arts. How else would anyone explain how he always seemed to know what to do before the markets change?'

'Jealous fools,' was Leontia's firm opinion.

'But I did not believe such a thing.' Neferet ignored her sister-in-law.

'Did not?'

'He was my husband, and I love him still, but if everyone says a thing is so, in the end . . .' Her voice trailed off for a moment. 'I believe he was trying to tell me that if his soul was freed, he must face the judgement of the lords of the dead, weighing his heart against the feather of truth. Why would he be afraid of judgement if he had done no wrong? Perhaps it is true that he did dabble, as they say. And he sent the dream to ask me to save him from his punishment.'

'The feather of truth is nothing but Egyptian nonsense,' her sister-in-law pointed out.

'But you see, he wanted so much to make me feel at home, even though I told him I hardly remembered Alexandria. I was so young when mother and I left. He built this lighthouse, he studied our religion and even learned a little of the language. So it is not so surprising that he chose to speak to me in a way I would understand when he sent his appeal from – wherever he is.'

'My brother was a practical man. At least until he met you. He wouldn't speak in strange symbols, even from the dead.'

'Perhaps, Leontia, you didn't really know your brother.' Neferet's voice trailed off. She swayed and John caught her arm. Isis spoke softly to the girl. Much to Leontia's consternation, the other three exchanged words in the language she had just described to John as sinister.

122

'Neferet has agreed to leave her husband's side,' John translated for the older woman, turning to her, 'on condition we secure the room. Temporarily, that is, until the appropriate arrangements are made.'

Leontia nodded her approval and reluctantly preceded the others from the octagonal office and on to the covered colonnade that led away from it, past the bath house, to the villa. Neferet walked slowly, leaning against Isis, looking frail and small beside the larger woman. As they moved away, Leontia turned to John, who had remained in the doorway.

'I apologise if I seemed impolite, Lord Chamberlain. Of course, someone in your position knows the most discreet way to deal with these situations. We will cut that lock of hair now and be done with it.'

'If you imagine I was trying to trick her, you're mistaken,' John said quietly. 'I made a promise that the room would be secured. The room *will* be secure.'

Leontia's long face darkened with anger. 'A promise? You . . . the Lord Chamberlain . . . you would keep a promise to a girl from one of those houses?'

Before she could say more, a man of regal bearing emerged from the villa, striding along the colonnade toward them.

'Is this the partner, Hippoklides?' John asked.

Leontia turned to look, and let out a harsh laugh. 'Partner? That is only Castinus, the slave!'

When Leontia had gone into the villa, John placed Castinus on guard at Krateros's office door, and proceeded to examine the octagonal room. Despite its eccentric façade, inside it was clearly a place of business. The old merchant had apparently not bothered to order his groundskeepers to trim the thick branches of the fig tree which all but blocked the view of the Sea of Marmara from the single rectangular window. The walls were plain and plastered. Against one stood a large wooden table, scattered with writing implements and a pile of parchments next to an empty ceramic goblet. A shelf held scrolls and codexes. The only anomaly was a small lacquered table, on which sat a vase of roses and a statuette of Bast, the cat goddess of Egypt.

There was a round opening in the low ceiling which, John surmised, gave access to the cylindrical apex of the imitation lighthouse. Climbing on to a stool, he pulled himself up into the cramped chamber above. There he found a brazier and a mirror, miniatures of those in the Alexandrian lighthouse. At night, with the fire lit and the mirror reflecting a blaze of light out through the tower's tall windows, the illusion must have been quite convincing.

However, it appeared to have been some time since Krateros had sought to, as it were, transport his young bride back to her homeland. The ashes in the brazier were cold and the wind, entering through one partially opened window, had scattered some of them, along with a few brown leaves, across the floor. The mirror was dusty and streaked, an instrument of dreams reduced to an occasional perch for birds.

John took a quick glance through the windows at the surrounding estate. It was much as other estates he had seen, with olive groves, cattle pens, dovecotes, bee hives, stables, an herb garden where a gardener toiled. Here and there were scattered fig trees and ornamental bushes, some trimmed into pyramids. Then he climbed back down into the room below.

Taking one last look around the lower room before leaving, his attention was caught by a metallic gleam in one corner.

Neferet held the silver vial towards her reddened eyes, examining its delicate lotus design. It was the sort of vessel that, stoppered, might hold perfume or unguents.

'Or poison,' John pointed out. 'Be careful. The inside appears blackened, although it might just be tarnished.'

They were alone in one of the villa's sitting rooms, Neferet, more decently dressed, on a couch, John standing. Isis had withdrawn as John entered, to inquire about dinner, she said. For a moment the silence was broken only by the splash of a fountain in the atrium beyond.

'Even if it were an assassin, it makes no difference for his soul,' Neferet finally said, dully.

'Nevertheless, those of us still living must concern ourselves with the crime, if one occurred.' John did not add that it was a problem with which he felt he could grapple, as opposed to Neferet's insubstantial demons. 'You have never seen it, then?'

Neferet shook her head as she handed the vial back. 'No one would have wanted to kill my husband.'

John wished he could have avoided having to ask her the next question. 'Is there any reason why your husband might have taken his own life?'

Neferet stiffened with outrage. 'You've been talking to Leontia. Krateros wasn't as ill as that. He'd had some weakness lately.'

'I didn't realise—'

'Castinus did help him from the bath to the office each morning. The tiles can be slippery, and then there are the stairs down to the pools.'

'More than one young man has slipped and cracked his head open in the baths,' John said, diplomatically, then changed the subject. 'Who had access to the office?'

'My husband and myself, and Castinus. Though I rarely went there and Castinus only if Krateros needed something.'

'Where did he see visitors?'

'He spoke to them in a sitting room. Castinus would show them in.'

'Could he have had an otherwise unannounced visitor yesterday?'

'Not without someone in the household noticing. And then there are walls around the interior of the estate, so it would be difficult for someone to get in unnoticed. Even so, we do keep geese in the courtyard.'

John nodded. 'They are the best watch-dogs. Am I right to assume the office was locked at all times?'

'Of course. The business records were kept there.'

John paced over to a window. It looked into an interior garden. He picked up a shell from a tray sitting on a table beneath the window.

'And what about his business partner, Hippoklides?' he asked, turning the shell over in his hands.

'Business? It is a mystery to me.' Neferet smiled wanly. 'Aren't those shells lovely? The sea was good to us. We collected the shells on the way to Trebizond, just after we married. A small holiday.' She paused to regain control of her wavering voice. 'He used to say . . . he used to say that the sea was kind to him in all matters, for it was from across the sea that I had journeyed to him.'

John moved back to the couch and laid a gentle hand on hers. 'He loved you very much, I can see that. And you him.'

She closed her eyes, as if better to see happier times. 'As I told you. I tried to learn something of his culture. Roses. They are sacred to lovers. So I would ensure that there were always roses here.'

'Hippoklides? I understand my brother was pleased with his services, despite his youth. He's little older than that wretched girl Krateros married.'

John had found Leontia walking in the garden behind the villa. Overhead, ragged clouds, a memory of the recent storm, were reddening as the sun fell into the arms of night.

'I understood him to be a partner?'

'Of course. I believe Krateros allowed him half the profits. My brother's health has suffered recently. Hippoklides travelled for him.'

'He has been sent for?'

'Yes. He had intended to spend several days just down the coast, with the Prefect in Rhegion, but this dreadful event will cut his visit short.'

John, who had turned his thoughts away from demons and towards murder and possible suspects, knew it would be easy to confirm whether the partner had been with the Prefect when Krateros was poisoned. If, indeed, he had been poisoned. On the other hand, widow and business partner were both young, the husband old and rich. It had been a lethal combination before and would be again.

'Have you seen this, or one like it?' John showed Leontia the vial. While she denied any familiarity with the object, John paid greater attention to her face than her words. A thought had occurred to him.

'Do you know the contents of your brother's will?' John asked bluntly.

Leontia's eyes narrowed. 'A strange question, Lord Chamberlain. I thought you and . . . that woman . . . were here to calm my brother's wife. His body still lies on the cold floor of that ridiculous room, his soul still wanders. I implore you, let me snip a lock of hair. She will never notice.'

They had come to one of the bushes which Krateros had ordered cut into a pyramid. Leontia stopped beside it and looked out towards the sea. In the fading light John noticed something that took him by surprise, but probably should not have. Leontia's eyes glistened with tears.

Isis, though an imposing figure to those who did not know her, was still one in whom all manner of people confided. She attributed this to her sympathetic face, while John tended to think it was more a talent developed during the course of her long career. In any event, John was not surprised when the plump Madam intercepted him on his way back to the house, to relate something she had learned from the cook.

Isis and John stood at the end of the colonnade. Lights were springing up in the villa as slaves went from room to room, lighting torches.

'The cook was distressed about the dinner. Squab. A speciality of his and a favourite of Neferet, he said. But having it tonight, under these circumstances, would she ever want to look at such a meal again? He may have a point. Strange how our ideas colour our appetites. But you know, I'll have someone's life story before his name. I persuaded him to tell me something about the household.'

John broke into his friend's soliloquy. 'You can ascertain a lot about a household from its servants.'

'And more importantly a lot about it by what they say once the master is safely dead. In this case, the cook told me he had been wondering if the business was failing.'

'What made him come to that conclusion?'

'Well,' Isis rustled her silks with satisfaction, 'it seems that, when Krateros first engaged Hippoklides, the young partner came to visit often. Now, these past few months, he rarely displays his features in this house, as the cook colourfully put it.'

'Perhaps I should ask him about that when he finally arrives.'

'Another odd thing,' Isis said thoughtfully. 'The cook mentioned that, when he is here, Hippoklides rarely stays long. So as not to lose business, he thinks. He's here only a few hours and then departs, quite often after dark.'

'Didn't he fear being waylaid?'

Isis shook her head. 'No, and in fact, he travels without guards, which is foolhardy to my mind. The more so as apparently he's often carrying – well – something of value.'

126

'I expect now you will tell me you've fathomed this secret as well?'

'Unfortunately, I cannot. Except it's large. His horse is always burdened with large baskets when he departs.'

'Sneaking off with the silver in the middle of the night?'

'That's what the cook thinks. His theory is that Hippoklides was stealing goods and information from the old man, setting up in business for himself. When he'd accomplished that, there was no reason for him to consult Krateros, especially since he would be familiar with most of the business contacts.'

John commented that it seemed Isis's investigations had been more fruitful than his.

'Ah,' she said, looking pleased, 'but you have not heard all that I learned. It's common gossip in the household that Hippoklides was not content to steal Krateros's riches and business, he also intended to steal the old man's young bride.'

When Madam Isis hurried back to the house to sit with Neferet, John realised that she had failed to question him about his opinions on the merchant's rumoured transactions with demons. However, having known her a long time, it didn't surprise him that the Madam took little interest in fleshless beings.

With supernatural speculation engaging his mind, John was momentarily startled by a shadowed figure in the courtyard below the colonnade. It was the servant Castinus, who had left his post at the office door.

'Lord Chamberlain!' he said familiarly. 'Don't worry, I've assigned one of the house servants to guard the body. How is the Mistress? Have you talked her out of her hysteria yet?'

'Isis has gone to comfort her. It seems she is still firm in her intention that her husband's soul be allowed to wander here, rather than being released to the demons.'

'Krateros had nothing to do with black arts. He was a man of this world.'

John asked him how well he had known his late master.

'Like a brother. You know how it is, John. I was his manservant, just as you are manservant to the Emperor.'

'Technically, that is true.' John ignored the man's insolence.

'But, I imagine, you do not have to help Justinian to the baths each morning, or clothe him? At least not yet. I'm afraid if Krateros wanted to summon demons, he would have required my assistance.'

John nodded. 'You were in your master's confidence then?'

'Do you not have Justinian's confidence?' Castinus moved a step nearer to John, speaking in a whisper. 'He confided all to me. His sister, this partner of his . . . what did they know of the man? Last month he sent me into the city to fetch a love potion. He had been ill and was having . . . problems. He was solicitous of his young wife. There was nothing he withheld from me.'

'What about the contents of his will?'

'What do you mean?'

'It is not uncommon for a master to manumit a trusted slave.'

Castinus looked thoughtful. 'I hadn't considered that. The death was so sudden. I might be a freed man even now.'

John did not point out that a slave who knew he would gain freedom upon the death of his master had a powerful motive for advancing that death. 'Have you seen one of these in the office before?' John held the silver vial up toward the light of a nearby torch.

'Krateros kept nothing like that, I am sure. It was not the kind of thing in which he dealt.'

John suggested the possibility that it might have been a new venture.

Castinus shook his head. 'Even so, he did not keep goods in his office. And I am sure he would have shown it to me.'

John had his own thoughts on that, but continued to question the slave. 'Did he leave his office during the day?'

'Never without my assistance.'

'Did his callers go to his office?'

Castinus shook his head. 'Hippoklides was the only business associate who ever entered, and he has not been here for some time. I was the only other person allowed into it. Callers were seen in the villa.'

A torch sputtered and sent an explosion of sparks into the air. From somewhere close by in the dark gardens came the scent of roses.

'So,' said John wearily, 'this deadly vial must have been transported to his hand by magick.'

Hippoklides finally arrived, tramping mud from the Via Egnatia across the atrium. He had embraced Neferet, murmuring a few words of solace, and then gone to the octagonal room to stand in respectful silence by the body of Krateros for a moment or two.

'I've had hours of hard riding to accustom myself to this shocking thing, but . . . still . . . still . . .' he had said, rubbing tired eyes. Younger than John, he had a hawkish look about him. He had soon withdrawn to the villa, leaving John alone with the old man and his thoughts.

It was a solemn group that sat down to dinner that evening. Isis had instructed the servants to bring out wooden chairs. It was not, she insisted, an occasion for reclining on couches. Neferet stared into her wine goblet, drinking little, eating nothing. Hippoklides leaned close to speak to her, occasionally eliciting a faint smile.

Leontia sat stiffly, glaring occasionally towards Madam Isis, her rigid back and outraged expression making plain her distaste at sharing a table with such a woman. Finally she could tolerate it no longer. 'I am not familiar with uncomfortable chairs such as these,' she finally announced, before stalking out of the room.

'Her façade is as hard as a mosaic,' remarked Hippoklides, 'but she loved her brother.'

John took a bite of the honeyed squab on his plate. He was not hungry, but as a former soldier, he understood that the body must be nourished, whatever the circumstances.

'Krateros was a man of great business acumen, I understand,' he said mildly.

Hippoklides nodded. 'Earlier this year a merchant ship filled with amphorae for the May celebrations ran aground. Before word reached the Palace, Krateros had already purchased half the wine in Constantinople. No doubt the merchants were amused he would pay high prices. Ah, but a day later . . .' He took a gulp of wine himself. 'If you heard Krateros had invested in wheat, you could be sure the Emperor was about to raise the price of bread. Of course, there were those who said . . .'

Neferet burst into tears.

Isis patted her arm, glaring at Hippoklides. 'Just because someone is good at what they do, doesn't mean they're practising magick. Do you think demons tell me how to run my business? Indeed not!'

Hippoklides put an arm around Neferet's trembling shoulders. She hesitated, then let her head sink down to rest against his chest.

'I did not believe it of him,' she sobbed, 'until he begged my help in that dream.'

Could it be possible, John wondered, that Krateros, who cared so much for his wife, had spoken to her in a dream, using her Egyptian beliefs? And if he had spoken thus, would it have been to protect himself? Or, he thought, watching Hippoklides caress the grief-stricken widow's dark hair, had it been to protect Neferet? And what was it she had dreamed about? A sandstorm that changed into down. He looked at his plate. Down, she had said. What could it mean? Suddenly a grim thought struck through his puzzling.

'Leontia,' he said, standing. 'Did she go to her room?'

Before they reached Krateros's lighthouse they saw a fitful glow in the tower. There was movement there and in the pallid beams of flickering light lying across the gardens.

Inside the octagonal office, Leontia stood, shears in hand. Wild light from hastily prepared lamps climbed the walls and fell back. Too many corners, too many shadows, formed the impossible architecture of nightmare. On a plate on the lacquered table, beside the vase of wilted roses, a smoky ember burned like the eye of Anubis.

Neferet shrieked, 'She has burnt his hair! They are here! They have come for his soul!'

She threw herself on to her husband's corpse as a great winged shadow closed over her.

Hippoklides, entering the room just behind John, stepped forward, then his face registered horror and he retreated. A white shape flashed and flapped in the small room. He flailed wildly at it. Isis screamed for the first time since John had met her. He pushed Hippoklides aside, grabbing at the air. A few feathers floated lazily in the smoky room.

'My dream!' wailed the young widow, wild-eyed.

Those who were less hysterical saw that the Lord Chamberlain was holding a pigeon.

'Birds, like this one, are what you carried off in baskets,' he told Hippoklides. 'Trained to return home to the lighthouse. These swift messengers, not demons, account for Krateros's mysterious knowledge. Their shadows, magnified by the mirror on such nights as the fire above was lit, account for those wild tales of demons and lightning flashes that we've heard about. Krateros would admit no one to his office, because he could never be sure when one of the birds might arrive.'

Castinus was suddenly in the doorway, his expression shocked. 'He never told me about the birds,' he said, sounding hurt. 'They used to roost in the fig tree.'

Leontia turned on him. 'Why should he have told a slave?'

'You see, now, my dear,' Madam Isis was telling Neferet, as she gently helped the girl to her feet, 'you no longer need to fear for your dear husband. There were never demons.'

'But he sent the dream . . .' she faltered.

'You might say that the down represented the feather of truth, but not in the way in which you interpreted it,' John replied. 'He was perhaps trying to make you think of birds, and not just the squab we have left cooling on the plates. Although what better reason to keep plenty of pigeons on an estate? A few more would not be noticed, after all.'

With a quick movement John tossed the bird he was holding up into the air. It vanished through the ceiling opening leading up into the tower. But in his hand John held the silver vial he had taken from the bird's leg, identical to the vial he had found in the office, except that this one was securely stoppered.

'Vials tied to the birds' legs held messages. But when Krateros asked you to seek out and secretly send him a love potion, for after all a man cannot continually send out a servant for such a thing, you decided such a vial could just as easily hold a love potion. Or poison.'

Hippoklides laughed harshly. 'You have no proof I murdered him.'

'No. Because you did not. I have no doubt that Krateros, who had been ailing, died of natural causes. The pigeon who just arrived here was delayed by last night's dreadful storm.' John removed the stopper from the silver vial. 'If this substance you sent him so secretly is indeed not poison, you will no doubt humour us by sampling it.'

130

★   ★   ★

'No,' admitted John the following morning, as Isis' litter-bearers passed between the estate's gates on the way back to Constantinople after Krateros's funeral. 'It could probably not be proved without doubt that Hippoklides attempted murder. But in my experience, a court of law is the last place one looks for justice in this world. I think it is safe to predict that Leontia will ensure that from now on few doors will be open to him, and most of those with whom he had business dealings will suddenly be unavailable.'

'More importantly, Neferet has been saved from him,' Isis paused. 'Now, John, you've explained that certain oracles depended not on revelations from the gods but rather on trained birds bringing news of distant events with which to astound their clients. What about Neferet's dream, however? Was that truly a revelation, a message from the dead?'

But, as Isis had half-anticipated, the Lord Chamberlain made no reply beyond a thin smile.

History gave me my start in the crime business. I was twenty-three and, for my sins, studying towards a PhD on the novels of Muriel Spark. Spark is best known for *The Prime of Miss Jean Brodie*, and Jean Brodie boasts that she is a descendant of Deacon Brodie, a real-life Edinburgh criminal and the model for Robert Louis Stevenson's *Jekyll and Hyde*. As part of my research into Spark, I began studying Edinburgh's past. I decided that the city's dualism, the feel I had of it representing 'public probity and private vice', was as true in the 1980s as it had ever been. I wrote a book that I hoped was a modern twist on *Jekyll and Hyde*, and blithely decided to make my hero a policeman, a CID officer called John Rebus. I haven't written any historical novels – not yet. But BBC Radio 4 broadcast two of my full-length plays set in the Edinburgh of the 1790s and starring a character called Cullender, this being the Scots word for a sieve. Cully himself was conceived as a moral sieve, a man as dark and crooked as some of the old city's wynds. One day I'd like to write about him at greater length.

Ian Rankin

The Serpent's Back

Ian Rankin

This was, mind you, back in 1793 or '94. Edinburgh was a better place then. Nothing ever happens here now, but back then . . . back then *everything* was happening.

Back then a caddie was indispensable if you happened to be visiting the town. If you wanted someone found, if a message needed delivering, if you wanted a bed for the night, fresh oysters, a shirt-maker; or the local hoor, you came to a caddie. And if the claret got the better of you, a caddie would see you safely home.

See, the town wasn't safe, Lord no. The streets were mean. The hifalutin' were leaving the old town and crossing the Nor' Loch to the New. They lived in Princes Street and George Street, or did until they could no longer stand the stench. The old loch was an open sewer by that time, and the old town not much better.

I was called Cullender, Cully to my friends. No one knew my first name. They need only say 'Cullender' and they'd be pointed in my direction. That's how it was with young Master Gisborne. He had newly arrived by coach from London, and feared he'd never sit down again . . .

'Are you Cullender? My good friend Mr Wilks told me to ask for you.'

'Wilks?'

'He was here for some weeks. A medical student.'

I nodded. 'I recall the young gentleman particularly,' I lied.

'I shall require a clean room, nothing too fancy. My pockets aren't bottomless.'

'How long will you be staying, Master?'

He looked around. 'I'm not sure. I'm considering a career in medicine. If I like the faculty, I may enrol.'

And he fingered the edges of his coat. It was a pale blue coat with bright silver buttons. Like Master Gisborne, it was overdone and didn't quite fit together. His face was fat like a whelp's, but his physique was lean and his eyes shone. His skin had suffered neither disease

135

nor malnourishment. He was, I suppose, a fine enough specimen, but I'd seen fine specimens before. Many of them stayed, seduced by Edinburgh. I saw them daily in the pungent howffs, or slouching through the narrow closes, heads bowed. None of them looked so fresh these days. Had they been eels, the fishwives would have tossed them in a bucket and sold them to only the most gullible.

The most gullible, of course, being those newly arrived in the city.

Master Gisborne would need looking after. He was haughty on the surface, cocksure, but I knew he was troubled, wondering how long he could sustain the act of worldliness. He had money but not in limitless supply. His parents would be professional folk, not gentry. Some denizens would gull him before supper. Me? I was undecided.

I picked up his trunk. 'Shall I call a chair?' He frowned. 'The streets here are too narrow and steep for coaches. Haven't you noticed? Know why they're narrow?' I sidled up to him. 'There's a serpent buried beneath.' He looked ill at ease so I laughed. 'Just a story, Master. We use chairmen instead of horses. Good strong Highland stock.'

I knew he had already walked a good way in search of me, hauling his trunk with him. He was tired, but counting his money too.

'Let's walk,' he decided, 'and you can acquaint me with the town.'

'The town, Master,' I said, 'will acquaint you with itself.'

We got him settled in at Lucky Seaton's. Lucky had been a hoor herself at one time, then had been turned to the Moderate movement and now ran a Christian rooming house.

'We know all about medical students, don't we, Cully?' she said, while Gisborne took the measure of his room. 'The worst sinners in Christendom.'

She patted Master Gisborne on his plump cheek, and I led him back down the treacherous stairwell.

'What did she mean?' he asked me.

'Visit a few howffs and you'll find out,' I told him. 'The medical students are the most notorious group of topers in the city, if you discount the lawyers, judges, poets, boatmen, and Lords this-and-that.'

'What's a howff?'

I led him directly into one.

There was a general fug in what passed for the air. Pipes were being smoked furiously, and there were no windows to open, so the stale fumes lay heavy at eye level. I could hear laughter and swearing and the shrieks of women, but it was like peering through a haar. I saw one-legged Jack, balancing a wench on his good knee. Two lawyers sat at the next table along, heads close together. A poet of minor repute

136

scribbled away as he sat slumped on the floor. And all around there was wine, wine in jugs and bumpers and bottles, its sour smell vying with that of tobacco.

But the most noise came from a big round table in the furthest corner, where beneath flickering lamplight a meeting of the Monthly Club was underway. I led Gisborne to the table, having promised him that Edinburgh would acquaint itself with him. Five gentlemen sat round the table. One recognised me immediately.

'Dear old Cully! What news from the world above?'

'No news, sir.'

'None better than that!'

'What's the meeting this month, sirs?'

'The Hot Air Club, Cully.' The speaker made a toast of the words. 'We are celebrating the tenth anniversary of Mr Tytler's flight by montgolfier over this very city.'

This had to be toasted again, while I explained to Master Gisborne that the Monthly Club changed its name regularly in order to have something to celebrate.

'I see you've brought fresh blood, Cully.'

'Mr Gisborne,' I said, 'is newly arrived from London and hopes to study medicine.'

'I hope he will, too, if he intends to practise.'

There was laughter and replenishing of glasses.

'This gentleman,' I informed my master, 'is Mr Walter Scott. Mr Scott is an advocate.'

'Not today,' said another of the group. 'Today he's Colonel Grogg!'

More laughter. Gisborne was asked what he would drink.

'A glass of port,' my hapless charge replied.

The table went quiet. Scott was smiling with half his mouth only.

'Port is not much drunk in these parts. It reminds some people of the Union. Some people would rather drink *whisky* and toast their Jacobite "King O'er the Water."' Someone at the table actually did this, not heeding the tone of Scott's voice. 'But we're one nation now,' Scott continued. That man did like to make a speech. 'And if you'll drink some claret with us, we may yet be reconciled.'

The drinker toasted Bonnie Prince Charlie; another lawyer, whose name was Urquhart, now turned to Gisborne with his usual complaint to Englishmen. '"Rule Britannia,"' he said, 'was written by a Scot. John Bull was *invented* by a Scot!'

He slumped back, having to his mind made his point. Master Gisborne looked like he had tumbled into Bedlam.

'Now, now,' Scott calmed. 'We're here to celebrate montgolfiers.' He handed Gisborne a stemless glass filled to the brim. 'And new arrivals. But you've come to a dangerous place, sir.'

'How so?' my master enquired.

'Sedition is rife.' Scott paused. 'As is murder. How many is it now, Cully?'

'Three this past fortnight.' I recited the names. 'Dr Benson, MacStay the coffin maker, and a wretch called Howison.'

'All stabbed,' Scott informed Gisborne. 'Imagine, murdering a coffin maker! It's like trying to murder Death himself.'

As was wont to happen, the Monthly Club shifted to another howff to partake of a *prix fixe* dinner; and thence to another, where Scott would drink champagne and lead a discussion of 'the chest.'

The chest in question had been found when the Castle's crown room was opened during a search for some documents. The crown room had been opened, according to the advocate, by special warrant under the royal sign manual. No one had authority to break open the chest. The crown room was locked again, and the chest still inside. At the time of the union with England, the royal regalia of Scotland had disappeared. It was Scott's contention that this regalia – crown, sceptre, and sword – lay in the chest.

Gisborne listened in fascination. Somewhere along the route he had misplaced his sense of economy. He would pay for the champagne. He would pay for dinner. A brothel was being discussed as the next destination . . . Luckily, Scott was taking an interest in him, so that Gisborne's pockets were still fairly full, though his wits be empty.

I sat apart, conversing with the exiled Comte d'Artois, who had fled France at the outset of revolution. He retained the habit of stroking his neck for luck, his good fortune being that it still connected his head to his trunk. He had reason to feel nervous. Prompted by events in France, sedition was in the air. There had been riots, and now the ringleaders were being tried.

We were discussing Deacon Brodie, hanged six years before for a series of housebreakings. Brodie, a cabinetmaker and locksmith, had robbed the very premises to which he'd fitted locks. Respectable by day, he'd been nefarious by night – to the Comte (who knew about such matters), this was merely 'the human condition.'

I noticed suddenly that I was seated in shadow. A man stood over me. He had full thick lips, a meaty stew of a nose, and eyebrows which met at the central divide the way warring forces sometimes will.

'Cullender?'

I shook my head and turned away.

'You're Cullender,' he said. 'This is for you.' He slapped his paw onto the table, then turned and pushed back through the throng. A piece of paper, neatly folded, sat on the wood where his hand had been. I unfolded it and read:

'Outside the Tolbooth, quarter before midnight.'

The note was unsigned. I handed it to the Comte.

'You will go?'

It was already past eleven. 'I'll let one more drink decide.'

The Tolbooth was the city jail where Brodie himself had spent his final days, singing airs from *The Beggar's Opera*. The night was like pitch, nobody having bothered to light their lamps, and a haar rolled through from the direction of Leith.

In the darkness, I had trodden in something I did not care to study and was scraping my shoe clean on the Tolbooth's cornerstone when I heard a voice close by.

'Cullender?'

A woman's voice. Even held to a whisper, I knew it for that. The lady herself was dressed top to toe in black, her face deep inside the hood of a cloak.

'I'm Cullender.'

'I'm told you perform services.'

'I'm no minister, lady.'

Maybe she smiled. A small bag appeared and I took it, weighing the coins inside.

'There's a book circulating in the town,' said my new mistress. 'I am keen to obtain it.'

'We have several fine booksellers in the Luckenbooths . . .'

'You are glib, sir.'

'And you are mysterious.'

'Then I'll be plain. I know of only one copy of this book, a private printing. It is called *Ranger's Second Impartial List . . .*'

'. . . *of the Ladies of Pleasure in Edinburgh . . .*'

'You know it. Have you seen it?'

'It's not meant for the likes of me.'

'I would like to see this book.'

'You want me to find it?'

'It's said you know everyone in the city.'

'Everyone that matters.'

'Then you can locate it.'

'It's possible.' I examined my shoes. 'But first I'd need to know a little more . . .'

When I looked up again, she was gone.

At The Cross, the caddies were speaking quietly with the chairmen. We caddies had organised ourselves into a company, boasting written standards and a Magistrate of Caddies in charge of all. We regarded ourselves superior to the chairmen, mere brawny Highland migrants.

But my best friend and most trusted ally, Mr Mack, was a chairman. He was not, however, at The Cross. Work was nearly over for the night. The last taverns were throwing out the last soused customers. Only the

139

brothels and cockpits were still active. Not able to locate Mr Mack, I turned instead to a fellow caddie, an old hand called Dryden.

'Mr Dryden?' I said, all businesslike, 'I require your services, the fee to be agreed between us.'

Dryden, as ever, was willing. I knew he would work through the night. He was known to the various brothelkeepers and could ask his questions discreetly, as I might have done myself had the lady's fee not been sufficient to turn me employer.

Me, I headed home, climbing the lonely stairs to my attic quarters and a cold mattress. I found sleep the way a pickpocket finds his gull.

Which is to say easily.

Next morning, Dryden was dead.

A young caddie called Colin came to tell me. We repaired to the Nor' Loch, where the body still lay, face down in the slime. The Town Guard – 'Town Rats' behind their backs – fingered their Lochaber axes, straightened their tall cocked hats, and tried to look important. One of their number, a red-faced individual named Fairlie, asked if we knew the victim.

'Dryden,' I said. 'He was a caddie.'

'He's been run through with a dagger,' Fairlie delighted in telling me. 'Just like those other three.'

But I wasn't so sure about that . . .

I went to a quiet howff, a drink steadying my humour. Dryden, I surmised, had been killed in such a way as to make him appear another victim of the city's stabber. I knew, though, that in all likelihood he had been killed because of the questions he'd been asking . . . questions *I'd* sent him to ask. Was I safe myself? Had Dryden revealed anything to his killer? And what was it about my mistress's mission that made it so deadly dangerous?

As I was thus musing, young Gisborne entered the bar on fragile legs.

'Did I have anything to drink last evening?' he asked, holding his head.

'Master, you drank as if it were our last day alive.'

Our hostess was already replenishing my wine jug. 'Kill or cure,' I said, pouring two glasses.

Gisborne could see I was worried and asked the nature of the problem. I was grateful to tell him. Any listener would have sufficed. Mind, I held back some. This knowledge was proving dangerous, so I made no mention of the lady and her book. I jumped from the messenger to my words with Dryden.

'The thing to do, then,' my young master said, 'is to track backwards. Locate the messenger.'

I thought back to the previous evening. About the time the messenger had been arriving, the lawyer Urquhart had been taking his leave of the Monthly Club.

'We'll talk to Urquhart,' I said. 'At this hour he'll be in his chambers. Follow me.'

Gisborne followed me out of the howff and across the street directly into another. There, in a booth, papers before him and a bottle of wine beside them, sat Urquhart.

'I'm pleased to see you,' the lawyer announced. His eyes were bloodshot, his nose like a stoned cherry. His breath I avoided altogether. Aged somewhere in his thirties, Urquhart was a seasoned dissolute. He would have us take a bumper with him.

'Sir,' I began, 'do you recall leaving the company last night?'

'Of course. I'm only sorry I'd to leave so early. An assignation, you understand.' We shared a smile at this. 'Tell me, Gisborne, to which house of ill fame did the gang repair?'

'I don't recollect,' Gisborne admitted.

Urquhart enjoyed this. 'Then tell me, did you awake in a bed or the gutter?'

'In neither, Mr Urquhart. I awoke on the kitchen floor of a house I did not know.'

While Urquhart relished this, I asked if he'd taken a chair from the tavern last night.

'Of course. A friend of yours was front-runner.'

'Mr Mack?' Urquhart nodded. 'You didn't happen to see a grotesque, sir?' I described the messenger to him. Urquhart shook his head.

'I hear a caddie was murdered last night,' Urquhart said. 'We all know the Town Rats can't be expected to bring anyone to justice.' He leaned toward me confidentially. 'Are you looking for justice, Cully?'

'I don't know what I'm looking for, sir.'

Which was a lie. For now, I was looking for Mr Mack.

I left Gisborne with Urquhart, and found Mack at The Cross.

'Yes,' he said, 'I saw that fellow going in. A big fat-lipped sort with eyebrows that met in the middle.'

'Had you seen him before?'

Mack nodded. 'But not here, over the loch.'

'The new town.' Mack nodded. 'Then show me where.'

Mack and his fellow chairman carried me down the steep slope towards the building site. Yes, building site. For though Princes Street and George Street were finished, yet more streets were being artfully constructed. Just now, the builders were busy on what would be called Charlotte Square. We took the simpler route, down past Trinity Hospital and the College Kirk, then along Princes Street itself. There were plans to turn the Nor' Loch into either a canal or formal gardens, but for the moment it was a dumping ground. I avoided looking at it and

141

tried not to think of poor Dryden. Joining the loch to the old town sat The Mound, an apt name for a treacherous heap of new-town rubble.

'All change, eh, Cully?' Mr Mack called to me. 'Soon there'll be no business in the old town for the likes of you and me.'

He had a point. The nobility had already deserted the old town. Their grand lands now housed wheelwrights and hosiers and schoolmasters. They all lived in the new town now, at a general distance from the milling rabble. So here the foundations were being laid not for the new town alone but for the death of the old.

We passed into George Street and the sedan chair was brought to rest. 'It was here I saw him,' Mr Mack said. 'He was marching up the street like he owned the place.'

I got out of the chair and rubbed my bruised posterior. Mr Mack's companion had already spotted another likely fare. I waved them off. I must needs talk to my mistress, and that meant finding her servant. So I sat on a step and watched the work carts grinding past overloaded with rocks and rubble. The day went by pleasantly enough.

Perhaps two hours had passed when I saw him. I couldn't be sure which house he emerged from; he was some way along the street. I tucked myself behind some railings and watched him head down towards Princes Street. I followed at a canny distance.

He was clumsy, his gait gangling, and I followed him with ease. He climbed back up to the old town and made for the Luckenbooths. Here he entered a bookshop, causing me to pause.

The shop belonged to a Mr Whitewood, who fancied himself not only bookseller but poet and author also. I entered the premises quietly and could hear Whitewood's raised voice. He was towards the back of his shop, reciting to a fawning audience of other *soi-disant* writers and people to whom books were mere fashion.

The servant was pushing his way to the front of the small gathering. Whitewood stood on a low unsteady podium and read with a white handkerchief in one hand, which he waved for dramatic effect. He needed all the help he could get. I dealt daily with the 'improvers,' the self-termed. 'literati.' I'll tell you now what an improver is, he's an imp who roves. I'd seen them dragging their carcasses through the gutter and waylaying hoors and scrapping with the tourists.

The servant had reached the podium, and the bookseller had seen him. Without pausing mid-stanza, Whitewood passed the wretch a note. It was done in an instant and the servant headed back towards the door. I slipped outside and hid myself, watching the servant head as if towards the courts.

I followed him into the courthouse and into one particular court . . . and there was brought up short.

Lord Braxfield, the Hanging Judge, was deciding a case. He sat in his wig at his muckle bench and dipped oatcakes into his claret, sucking loudly on the biscuits as he glared at the accused. There were three of them, and I knew they were charged with sedition, being leaders of a popular convention for parliamentary reform. At this time, only thirty or so people in Edinburgh had the right to vote for the member of parliament. These three sad creatures had wanted to change that, and a lot more besides.

I glanced at the jury – doubtless hand picked by Braxfield himself. The accused would be whipped and sent to Botany Bay. The public gallery was restless. There were guards between the populace and the bench. The servant was nodded through by one of the guards and handed Whitewood's note to Braxfield. Then he turned quickly and left by another door. I was set to follow when the Hanging Judge noticed me.

'Cullender, approach the bench!'

I bit my lip, but knew better than to defy Braxfield, even if it meant losing my quarry. The guards let me through. I forbore to look at the accused as I passed them.

'Yes, my Lord?'

Braxfield nibbled another of his infernal biscuits. He looked like he'd drunk well, too. 'Cullender,' he said, 'you're one of the least honest and civil men in this town, am I correct?'

'I have competitors, my Lord.'

He guffawed, spitting crumbs from his wet lips. 'But tell me this, would you have a man live who committed treason?'

I swallowed, aware of three pairs of eyes behind me. 'I might ask myself about his motives, my Lord.'

Braxfield leaned over the bench. He was unquestionably ugly, eyes black as night. In his seventies, he grew increasingly eccentric. He was what passed for the law in this city. 'Then it's as well *I'm* wearing this wig and not you!' he screeched. He wagged a finger, the nail of which was sore in need of a trim. 'You'll see Australia one day, my friend, if you're not careful. Now be gone, I've some justice to dispense.'

It had been a long time since Braxfield and 'justice' had been even loosely acquainted.

Outside, the servant was long gone. Cursing my luck and the law courts both, I headed down to the Canongate.

I engaged Mr Mack's services regarding my lady's book, warning him to be extra vigilant and telling him of Dryden's demise. He suggested going to the authorities, then realised what he was saying. The law was as effectual as a scented handkerchief against the pox, and we both knew it.

I sat in a howff and ate a dish of oysters. Having been to look at the university, Master Gisborne joined me.

'It'll be fine when it's finished,' was his opinion.

143

I supped the last of the juice and put down the platter. 'Remember I told you about the serpent, Master?'

His eyes were red-rimmed, face puffy with excess. He nodded.

'Well,' I continued thoughtfully, 'perhaps it's not so far beneath the surface as I thought. You need only scratch and you'll see it. Remember that, even in your cups.'

He looked puzzled, but nodded again. Then he seemed to remember something, and reached into his leather bag. He handed me a wrapped parcel.

'Cully, can you keep this somewhere safe?'

'What is it?'

'Just hold it for me for a day or so. Will you do that?'

I nodded and placed the parcel at my feet. Gisborne looked mightily relieved. Then the howff door swung inwards and Urquhart and others appeared, taking Gisborne off with them. I finished my wine and made my way back to my room.

Halfway there, I met the tailor whose family lived two floors below me.

'Cully,' he said, 'men are looking for you.'

'What sort of men?'

'The sort you wouldn't have find you. They're standing guard on the stairwell and won't shift.'

'Thanks for the warning.'

He held my arm. 'Cully, business is slow. If you could persuade some of your clients of the quality of my cloth . . . ?'

'Depend on it.' I went back up the brae to The Cross and found Mr Mack.

'Here,' I said, handing him the parcel. 'Keep this for me.'

'What's wrong?'

'I'm not sure. I think I may have stepped in something even less savoury than I thought. Any news of the *List*?'

Mack shook his head. He looked worried when I left him; not for himself, but for me.

I kept heading uphill, towards the Castle itself. Beneath Castle Hill lay the catacombs where the town's denizens used to hide when the place was being sacked. And here the lowest of Edinburgh's wretches still dwelt. I would be safe there, so I made my way into the tunnels and out of the light, averting my face where possible from each interested, unfriendly gaze.

The man I sought sat slouched against one of the curving walls, hands on his knees. He could sit like that for hours, brooding. He was a giant, and there were stories to equal his size. It was said he'd been a seditionary, a rabble-rouser, both pirate and smuggler. He had most certainly killed men, but these days he lay low. His name was Ormond.

He watched me sit opposite him, his gaze unblinking.

'You're in trouble,' he said at last.

'Would I be here otherwise? I need somewhere to sleep for tonight.'

He nodded slowly. 'That's all any of us needs. You'll be safe here, Cullender.'

And I was.

But next morning I was roused early by Ormond shaking me.

'Men outside,' he hissed. 'Looking for you.'

I rubbed my eyes. 'Is there another exit?'

Ormond shook his head. 'If you went any deeper into this maze, you could lose yourself forever. These burrows run as far as the Canongate.'

'How many men?' I was standing up now, fully awake.

'Four.'

I held out my hand. 'Give me a dagger; I'll deal with them.' I meant it too. I was aching and irritable and tired of running. But Ormond shook his head.

'I've a better plan,' he said.

He led me back through the tunnel towards its entrance. The tunnel grew more populous as we neared the outside world. I could hear my pursuers ahead, examining faces, snarling as each one proved false. Then Ormond filled his lungs.

'The price of corn's to be raised!' he bellowed. 'New taxes! New laws! Everyone to The Cross!'

Voices were raised in anger, and people clambered to their feet. Ormond was raising a mob. The Edinburgh mob was a wondrous thing. It could run riot through the streets and then melt back into the shadows. There'd been the Porteous riots, anti-Catholic riots, price-rise riots, and pro-revolution riots. Each time, the vast majority escaped arrest. A mob could be raised in a minute and could disperse in another. Even Braxfield feared the mob.

Ormond was bellowing in front of me. As for me, I was merely another of the wretches. I passed the men who'd been seeking me. They stood dumbfounded in the midst of the spectacle. As soon as the crowd reached the Lawnmarket, I peeled off with a wave of thanks to Ormond, slipped into an alley, and was alone again.

But not for long. Down past the Luckenbooths I saw the servant again, and this time he would not evade me. Down towards Princes Street he went, down Geordie Boyd's footpath, a footpath that would soon be wide enough for carriages. He crossed Princes Street and headed up to George Street. There at last I saw him descend some steps and enter a house by its servants' door. I stopped a sedan chair. Both chairmen knew me through Mr Mack.

'That house there?' one of them said in answer to my question. 'It used to belong to Lord Thorpe before he left for London. A bookseller bought it from him.'

'A Mr Whitewood?' I asked blithely. The chairmen nodded. 'I admit I don't know that gentleman well. Is he married?'

'Married, aye, but you wouldn't know it. She's seldom seen, is she, Donald?'

'Rarely, very rarely,' the second chairman agreed.

'Why's that? Has she the pox or something?'

They laughed at the imputation. 'How would we know a thing like that?'

I laughed too, and bid them thanks and farewell. Then I approached the front door of the house and knocked a good solid knock.

The servant, when he opened the door; was liveried. He looked at me in astonishment.

'Tell your mistress I wish to speak with her,' I said sharply.

He appeared in two minds at least, but I sidestepped him and found myself in a fine entrance hall.

'Wait in here,' the servant growled, closing the front door and opening another. 'I'll ask my Lady if she'll deign to see you.'

I toured the drawing room. It was like walking around an exhibition, though in truth the only exhibition I'd ever toured was of Bedlam on a Sunday afternoon, and then only to look for a friend of mine.

The door opened and the Lady of the house swept in. She had powdered her cheeks heavily to disguise the redness there – either embarrassment or anger. Her eyes avoided mine, which gave me opportunity to study her. She was in her mid twenties, not short, and with a pleasing figure. Her lips were full and red, her eyes hard but to my mind seductive. She was a catch. But when she spoke her voice was rough-hewn, and I wondered at her history.

'What do you want?'

'What do you think I want?'

She picked up a pretty statuette. 'Are we acquainted?'

'I believe so. We met outside the Tolbooth.'

She attempted a disbelieving laugh. 'Indeed? It's a place I've never been.'

'You would not care to see its innards, Lady, yet you may if you continue in this manner.'

No amount of powder could have hidden her colouring. 'How dare you come here!'

'My life is in danger, Lady.'

This quieted her. 'Why? What have you done?'

'Nothing save what you asked of me.'

'Have you found the book?'

'Not yet, and I've a mind to hand you back your money.'

She saw what I was getting at, and looked aghast. 'But if you're in danger . . . I swear it cannot be to do with me!'

'No? A man has died already.'

'Mr Cullender, it's only a book! It's nothing anyone would kill for.'

I almost believed her. 'Why do you want it?'

She turned away. 'That is not your concern.'

'My chief concern is my neck, Lady. I'll save it at any cost.'

'I repeat, you are in no danger from seeking that book. If you think your life in peril, there must needs be some other cause.' She stared at me as she spoke, and the damnation of it was that I believed her. I believed that Dryden's death, Braxfield's threat, the men chasing me, that none of it had anything to do with her. She saw the change in me and smiled a radiant smile, a smile that took me with it.

'Now get out,' she said. And with that she left the room and began to climb the stairs. Her servant was waiting for me by the front door, holding it open in readiness.

My head was full of puzzles. All I knew with certainty was that I was sick of hiding. I headed back to the old town with a plan in my mind as half-baked as the scrapings the baker tossed out to the homeless.

I toured the town gossips, starting with the fishwives. Then I headed to The Cross and whispered in the ears of selected caddies and chairmen. Then it was into the howffs and dining establishments, and I was glad to wash my hard work down with a glass or two of wine.

My story broadcast, I repaired to my lodgings and lay on the straw mattress. There were no men waiting for me on the stairwell. I believe I even slept a little. It was dark when I next looked out of the skylight. The story I'd spread was that I knew who'd killed Dryden and was merely biding my time before alerting the Town Rats. Would anyone fall for the ploy? I wasn't sure. I fell to a doze again but opened my eyes on hearing noises on the stair.

The steps to my attic were rotten and had to be managed adroitly. My visitor – a lone man, I surmised – was doing his best. I sat up on the mattress and watched the door begin to open. In deep shadow, a figure entered my room, closing the door after it with some finality.

'Good evening, Cully.'

I swallowed drily. 'So the stories were true then, Deacon Brodie?'

'True enough,' he said, coming closer. His face was almost unrecognisable, much older, more careworn, and he wore no wig, no marks of a gentleman. He carried a slender dagger in his right hand.

'I cheated the gibbet, Cully,' he said with his old pride.

'But I was there, I saw you drop.'

'And you saw my men cut me down and haul me away.' He grinned

147

with what teeth were left in his head. 'A wooden collar saved my throat; Cully. I devised it myself.'

I recalled the red silk he'd worn ostentatiously around his throat. A scarf from a female admirer, the story went. It would have hidden just such a device.

'You've been in hiding a long time,' I said. The dagger was inches from me.

'I fled Edinburgh, Cully. I've been away these past five and a half years.'

'What brought you back?' I couldn't take my eyes off the dagger.

'Aye,' Brodie said, seeing what was in my mind. 'The doctor who pronounced me dead and the coffin maker who was supposed to have buried me. I couldn't have witnesses alive . . . not now.'

'And the others, Dryden and the wretch Howison?'

'Both recognised me, curse them. Then *you* started to snoop around and couldn't be found.'

'But why? Why are you back?'

The dagger was touching my throat now. I'd backed myself into a corner of the bed. There was nowhere to go. 'I was *tempted* back, Cully. A temptation I could not resist. The crown jewels.'

'What?'

His voice was a feverish whisper. 'The chest in the crown room. I will have its contents, my last and greatest theft.'

'Alone? Impossible.'

'But I'm not alone. I have powerful allies.' He smiled. 'Braxfield, for one. He believes the theft of the jewels will spark a Scots revolution. But you know this already, Cully. You were seen watching Braxfield. You were seen in Whitewood's shop.'

'Whitewood's part of it, too?'

'You know he is, romantic fool that he is.' The point of the dagger broke my skin. I could feel blood trickle down my throat. If I spoke again, they would be my last words. I felt like laughing. Brodie was so wrong in his surmisings. Everything was wrong. A sudden noise on the stair turned Brodie's head. My own dagger was hidden beneath my thigh. I grabbed it with one hand, my other hand wrestling with Brodie's blade.

When Gisborne opened the door, what he saw sobered him immediately.

Brodie freed himself and turned to confront the young Englishman, dagger ready, but not ready enough. Gisborne had no hesitation in running him through. Brodie stood there frozen, then keeled over, his head hitting the boards with a dull dead sound.

Gisborne was the statue now. He stared at the spreading blood.

I got to my feet quickly. 'Where did you get the blade?' I asked, amazed.

Gisborne swallowed. 'I bought it new today, heeding your advice.'

'You saved my life, young Master.' I stared down at Brodie's corpse. 'But why are you here?'

Gisborne came to his senses. 'I heard you were looking for a book.'

'I was. What of it?' We were both staring at Brodie.

'Only to tell you that I am in possession of it. Or I was. The lawyer Urquhart gave it to me. He said I would doubtless find it useful . . . Who was this man?'

I ignored the question and glared at him. '*You* have the book?'

He shook his head. 'I daren't keep it in my room for fear my landlady might find it.'

I blinked. 'That parcel?' Gisborne nodded. I felt a fool, a dumb fool. But there was Brodie's corpse to dispose of. I could see little advantage in reporting this, his second demise, to the authorities. Questions would be asked of Master Gisborne, and a young Englishman might not always receive a fair hearing, especially with Braxfield at the bench. God no, the body must be disposed of quietly.

And I knew just the spot.

Mr Mack helped us lug the guts down to the new town, propping Brodie in the sedan chair. The slumped corpse resembled nothing so much as a sleeping drunk.

In Charlotte Square we found some fresh foundations and buried the remains of Deacon Brodie within. We were all three in a sweat by the time we'd finished. I sat myself down on a large stone and wiped my brow.

'Well, friends,' I said, 'it is only right and proper.'

'What is?' Gisborne asked, breathing heavily.

'The old town has its serpent, and now the new town does too.' I watched Gisborne put his jacket back on. It was the blue coat with silver buttons. There was blood on it, and dirt besides.

'I know a tailor,' I began, 'might make something fresh for an excellent price . . .'

Next morning, washed and crisply dressed, I returned to my Lady's house. I waved the parcel under the servant's nose and he hurried upstairs.

My Lady was down promptly, but gave me no heed. She had eyes only for the book. Book? It was little more than a ragged pamphlet; its pages were thumbed, scribbled marginalia commenting on this or that entry or adding a fresh one. I handed her the tome.

'The entry you seek is towards the back,' I told her. She looked startled. 'You are, I suppose, the Masked Lady referred to therein? A lady for daylight assignations only, and always masked, speaking in a whisper?'

Her cheeks were crimson as she tore at the book, scattering its shreddings.

'Better have the floor swept,' I told her. 'You wouldn't want Mr Whitewood to find any trace. That was your reason all along, was it not? He is a known philanderer. It was only a matter of time before he got to read of the Masked Lady and became intrigued to meet her.'

Her head was held high, as if she were examining the room's cornices.

'I'm not ashamed,' she said.

'Nor should you be.'

She saw I was not mocking her. 'I am a prisoner here, with no more life than a doll.'

'So you take revenge in your own particular manner? I understand, Lady, but you must understand this. Two men died because of you. Not directly, but that matters not to them. Only one deserved to die. For the other . . .' I jangled the bag of money she'd given me that first night. 'These coins will buy him a burial.'

Then I bade her good day and left the whole shining new town behind me, with its noises of construction and busyness. Let them build all the mighty edifices they would; they could not erase the stain. They could not erase the real town, the old town, the town I knew so intimately. I returned to the howff where Gisborne and Mack awaited me.

'I've decided,' the young master said, 'to study law rather than medicine, Cully.' He poured me a drink. 'Edinburgh needs another lawyer, don't you think?'

The image of Braxfield came unmasked into my mind. 'Like it needs another plague, Master.'

But I raised my glass to him anyway.

F. Paul Wilson, one of my favourite writers, noted that 'private eye fiction is a snapshot of our time.' The same holds true, I think, of historical mystery fiction. One of the things I hope to show here is that life in the Midwest wasn't much different a hundred years ago than it is today. Some of the props may have changed but the human heart remains the human heart. Someday there'll be a collection of Anna Tolan short stories. An Anna novel, *Night of Shadows*, was published several years ago.

Ed Gorman

Anna and the Players

Ed Gorman

At least they didn't have her running out and getting lunch for them any more, Anna thought. That in itself was a sort of promotion. She yawned.

As the lone female on the ten-man Cedar Rapids Police Department in the year of Our Lord 1883, police matron Anna Tolan had spent the previous night studying the work of a French criminal scientist named Marie François Goron. The field was known as criminology and both Scotland Yard and its French counterpart were expanding it every day. Using various methods she'd learned from Goron's writings, Anna had solved three murders in the fourteen months of her employment here. Not that anybody knew this, of course; two detectives named Riley and Czmeck had been quick to claim credit on all three cases.

Anna yawned again. Her sweet landlady Mrs Goldman had come to her door late last night and begged Anna to turn off the kerosene lamp and get some sleep. 'You push yourself way too hard with this police thing, Anna.'

Yes, and for what reason? Anna thought. It was doubtful she'd ever be promoted to full police officer. There were people in town who thought it was sinful for her to be on the police force at all. A woman. Just imagine. Tisk-tisk. They even stood before the mayor in city council meetings and quoted scripture to her that 'proved' that God didn't want women police officers. Apparently, God had opinions on everything.

Thunder rumbled down the sky. The chill, rainy October morning was at least partly responsible for Anna's mood. Rain affected her immediately and deeply, made her feel vulnerable, melancholy. Even as a child back on the farm near Parnell, Anna had been this way. Rain always brought demons.

She looked up at the list of rules she'd had to follow as a teacher. At least she wasn't labouring under that yoke any longer. She kept the list up there to remind her that no matter how frustrating police work got, it wasn't anywhere near as bad as teaching.

153

The teacher should not go out with any man except her father or brothers.
The teacher should not dress in bright colours.
The teacher should not use face powder or paint her lips.
The teacher should not loiter in or around an ice cream parlour.

'There's a lady up front who won't talk to me,' a male voice said. 'Said she wanted to talk to the one and only Anna Tolan.'

The loud voice, the smell of cheap cigars and the dog-like odour of rain on a wool suit meant that Detective Riley was leaning in the door of Anna's office in the back of the station house.

'Something about ghosts,' Riley said.

Anna turned in her chair and looked at him. Fifty pounds ago he'd been a good-looking man. But early middle-age hadn't been kind to him. He looked puffy and tired. Ten years ago, he'd pitched a no-hit game against Des Moines and had been town hero for several years following. Now, he looked like the bloated uncle of that young man, only the faintest resemblance showing.

'Ghosts?'

'That's what she said.'

'Nice of you to give it to me.'

Half the cops were nice to her and helped her in every way possible. They recognised her for the competent law officer she was. This, thank God, included the Chief. The other half gave her all the cases they didn't want. But she was glad to get even the bad ones because otherwise her day would consist of checking the jail three times, walking around town in her light blue pinafore and starched white blouse and asking merchants if everything was going well with them – no break-ins, no robberies, nobody hassling them. One of the reasons that Cedar Rapids had grown so quickly was that it knew how to attract and keep businesses. Twenty-five thousand citizens. More than four hundred telephones. Electricity. In two or three years, there'd be steam trolleys to replace the present horse-drawn ones. There was even an opera house that featured some of the world's most notable theatrical attractions. Chief Ryan once said, 'It sure doesn't hurt to have a pretty little slip of an Irish girl – and with beautiful red hair yet – talking to the merchants to see that the town keeps them happy. It sure doesn't, Anna.'

'I thought you wanted any cases we gave you,' Riley said. 'If you want me to, I'll give it to somebody else.'

'I'm sorry. I'm just in kind of a crabby mood today.'

'Trace Wydmore bothering you to marry him again?'

'I wish you'd leave him alone. He's a decent man.'

'If he's so decent, why don't you marry him?'

'That really isn't any of your business.'

154

'Tell him to give me some of his money. He's got plenty to go around, that's for sure.'

Trace Wydmore was intelligent, handsome, pleasant, fun and kind. He was also very, very rich. About every three months, even though they'd long ago quit seeing each other, Trace would suddenly reappear and ask her to marry him. She felt sorry for him. But she didn't love him. She liked him, admired him, appreciated him. But she didn't love him.

She changed the subject. 'You're right, Riley. I *do* want the case. Thank you for giving it to me. I guess I'm just in a bad mood. The rain.'

'You and my old lady,' he said. 'If it's not her monthly visitor, it's the weather. There's always some reason she's crabby.' Then he waggled his fingers at her wraith-like and made a spooky noise. 'I'll go get the ghost lady.'

Her name was Virginia Olson, a bulky, middle-aged woman with a doughy face and hard, bright, not terribly friendly blue eyes. She cleaned rooms at the Astor hotel, a somewhat seedy place along the river. She wore a pinafore, not unlike Anna's in cut and style, but stained and smudged with the indelicacies of hotel guests. When she talked, silver spittle frothed up in the corners of her mouth and ran down the sides of her lips. She said, 'Oh, I seen her all right.'

'Anthea Murchison?'

'Anthea Murchison. Right in front of my eyes.'

'She's been dead over a year now. Her buggy overturned over in Johnson county and she went off a cliff.'

'I don't need no rehash, Miss,' she said. 'I read the papers. I keep up.'

'Then if you keep up,' Anna said, staying calm and patient, 'and if you think it through, what you're saying is impossible.'

'That a dead woman was in the hotel last night? Well, she was.'

Anna sighed. 'Exactly what would you like me to do?'

'You're just as snooty as the men officers. You try'n give the coppers a tip and look what you get.'

'I'm sorry, Mrs Olson.'

'Miss Olson.'

'Miss Olson, then.'

'Not that I never had no chances to be *Mrs* Olson.' She sucked up some of the frothing spittle.

'I'm sure you had plenty of chances.'

'I wasn't always fat. It's this condition I have. And my hair used to be black as night, too. But then I got this here condition.'

'I'm sorry. Now, if you'll just tell me—'

'She wore this big picture hat. You know what a picture hat is?'

'Yes.' They were fashionable these days, hats with huge brims that covered half a lady's face.

'She also had some kind of wig on when she came in the hotel. That's why I didn't recognise her. Her disguise. But I was goin' to my own room – the hotel gives me room and board except the food is pig swill – anyway, later on I'm goin' to my room and I seen her door was partly open and I just happened to glance inside and there she was without her hat and her wig and I seen her. Anthea Murchison. Plain as day.'

'Did she see you?'

'I think she must've because she hurried quick-like to the door and practically slammed it.' She paused to suck up some more spittle. Anna wondered if the spittle had anything to do with the woman's 'condition'.

'You'd seen the Murchison woman before?'

Miss Olson smirked. 'You mean when she was alive?'

'Yes.'

'Oh, I seen her all right. Plenty of times.'

'Where?'

'The hotel. That's why I recognised her so fast. Her and her gentleman friend used to come up the back way.'

'When was this?'

Virginia Olson thought about it for a time. 'Oh, six, seven months before she died.'

'How often did they come there?'

'Once a week, say.'

'They didn't check in at the front desk?'

'No. They had – or she had, anyway – some kind've deal worked out with Mr Sullivan. The manager. Poor man.'

'Poor man?'

'The cancer. He weighed about eighty pounds when they planted him. Liver. He was all yellow.'

'That's too bad.'

'No, it isn't.'

'It isn't?'

'I mean, I didn't want to see him die that way – I wouldn't want to see *any*body die that way – but he was a mean, cheap bastard who never did a lick'a work in his life.'

'I'm sorry to hear that. But let's get back to Anthea Murchison.'

'They were havin' it on.'

'I gathered that. Did you know who he was?'

'I almost got a look at him once. But he always moved real fast. And he wore this big fake black beard and this big hat that covered a lot of his face.'

'Like her picture hat?'

'I never thought of that. But you're right. It was sorta like a picture

156

hat except it was for a man. Like somethin' you'd see on the stage, I guess. That a villain would wear or somethin'.'

She took a railroad watch from the pocket of her pinafore and said, 'I got to get back. I'm just here on my break.'

'I still don't know what you want me to do, Miss Olson.'

'Come over there and look at her. See if it ain't Mrs Murchison in the flesh.'

The woman wasn't going to be Mrs Murchison, of course. But it'd be better than just sitting here on this gloomy morning. And on the way back, she could swing past the jail and make one of her morning inspections. Make sure things were being run properly. Chief Ryan prided himself on his jail. He wanted it clean, orderly and without a whisper of scandal. He hoped to run for mayor someday, Chief Ryan did, and he didn't want some civic group pointing out that his jail had been a hell-hole, like something you'd see in Mexico. Their jails were much in the news lately. A lot of men died mysteriously in those jails.

'I'll walk back with you,' Anna said, standing up.

'I got to hurry,' Miss Olson said. 'Mr Sanford's worse than Mr Sullivan ever was. Now Mr Sanford, I sure wouldn't mind seein' him get the cancer. I surely wouldn't.'

Hotel rooms always saddened Anna. She'd seen too many suicides, murders and bad illicit love affairs within their walls. One problem with being a copper was that you generally saw the worst side of people, even in a nice little town like Cedar Rapids. The grubby hallway of the Astor's third floor told her that the room she was about to see would be grubby, too. The Olson woman had gone back to work.

The hallway offered eruptions of sounds on both sides – tobacco coughs, singing-while-shaving, snoring and gargling, presumably with 'oral disinfectant' as the advertisements called it.

Room 334. Anna put her ear to it. Listened. Silence. Just then a door down the hall opened and a bald man in trousers, the tops of long johns, and suspenders peeked out and picked up his morning paper. He gave Anna a very close appraisal and said, 'Morning.'

Anna smiled, wanting to remain silent, and nodded good morning back.

She put her ear to the door again. If the woman inside was moving around, she was doing so very, very quietly. Maybe she had gone out the back way. While the desk clerk had assured Anna that the woman had not come down yet this morning, he obviously didn't know for sure that she was in her room.

Anna knocked gently. Counted to ten. No response. Knocked again. Still no response.

Sounds of doors opening and closing on all three floors of the hotel; morning greetings exchanged; smells of cigarettes, pipes, cigars; men with leather sample bags of merchandise carted out here from points as distant as New York and Cincinnati and Chicago suddenly striding past her in the hall. A quarter-to-eight and the business day just beginning.

Anna knocked again.

One of the officers friendly to her had given her a couple of tools resembling walnut picks; showed her how to use them on virtually any kind of door. He'd also given her several skeleton keys. She could get into virtually any room or house.

The room was about what she'd expected: double bed; bureau; faded full-length mirror hanging on a narrow closet door; window overlooking the alley on the east side of the hotel. What she hadn't expected was the woman in the bed. She lay in a faded yellow robe, with her arms spread wide. She was otherwise naked. Somebody had cut her throat. There was a necklace-like crust of dried blood directly across the centre of her throat.

The woman was Anthea Murchison.

Anna's first instinct was to hurry downstairs and send somebody to summon the Chief. But then she forced herself to calm down. She wouldn't get much of a chance to scientifically appraise the room – the way her idol Goron would want her to – with other cops present.

She spent the next twenty minutes going over everything. In the purse, she found various documents bearing the name Thea Manners, obviously the name the Murchison woman had used during the past year. But where had she been? What had she been doing? Anna inspected the bed carefully, looking for anything that might later prove useful. She found red fibres, hair strands that looked to belong to Anthea Murchison, a piece of a woman's fingernail. She checked Anthea's fingers. A slice of her right index fingernail had broken off. The piece Anna held fit the maimed nail perfectly. A couple of times, Anna noticed the small, odd indentation in the wooden headboard. She took a piece of paper and held it tight to the headboard. Then she scribbled lead over the indentation. It showed a symbol: H. The style was rococo, and a bit too fancy for Anna's tastes. She put the paper in her pocket. Then she started in on the floor. Down on her hands and knees, looking for curious footprints, or something tiny that might have been dropped. She found a number of things worth placing in the white evidence envelope she'd made up for herself. A plain black button interested Anna especially. She checked it against Anthea's clothes in the closet. There was no match. The button belonged to somebody else. The way fashions were getting so radical these days – an Edwardian craze was sweeping the country – it was impossible to know if the button had come from male or female attire.

Fifteen minutes later, the room was filled with police officers. Anna was pretty much pushed aside. She went downstairs to the porch and stood looking out at the street. The rain had let up but the overcast, chill autumn day remained. Wagons, buggies, surreys and a stray stagecoach or two plied the muddy streets. Somewhere nearby, the horse-drawn trolley rang its bell. Then she realised that the trolley could take her very close to where she needed to go.

She hurried to the corner. The trolley stopped for her. On a day like this one, the conveyance was crowded, the bowlers on men and bustles on women bobbing as the trolley bounced down the bumpy streets. Horse-drawn taxi cabs were busy, too. The rain had started in again.

Ten years ago, the large red barn had housed two businesses, a blacksmith and a farm implement dealer. It now housed the Players, a local theatrical group that did everything it could to create controversy, and thus sell tickets. Kevin Murchison was a dentist by day, but at night he oversaw production of the plays. His partner was David Bailey, a medical doctor. The men had much in common. They were in their early thirties, literary, handsome and were widely held to have slept with half the women, married or not, who took roles in the various plays. Kevin was tall, pale and blond; David was short and dark, with an air of not only malice but violence. His bedside manner was rarely praised. In fact, it was well-known that most of the other doctors in town regretted ever letting him practise here. One practised in Cedar Rapids only at the sufferance of the docs already in place. Many were called; few were chosen. David Bailey was generally regarded as a terrible choice.

The playhouse was empty when Anna arrived. She stood at the back of the place, listening to the rain play chill ancient rhythms on the roof of the barn. The stage was set for a French bedroom farce advertised outside as 'DEFINITELY NAUGHTY!' – THE NEW YORK TIMES. Who could resist? Word was that this was the most successful play of the past three years, so successful in fact that both dentist and doctor were thinking of quitting their respective practices and joining the Players full-time.

'It's lovely, isn't it?' The voice definitely male but practised and just this side of being 'cultured'.

She turned to find three people standing there: Dr Murchison, Dr Bailey and Bailey's gently beautiful wife, Beatrice.

Anna said, 'You've done a nice job.'

Murchison said, 'The finest theatre outside Chicago.'

Beatrice actually blushed at the hyperbole. 'Or so we like to think, anyway.'

There was no clue on their faces or in their voices that they'd heard about their friend Anthea. She was probably at the undertaker's by now.

Murchison, whose Edwardian suit complemented his clipped good looks and slightly European curly blond hair, said, 'I'm sure you're here about Anthea.'

So they did know.

159

'It's terrible,' Beatrice said.

'I hope there'll be an investigation,' Bailey added. His stocky form looked comfortable in Levi's and work shirt. The odd thing was, Murchison, who looked almost effete, had been raised on a farm, while Bailey, who'd come from Boston money, could have blended in with a crew of railroad workers. 'I was the one who pronounced her dead after the accident. I've got my reputation to think of.' Then he made an awkward attempt to touch his hand to Murchison's shoulder. 'I'm sorry, Kevin. You're grieving and all I can talk about is my reputation.'

There was something rehearsed about the little scene she'd just witnessed. Or was there? Theatre people – or so she'd read in one of Mrs Goldman's eastern magazines – sometimes carried their acting over into real life. Ham was the word Anna was looking for.

'Did any of you see her last night?'

'No,' said Murchison. 'I wished I would have. My God, I had so many questions for her.' Tears filled his eyes and Beatrice, tall, regal Beatrice, took him in her arms and held him.

'Why don't we step into the office?' Bailey said to Anna. 'We can talk there.'

Theatre posters lined the walls of the small office with the roll-top desk and the long table covered with leaflets for the present production. 'Uncle Tom's Cabin', 'The Widow's Revenge', 'A Cupid For Constance' were listed as forthcoming. The Players were an eclectic bunch. They mixed tame fare with the occasional bedroom farce and seemed to be surviving quite nicely.

'She was dead when we put her in the ground,' Bailey said. 'I'd swear to that.'

'You'll have to, Doctor. There'll be a lot of questions about the autopsy report you signed.'

A tic troubled his right eyelid suddenly. She said, 'You didn't see her last night?'

'I believe I already answered that question.'

'I'd appreciate you answering it again.'

'Neither of us saw her last night,' Beatrice said as she came into the office. 'Poor Kevin's lying down in his private office.' She went over and took a straightback chair next to her husband. 'We worked at the theatre until nearly midnight and then went home and went to bed.'

'I see.'

Beatrice smiled. 'I was just wondering if you're even authorised to ask us questions. I remember you had some trouble with the city council and all.'

'The Chief will back me up, if that's what you mean.' Then, 'I'm going to ask for the grave to be disinterred this afternoon.'

'And why would you do that?' Bailey asked.

'I want to see what's in the coffin.'

'Well, obviously *Anthea* won't be,' Bailey said. His eye tic was suddenly worse.

'How did Anthea and Kevin get along?'

'Just wonderfully,' Beatrice said.

'There were a lot of rumours.'

Beatrice smiled. 'Of course there were rumours, dear. This is a rumour kind of town. Anybody who shows a little flair for anything even the slightest bit different from the herd – well, rumours are the price you pay.'

'Then they were happy?'

'Very.'

'And there was no talk of divorce?'

'Of course not.'

They weren't going to cooperate and Anna knew it. They had pat little answers to turn aside her questions. And that was all she was going to get.

She stood up. 'Where's Dr Murchison's office?'

'Just down the hall,' Beatrice said. 'But he really does want to be alone. He's very confused and hurt right now.'

'I'll keep that in mind,' Anna said. 'And thank you for your time.'

As she was turning to the door, Bailey said, 'You've been incredibly insensitive. I may just talk to the Chief about it.'

'That's up to you, Dr Bailey.'

They stared at each other a long moment, and then Anna went down the hall.

Just as she reached Murchison's door, she heard a female voice behind it say, 'Oh, Kevin, why lie about it? You sleep with all the ingénues and then get tired of them. That's what's happening to us. You're tired of me but you don't want to hurt my feelings by telling me.'

'I just need some time to – think, Karen. That's all. Especially after this morning. My wife and everything.'

'You should be grateful to her,' Karen said. 'She gave you a perfect excuse for not seeing me tonight.' By the end, her voice had started to tremble with tears. 'Oh, I was stupid to think you were really in love with me.'

Anna had always been told that in amateur theatre groups, the real drama went on off-stage. Apparently so. She hated to embarrass Karen by knocking now but she had work to do. She knocked.

Murchison opened the door quickly, obviously grateful for any interruption. But he frowned when he saw Anna. 'Oh, great, just what I need. More questions.'

'I just need a few minutes, Dr Murchison.'

The word 'ingénue' had misled Anna into picturing a slender, some-what ethereal young woman. While Karen was still an exquisite-looking

161

woman, her years were starting to do damage, the face a bit fleshy, the neck a bit loose, the high bustline matronly now. She was a fading beauty, and there was always something sad about that. She wore a large wedding ring on the appropriate finger. But it was the other ring she kept touching, fingering, a large red ruby with the letter H imposed on it in fretted metal. She worried it like a touchstone.

'I'll talk to you tonight,' Murchison said, 'if Miss Tolan here doesn't put me in jail for some reason.' He didn't even try to disguise the bitterness in his voice.

Karen whimpered, pushed past Anna, and exited the room.

'I suppose you heard it all while you were standing by the door,' Murchison said, 'and will run right down to her husband's office and tell him.' Anna suspected that this was the real Murchison. The mild man she'd met earlier had been a masque.

'I don't even know who her husband is,' Anna said.

'Lawrence Remington,' Murchison said. 'He has a very successful law practice in the Ely building. On the second floor, in case you're interested.' He smirked. 'I only commit adultery with the upper-classes. I guess I'm something of a snob.' He took out a packet of Egyptian cigarettes. Nobody was more pretentious than certain amateur theatre types. 'She's not as beautiful as she used to be. But Remington doesn't seem to notice that. He's insanely jealous.'

'Maybe he loves her.'

But love didn't interest him much. He merely shrugged.

'I'm told that you and your wife were on the verge of divorce at the time of her supposed death.'

He glared at her. 'You don't waste any time, do you? Have you ever thought that I might be grieving? I thought my wife was dead – and then she suddenly turns up. And now she's dead again.' She could see why he produced the shows instead of starred in them. He was a terrible actor.

'Did you see her last night?'

'I've already told you no.'

'What if I said somebody saw her slipping into your house?'

He didn't hesitate. 'Then I'd say you're lying.'

Sometimes the trick Chief Ryan had taught her worked. Sometimes it didn't. She tried a trick of her own, 'I found a cuff button in your wife's hotel room.'

'Good for you.'

'I'm sure you'd be happy to let me look through your shirts.'

He met her eye. He seemed to be enjoying this, which did not do much for her police officer ego. 'Would you like to go to my place and look through my shirts?'

Once again, she changed the subject, now uncertain of herself and the direction of her questions. 'The night clerk said he saw a man going up to her room late last night.' One last attempt to trap him.

'Oh? Maybe you'd like me to stop by so he can see me.' He laughed. 'I'll cooperate with you any way you want, Miss Tolan. I have nothing to hide.'

Maybe he didn't, after all. Or maybe he was clever enough to offer himself up this way, knowing she wouldn't call him on it. She felt slow-witted and dull. She was sure she'd been the brunt of many jokes told after-hours at the Players' notorious wine parties. She was just glad Chief Ryan wasn't here to see this sorry interrogation. She wanted to be home suddenly, in Mrs Goldman's parlour, listening to Mrs Goldman's stirring stories about the Civil War, and how the ladies of Iowa had worked eighteen-hour days making bullets and knitting sweaters and stockings and mittens for their Union husbands and sons and brothers. Mrs Goldman said that they'd even loaded up the steamboats when no men could be found.

She angled herself toward the door. 'I guess I'll be going now.'

'I was just starting to have fun.' Then, 'You're very pretty, Anna. Have you ever thought of trying out for one of our plays?'

She knew she was blushing. His compliment had cinched his victory. He'd reduced her status from detective to simple young woman.

'I'll talk to you later,' she said, and hurried out of his room. He laughed once behind her – an empty, fake laugh that was yet another example of his bad acting.

Anna was about to walk out through the front door when she heard weeping in the deep shadows to the side. She squinted into the gloom and saw nothing. But the weeping sound remained constant. Anna made her way carefully toward the far wall. A shape began to form. Karen Remington. She paused long enough to say, 'Do you have a cigarette?'

Good girls don't smoke, Anna wanted to say. Or so her farmer parents had always told her, anyway. And Anna couldn't get away from their influence, much as she wanted to sometimes. Any woman she saw smoking a cigarette, she automatically downgraded socially if not morally. 'I'm afraid I don't smoke.'

'I must look terrible. My make-up.'

Anna smiled. 'Actually, I can't see you very well.'

The Remington woman laughed. And that made Anna like her. 'If that's the case, I should probably stay here the rest of my life. In the shadows. Then I won't have to see how old I'm getting.' She paused, snuffled tears, dabbed a lace handkerchief to nose and lips. 'I've always read about women like myself – that's why I can't stand to read Henry James. I see myself in so many of his silly, middle-aged women. Vain and desperate.' More snuffling. 'I told myself that the Players would be good for me. My son was off to Princeton, my husband was always busy.

163

I felt – Oh, it's all such a cliché. You know how I felt. So I decided to help out with publicity. Then I helped with costumes. Then I tried out for a part in a play. And then I got involved with dear Kevin. You know the funny thing? He not only seduced me – though of course I *wanted* to be seduced – he convinced me to give him money. And large amounts of it. My husband was furious when he found out. Even threatened to divorce me. I actually think he resented the money even more than he resented my being unfaithful. He's not a generous man. But I didn't care. Kevin and I were going to run off and start another theatre someplace. I wanted to go east, to be nearer my son. Kevin led me to believe—'

'Nasty Kevin,' a male voice said on the other side of the gloom. 'Nasty, nasty Kevin.'

It was Kevin, of course.

'I didn't "lead her to believe" anything, Miss Tolan. She believed what she *wanted* to believe.'

'Unfortunately,' the Remington woman said, 'that's true.' And promptly began sobbing again, even more violently than before.

Soon enough, Anna was on the trolley again, headed downtown once more. The sun was out now; the temperature was up in the forties. Anna looked longingly at the stately buildings of Coe College, Main Building and Williston Hall, as they were known. She hoped to take classes there someday. She'd seen photographs of college girls in crisp spring dresses, how intelligent and poised and professional they looked. Her secret dream was to be one of them. Anna Tolan, college girl.

Anna had no trouble with Chief Ryan. He understood exactly why she wanted the Murchison woman's coffin dug up. Judge Rollins, who could sometimes be a problem, also understood and approved her request.

At four that afternoon, Anna, Chief Ryan, and two scruffy gravediggers, stood over Anthea Murchison's gravesite. The air was fresh, cleansed by the recent rain, and the gravestones glistened as if they'd been scrubbed. Some of them dated as far back as the late 1700s, when some Frenchmen down from Green Bay, Wisconsin, had started trading iron kettles, cloth and knives for some of the Iowa Indians' animal skins. An influenza outbreak had killed at least a dozen of the French traders.

'If there's a body in there, Anna,' Chief Ryan said. 'I want you to look away. Otherwise, it'll stay in your mind the rest of your life.'

Chief Ryan was every bit as grandfatherly as he sounded, a big, broad, grey-haired man with the red nose of a drinker and the kind eyes of a village priest. His grandparents had come from County Cork two generations ago. Every Ryan male since had been a law officer of some kind.

'I'll be fine, Chief.'

'You're not as tough as you think, young lady.'

164

Remembering her wretched questioning of the glib Kevin Murchison, she had to silently agree.

The exhumation went quickly. The gravediggers knew their business. When they reached the wooden coffin with the cross in the centre of the lid, the taller of the two jumped down into the grave with his crowbar. He was able to balance himself against the walls of the grave and open the coffin lid. He prised it open and flung it back.

'Empty, sir,' he shouted up to the Chief.

'Empty,' the Chief repeated. 'Empty.'

When they got back to the station, Anna found a man waiting for her. She saw him around town frequently but didn't know who he was or what he did.

He doffed his derby and said, 'My name is Peterson. Pete Peterson. I sell insurance.'

'This is a bad time to sell me anything, Mr Peterson.'

He smiled. He had a boyish face emphasised by the youthful cut of his checkered suit. Salesmen, or drummers as they were popularly called, had come to favour checks. They felt that the pattern put people in a happier frame of mind than, say, dark blue or black. 'I'm here about Anthea Murchison.'

'Oh?'

'My company issued her a life insurance policy for $50,000 eight months before she died.'

'Oh,' Anna said, catching his implication instantly.

They sat in her office for the next hour. The day shift was winding down. Men called goodbyes to each other. The handful of night-shifters came on, their leather gunbelts creaking, their heavy shoes loud on the wooden floors.

'Insurance fraud is what we're looking at,' Peterson said. 'If we can prove it.'

'Why couldn't you prove it?' Anna said. 'The coffin was empty. And Dr Bailey signed the death certificate. He had to know she wasn't dead.'

'I think it was for that theatre of theirs.'

'The money, you mean?'

Peterson nodded. 'The way I understand it, they couldn't get any more investors. They'd borrowed everything they could. The theatre was going under.'

'So they staged Anthea Murchison's death.'

'And collected $50,000.'

'Your company didn't investigate?'

'Of course we investigated. But as you said, we had a signed death certificate. There was no reason to go into an all-out investigation. We didn't spend all that much time on it. Now, it's obvious we were defrauded.'

165

'They'll probably try to leave town.'

'If they haven't already.'

'I'm not sure how long I can hold them on what we have now, though.'

'But we *know* what happened, Anna.'

'Yes, we know it. But can we prove it? Defence attorneys are very creative people, Pete.'

'Don't I know it. They've helped cheat my company out of millions of dollars.' Whenever he spoke of the company, his tone became downright reverent. Like a cardinal invoking the name of the Vatican.

'I need to talk to the Chief about all this, Pete. There's also a murder investigation going on. He'll want to move carefully.'

'What's he afraid of?'

'What he's afraid of, Mr Peterson,' Chief Ryan said, walking into Anna's office, 'is that you'll get your fraud case all resolved, and we still won't know why Anthea Murchison came back to town last night – and why one of them killed her.'

Peterson frowned. 'So you're not going to arrest them?'

'Not right now,' Ryan said, 'and I don't want you approaching them, either. You understand?'

'My company isn't going to be happy.'

'I'm sorry about that, Mr Peterson,' Ryan said. 'But that's the way it has to be for a little while longer.'

Mr Peterson's checkered suit seemed to fade slightly in intensity. Even the magnificently bogus gleam in his eyes had dulled. His company wasn't happy, and neither was he.

'Now, if you don't mind, Mr Peterson, Anna and I need to get back to work.'

Mr Peterson dragged himself to his feet. He looked weary, old. He took his faded suit and faded eyes to the door and said, 'I'll have to go and send my company a telegram, I guess.' And with that, he was gone.

A moment later, Chief Ryan said, 'The mayor wants me to put Riley on the case.'

'I figured that would happen.'

'You know this isn't my decision. But there's an election coming up and he doesn't want to have an unsolved case like this hanging over his head.' Ryan smiled. 'But nobody can stop you from working on the case on your own, Anna.'

Their usual bargain had been struck. Anna worked on the case and secretly reported back to the Chief.

Anna smiled. 'I guess I do have a little time on my hands tonight.'

'Glad to hear it.'

After dinner with Mrs Goldman, Anna took the evidence up to her room and started sifting through it. Goron had instructed would-be detectives to store all evidence in the same box, and to tag it alphabetically. Fingerprints were beginning to play a role in detective work. Even though law enforcement in the United States was still sceptical of such evidence – and no court would allow it to be used – Goron insisted that all pieces of evidence remain as pristine as possible; and that fingerprints were also the surest way to identify a killer. Find a print on a murder weapon and you had your man.

Anna worked till after midnight. On her bed was the button she'd found on Anthea Murchison's hotel floor, the sketch she'd made of some strange footprints on the hotel room floor, a cigarette made of coarse tan paper and heavy tobacco leaves, a man's comb with grey hair in it, a drinking glass across which were smeared two or three different sets of fingerprints, and the curious H marking she'd found on the headboard of Anthea's hotel bed. The trouble with all her evidence was that she couldn't date it. It might have been in the room for a month. Even the cigarette butt didn't tell her anything decisive. A sloppy cleaning woman might have left it behind a few weeks ago.

There would be no trouble proving that the owners of the Players had perpetrated a fraud; proving that one of them had perpetrated a murder might be something else again.

Kevin Murchison had planned on only one drink at the River's Edge. He had four in less than an hour. On an empty stomach. Which was not exactly wise. With the law having him under suspicion – even that stupid insurance investigator Pete Peterson should be able to figure things out now – he needed to remain sharp and clear-headed.

But somehow his fear (oh he'd do just dandy in prison, wouldn't he?) and self-pity (why shouldn't a nice decent fellow like himself be able to get away with a little fraud now and then?) and loathing (he hated the taverns of Cedar Rapids; all the silly yokel chatter, never a word about theatre life or the latest Broadway scandal, which Kevin kept up on via *The New York Times*) forced him to drink more.

By the time he was ready to walk home, he had to make himself conscious of his gait. Didn't want to appear drunk. Drunk meant vulnerable and oh how that pretty little piece of a police matron or whatever the hell she was would love to get him when he was vulnerable.

The autumn dusk was chill and brief and gorgeous, the sky layered in smoky pastels of gold and salmon. His Tudor-style home was dark when he reached it. He'd let the last of his servants go shortly after Anthea's 'death'. He could no longer afford the pretence. Anyway, he needed the town's sympathy – the bereaved husband and all that – to allay suspicion that Anthea's death had been suspicious. People in a place like Cedar Rapids were never sympathetic to people who had servants.

167

He reheated this morning's coffee and then went to the north wing of the house, where the den was located. He'd just touched a match to the desk lamp when the smell filled his nostrils. He wanted to vomit.

She lay over by the fireplace, the fire poker next to her fine blond head. The tip of the poker gleamed with her blood.

He knelt next to her. Once or twice, he reached out to touch her, but stopped himself. He didn't want to remember her flesh as cold. In life, it had been so warm and supple and erotic. He had never loved anyone as much as he'd loved Beatrice. They'd been planning to run away tonight, leaving her husband David to explain things to the police – the insurance fraud and Anthea's murder last night.

Now he knew who had murdered Anthea. David Bailey. Anthea had stopped by the house late last night and demanded more money, said she'd been living in New Orleans but had run out of money. They'd been planning to divorce anyway at the time they faked her death, so she took one-third of the insurance money and fled, and they put the rest of the money into the theatre. He'd lied to her last night and said he'd get her more this morning. Anything to get rid of her. So apparently she'd next gone to blackmail Bailey. And he must have killed her. As he'd killed poor Beatrice tonight. Bailey, a jealous man for all his own unfaithfulness, had likely learned about Beatrice and Kevin. And killed her for her betraying him.

He wasn't given to tears and so his sobs were fitful. He leaned in. He couldn't help himself. He kissed her cold dead lips.

And then he stood up and knew what he had to do, where he had to go.

Right now, nothing else mattered. Nothing else at all.

'You could've killed Beatrice,' Anna said.

'No, I couldn't,' Murchison said. 'I loved her too much.'

'So,' the Chief said, 'you admit to the insurance fraud.'

'Yes, of course. I've told you that already. We were just trying to save the theatre.'

'But not to murdering your wife,' Anna said.

'Or Beatrice,' the Chief added.

It was near midnight in the small back room of the station used to question suspects. The room was bare except for a few fading dirty words prisoners had scribbled on the wall from time to time.

Kevin Murchison had gone straight to Anna's and told her what happened. His version of it, anyway. Then she'd taken him downtown and used the telephone to call the Chief and ask him to come down, too. She still got a thrill every time she used the telephone. They'd spent the last two hours going over and over Murchison's story. The atmosphere wasn't hostile but it was certainly intense. The dancing light of a kerosene lamp threw everything into soft shadow.

'Who do you think killed them, then?' Anna said.

'I've told you that already.'

'I wish you'd quit saying that,' the Chief said, lighting his pipe with a stick match. 'We're well aware we keep asking you the same questions over and over.'

'It's damned annoying is what it is.'

'So,' the Chief said, 'who do you think killed the two women?'

Murchison glared at him. Sighed. 'I've told you and told you. David killed them.'

'Why would he kill them?'

'He's got a terrible temper. Anthea must've seen him last night and demanded money. The same way she did from me. He got angry and killed her.'

'But why would he kill Beatrice?' Anna asked.

'Because he found out about us. Not only that we were lovers but that we were running away together.'

'And so he killed her?' Anna said.

'You'd have to see him lose his temper to understand how easily he could kill somebody. He's terrifying when he's like that.'

A knock. The Chief said, 'That's probably Henning, Anna. Why don't you take it? I'll keep on questioning our friend here.'

'I didn't kill either of those women,' Kevin Murchison said, sounding like a sad little boy. 'I really didn't.'

Anna opened the door. Henning was one of the older officers, a big, bald man with bushy eyebrows and a chin scar from a long-ago altercation with a hobo. Anna stepped out into the hall. 'Bailey wasn't at home,' he said.

'Did you find a train schedule?'

Henning nodded, handed her a pamphlet.

'Thanks,' she said.

'I need to make my rounds.'

She nodded. There was a train leaving for Chicago in forty-five minutes. She opened the door of the small back room, peeked in and said, 'I'm going over to the train depot.'

'Good idea,' the Chief said. 'You know where my Navy Colt is. Take it.'

'I probably won't need it.'

'Take it, anyway.'

While Anna didn't much like firearms, the Chief had turned her into a fair marksman. She preferred to think of herself as a Goron-type of peace officer. 'Brain power' Goron often said was more important than 'brute power'. But she reluctantly went into the Chief's office, opened the wide middle drawer of his desk, and took out the Navy Colt.

Cedar Rapids had a crush on its train depot, one of those crushes that made folks just about absolutely goofy. Some folks would bring their own chairs to the depot so they could sit and watch trains arrive and depart all day long. Other folks brought picnic lunches, just to sit and watch the panoramic show that trains put on. People loved everything about trains, the bold colours of the engine cars, the grey billowing smoke, the stink of coal, the smell of oil, the clatter of couplings. They were especially interested in the fancy dining cars and parlour cars. 'The envy of sultans!' as one advertisement boasted. They liked to see exotic strangers disembark, New York people or Chicago people or Boston people, fancy people stepping down to stretch their legs before the train roared away again, women in huge capes and big important hairstyles, and men in dove-grey vests and top hats and spats, with money and culture and a self-confidence that Cedar Rapids folks could only daydream of.

Because the temperature had dipped several degrees, most of the waiting passengers were inside the depot, on the benches close to the pot-bellied stove. The fog had discouraged them, too, a damp, thick, gritty fog. There weren't many people inside, mostly drummers on to the next burg, derbys down on their faces as they snored off weariness and whiskey.

She searched all the obvious places inside. Bailey wasn't in any of them. She described him to everybody she saw. Nobody had seen him. Not even the ticket seller recalled seeing him.

She'd been there fifteen, twenty minutes when the drunk came reeling in. She'd arrested him a few times. His name was Henry. He'd used so many aliases neither she nor the police were sure of his last name. He was mostly a small-time grifter preying on elderly folks. He was a decent-looking man but you couldn't tell it beneath the layers of grime and bar liquor.

He went over to the ticket window. Moments later, he was shouting at the ticket man. Anna went over.

'Where the hell is he?' Henry wanted to know.

'Where is who?' the ticket man said several times. 'I don't know who you're talking about.'

'That doctor.'

'What doctor?' Anna said.

Henry turned awkwardly and glared at her. He looked to be near collapse, the final stages of this particular bender. He'd stay dry for a few months, working his grifts, and then do another bender for five, six weeks. 'You got no call to arrest me.'

'I just want to talk to you.'

'That's what you said las' time.'

For a drunk, he had a good memory. She took his elbow, angled him away from the ticket window. 'Who's the doctor you're looking for?'

'None of your damn business. I got rights, you know.'

170

'You keep it up, Henry, and I *will* arrest you. Now who's the doctor?'

He needed a shave, two or three baths, and his dirty black suit needed all sorts of sewing. He glared silently at her as long as he could. Then he sighed and said, 'Bailey.'

'I thought so. Why're you looking for him?'

'He promised me five dollars.' Five dollars would buy a lot of bad liquor.

'For what?'

'For buying his train ticket.'

So that's how Bailey had worked it. He knew the police would be watching the depot. 'Where'd you see him last?'

Henry nodded eastward. 'Out by the baggage carts.'

The plan was becoming obvious. Bailey had sent Henry in to buy a ticket. That's why nobody had seen him. Then he'd wait till the very last minute and jump out of the shadows and board the train. He'd hide somewhere aboard until the train was thirty, forty miles down the line.

'Where was the ticket to?'

'Chicago.'

A good place to get lost in, Anna thought.

'He said he'd pay you five dollars?'

'Yeah. But he only paid me two. Said that was all the cash he had on him. I went over and started drinkin' and the more I thought of it, the madder I got. So I come back here.'

'I appreciate this, Henry.'

'You see him, you tell him he owes me three dollars.'

'I'll tell him, Henry. Don't worry.'

Things were working out for Bailey. A heavy autumnal fog was even heavier, rolling in, snaking silver across everything. You couldn't see more than a yard or so in front of you.

She started making her way down the platform. She'd decided to use the Chief's Navy Colt if necessary, after all. She gripped it tight in her right hand.

She heard somebody walking toward her and ducked behind an empty baggage cart, one as large as a small horse-drawn utility wagon. She raised the gun, ready to fire.

An older couple, the Mayples, appeared out of the fog. Selma Mayples had on the tiny straw hat with the merry red band she wore whenever she left the house. Stout Sam Mayples was carrying a small suitcase. Selma must be visiting her sick sister in Rock Island again.

After they passed, she resumed her search. She walked up and down the platform twice, searching in, under and around anything that looked even vaguely like a hiding place. She had no better luck outside than she'd had inside.

She was about to give up when she heard a horse neigh somewhere

171

in the gloom. The cabs. This late at night, there'd be only one working, but a couple of the drivers always left their cabs here. The livery was close by. They'd just walk their horses over in the morning and they'd be ready to go.

She found the shapes of three empty cabs down by the wagons. In the fog, the wagon beds resembled coffins. Again, she had her gun drawn, ready.

Night sounds. Piano music from a tavern somewhere. The rail-thrumming buzz of a distant train. Fog-muted conversation from inside the depot.

She walked up to the first wagon. Checked out the bed. Empty. Moved on to the second wagon. Also empty.

She was just moving to the third wagon when he suddenly lurched from the murk – the smell of whiskey, the rustle of his wool suit – and brought the handle of his six-shooter down on the side of her head. But she'd been turning away from him and so the impact of his blow lost most of its effectiveness.

Bailey made the mistake of trying to hit her a second time. He moved too far in and this time – despite the pain he'd inflicted – she was ready for him. He found himself facing the barrel of her Colt.

'Give me your gun.'

He hesitated. Then she put the barrel of her weapon directly against his left eye and slowly eased back the trigger.

'Your gun.'

He handed her the gun.

'The Chief wants to talk to you,' Anna said.

'For what?'

'For killing Anthea last night, and your wife Beatrice tonight.'

She couldn't see him well enough to read his expression. But when she mentioned Beatrice, an animal cry seemed to stick in his throat. 'Beatrice? Beatrice is dead?'

'You don't know anything about it, of course?'

'My God. You're talking about my wife. I would never kill her.'

She thought of Murchison saying essentially the same thing about his own wife's death. They were both apparently reading from the same bad play.

'I didn't kill her, Anna. I really didn't.'

'We'll talk to the Chief about that.'

She took his shoulder, turned him around so that he faced the depot. 'We'll walk to the depot then take the alley over to the station. Just remember I have a gun.'

'He must have done it.'

'Who?'

'Kevin. He thought she loved him. She must've changed her mind and then he killed her. He was never satisfied with just seducing them.

172

They had to fall in love with him, too.' His words were bitter yet tired, the force of them fading in the fog. 'The way he got Karen Hastings to fall in love with him. He thought that was such a conquest.'

'Who's Karen Hastings?'

'You met her yesterday. At the theatre. In Kevin's office.'

'I thought her name was Remington.'

'Oh – sorry, Hastings was the name she used at the theatre. It was her maiden name.'

'C'mon, now. Move.'

'But I didn't do anything. I really didn't.'

'You're part of an insurance fraud if nothing else.'

She nudged him with the gun.

The tracks thrummed louder now. The train was approaching. Passengers were drifting to the platform, carrying carpetbags and suitcases and even a trunk or two. This late at night, and the fog so heavy, the festive air common to the depot was gone. The passengers just wanted to get on board and be gone. A couple of Mesquakie Indians shivered inside the colourful blankets they had wrapped around themselves.

And then Anna saw the woman they'd just been talking about, Karen Remington. She was hurrying out the depot door to the platform. She wore a vast picture hat that did a good job of concealing her face, as the Russian-style greatcoat concealed her figure. Anna wouldn't have recognised her but Bailey did. 'Karen!'

The Remington woman swung her face away from Bailey and tried to hurry to the edge of the platform. Obviously, she didn't want to be seen. Bailey started to reach out for her but Karen Remington raised her hand to keep him away.

And when Anna saw the large, pale hand – and the ring with the H on the large, pale hand – she remembered the indentation on the headboard in Anthea Murchison's hotel room. A ring had put that indentation in the headboard, probably when the hand was flung against the wood as the killer was wrestling with her. A ring with the letter H on it. Karen Hastings Remington was the killer Anna was looking for.

It was dawn before Karen Remington told Anna and the Chief what had really happened. When Karen learned that Anthea was back in town, she was afraid that she would steal Kevin back. So she killed her. Then when Kevin spurned her for Beatrice, she decided to end his life in an especially nasty way – kill the woman he loved, and see to it that he was hanged for that murder.

Anna used the new typewriter to pound out a confession for Karen Remington to sign. By this time, Karen's blustery husband was in the station making all sorts of threats to the Chief and talking about the outrage of even *suspecting* a woman of such high reputation of murder.

173

He even summoned a few more of his firm's lawyers to come to the station and badger the Chief.

Anna reached home about noon. Mrs Goldman fed her warm tomato soup and a cheese sandwich. Anna took the latest Nick Carter suspense story upstairs with her. She didn't get much further than the part where Nick disguised himself as a blind Chinese wise man so he could infiltrate the Tong gangs that had been plaguing the city.

Nick would have to wait. So would everything and everybody else. She slept.

I have always been interested in the past; I took a degree in history and for a time I was what you might call a professional historian, a medieval historian, and one interested in legal history at that.

But the truth is my interest was more imaginative than academic. I liked to look at the great henges that dot the English countryside and wonder about the people who constructed them, what they used them for, and to marvel that their use lasted for a thousand years. Walking round the remains of a great Norman castle I would meditate on the life that must have been lived within it, not the life of the lord and his lady, but of the servants – the cooks, the cleaners and the laundry women.

No one can live in England without thinking about the generations, going back to Neolithic man, that cleared the trees, shaped the landscape and handed on this world to their descendants who built and rebuilt the villages and towns. The past not only made the present but sometimes bangs into it. When you walk around a city like London and read place names such as Piccadilly, and street names such as the Strand, Leathergate and Covent Garden, you know you are walking over its history. And so it is in a much newer city like Birmingham: Rope Walk, Mill Street and Raddleburn Road remind us that this was once a farm with rams to be marked before mating; they tell you what once went on there.

All this fascinated me and continues to do so, but I did not want to write fiction about the Picts, the Normans or even the Tudors. I wanted to recreate the world of the late eighteenth century because, aided by the many diaries, letters and novels of the period, I felt I could move around it with some ease, creating characters into whose lives, whose sorrows and joys I could enter.

Perhaps one day I may write a story about a stone age woman finding a dead body, and being pursued by an axe murderer . . . Who knows?

Gwendoline Butler

Bloody Windsor

Gwendoline Butler

It was the best of times, it was the worst of times.

In Paris the Tricolour flew, and the crowds sat watching Madame Guillotine receive her passing guests.

In Windsor all was normal except for a few apprentices and mechanics who held a meeting in Thames Street but were soon dispersed, one or two to the hulks and then on to Australia. The navy was offered as an alternative but few chose it and rightly so, Denny thought.

'I can't see that the death of the Queen serves any purpose,' said Major Mearns, over his *Times*, to Sergeant Denny. 'Seeing that she was helpless to hurt anyone and might have served as an hostage with the Emperor of Austria.'

'Ah,' said Denny, drawing on his pipe. 'All quiet here, though.'

'I hear of a bad tumult in Ireland.'

'Ah,' said Denny again. 'There would be. In Ireland.'

The room where the two men were breakfasting, in the deep wards of the great Castle of Windsor itself, was warm and comfortable if on the dark side. This did not worry them, they were used to darkness.

The two men were servants of the government rather than the King. They were there to protect the peace, search out criminals and cause them to be arrested. They had served together in India where they had, more by chance than plan, discovered the murderer of a high-ranking officer. Back in London, they had stumbled into a plot against the government. In consequence, they had been sent together to keep an eye on Windsor Castle, to keep an eye on the King, the court, and the Prince of Wales.

These were heady times, with revolution afoot in France, and the government trusted no one.

The court, arranged in layers like a very rich cake, had no interest in what lay at the bottom of the cake so that the King, when in his right mind, would bow when he saw the Major but distantly, not knowing that the Major, with Sergeant Denny, was stowed away in his own basement.

177

When a dead body was found hanging in the wine vaults, it was the Major and Sergeant Denny who sorted the matter out and recognised it for murder and not suicide. When an unknown woman died of a stab wound in the entrance to the silver vaults, it was the same pair who decided it was suicide and got the lady decently buried. It was never discovered who she was.

'Anyone who thinks a royal castle is an orderly place, needs to think again,' declared the Major.

He reported to Lord Charleston in the government, knowing that he was not the only source of information; his lordship had others. It is the way with governments when there is civil unrest to be feared.

Major Mearns was able to assure his lordship that the King was indeed mad in patches, and then sane again; that the Prince of Wales had married Mrs Fitzherbert but the marriage was a fake, a put up job, which the poor lady had no idea of. These stories his lordship knew already but the Major knew it was his duty to report them. Repetition made for truth.

While in Windsor, they had had the luck, or bad luck, to trap a murderer of women.

And trap was the word, thought Denny with a shudder, remembering what they had been forced to do.

While never forgetting the difference in rank between them, the two men were friends. They had fought together in the American war and then in India. Both had been wounded, both knew themselves to be survivors. They kept details about their lives private, but Sergeant Denny knew that the Major's young wife had died in childbirth, as many did, while he was in Canada, and that on the day of her death he wore a white sprig in his lapel. Denny himself had never married but one evening when the wine was red in his veins, he had told the Major that he had left a girl behind when he went abroad; she had promised to wait, but when he came back she was gone.

'Into marriage or the streets,' he had said. He was bitter; when a soldier goes to fight, he wants his woman to be there when he comes back. He could write, had written, but got no reply. He had written letters for other men, as war was hard on men who could not write. Then he had read the letters as they came back. None for him, though.

'You had plenty of women in India,' the Major had answered. 'Did myself. Splendid creatures.'

'But not to marry.'

'No, not to marry.' Although some men did, but never brought them home to England. 'It doesn't break your heart like the poets make out,' confided the Major, the wine still red in his veins and brain, 'but it cuts it in half. I have but half a heart.'

'A half is better than nothing,' said Sergeant Denny. The big dog stirred by the fire and the cat purred from the windowsill; half a heart was enough for them.

The subject never came up again, although it was not forgotten. They had but one heart between them, the Sergeant thought and his half was frozen too.

The cat stirred and stretched on the windowsill. Denny rose to join her at the window, rnnning his hand over her plump form. 'What, in kitten you wretch?'

'I won't drown them,' said the Major from his armchair. 'You must do it.'

Denny could see down the slope to the arched entrance with a view of the houses of the Poor Knights of Windsor across the way. A pretty sight. But not pretty inside, as he knew, for the old soldiers were a drunken, quarrelling lot with no taste for housekeeping.

'There goes old Tossy,' he said, seeing a short, stout caped figure making an unsteady path up the hill from the gate to where he worked for the Poor Knights.

'Old sot,' complained the Major. 'I wonder they employ him.'

'He has his uses.' Sergeant Denny grinned.

'Yes: the best informant in the city. He knows all the dirt and the dirtier it is the closer it clings to his pockets.'

Denny turned away from the window. 'He is coming over . . .' He held up his right hand, rubbing thumb and forefinger together. 'Money. Spondulick.'

Major Mearns had a rule: never pay him as much as you promise, always keep him short, so that he comes back. A hard man, the Major.

A tap on the door. Tossy was in without waiting for a word. There was steady grubbiness about his face, hands and clothes, but hot water and soap did not come his way readily. What money he had, he preferred to use on drink.

The Major stood up, rattled a few coins in his pocket.

'So, what have you got for me?'

Tossy pursed his lips as if debating what to say. The big black dog who unaccountably liked the man, came up to fawn on his boots. 'I 'ave 'eard that a grand lady of the town is about to be taken up . . .'

'Is she a whore?' demanded the Major.

'No, none of that, an important, respectable lady, who is about to be taken up for procuring young girls.'

'Very respectable, indeed,' said Denny. 'So who is this lady?'

At this Tossy had to admit he did not know. 'What I give is worth something.'

When he had gone off, muttering at the smallness of his reward, the two looked at each other.

'He knows more,' said Denny, 'and he is frightened, Tossy is frightened.' And nothing frightened Tossy except death. His own.

179

'So I suspect, but we shall get at it in the end . . . if it is worth anything. However, it cannot be of importance to us here in the castle.'

In truth, Mearns and Denny took an alert interest in anything that might worry the government. They had honed their skill in America and India and so were a valuable team.

'I don't think we need worry about the poor King . . . he lives in the past.'

'And the Prince of Wales only desires plump middle-aged ladies.'

'Of which there is no shortage willing to oblige . . . however, there is the Duc de Chancey-Melun.'

Monsieur le Duc was a refugee from the French Revolution who had had the good luck to be staying in London, having his tailor fit his coat, when the Bastille was stormed. Reading the signs accurately, he had decided to stay.

'Could he afford it, they don't come cheap these girls.' M. le Duc had no money but kind friends.

'He might be the procurer himself . . . taking his profit.'

'Both ways?'

The Major laughed. 'He is not a clever man, able to dissemble, and is certainly in debt, but I have never heard of him knowing a notable lady in Windsor, nor of having a liking for young girls . . . his tastes run quite the other way.'

'A pity,' regretted Denny. 'I would like to have got him; I saw him kick a dog the other day.'

'Then we must certainly see he is punished for something,' said the Major, running his hand over the black cat's thick coat. 'I daresay we might manage it between us.'

He got up. 'We must go out into the town and see what we can grub up.'

Major Mearns shrugged himself into a greatcoat while the Sergeant put a muffler round his neck twice, the ends hanging. When they were alone, the rank difference was pretty well ignored, they were working partners, but in the world outside they marked the social barrier with different clothes.

They passed down the long corridor on whose walls hung some of the less choice pictures of the Royal collection. One was a female saint with her head in her arms.

'I never fancy that one,' grumbled Sergeant Denny. 'I can't abide a head on the loose. Seen too many in India.'

'They have here the shirt King Charles the First was wearing when his head was cut off. Clean as a whistle, not a blood stain on it.'

'Washed, I suppose.'

'Or fake,' said the Major sceptically. He believed in very little.

Slowly the two men, well-known in the town, walked down the

180

Castle Hill towards the Marlborough Arms, one of the most popular if rowdiest drinking places in Windsor. If you wanted gossip, information, you supped your ale in the Marly . . . for as such it was known.

The Major stopped suddenly. 'Denny,' he said. 'Do you know you have blood on your sleeve?'

Denny drew his left sleeve up. 'By God, sir, so I have.' There was a long thin streak of red on the sleeve of his coat. He touched it; his finger came away with blood on it. 'Still wet. I must have rubbed against something.'

'And not long ago,' said the Major. 'I like a bit of blood,' he added thoughtfully. 'You know where you are with blood.'

They looked at each other.

'Was Tossy bleeding?'

'I did not see him bleed.' Denny pursed his lips. 'That's not to say he wasn't. He was worried about something. More than he told us.'

'I'll have it out of him,' said the Major with decision. He half turned back. 'He will still be with the old soldiers, all as drunk as each other. Where does he drink in the town?' They both knew that Tossy had been drinking.

'Mostly in the Marlborough.'

'They will likely know what he has been up to. Blood, indeed. His own or someone else's?'

The town was busy in its usual quiet way: a donkey pulling a cart with a boy in charge was bearing down on Mr Turvey, owner of the tailor's shop on the corner of Peascod Street, while a smart phaeton was whipped along by a dapper young man, splashing through a puddle and causing the lad with the donkey to shake a fist.

'That's how revolutions start,' said Denny, still cross.

At the bottom of the hill they could see a slender form leading a procession of twelve young ladies across the road. At their tail came a more imposing form, well bonneted and poking at the pavement with her parasol.

It looked like a poke, the Sergeant decided, as if she was put out, annoyed, even angry.

A stout man was hurrying up the hill as if he had just been speaking to her.

'And there is John Armour coming our way,' said Major Mearns.

Mr Armour was a lawyer who lived in the town and managed the affairs of the most prosperous of the citizens from his handsome Queen Anne house where he both dwelt and kept his office. A plump, cheerful man with white hair and rumpled clothes, he looked more harmless than he was. Now he came rushing towards them.

'Major, Major Mearns, sir, I am glad to to see you. How do you do, how do you do.' He addressed himself to the Major, ignoring Sergeant Denny, but he was one of the few who grasped that Denny was as powerful in the world of keeping the King's Peace as the Major. Possibly more so, since he could gather information in circles closed to the Major. A pot boy or the kitchen cleaning wench would not talk to Major Mearns, a gentleman (which he was not and knew he was not), but they could to Sergeant Denny.

'I was about to call on you, Major.' He did include Sergeant Denny at this point with a swift glance his way, knowing as he did that to consult Mearns was to consult Denny also. 'You are one who knows how to go about finding out where the truth lies. You ask questions and get answers. You investigate, sir.' His eyes did not miss the smear of blood on Denny's jacket sleeve, but he said nothing.

'Yes, sir,' replied Major Mearns in a judicial way. 'I have an investigatory capacity. Learnt in the army, sir.'

'Of course.'

'And honed in civic life.'

Now what's he up to, Denny thought, he's not usually so pompous.

'We must talk, Major.' He looked around him at the street where a carriage was passing and where a mother with a child spinning a hoop was passing by, and an urchin was kicking something round which might have been a ball or a dead cat or a cabbage in the gutter. 'But not here . . .'

'Let's go to the Marly?'

Mr Armour said doubtfully, 'It is not the sort of place that I usually go to.'

The Major ignored this plea. He put his arm firmly round Mr Armour's shoulders. 'Then now is the time to start.'

The Marlborough was crowded as usual.

'My friend and valued client Mrs Breakspere, a remote descendant of the famous Archbishop . . .' began the lawyer.

Mearns nodded politely although he had never heard of the said Nicholas Breakspere.

'A lady of dignity.'

She must be fat, thought Denny with some cynicism.

'She is the proprietor of the school for young ladies; some six couples follow her to church, St Leonard's in Grancy Road, where I go myself when not at the Chapel Royal in the Castle . . .' went on Mr Armour.

Wordy as usual, noted Denny silently, and every word on his bill. Mrs Breakspere must pay her bills since he speaks so well of her. Wonder how she pays? He is a bit of an old lecher.

'On this exemplary lady has fallen the most terrible accusation.'

Here we go, thought Denny, preparing to look surprised.

'She has been accused of—' the lawyer hesitated, seeking words chaste enough to suit the lady's virtue. '—Of procuring young girls for the stews of London,' he finished in a rush, abandoning all restraint of language.

He had gone quite pink as though even the very words excited him.

'Who accuses her?' asked the Major coolly.

'The father of one of her pupils.'

'Ah.'

'A culumny, a foul culumny.' He leaned forward almost knocking over the glass of gin and water with which the Major had provided him. 'She wishes to engage you in investigating the lie.'

He did not mention the word payment but he knew that the Major would expect to be paid. Never mind how, maybe in information when needed or a patronage when desired, but there would be payment.

And I shall expect my whack, decided Denny.

'So we go when it is dark, invisible to the young ladies.' The Major was contemptuous as they marched back to the Castle. Once inside, walking towards the picture of the decapitated saint, the Major said: 'Denny, do you see any blood? Look around for blood.'

No blood.

They had left Mr Armour still in the Marlborough. 'He's a bit of a bum boy, isn't he?' Denny had said idly as they left him behind.

A bleeding saint on the wall, but otherwise no blood.

'Wait.' Denny had caught sight of something on one of the paler of the stone flags which made up the floor. It was the faint shape of a bloody footmark.

'Find and fetch Tossy,' was the Major's order. 'Don't forget the bath house.'

'Tossy does not bath much.'

'Other things go on there, as you know,' said Mearns sharply.

The bath house was a long-established institution in Windsor, if not much talked about in polite circles. Some said it went back to Queen Anne. The bath house had baths, hot water and benches for sitting out. It also had more private rooms for those who wished to rest after the hot bath. Those who did so were rarely alone, and it was thought that they met by arrangement with the ladies of their choice who made their entrance through a small side door. The bath house was run at present by a middle-aged couple, Mr and Mrs Jones. He was an old soldier but many thought she was the stoutest soldier of the two. Sergeant Denny, not a patron of the baths, approached her with caution.

She emerged from stoking the furnace, red-faced and damp as she always seemed to be from the steam of the baths, to say that she had not seen Tossy, and he should've been here feeding the furnace, a job for which she paid him, and if he did show his face she would give him he knew what. One stout red arm suggested she knew what too.

On an impulse, Denny turned back. 'Do you know Mrs Breakspere?'

Sarah Jones did not answer, her eyes wary. 'She don't visit here.'

'Never thought she did. But you know her?'

'Know her looks, never had speech, Sergeant.'

'You know who I am?'

'Everyone knows you and knows the Major.'

'Do you find enough young, really young, women to please your customers? Supply running short, is it?'

'Not everyone fancies a slice of chicken.'

'A true word,' and as Denny walked away he remembered that word had it that she obliged herself when asked.

The lodgings of the Poor Knights of Windsor did not harbour Tossy, nor did the Marlborough Arms, Ma Bradley's Chop House, and the Watermen's ale house down by the river knew him not. He lodged with many others in a large, run-down house with no drains, run by a small dark woman who called herself Mrs Dodge, and was known as the Artful Dodger.

Nowhere was Tossy to be found, so Denny returned to the Castle to report no success.

'I don't care for this disappearing,' said the Major, with a frown. 'He was frightened and he had blood on him.'

Several other matters came up in the day, such as the disappearance of a dozen bottles of the best claret from the royal cellars, and the appearance on the wall of the kitchen of a drawing of a tricolour and the words: REVOLUTION NOW.

The latter was found to be the work of a drunken scullion who may have been at the claret, although it was suspected he had sold the wine. He was dismissed from the royal service and given the choice between the navy and the army. He chose the navy.

By evening, they were ready to visit Mrs Breakspere. The night was dark and heavy with a light rain falling.

The Academy for Young Gentlewomen was housed in a sprawling red brick building hidden behind trees and shrubberies. A heavy iron gate leading to a winding drive protected the young ladies from rude gazes from the road.

The two men pushed through the gate which Sergeant Denny then closed after them. It needed a good shove, and he stepped back a pace to get more force.

His foot hit something which rolled away.

Major Mearns turned back. 'What's that, a ball? Young ladies shouldn't play with balls. It don't do their figger any good.'

Denny bent down to look. But he already knew, his feet had told him what had felt that way before. On the battlefield.

'No, sir. A head.'

There was silence for a moment. 'Are you sure?'

'Yes, sure.'

Another pause.

'Is it Tossy?'

'No, sir, it is not Tossy.'

The bloodied head was of a younger man, with a crop of fair hair.

Major Mearns swore under his breath as he made his way to the bushes to look for himself. The head stared up at him, cheeks covered in blood and mud.

'And where is the body?'

There was no body.

The Major did what he would have done in the middle of a battle; he moved the head further into the bushes and nodded towards the house.

'Deal with this later, Sergeant. It'll need the Coroner, the Town Officer and the Magistrate. So we will see Mrs Breakspere first.'

'Think she knows anything about it?' asked Denny, stumbling after him. He was out of breath. In spite of the training of war, death for him was still death. He could not accommodate its presence in the garden of an academy for young ladies in the way the Major seemed able to do. Officers are different, he told himself, although he knew that Major Mearns was an officer like no other.

The door was opened at their approach by an elderly manservant, as if they had been watched for. He was wobbly on his feet, frail-looking and nearly blind. A poor protector of this household of women. But also too old and and weak to do anything to the young ladies even if he wanted to.

Don't you believe it, Denny told himself; age and weakness are not a bar if you want it enough.

Mr Musket, for that was his name, was being hailed from the stairs by a tall and handsome young woman, and behind her a chain of the young pupils. They were to get a sight of the inmates and be seen by them after all.

The teacher in charge led her pupils round the corner without a glance at the two men, but the young ladies took them in with discreet glances.

Born to it, he thought, the young devils. One especially, with big blue eyes and a tiny waist almost gave the Sergeant a smile.

Almost but not quite. There was something familiar about her.

He dismissed the thought; there was a feeling about this place that gave you such ideas. But the Major's face looked cold and angry, reminding Denny what a strong, hard man he was underneath his cheerful, drinking-companion friendliness.

'The handsome young woman, who is not so young as she looks, is Miss Tong, and she is a wonderful storyteller to the young ladies with a great turn of phrase. She is leaving to live in Chatham with her married sister, a Mrs Dickens.'

185

'You know her?'

'While you were out looking for Tossy I employed my contacts. I can tell you that Mrs Breakspere is a widow, or calls herself so, who came to Windsor to set up her school with a small inheritance.'

She has done well with it, thought Denny, looking around him. The hall and staircase were carpeted with bright Indian rugs, the brass and mahogany on the banisters were well polished. It all said prosperity.

Down the stairs, treading with a dignity that became her status, came Mrs Breakspere. There was no mistaking her. She was dressed in heavy green silk, well cut and nicely trim. Sergeant Denny stared at her as if he could see through the solid flesh and out the other side. 'That's a strong woman,' murmured the Major into the Sergeant's ear. 'Look at the shoulders on her. We could have done with her in the regiment.'

Denny did not answer, but he was thinking that there was a pretty face embedded in all that flesh.

Mrs Breakspere held out her hand and the Major bowed over it. 'Ma'am,' And then as he was rising from the bow, 'A wicked business.'

'You know all?'

Another bow. 'Mr Armour.'

Mrs Breakspere gave a great sigh. 'An adviser and friend. He told me that he would speak to you. I thank you for coming. Of course, you understand that there is no truth in this slander?'

'Never believed it for a minute, ma'am, but we must get to the bottom of it and put an end to it. Who tells this story?'

With another sigh, Mrs Breakspere admitted that it was the father of a pupil. She began to shake a little as she told her story. How the man had come to her, told her that he had learnt what was taking place, he had not shouted at her, no, she could have supported that better, but he had been cold and clear. He would see her school was closed.

'Calm, dear madam. Tell me his name and where he resides. A Windsor man? So, easy to find. And with Sergeant Denny I will talk to him.'

'He lives in Egham, sir, a small town on the river.'

'I know it.'

She added: 'Mr Vavasour.'

'An aristocratic name.' He kept his eyes on her, so Denny noticed.

She hesitated before agreeing that, yes, it was indeed an aristocratic name. She had led them into her own room from where she ran the school. There was a large, handsome desk from which she drew a sheet of writing paper on which she wrote an address.

'A good-looking man, is he?' asked Major Mearns, pocketing the sheet. 'Oldish, I suppose.'

'No, young, very pleasant to see, with fair hair and bright blue eyes.'

The Major took this in, giving Denny a quick glance. 'I may have

186

seen him, madam. And like his daughter? Eye colour does run in families.'

Mrs Breakspere agreed that the girl was a pretty girl with blue eyes. She seemed to reserve opinion on the family resemblance.

'I must ask if we can move around the school, ma'am.'

Surprised, Mrs Breakspere said she would ring for the butler.

'Better not. Let me make my way alone. Best on my own.'

Outside the door, he paused, then laid his hand on the door knob.

'Back in?' asked Denny, surprised.

'Advice to you: let the ladies think they have got away with something, then go back in and give them a shock.'

Denny, who thought he knew a bit about shocks himself, followed him in.

Mrs Breakspere was sitting at her desk; she jerked her head towards them as they came in.

'Just a question, ma'am. Mr Vavasour . . . he is not the girl's father.' It was not a question, after all, but a statement.

He waited. And waited.

Slowly, Mrs Breakspere rose. 'No,' she said. 'He is . . .' she hesitated. 'He is her guardian; he is educating her to be his wife.'

'And this he told you?'

'I guessed. I have met the arrangement before.' She raised her head high. 'In fact, my own marriage was arranged so.'

Ah, was it, thought Sergeant Denny.

'I so much desired an education. It was a passion with me.'

'And you think this is why he told the story about procuring the girls for the stews of London? A punishment, to keep you quiet?'

She flinched at the words, then nodded, her face white.

Mrs Breakspere seemed about to ask her own questions of the Major but he spoke first.

'Keep your young ladies close in the house, that's my advice. And stay there yourself.'

Before she could speak, he had the two of them out of the door, and led the way down the stairs. 'You think she spoke the truth?'

Denny considered. 'Some of it,' he said with caution.

Major Mearns nodded. 'You are learning, lad.' He continued down the stairs. 'To the servants. Always learn more there.'

In the hall they met Musket, who made a feeble attempt to direct them out. 'Stay where you are, Musket,' commanded the Major, although the butler showed no sign of even thinking of leaving the house. 'Orders.'

A feeble bleat followed them down the winding staircase where carpet gave place to bare stone. At the bottom of the stair three doors stood wide open. One door led to the kitchen, a second to a pantry and the third to a washhouse. All three were filled with active young women, working and shouting. Over all presided a woman of size who dwarfed

187

even Mrs Breakspere; where she was large, this woman was huge, with muscles standing out on her bare arms. She was beating a mixture in a large bowl with hard, directed energy. Her complexion was red and sweaty, her eyes cold and blue.

Give her a whip and she would make a fine slave driver. No, thought Denny, observing the kitchen girls at work, she *is* a slave driver, fully formed and in good working order.

Now how is the guvnor going to introduce himself, Denny wondered. And the answer was easy: he did not. Just sailed on as if he was an expected visitor.

Perhaps he was.

'Plenty of help, I see.'

'It's my job to train the gals and send them out into the world,' said Mrs Badgett stiffly. 'I am the housekeeper as well as the cook.'

'And do they stay long with you?'

There was a pause. 'Girls always move on, it's their nature.'

'So it is, so it is.' He was most genial. 'Still, it's a nuisance for you, always training new girls.'

'I should be obleeged if you would leave my kitchen, sir, we are busy.'

Outside, Mearns turned to Denny. 'You guess where we are? She is the organiser and those poor frightened girls are the ones she transports . . .'

'To where?' But Denny was already guessing. 'How do you know?'

'Who sent you to the bath house? I always know more about this town than you may guess.'

There was a narrow window high on the wall and rain was beating against it. Denny thought of the bloody head with the curly hair on which the rain was now falling. Was rain merciful and cleansing?

At the door, they found the pretty young girl with big blue eyes, cape drawn down over her head, about to open it. Musket was nowhere to be seen. No doubt always bribeable.

Mearns put his hand on her arm. 'Young lady, you must not go out.'

'I am only going to meet my father, sir.'

'Your father? Come, I know better than that.'

She drew in a deep breath.

'What is your name?'

'Nell.'

'And he is not your father, Nell.'

There was something in Major Mearn's demeanour that made her hang her head. 'No, sir.'

'And so?'

'John wants me for his wife . . . I was to learn here how to be a

188

lady . . . I am a quick learner, sir. I have performed. On the City Theatre in Bow. That was where Mr Vavasour saw me.' Her voice was proud.

'How old are you, Nell?'

'Thirteen, sir. I think thirteen.'

Mearns looked at her sadly. 'Who is your friend in this place?'

'Alice Ellis, sir. And then Miss Tong.'

'Go to Miss Tong, Nell.' He looked at the Sergeant. 'Denny, set Miss Nell on her way.'

Denny led Nell to the stairs and watched her walk up, her eyes always looking backward. Too easy, too malleable, too lost, he thought.

He followed the Major silently down the path.

'I am glad to be out of that house,' said the Major. 'That woman would have killed us if she could.'

'To the bath house, is it?' asked Denny. 'Won't we be in danger there?'

'The two large women are sisters, Badgett and Jones, you saw the likeness?'

Denny nodded. It seemed to him that he had been seeing a likeness of one sort or another ever since they entered the school.

'Yes, we shall be in danger but we shall be on our guard,' and the Major drew a pistol from his pocket.

Denny was thinking about the head which must be still lying there, waiting to be rejoined to its body. He started as a figure crept out of the bushes. 'Tossy! What are you doing here?'

'Followed us, I daresay,' said Mearn.

'I was waiting . . . I knew you would get here, sir.' He was carefully standing well away from the head of John Vavasour.

Mearns dragged him by the shoulder and turned him to see the dead face. 'How did that get here? Tell me all you know or by God you will go to the gallows yourself. There was blood on you, Tossy, and you will tell me how you came by it.' He gave Tossy a shake to add force to his words.

Trembling, Tossy admitted that he had been at the bath house when John Vavasour had come there to lay his accusation against the sisters: that girls were brought into Mrs Breakspere's school to work, then sold on to the bath house.

'He shouted out that he had thought Mrs Breakspere guilty, but now he blamed but the sisters. He shouted so loud that Mrs Jones knocked him to the ground with a single blow . . .'

'And who cut his head off?'

'Jones, sir. I was there watching through a crack in the door. He did it with an axe and the blood spurted everywhere, some came my way, they are washing it still I will say.'

'And the head?'

189

'Jones carried it up here, meaning to bear witness against Mrs Breakspere. I followed and watched. They hate her, sir, say she is a strict, mean mistress.'

'Not strict enough,' said the Major, letting him go. 'Bend over.'

With fear, Tossy did so. Denny waited for the execution. But the Major tore a page from his notebook and wrote on it with a black crayon.

'Here, take this note to the Magistrate, Mr Jennings, and tell him to come down to the bath house with two constable and a cart,' he ordered Tossy. 'And you and I Denny will be off to the bath house to start the arrest.'

'What about the head?'

'It will not walk away,' said the Major, beginning to march. 'To the bath house, Denny.

The bath house was a long, low building with a single flambeau burning over the door. Dim lights could be seen as the two men approached and there was a smell of steam.

'Business as usual,' said the Major.

They looked at each other. The door would have opened at their knock, but the two men were seasoned campaigners and knew you did not approach the enemy at his strongest point.

'Round the back,' murmured Denny.

A cobbled yard lay behind the bath house, where the flicker of flames from the furnace which heated the water could be seen from a small window. In one corner of the yard was a wagonette with no horse, and in the protection of a roofed shed stood a hand cart.

Denny walked over to the hand cart to take a look at the bundle resting within. He raised the sacking and looked, then shook his head and walked back to Major Mearns.

'The body is there, and an axe . . . it will be buried or else burnt.'

'It would burn,' commented Mearns, 'if jointed, and smell no worse than the Jones's usual supper when cooked.'

The faint hint of cannibalism sickened Denny who turned away. 'God help us,' he thought, 'we must prevent this.' He thought the Joneses, husband and wife, capable of anything. 'Let us break in, and not wait for the constables and the Magistrate.'

Mearns nodded and drew out his pistol.

But before they could move, the back door opened and Jones and his wife stood there. She carried a great dish and a jug and he held a cleaver.

'A fine dish,' said Jones. 'If nicely boiled.'

'It will do for the guests and the gals, jugged with the blood, and an onion or two,' replied his wife. 'But I shan't touch it myself. Get on with it now.'

The Major advanced towards them, his manner easy but his pistol in his hand.

'Well, Jones, so this is what you do with your friends; kill them and cook them for dinner?'

Mrs Jones, brave and huge, raised her great arms and moved towards him.

'Yes, Mrs Jones,' said Mearns, 'and will your sister, Mrs Badgett, help with the cooking?'

Denny moved up behind the Major in support, but the stamp of the constables' feet announcing the arrival of the Magistrate made her draw back, while her husband turned and ran into the house

'It might have been a near run thing if she had made a fight of it,' said the Major later. 'I swear she is stronger than me.' He turned to Denny. 'You caught the husband, but she's the worst of the two.'

'He's bad enough.' Denny was terse. 'I found him trying to escape from the hatch that lets the coal in, and gave him a blow that made him squeal.'

In a basement of the bath house, next to the coal cellars, was a locked room. Denny had dragged Jones to the door, and forced him to open it.

Inside, he saw a huddled group of young girls.

'And who are these?' he demanded of Jones. 'What do you mean to do with them?' He gave Jones another blow to help him answer.

Wincing, Jones gasped, 'The plain ones we keep to work Windsor and the pretty ones who will fetch a better price we take to London to be used there.'

'They will hang together, side by side,' said the Major with satisfaction.

As the two men walked back to the Castle along an unlit road in the rain, Denny said: 'And what will happen to all the young critters that have been caught up in this, the girls in the kitchen at the school, the ones already down at the bath house, the plain ones and the pretty ones all ready to be sold on?' Tossy too for that matter, but he knew Tossy would survive.

The Major marched on. 'I don't know. We can't know the end of every story.'

Denny was silent. After a minute, he said, 'I know the end of one story now. You remember my girl that I left behind when I went to fight? I saw her again this evening. I believe she recognised me too.'

Major Mearns stopped short. 'Not the lovely Miss Tong?'

'No, the other one. Mrs Breakspere.'

For moment, all was silence as they walked on, then the Major started to laugh. 'You are a lucky fellow indeed. It is all over.'

191

* * *

Not so. Events seed themselves if they fall on fertile ground and eventually bear fruit. Thus it was with the meeting between Miss Tong, aunt to Charles Dickens, and little Nell.

W hat is the distance from twelfth-century England to Tokugawa Period Japan? Not so far across space and time, as I know because I've travelled that road.

The first historical mystery novel I ever read was *A Morbid Taste of Bones*, from Ellis Peters' Brother Cadfael series. I read it at a time when I was working as a scientist, before I had any notion of becoming a writer. I was fascinated by the setting (so rich in atmosphere and so different from the modern environments of most mystery fiction), the detective hero (a monk with a different code of behaviour from a police detective or private eye, but with the same desire for truth and justice), and the whole idea of transporting a classic genre to a past that seemed fresher than the present because the physical, social, and spiritual parameters of life there were unfamiliar.

Some fifteen years passed before I began writing my own mystery series, but Ellis Peters' work made a lasting impression on me, and I reached back in time to create a detective in a rich historical setting where arcane rules applied. I write about seventeenth-century Japan instead of a medieval England, but I like to think of my samurai detective as a distant cousin of Brother Cadfael. For me, Ellis Peters opened a gate into the past. I wonder how many other mystery authors have passed through that same gate, following many other paths to destinations varied and wonderful.

Laura Joh Rowland

The Iron Fan

Laura Joh Rowland

Edo, Genroku Period, Year 2, Month 5 (Tokyo, June 1689)

'**S**ano-*san*, I have a new, ahh, assignment for you,' the shogun said. Dressed in brocade robes and the black cap of his rank as Japan's supreme military dictator, he sat on the dais in the audience chamber of Edo Castle. 'You must prevent a murder. The intended victim is the, ahh, Honourable Left Magistrate Okido, with whom I believe you are acquainted?'

'Yes, Your Excellency.' Sano, the shogun's Most Honorable Investigator of Events, Situations, and People, knelt before the dais. He exchanged bows with the man seated beside him.

Magistrate Okido was one of two officials responsible for maintaining law and order in Edo. A dignified man in his early fifties, he supervised the police force, conducted trials, and settled disputes. His head seemed too large for his slight body; the bold intelligence in his eyes offset a weak chin. Sano knew and respected Okido's reputation for integrity.

'Recently I presided over the trial of the leader of a crime gang,' Okido said. 'I condemned him to death for murdering a shopkeeper who resisted the gang's extortion attempts. Now his brother – a hoodlum named Kajiro – has sworn revenge upon me. He's a dangerous fighter whose favourite weapon is the war fan.'

Because the law restricted the use of swords to the samurai class, commoners relied upon other weapons. The war fan, made of paper and bamboo, resembled an ordinary folding fan, except for its heavy iron outer ribs. These could be used to parry sword cuts, injure, or kill.

'My wife is ill, and I'm taking her on a pilgrimage to Ise Shrine, in hope of a cure,' Magistrate Okido informed Sano. 'We leave tomorrow. I fear that Kajiro will follow and attack me along the way. Therefore, I have asked His Excellency to lend me your service as a bodyguard.'

'Accompany Magistrate Okido on the pilgrimage,' the shogun ordered Sano. 'Guard his life, and, ahh, capture Kajiro.'

★　　★　　★

The highway meandered through fields and villages, across rivers and over hills. Clear, warm weather graced the first morning of the fifteen-day journey to Ise. Mounted on a bay stallion, Sano rode at the head of a procession which included Magistrate Okido, his son, chief retainer, and ten guards, all on horseback, and the magistrate's wife and concubine in palanquins. Attendants lugged baggage. Sano's chief retainer Hirata followed with their own troops and servants.

The procession entered a forest. Sunlight filtered through pine boughs, birds twittered, the pungent scent of resin laced the air. However, Sano paid little attention to nature's beauty. This was a perfect spot for an ambush, and he remained alert for signs of the hoodlum Kajiro. He also had a disturbing sense of something wrong.

Behind Sano, a heated argument raged. 'I'm sick of your complaints about your boredom,' Magistrate Okido said angrily.

'Well, you shouldn't have forced me to come,' retorted his son, Monzaemon.

Sano glanced backward at the pair riding together. Monzaemon, aged twenty-five, was tall and husky, clad in a gaudy kimono. With his bold features, he might have been handsome, if not for his surly expression.

'This trip is necessary for your mother's health,' Magistrate Okido said, 'and I want my family to be together.'

'She's my stepmother.' Antipathy edged Monzaemon's words. 'And I wish I were back in Edo.'

Okido gave a harsh laugh. 'What for? To drink and gamble, or dally with prostitutes? I'm tired of financing your amusements while you're too stupid and lazy to do the simplest work.'

'Serving as your errand-boy is beneath my dignity,' Monzaemon flared. 'Especially since your fortune and position will be mine some-day.'

'Not until I die,' the magistrate said grimly.

Why, Sano wondered, was his own presence necessary, when Magistrate Okido had brought enough men to thwart any assassin, and seemed less concerned about the threat of an attack than occupied by strife within his own party?

The procession reached a clearing in the forest. 'My Lord,' called a woman's voice. 'Can we stop and eat now?'

Sano turned and saw the magistrate's concubine Chiyoko peering out the window of her palanquin.

'Of course, my dear.' Dismounting, Okido ordered the procession to halt.

Alarmed, Sano said, 'I advise against it. You're too vulnerable to attack here.'

The magistrate's chief retainer Araki joined them. In his mid-forties, he was a classic samurai: tough, stoic, an expert swordsman, and fiercely devoted to his master. 'I agree,' Araki said. 'Even if Kajiro doesn't attack, bandits may. We should continue on to the next village.'

Chiyoko climbed out of her palanquin, flounced over to Magistrate Okido, and pouted. 'But I want to stop now.'

She was a voluptuous beauty, half the magistrate's age, dressed in a pink silk kimono. Lustrous black hair flowed over her shoulders; her face was made up with white powder and crimson rouge. She batted almond-shaped eyes at Okido.

He smiled fondly at her, then told Araki and Sano, 'We won't stay long.'

Chiyoko flashed a triumphant glance at Araki, who frowned. Sano guessed that the two often clashed, and Araki resented losing disputes to his master's concubine.

Servants laid out a picnic. Sano called to his retainer Hirata, a young samurai of earnest manner and boyish looks. 'Position our troops around the magistrate's party, then scout the area.'

Hirata went off to obey, while Sano stood guard near Magistrate Okido. Chiyoko sat in the place of honour at his right. Toward them came two attendants, carrying the magistrate's invalid wife. She was small and delicate, wrapped in a quilt.

'You're in my place,' Madam Okido said to Chiyoko. 'Move!'

The concubine turned to Magistrate Okido. 'Do I have to?'

Magistrate Okido patted Chiyoko's arm. 'Stay where you are. Honourable Wife, you may sit on my other side.'

The attendants settled Madam Okido in this less desirable location. It was common knowledge that the magistrate had taken Chiyoko, the daughter of a respected samurai family, as a concubine last year, after his second wife developed severe muscle weakness, pains and tremors. Now Madam Okido's sunken eyes burned with hatred as her attendants fed her. Despite the ravages of sickness and middle-age, her pale, elegant face was still lovely. Sano pitied the woman. How humiliating to be cast aside in favour of a younger, healthier rival!

Hirata returned. 'No sign of Kajiro or any other problem.'

While everyone ate, Sano noticed Chiyoko's flirtatious gaze lingering on Monzaemon, who sat apart from the others. She made silly remarks in a voice loud enough to reach him. Gulping *sake*, Monzaemon watched her and his father, his expression stormy. The attendants opened a medicine chest and mixed potions to ease Madam Okido's pains. Araki glowered. At last, the group prepared to depart. Magistrate Okido helped Chiyoko into her palanquin. Servants shouldered their loads and guards mounted horses, while Monzaemon crouched beside Madam Okido for a brief, tense conversation.

Hirata said to Sano, 'For a man who fears for his life, the magistrate seems unconcerned about security. If he won't follow your advice, why did he ask you to come?'

'I wish I knew. Unfortunately, it's not our place to question the shogun's orders.'

Even more unfortunately, Sano sensed that what he didn't know might affect his ability to protect Magistrate Okido. If he failed, he could lose not only the life of his charge, but also the shogun's favour, his post, and his honour.

The sky was awash in fiery sunset by the time the procession reached the village of Totsuka. Teahouses, restaurants and inns lined the main street. The travellers found lodgings in a quaint inn secluded within bamboo fences. A servant boy showed them to their rooms.

'You have separate quarters all to yourselves,' he said, stopping outside one of three low buildings with thatched roofs and barred windows.

Sano approved of the accommodation. He and his men could easily guard the doors and patrol the grounds. If Kajiro came, he wouldn't get near Magistrate Okido. Entering the front of the building, Sano found five spacious interconnecting rooms along a corridor, each furnished with *tatami* mats, a table, lamp, and a large, built-in cabinet for bedding. The rear of the building contained smaller compartments.

Magistrate Okido took the centre room at the front. His wife appropriated the room on his right, and Araki the one on the left. That left the two end rooms for Chiyoko and Monzaemon, with Sano, Hirata, and the entourage sharing the rear compartments.

Monzaemon, flushed from liquor consumed during the trip, muttered, 'Excuse me,' and departed.

Chiyoko whined to the magistrate, 'I want a room beside yours.'

'Don't fret,' Okido said. 'You shall spend the night with me.'

The servant boy fetched the guests' baggage, chattering constantly: 'The privies and bath house are over there. Dinner will be served soon. Would you like a guided tour of the village later?' He was about twelve years old, thin and agile, with knobby knees, sharp eyes and a wide grin. 'If you need me, please call. My name is Tadeo.' He hovered around until Araki tipped him a few coins.

Before the party settled in for the night, Sano inspected the building. All was secure, with everyone in their rooms except Monzaemon, who hadn't returned. Then Sano rested while Hirata supervised an uneventful first watch. An hour before midnight Sano took up his post on the veranda outside the door. He watched the full silver moon shine upon the garden and his patrolling troops. Music drifted from the street. The night was warm and peaceful. Araki came out, greeted Sano, and headed toward the privy. Then the servant boy Tadeo joined Sano.

'What are you doing?' Tadeo asked curiously.

'Guarding the magistrate,' Sano answered.

'Why?'

198

'Because he's an important man with dangerous enemies. Why are you up so late?'

'Oh, I work as long as there are guests awake who might want my services, and chances to make extra money. Since my father died, I help support my mother.'

Just then, the inn's proprietor called, 'Tadeo! Stop bothering the guests. Go home!'

'Yes, master,' Tadeo answered. He bowed to Sano and ran off.

Time passed. Then the bell at a nearby temple heralded midnight with several deep, loud peals. Above its last echoes, a shout arose from the darkness beyond the garden: 'Halt!'

Excitement propelled Sano off the veranda. Ordering a patrol guard to take over his post, he ran between buildings and into a courtyard. There he found three of his troops, their swords drawn, surrounding a stocky man who clutched a slender object as long as his forearm: a folded war fan. The moonlight illuminated his startled face.

'Kajiro, drop the fan,' Sano ordered. 'Surrender.'

Suddenly Araki ran into the courtyard, brandishing his sword and yelling, 'You tried to kill my master. You'll die for this!'

'No!' Too many of Sano's investigations ended in violent death. 'Capture him alive!'

Araki charged and slashed at Kajiro. Kajiro dodged. Whirling, he clubbed Araki's shoulder with his iron fan. Araki went reeling into a wall. Then Kajiro attacked Sano's troops. The fan battered their waving blades, thudded against flesh. Cries pierced the night. Around the inn, lamps lit windows as people hurried to see the excitement. Sano drew his sword, lunged, and sliced at Kajiro's legs, but the man leapt away, swung the fan around, and dealt Sano's arm a painful glancing blow. Kajiro fought with skill and desperation, but he couldn't defeat four swordsmen. Blades cut him. When Sano's sword gashed his thigh, he dropped his fan and fell to the ground, clutching the bloody wound.

'Kill him!' Araki yelled.

'That's not necessary. He can't hurt anyone now.' Sheathing his sword, Sano picked up the heavy iron fan. Carved dragons decorated the outer ribs. He opened it, examining the inner bamboo blades and the red sun painted on the arc of pleated gold paper. It was a fine, expensive weapon. Sano refolded the fan and inspected Kajiro. 'His injury isn't mortal. We'll take him back to Edo to be tried for attempted murder.'

'What?' Kajiro stared in shock. He was in his twenties, with crude tattoos on his arms and legs. Sweat drenched his short hair and beaded a face toughened by old knife scars. 'But I didn't— you can't—'

Sano and his men hauled the struggling, incoherent Kajiro to the

199

magistrate's quarters, where Hirata stood outside with Okido's attendants. The door opened, and Magistrate Okido stumbled onto the veranda, crying, 'Help! Help!'

Perplexed, Sano said, 'You're safe now. See – we've captured Kajiro.'

The magistrate knelt and wept. 'Chiyoko is dead. She's been murdered!'

In the light of lanterns in Magistrate Okido's room, Sano and Hirata crouched beside Chiyoko. She lay on her back upon the futon; a quilt covered her body. From the neck up she was an ugly ruin of shattered bone and bloody tissue. The killer had bludgeoned her face. Sano touched Chiyoko's neck. She was still warm, the blood still liquid.

Hirata pointed to a pattern of small indentations on Chiyoko's forehead. 'What's this?'

With a sense of foreboding, Sano held Kajiro's iron fan beside the corpse. The pattern matched the carved scales of the dragon on the outer ribs, which had blood between them. Looking up, Sano saw his own surprise reflected in Hirata's eyes.

'Kajiro couldn't have done it,' Hirata said. 'You caught him before he got here.'

From the doorway, Araki said, 'Obviously, Kajiro evaded your defence and entered through the skylight. In the darkness, he must have mistaken Chiyoko for the magistrate. He killed her, and you caught him as he was leaving.'

'That's impossible.' Sano faced Araki's accusing stare. 'No one could have got past us.'

Yet a shard of doubt pierced Sano. Had his men relaxed their guard? Could he have failed to notice Kajiro sneaking into the building? The weapon in his hand said yes.

'You've captured the enemy,' Araki said, 'but not soon enough to prevent murder.'

It was a terrible blow to Sano's samurai honour. That he'd let a murder occur on his watch would destroy his professional reputation. He could lose the shogun's favour and his position.

The village authorities had come to take a report of the incident; they'd removed the corpse to the mortuary and Kajiro to jail. Magistrate Okido had moved to his wife's room. Everyone else had gone to bed. Now Sano and Hirata sat alone in the dark garden.

'I don't believe Kajiro got inside Okido's room,' Sano said. 'The men who were stationed around the building say they never left their posts, never dozed off or got distracted, and I trust them. No one, including myself, noticed anything.'

'What shall we do?' Hirata asked, his expression clouded by concern for his master, and his own fate.

Sano pondered the tensions within the magistrate's family. 'The murderer could be someone who was already in the building, because we weren't expecting an attack from inside. We won't concede failure until we find out exactly what happened. We'll begin by questioning Kajiro.'

They walked down the road to the checkpoint where government officials monitored activities along the highway. At three hours till dawn, the village gate was closed, the checkpoint office dark. A guard led Sano and Hirata to the small, dingy jail, pointed out the barred window of Kajiro's cell, gave them a lantern, and left.

Sano shone the lantern through the window. Inside, Kajiro sat on the dirt floor, squinting at the light. A bandage girded his wounded thigh; his tattooed body, naked except for a loincloth, was covered with cuts, blood, and grime. 'Who's there?' he demanded.

After introducing himself, Sano said, 'I'm investigating the murder of the magistrate's concubine.'

'I didn't kill anyone!' Leaping up, Kajiro grasped the window bars, his scarred face taut with angry desperation. 'Let me out! I'm not a murderer!'

'You swore revenge upon Magistrate Okido for condemning your brother to death,' Sano said. 'You followed him here to kill him.'

'I admit I threatened the magistrate,' Kajiro said, 'but I came because he invited me. A few days ago, I got a message saying he wanted to make peace, and I should meet him tonight in Totsuka at midnight. He offered me money to spare his life.' Kajiro scowled. 'The message must have been a trick. Someone lured me here, killed the woman, and framed me.'

Hope rose in Sano. If it had happened that way, with Chiyoko the intended victim, perhaps he didn't deserve the blame, because how could he have known about a plot against a person he hadn't been assigned to guard? Striving to maintain his objectivity, Sano said, 'Show me the message.'

'I can't. It was delivered by word of mouth, by a man who said he worked for Okido.'

'How did you get inside the magistrate's room?'

'I didn't.' Kajiro stirred uneasily. 'I was surrounded the moment I got to the inn.'

If Sano had indeed captured Kajiro before the murder, then he'd done his duty. Still, he cautioned himself against accepting Kajiro's story just because he wanted to believe it.

'How did the design on your fan get on the victim's face?' he said.

'I don't know. My fan never left my sight until you took it away.'

Stepping away from the window, Sano beckoned Hirata. 'If he's telling the truth, the killer used a fan similar to Kajiro's.'

201

'Then where is the murder weapon?' Hirata said. 'We didn't find it by the body. And I have a feeling Kajiro's hiding something.'

'So do I,' Sano said, 'but there are enough discrepancies to justify further investigation.'

He intended to learn the truth, clear his reputation, and reclaim his honour.

'I was awakened by the temple bell,' Magistrate Okido said. 'Then I heard a commotion outside. I lit a lamp and saw Chiyoko lying dead beside me.'

He, Sano and Araki sat on the veranda, eating breakfast. Theirs was the only party left at the inn. Maids swept rooms; voices and hoof-beats clamoured in the street.

'You didn't see anyone enter or leave your room, or hear any noises?' Sano asked.

'No. I was fast asleep.' In the sunlight, Okido's face looked haggard and sickly.

Perhaps the bell had drowned the sounds made by an intruder, Sano speculated. From his examination of Chiyoko's body, he knew she'd died soon before Okido had announced the news of her murder. But if there'd been no intruder, then Okido was the person with the best opportunity to commit the crime.

'Kajiro says you were expecting him.' Sano related the hoodlum's story.

Magistrate Okido frowned. 'I did not invite Kajiro. I loved Chiyoko, and I could never have hurt her. I was the target of the attack. Kajiro is inventing ridiculous lies to save himself.' Okido turned an affronted gaze on Sano. 'And you're trying to excuse your own incompetence.'

Reluctantly, Sano acknowledged the partial truth of the accusation. He'd expected Okido to deny Kajiro's story, but was Okido telling the truth? His grief and indignation seemed genuine, and his good reputation supported his innocence, yet officials like Okido excelled at the art of dissembling.

'I must insist that you remain in Totsuka while I investigate the situation,' Sano said. 'My retainer has questioned the other guests at the inn and is now interviewing the staff.' The guests had seen nothing, but the staff might have useful information. 'We'll need to search your quarters and interview your party.'

'That's impossible,' Araki said angrily. 'We must continue the pilgrimage. How dare you treat us like suspects when the killer is already under arrest?'

'Until I discover the truth, everyone is a suspect,' Sano said. 'Your room adjoins the magistrate's. Did you see or hear anything before you left the building last night?'

'Nothing except my master and his concubine breathing next door,' Araki said.

If Araki was telling the truth, then Chiyoko had been alive when he went outside. Yet Sano wondered if Araki had entered Okido's room through the connecting door, killed Chiyoko, then walked past him as though nothing had happened.

'You disliked Chiyoko,' Sano said.

'Araki wouldn't have harmed my concubine.' Sudden doubt tinged Magistrate Okido's glance at his retainer.

'I disapproved of her influence over you,' Araki said, 'but I didn't kill her.' He addressed Sano: 'The walls are thin. The blows that struck Chiyoko must have been loud. If I had killed her, everyone would have heard me.'

If the murder had occurred after Araki left the building, then someone else had struck while the bell tolled. 'Where's your son?' Sano asked Okido, because Monzaemon apparently hadn't returned from wherever he'd gone yesterday evening.

'I've no idea, and I'm very concerned about him. If you see him, tell him we're leaving immediately. Since Kajiro has been captured, I don't need you for a bodyguard any more. You are free to do as you wish.'

'You can't keep us here against our will,' Araki added.

'As the shogun's investigator, I order you to cooperate with my inquiries,' Sano said. 'If you won't, shall I assume it's because you have something to hide?'

Both men glared at Sano, then sighed in resignation.

In the corridor outside Madam Okido's room, Sano met Tadeo.

'Good morning, master.' Balancing a tray of dishes, the servant boy bowed.

Sano returned the greeting. 'I'm trying to determine what happened last night. Did you see or hear anything that might help me?'

'No, master.' Tadeo's gaze darted nervously. 'Please excuse me. I have work to do.'

He hurried away. Sure that Tadeo did know something, Sano decided to catch up with him later. Now Sano knocked on Madam Okido's door. A maid let him into the room, where the magistrate's wife reclined upon cushions. Attendants arranged her hair and massaged her feet. With her face powdered and rouged, she looked radiantly beautiful in a teal silk kimono.

When Sano explained about his investigation, Madam Okido said calmly, 'So you've come to interrogate me because my room adjoins the murder scene, and I hated Chiyoko.'

'You also benefit from her death,' Sano said, noting that the woman's quick understanding of the situation demonstrated a cunning intelligence.

'Yes.' Madam Okido smiled. 'With Chiyoko gone, I have my husband to myself again. I feel certain that the pilgrimage to Ise Shrine will cure me. Soon, life will be as it was before I took ill.'

'That may not happen as soon as you'd like,' Sano said, chilled by her pleasure in the girl's death. 'We'll be staying here until my investigation is finished.'

Alarm flashed in Madam Okido's eyes; her limbs began to tremble. 'No. I can't wait.' She obviously knew she couldn't regain her husband's affection unless she got well; perhaps she also feared that the investigation might harm her. 'How can you think I killed Chiyoko when I haven't the strength to walk, or lift anything heavy?'

Sano wondered if she deliberately exaggerated her symptoms, and he decided he couldn't accept them as an alibi. 'Where were you between the time you retired last night and Kajiro's arrest?'

'In my room, with my attendants.'

In reply to Sano's questioning glance, the four women nodded. He said, 'Did you hear any sounds from next door?'

Attendants and mistress shook their heads.

'Did any of you leave the room?'

'No,' said Madam Okido. 'I took my sleeping potion and didn't awake until I heard my husband calling for help. My attendants also stayed.'

'If you were asleep, how do you know?' Sano asked.

Madam Okido said firmly, 'We were all in my room together.'

Her steely gaze belied her body's weakness. The attendants grouped around her in a show of loyalty. Sano considered the possibility that they'd slain Chiyoko on her orders. However, she was smart enough to know that as long as they all stuck to their story, they were safe . . . unless Sano found evidence to disprove it.

Bidding Madam Okido farewell, Sano went off in search of Hirata.

'So far, the staff hasn't provided any clues,' Hirata said. 'Monzaemon is still missing. Our men are searching the inn, but they haven't found a second war fan. They did discover something else, however.'

Hirata led Sano through the village, which was crowded with travellers. Beyond the townspeople's houses, a stream flowed. Hirata and Sano descended the steep bank bordered by trees. Sunlight gleamed on the rippling water where peasant women were washing clothes. Hirata pointed to a gap between two large rocks near the water's edge. On their facing surfaces were pale scrapes and reddish-brown stains.

'Blood,' Sano said.

'Maybe the killer got splashed with Chiyoko's blood and washed here,' Hirata said.

'If so, then it wasn't Kajiro,' Sano said. 'Even if there was blood on him before the fight, he went straight to jail afterward. Madam Okido, her attendants, and Magistrate Okido didn't leave the building last night; neither the guards nor I saw them. It could have been Araki. I didn't get a close look at him, and he was gone long enough to get here and back. He's clever enough to slip past the patrols.'

'Why come here, when he could wash in his room?'

'Maybe to dispose of the murder weapon.' Sano gazed into the translucent water. 'The blood may have nothing to do with the murder, but we'll drag the stream just in case.'

When they returned to town, they found Monzaemon sitting in the open storefront of a teahouse, a *sake* cup in his hand.

Sano said, 'Where have you been?'

Monzaemon regarded them through red, bleary eyes. 'Drinking.' His face was bloated, his kimono dishevelled; he reeked of liquor.

'Chiyoko was murdered last night,' Sano said. 'Did you know?'

'Oh, yes. The news is all over the village.' Monzaemon's voice was apathetic, but his body stiffened.

'Where were you last night?'

Monzaemon drained his cup, then shrugged. 'I made a tour of the teahouses. I woke up this morning beside a ditch.'

'You never went back to the inn?'

'No.'

Observing the furtive movements of the young man's eyes, Sano said, 'Can anyone vouch for you?'

'I flirted with the teahouse maids, but I doubt if they'll remember me; there was such a crowd. I bought drinks for some travellers, but they've probably left town by now.'

Sano and Hirata exchanged a glance that registered the dubious nature of Monzaemon's alibi. Sano said, 'We'll walk you back to the inn. The pilgrimage is postponed, but your father is anxious about you.'

Monzaemon's face took on a queasy expression. Sano perceived that he was afraid to see the magistrate, but was it because Okido would punish him for getting drunk, or because he'd done something worse?

Recalling Chiyoko's flirtatious behaviour toward Monzaemon, Sano took a gamble: 'You and Chiyoko were lovers, weren't you?'

Monzaemon's complexion paled in horror. 'Please don't tell my father. He'll kill me!'

'Did Chiyoko tire of the old man and decide she'd rather have his young, handsome son instead?' Sano suggested. 'Did you and she plot to kill him and frame Kajiro?'

Monzaemon clapped a hand over his mouth and bolted into an alley. Retching sounds issued from it.

'He would have benefited from Okido's death by inheriting his wealth and post, as well as his concubine,' Hirata said. 'Maybe he ruined his plans by mistakenly killing Chiyoko instead of the magistrate.'

'The motive is plausible, but opportunity is a problem,' Sano said.

'We checked the building yesterday evening. Monzaemon wasn't there.'

Hirata reconsidered. 'This crime required intelligence and forethought. He doesn't seem capable of either.'

'I believe the killer staged the crime to coincide with Kajiro's arrival,' Sano said. 'If Magistrate Okido did invite Kajiro, could Monzaemon have known? Maybe the message to Kajiro was sent by someone else, but I can't envision Monzaemon – or Chiyoko – inventing such a clever scheme.'

'I'll check his story at the teahouses,' Hirata said.

Monzaemon, looking dazed and sick, emerged from the alley and reluctantly accompanied Sano back to the inn. At the gate, one of Sano's men met them and said, 'I've found a maid who has something interesting to tell you.'

The maid was plain of face and quiet in demeanour. As she washed laundry in the courtyard, she told Sano, 'I was working in the bath house last night. The magistrate and his retainer talked while I was scrubbing their bodies. The magistrate said it would ruin him if the government knew he'd let gangsters run gambling dens and brothels in Edo. He said he'd thought he would be safe after the man who bribed him was executed, but the secret came back to haunt him. His retainer told him not to worry, because by midnight the problem would be solved.'

They were probably so used to ignoring servants that they hadn't realised she was listening, Sano supposed. Now bitter enlightenment filled him. After thanking the maid, he paid a visit to Kajiro at the jail. Then he returned to the inn and found Magistrate Okido in his chamber, lying on the futon while Araki massaged his naked back.

'Have you finished your investigation?' Okido said in a derisive voice. 'May we go?'

'Not yet,' Sano said. 'First, I'd like to discuss the bribes that Kajiro's brother paid you.'

Araki's hands faltered. Okido's face became still and impassive. 'I don't know what you're talking about.'

'Yes, you do.' Anger swelled in Sano, and disappointment in this man he'd once respected. 'You accepted money from criminals to overlook their illegal business. But when Kajiro's brother killed that shopkeeper, you couldn't ignore a murder. You sentenced him to death. Kajiro knew about the bribes and blackmailed you. You were afraid of losing your post, so you sent a message, asking Kajiro to meet you last night and promising him money. Someone overheard you and Araki say as much. Kajiro has just confirmed it.'

Magistrate Okido sat up, his expression alarmed.

'Relax, master,' Araki said. 'He has no evidence except other people's lies.'

Shaking his head in resignation, Okido said, 'I was wrong to take the money, and a fool to think I could conceal the secret forever. Now I must tell the truth and clear myself of a worse crime.' Okido donned a dressing gown and turned to Sano. 'Yes, I lured Kajiro here, but I didn't kill Chiyoko. My intended victim was Kajiro.'

Belatedly, Sano understood. Outrage assailed him.

'Araki-*san* and I concocted a plan to retain you as a bodyguard so that you would catch Kajiro,' said Okido. 'He was supposed to resist capture and die in battle – at your hands – before he could talk. That way, no one would question his death or investigate our dealings.'

'And just in case Kajiro didn't resist, Araki was at the scene to provoke him into fighting.' Furious at being manipulated, Sano said, 'You set me up to kill your enemy, and you set him up to take the blame for Chiyoko's murder.'

Pity and scorn mingled in the magistrate's gaze. 'I apologise for using you. Charge me with graft and conspiracy if you like, but to prosecute me for Chiyoko's murder, you must show my motive. And I don't have one.'

With a sense of vindication, Sano said, 'What about Chiyoko's affair with your son?'

'What affair?' Okido demanded.

'Did you plan to destroy your enemy and your faithless concubine at the same time?'

Looking horrified, Okido turned to Araki.

Araki nodded sadly. 'Chiyoko and Monzaemon were lovers. I didn't know how to tell you.'

Magistrate Okido leapt up and ran down the corridor. Sano and Araki followed him to Monzaemon's room, where the young man lay on the futon. Okido kicked and punched his son, yelling, 'Despicable wretch! You violated my concubine. You deceived me. I'll kill you!'

'I'm sorry, Father,' Monzaemon cried, fending off blows. 'Please don't hurt me.'

Sano dragged Okido away from Monzaemon and told Araki, 'Take your master to his room and calm him down. We don't need another murder.'

Okido yelled curses as Araki led him away; Monzaemon lay sobbing and moaning. Sano considered the drama he'd just witnessed. While he now knew about the plot against Kajiro, did Okido's violent reaction mean he really hadn't known about the affair, and thus lacked a motive for Chiyoko's murder?

Night fell in Totsuka. Lanterns glowed along the eaves of teahouses and restaurants filled with travellers, music, and laughter. After their evening meal, Sano and Hirata walked along the stream.

'I found witnesses who saw Monzaemon in teahouses the evening before the murder and the morning after,' Hirata said, 'but during the time between, he seems to have disappeared.'

'I've checked on Araki's whereabouts,' Sano said, contemplating the shadowy trees to their left as they angled down the steep descent to the dark water on their right. 'If he left the inn's premises, no one saw him. There's no sign of the murder weapon. Magistrate Okido insists on leaving town tomorrow, and I can't restrain a man of his rank by force, especially since he's threatened to complain to the shogun that I'm persecuting his family. If we don't solve this case soon, we'll have to give up and let Kajiro take the blame.'

And Sano would have to accept failure and disgrace.

A rustling sound came from the trees. 'What was that?' Hirata asked.

Something hurtled through the darkness and struck his head. He fell.

'Hirata-*san*!' Kneeling beside his retainer, Sano touched the bloody wound and found a fist-sized rock nearby.

Hirata mumbled, 'I'm all right. Go after him.'

Heart pounding, Sano raced up the bank, sword drawn. He paused beneath the trees, listening. The night was quiet, except for the rippling water. Then Sano felt a prickling sensation of someone behind him. Instinctively he dodged to his left, turning at the same time.

He saw a movement; an air current swept him. A heavy blow missed his head but hit his shoulder. The explosion of pain knocked him to the ground. He heard rapid, retreating footsteps. Cursing, he jumped up and hurried after them, but his assailant had vanished into the night.

Sano and Hirata walked the short distance back to town, chastened and sore. 'We were attacked near the spot where we saw blood on the rocks,' Hirata said.

'Could it have been the killer, returning for the murder weapon and trying to prevent us from discovering it?' Sano pictured a war fan striking him.

In the village they found Magistrate Okido and his family dining in his chamber. Okido and Araki looked grim, Monzaemon nervous, and Madam Okido annoyed. Tadeo filled their *sake* cups.

Sano said, 'Were any of you down by the stream just now?'

'Why?' Okido said. 'What happened?'

After Sano described the attack, a tense quiet filled the room. Tadeo's eyes widened in alarm.

Then Okido said, 'We've been here together, all evening.'

The hostile gazes of the party said that they understood why Sano had asked, and they were united against his threat to them.

208

Early the next morning, Sano heard a knock on his door. He opened it and saw Tadeo.

'May I speak with you?' Anxiety pinched Tadeo's small face.

'What is it?' Sano asked.

'Not here. Please come with me.'

They walked into the countryside where birds soared and trilled over green rice fields and peasant huts, against a brightening blue sky. Tadeo said, 'The magistrate and his son did leave the chamber last night. So did Araki. I saw them.'

This information implicated the three in the attack by the stream, but Sano sensed that it wasn't all the boy had to tell, so he waited.

'When you asked me if I saw anything the night of the murder,' Tadeo continued haltingly, 'I lied.'

Sano had suspected as much. 'Why?' he said gently.

'I didn't tell you what I knew because I was only thinking of how I could get ahead by keeping it secret.' Tadeo scowled at the ground. 'But after what happened yesterday . . .' He lifted a troubled gaze to Sano. 'If I'd told the truth, you might already have caught the murderer. My lie almost got you killed. I want to make amends by helping you now.'

He led Sano to a hut with a thatched roof and weathered plank walls. Outside, chickens inhabited a fenced yard. Inside was a single room, shabbily furnished with a stove, cooking utensils, and other bare necessities of life.

'My mother is working in the fields.' Tadeo went to a cabinet, rummaged under worn bedding, removed an object and presented it to Sano.

It was a war fan, almost identical to Kajiro's. The iron ribs were shinier, the dragon designs sharper. When Sano unfolded the fan, inner ribs parted stiffly; crisp creases pleated the gilt paper. A few scratches marred its newness. Someone had acquired this second fan, probably from the same craftsman who'd made the original. Traces of blood between the dragon scales and on the edges of the paper confirmed it as the murder weapon.

Elated, Sano said, 'Where did you get this?'

'I was bathing in the stream on my way home that night,' Tadeo said, 'when I heard someone running through the woods. He stopped at the top of the bank and threw something. It crashed on the ground, and he ran away. I found that—' Tadeo pointed to the fan '—stuck between two rocks.'

Right where Hirata had shown him the blood, Sano realised; it had been left behind when Tadeo pulled out the fan. 'Who was the man?' Sano asked.

'I couldn't tell. It was too dark.'

Sano considered asking Kajiro for the name of the craftsman who had

209

made his fan, then sending Hirata to find out which suspect had ordered the replica. However, the trip to Edo and back would take two days, and Sano wanted to solve the case before Magistrate Okido's party left Totsuka.

'I heard your men say that the fan had killed the magistrate's concubine and saw them searching for it. But fancy weapons like this are valuable. I meant to sell it so my mother could buy food.' With adult dignity, Tadeo said, 'But I don't want anyone else to get hurt. So I'm giving it to you.'

'Many thanks,' Sano said, appreciating the sacrifice involved. Then he had an inspiration. 'Did the man see you?'

'I don't think so.'

'The killer must have tried to dispose of the fan in the stream,' Sano conjectured, 'and later realised he'd failed. When he went back to correct his mistake, Hirata and I were there. He attacked us to keep us from finding the fan.' Sano focused a speculative look on Tadeo. 'If he doesn't know you were there, he won't know you didn't recognise him.'

Temple bells signalled the hour of the boar. Darkness shrouded the deserted highway outside Totsuka. Clouds veiled the moon that shone upon the crossroads, where Tadeo stood. Hidden in the woods, Sano, Hirata, and their men, watched Tadeo.

Earlier, the boy had followed Sano's instructions. He'd mentioned to each suspect that he'd seen someone throw the fan from the bank; he'd hinted at his willingness to return the fan and keep quiet about what he'd seen, for a price. All the suspects had seemed disturbed, but although they'd postponed their plans to leave town, nobody had accepted Tadeo's invitation to meet at the crossroads to exchange the murder weapon for blackmail money tonight. Thus, Sano couldn't predict who – if anyone – would take the bait.

Then Sano heard footsteps coming from the village. Down the road appeared the dark silhouette of a samurai, his two swords protruding from his side. As he reached the crossroads, Sano recognised his shape and bearing.

'It's Araki,' Hirata whispered.

Sano felt a stab of surprise. He couldn't picture Araki bungling the disposal of the weapon and placing himself in the power of a black-mailer, or committing the clumsy attack against Sano and Hirata.

'Good evening, master,' Tadeo greeted Araki.

Araki seized Tadeo and pressed his short sword against the boy's throat. 'Where is the fan?' he demanded. 'Tell me!'

Swords drawn, Sano and his men rushed out of the woods and surrounded the pair. 'Let him go,' Sano ordered Araki.

Time and movement ceased. The only sound was the shrill of insects in the woods. Araki's dismayed expression registered the knowledge that he'd been trapped. Tadeo strained away from the blade, eyes round with terror.

Then Araki released Tadeo. Sano's breath joined the sigh of relief that issued from his team. Hirata confiscated Araki's swords; the troops bound his hands.

'Are you all right?' Sano asked Tadeo.

'Yes, master,' the boy said shakily.

Sano clasped Tadeo's shoulder. 'One of my men will take you home. In honour of your courage, you'll receive a reward of gold.'

A happy grin lit the boy's face.

Turning to Araki, Sano said, 'What have you to say for yourself?'

Araki stood proudly, as if accepting an honour rather than defeat. 'I killed Chiyoko.'

Lingering disbelief undermined Sano's triumph at solving the case. The solution seemed all wrong. On the way back to the village, Sano pondered the questions unanswered by Araki's confession. How could such a loyal retainer kill his master's beloved concubine, no matter what the provocation? How had Araki done it without anyone hearing? Where had Monzaemon been on the night of the murder? Sano thought of the schemes that had complicated the investigation. Now he had a sense of other machinations revolving around him. He recalled seeing Monzaemon and Madam Okido talking together during the trip, and a medicine chest of full of potions. As the group reached the inn, revelation dazzled Sano.

Magistrate Okido, his wife and son sat on the lantern-lit veranda. When they saw Sano's men escorting Araki, shock blanched their faces. Okido leapt to his feet.

'What is this?' he demanded.

Sano said, 'We caught Araki trying to recover the murder weapon from a servant who blackmailed him. He's confessed to killing Chiyoko.'

'No!' The magistrate stared, aghast.

Araki bowed his head. 'I'm sorry, master.'

'But he didn't kill Chiyoko,' Sano said. 'He's only sorry because he got caught in the trap I set for the person who did.'

The Okido family sat as though paralysed. Sano heard their collective gasp, saw the startled faces of his men.

'You mean we're not arresting Araki?' Hirata said.

'Indeed we are,' Sano said. 'We're also arresting Madam Okido and Monzaemon for the murder of Chiyoko, and the magistrate for attempting to subvert justice.' Sano addressed Madam Okido: 'You knew about your husband's plan to kill Kajiro. Before you left Edo, you bought a replica of his fan. You cleverly plotted to murder Chiyoko and frame Kajiro.'

211

'That's a lie!' Madam Okido exclaimed, but her body began trembling violently.

'The night of the murder, you drugged your attendants and your husband with your sleeping potion. But you couldn't manage the rest without an accomplice.' Sano looked at Monzaemon.

Terror filled Monzaemon's eyes. 'You're insane.'

'Your stepmother convinced you that if Chiyoko died and she regained your father's favour, she would make him be more generous and lenient toward you,' Sano continued relentlessly. 'She played upon your greed and foolishness and persuaded you to help her. You both put aside mutual dislike for the sake of common interests.'

'That's outrageous supposition,' Magistrate Okido blustered. 'I refuse to hear any more.'

Ignoring him, Sano said, 'Madam Okido hid Monzaemon in the cabinet in her room before I secured the building. That's why I didn't see him. When the temple bell rang at midnight, she let him out of the cabinet. She gave him the fan. He stole through the door to the next room and killed Chiyoko while the magistrate slept. Afterward he returned to Madam Okido's room and waited until the confusion of later events allowed him to escape undetected.

'But when Monzaemon tried to dispose of the weapon, he failed. Tadeo made his proposition. Fearing for their lives, Madam Okido and Monzaemon went to the magistrate, confessed what they'd done, and threw themselves on his mercy.' Sano's gaze swept the family. 'You discovered that the boy had approached all of you, and you guessed that he didn't really know who'd been at the stream, but you couldn't take the chance. Hence, the magistrate sent Araki to get the fan and silence the boy.'

As the story unfolded simultaneously in his mind and in his words, logic left Sano no room for doubt. 'Conspiracy was the underlying theme in this case from the start. Magistrate Okido and Araki conspired to lure Kajiro here to die by my sword. Madam Okido conspired with Monzaemon to murder Chiyoko. You all conspired together to retrieve the weapon. Now you're conspiring to protect the Okido clan from scandal and ruin by sacrificing Araki.'

'I killed Chiyoko,' Araki said with unwavering firmness. 'I acted alone. I must pay for my crime alone.'

'I can't allow that,' Sano said, though he admired the loyal retainer who was willing to die for his master's sake. To Hirata he said, 'We'll take everyone to Edo for trial. Our key witness will be the craftsman who made the duplicate fan; he'll name Madam Okido as his customer. The truth will come out eventually.' Sano turned to Magistrate Okido. 'I'll give you one last chance to reclaim your honour by confessing now. If you won't, you shall end your fine career on the public execution ground with your wife and son.'

212

Wildly, Okido looked around, as if seeking denial or escape; his mouth formed inaudible words. His wife and son stared at him in speechless entreaty.

Then the magistrate dropped to his knees; defeat and shame saddened his expression. 'Araki-*san*, I won't repay your service by letting you take the blame. I won't sacrifice your honour for the sake of those who have shed blood and deceived me.' He addressed Sano: 'You are right about everything.'

'Honourable husband!' cried Madam Okido, her face horror-stricken. 'No!'

Monzaemon clutched at his father with frantic indignation. 'But you promised to protect me!'

'I won't protect criminals any longer,' the magistrate said grimly, 'or evade justice.'

Madam Okido turned on Monzaemon. 'Everything would have been fine, except for your stupidity.' Rage distorted her features; her body shuddered. 'You were so drunk that you threw the fan on the rocks instead of in the water. You stayed out all night instead of coming right back the way you were supposed to. By the time I sent you to make sure the fan was safely hidden, it was too late. The boy already had the fan. And you risked getting caught when you attacked the detectives.'

'The murder scheme was your idea,' retorted Monzaemon. 'If you hadn't threatened to tell my father about me and Chiyoko, I never would have gone along with it.'

'This is all your fault,' Madam Okido raged at her husband. 'If you hadn't brought Chiyoko into our house, none of this would have happened.'

'You must suffer the consequences of your actions, as must I,' Okido told them coldly. 'I hereby resign my post. At dawn I shall commit ritual suicide. My life will not end in disgrace.'

Araki stood tall, his eyes burning with the glory of a samurai embracing his destiny. 'I shall have the privilege of acting as your second, then following you into death.'

After the troops placed the party under house arrest, Sano and Hirata reviewed the investigation over drinks in a teahouse.

'This case was like an iron fan, unfolding to reveal the ugly truth about a family bound together by love, hate, and need,' Hirata remarked.

Sano nodded thoughtfully. 'But the fan's blades were straight and strong. In the end, integrity prevailed over selfishness. Okido's decision salvaged his honour – and mine.'

History simplifies; mystery complicates. That sounds OK for a start, only it makes as much, or as little, sense if you put it the other way round. History complicates; mystery simplifies.

Most of us start with our simplified child's encyclopaedia templates of history: Athenians were intellectual, Medievals pious, Victorians respectable. A little more knowledge complicates things and reveals the occasional Athenian thicko, Medieval what-the-heller, or (as in the following story) Victorian middle-class porn pusher.

The job of the mystery story writer, as of the historian, is usually to complicate what seems simple. But unlike the historian, the mystery writer is expected to deliver a solution or, at least, a resolution – which means simplifying the complicated. History-mystery writers are on a pendulum between the two, which for people who deal in time seems a fair enough place to be.

Gillian Linscott

For All the Saints

Gillian Linscott

Saint Catherine was late. Ten o'clock was when Trillow had told her to get there, so as not to waste any of the March morning light. Ella was kneeling to put knobs of coal on the back of the fire in the studio because the saints needed warmth. Trillow had taken the hearth brush and was using it on an old broken-spoked cart wheel he'd borrowed from the coalman and propped up against the *chaise-longue* on the model's dais. Coal dust and flakes of black paint were scattered round it, sheets of screwed up drawing paper and charcoal sticks that had got broken and trodden into the boards.

'Ella, come over here, would you.'

She stood up at once. Trillow always talked to her like a brother to a younger sister. There were three of them in the household: Trillow the artist, his friend Ned, the engraver, and Ned's sister Ella. It wasn't a conventional arrangement, but Ned and Ella's mother had died three years ago, when Ella was thirteen, and it had either been move in with Ned and Trillow or go into service among strangers. They'd taken three rooms together in a tall house in Pimlico. Trillow had his studio on the first floor, Ned his print-making room upstairs, next to the kitchen where they ate, and Ella attended to the housekeeping and slept in a cupboard-bed alongside the fire. She was almost entirely happy. There was very little money to spare, but she knew all the saints watched over them. The saints paid the coal bills, kept bread on the table, provided Trillow's sticks of best quality charcoal and Ned's plates of shining copper and cakes of yellow beeswax. She put down the fire tongs and went obediently up to the dais. Trillow signed to her to stand alongside the coal-cart wheel, took her arm and draped it over the rim. She stood ecstatic, not moving a muscle, as he went over to his board and started drawing with quick strokes. Ella knew Saint Catherine had been martyred on a wheel, although she wasn't entirely sure how. When she was much younger she'd imagined her going slowly round and round on the wheel of the grocer's cart, gold hair trailing in the mud, and assumed she'd died from humiliation and

217

dizziness. But the how didn't matter. Saints in Triumph were what Ned and Trillow depicted, like Saint Catherine after martyrdom, radiant in virgin white, one arm resting on the transcended wheel, the other hand holding a palm frond. Children were given them as certificates for regular attendance at Sunday school. It was her dream that Trillow would ask her to model for one of the saints.

A knock on the front door one floor below, the confident knock of somebody who didn't expect to be kept waiting. Trillow sighed with relief and threw down his charcoal.

'Her at last. Go down and let her in, Ella.'

On her way out, she glanced at his drawing board. Only a hand on a wheel, that was all. She'd half hoped – more than half hoped – that a miracle would have happened and Trillow would have bestowed sainthood on her. As she went downstairs, the segs of her boots tapping on the uncarpeted boards, she tried to crush down her disappointment. Her face was too angular, body too thin, hair too ordinarily brown to make her a saint. Saints Triumphant had smooth faces, rounded bodies under their white draperies, swathes of black or golden hair.

Saint Catherine was waiting impatiently on the step. She was wearing a black velvet jacket over a skirt of yellow and black tartan, draggled with mud at the hem. A red shawl covered her head and the fringe that frizzed out of it at the front was as gold as fried egg yolk. She pushed past Ella without saying anything and went upstairs trailing a smell behind her. It was a warm, sourish smell, the sort you got when you knelt down to watch the mother cat feeding her kittens on the old blanket in the corner of the kitchen. As soon as Saint Catherine set foot on the landing the door to Trillow's studio opened. She went inside. The door shut.

'Come along, Kate dear, give a little more.'

'Me knee's stiff.'

'Rub it then. Ah, that's good. Keep your hand there like that. Don't move.'

'Thought you said I could rub it.'

'Shhh. Keep still.'

'Rub somewhere else if you want.'

'Only ten bob extra. Yes, I know.'

'So what's ten bob to you?'

'A lot of money. Now try lifting your petticoat up and holding it there on your knee. Knees apart for goodness sake.'

'Ten bob's not a lot when you're selling them for five guineas.'

'Who says we're selling them for five guineas?'

'Urse knows a man.'

'Ursula talks too much. Stop fidgeting.'

'Me titties are getting cold. I'll get goose pimples.'

'It's not cold in here.'

218

''Ow would you know? You've got a jacket on.'

'Alright, five minutes' break if you must.'

'Something to warm me up?'

'Help yourself. I only hope it puts you in a better mood.'

'Ten bob'd put me in a better mood.'

'Pity, because you're not getting it. We have a lot of expenses to cover.'

'Like bribing policemen to look the other way.'

'Just get your drink and sit down.'

'Only bribes don't always work, do they? You know Dutch Joe was raided last week? Took all 'is pictures and plates away and 'e's had to do a bunk.'

'Are you threatening me?'

'Ten bob.'

'I'll have to ask Ned.'

The door of Trillow's studio stayed closed. Ella and Ned lunched in the kitchen off tea, bread and cold mutton. His long hands were flecked with acid burns and a distinctive smell clung to him; of ammonia, linseed oil and resin, overlaid with the strong tobacco he smoked when he wasn't working to drive the chemical fumes out of his lungs. Ned had to sleep in his workroom. Through the winter his thin face had turned yellowish and there was a boil on his neck that wouldn't go away. When Ella had cleared up the lunch things, she went through to his room to help. There was a new batch of copper plates to be prepared, first cleaned with ammonia and whiting, then heated over a burner and spread with a fine film of wax. Ned had taught her the business as if she were a proper apprentice and she did all the preparation work and clearing up.

Ned stood at his big table by the window with a drawing Trillow had made the day before spread out in front of him, copying it on to a waxed copper plate with a sharp engraving tool. Ella left her first plate drying and went over to watch. The picture was of Saint Ursula and her eleven thousand virgins, a snaking line of them with their palm branches, stretching to infinity in correct perspective. Ursula was tall and stately, with dark hair stretching down nearly to her feet. Ella thought of Trillow's long charcoal strokes drawing it and felt as if her own hair were being stroked into sleekness by his hand. A little shiver went through her.

'She's beautiful, isn't she?'

Ned didn't answer. He'd seemed preoccupied over the past few days. She noticed that he kept passing his hand over his eyes.

'Eyes tired?'

'A little.'

'You're working too hard.'

219

She heard him from her cupboard bed next door working late into the night, coughing from the fumes of nitric acid.

'We have to work while the market's there.'

'Surely people always need saints.'

He laughed and it turned into a cough. 'Wouldn't you like to live in a house, Ella, with bedrooms and meals on a proper table and a skivvy to make up the fires?'

'I suppose so.'

'I suppose so too.'

'And Trillow?'

'Oh, I don't know what Trillow wants.'

The possibility that there might be a future without Trillow sent a different sort of shiver through her.

She said, diffidently, 'Trillow works too hard as well. He's out every night.'

Evenings were a good time to sell, Trillow said. It surprised her a little that Sunday school people should be doing business in the evenings. She waxed another plate and tidied the workroom. Artists like Trillow could work in confusion, but engravers had to be orderly: the sharp tools in racks on the walls, sheets of dampened paper piled between plates of glass ready for printing, bottle of linseed oil for mixing the ink, bottle of nitric acid for biting the design into the copper plates. Damping the paper, keeping the tools clean and the bottles topped up were part of Ella's work. At about half past three they heard feet stamping down the stairs and the front door slamming. Soon afterwards heavier feet tramped upstairs and Trillow came in, carrying a sheet of paper.

'That bloody woman . . .'

Ned gave him a warning look and glanced at Ella. Trillow went over to the work table and dumped his paper on top of the picture that Ned was copying.

'One Saint Catherine, as per specification.'

Ned looked at it, frowning.

'More of a sketch, isn't it?'

'The light was going. You can put in the detail when you're copying.'

'It's not that easy.'

'For heaven's sake, I have to deal with these women. It's all very well for you to sit up here and—'

'Ella dear, would you go and make us a pot of tea?'

She went obediently and, from the kitchen, was aware of low voices rumbling next door. She couldn't hear what they were saying, but knew it was an argument. It hurt her that the two people who meant most to her should argue.

'So I told her I'd ask you.'

'You decide.'

'No. You're not putting it all on me. Equal profits, equal risks.'

'It seems a lot of money. But then if she's a good model . . .'

'If you catch her quick between the third and fourth glass of gin she's not so bad. I'll bring the other ones up later, when Ella's out of the way.'

'So you mean, you think she's worth it?'

'Nothing to do with it. It's not a model fee she's asking, it's black-mail.'

Ned put down his engraver's point and stared.

'She wouldn't, would she?'

'She dropped a hint about Dutch Joe.'

'Oh God, don't you think we ought to leave off for a while?'

'No! With Joe out, we can take over his market. Every porter at every gentleman's club in London knew Joe. They'll need somebody to send their people to now he's gone.'

'We shouldn't get in so deep. Just a few months of it, we agreed.'

'Oh yes, enough for the rent on a little house in Barnes for you and your sister, then puppy dogs and prayer book markers for the rest of your life. Ned, there are thousands of pounds, tens of thousands in this – town house, flunkeys and carriage.'

'Is that what you want?'

'I certainly don't want to spend the rest of my life in a scrubby studio getting whores drunk.'

'Shhh.'

'Oh for goodness sake, your sister must have some notion of what's going on.'

'Of course she hasn't, and she's not going to.'

Trillow shrugged. 'So?'

'So?'

'Do we pay Kate's ten bob or don't we?'

'I don't know.'

The raid came three days later at around four in the morning while it was still dark. Ella, closed into her cupboard, heard the knock at the front door like something at the back of a dream, then woke as noises of outrage rose through the house, with tenants poking heads out of doors to ask what was happening, and heavy steps clacking on the stairs, strange voices. While she was sitting up and blinking, trying to separate reality from dream, she heard the door open and steps coming into the kitchen, soft steps, not like the ones on their way upstairs. The fire was out and the room quite dark.

'Ned? Ned, what's happening?'

Somebody pulled the cupboard doors open and stood close to her in the dark. Not Ned. Not Ned's smell.

221

'Ella, take these. Keep them in there with you and stay where you are.'

Trillow. He pushed something at her, something that dug against her ribs. Her hands closed around it and she knew at once what it was. Parcels of copper plates were as familiar to her as bread and cheese. Then the cupboard doors closed on her and Trillow was gone. She heard his voice out on the landing, louder and grander than usual.

'There's a sick girl in there. If you must go in, show some humanity.'

Then Ned's voice from the doorway, not at all loud or grand.

'Ella dear, I'm afraid there are some people coming in.'

Through a gap where the doors didn't quite meet she saw oil lanterns beaming over the kitchen, making ordinary chairs and bowls look sinister. Then steps towards her cupboard and Ned's voice, 'No, my sister . . .'

Trillow's voice, full of contempt, 'If they insist on violating a poor girl's sick bed, let's get it over and done with.'

The doors flapped back. She shrank against the wall from the lamplight, pulling the blanket up to her chin. The parcel of plates was pressed between her spine and the wall at the back of the cupboard. The light beamed at her for several heartbeats, making her screw up her eyes until a rough voice murmured, 'Sorry, miss,' and the doors shut on her.

She heard Trillow asking, 'Are you quite satisfied now?' in a voice as sharp as any engraving tool. Then the feet went clacking away downstairs.

Much later, when the house was quiet again, Ned came to her. She heard his apologetic whisper through the doors.

'Ella, are you awake?'

She sat up and opened the doors. He was carrying a candle in an enamel holder. His face in the light reminded her of a severed head in an engraving of a cannibal feast.

'What happened?'

He pulled a chair over and sat down.

'Ella, my dear somebody . . . oh, so much malice . . .'

'It was the police?'

'Yes. You see, when you're in trade, when other people see you doing well, you make enemies . . .'

'What did they want?'

'Our plates . . . you see, somebody who wanted to do us harm had told them we were . . . doing things we shouldn't. So they've taken the plates and . . .'

'Not all of them.'

She pulled the parcel of plates out from under the blanket. The candle wavered in his hand, sending shadows rocking across the room.

'How did they get there?'

'Trillow brought them.'

He turned away. 'I'll . . .' She waited, but he didn't say anything else, only put down the candle, grabbed the package from her and stumbled out.

Three days later, with casual apologies, a police constable returned fourteen engraved and etched copper plates of Saints in Triumph.

'We're safer now the police have made fools of themselves.'

Trillow leaned back on the *chaise-longue*, brandy glass in hand. Ned stood by the table, compulsively sorting sticks of charcoal into a neat length-graded row. His face was yellower than ever in the lamplight, the boil on the back of his neck more vivid.

'If they'd found the other plates . . .'

'Luckily, one of us didn't panic.'

'But to hide them in her bed . . . I don't see how you could think of it.'

'It was either that or harder beds for all of us – her included.'

'Not Ella, no.'

'She helps you, doesn't she?'

'Not with those.'

'Would the police believe that?'

Ned came up the step to the dais and stood at the end of the *chaise-longue*, hands clenched together.

'I'm getting out. Now. I want my share of the money and I'm getting out now.'

'Where to, Ned? And how long will a couple of hundred pounds last you? Give it a few more weeks with the plates we've got and an open field and I'll guarantee you ten times that.'

'What if the police come back?'

'Unlikely.'

'And Kate?'

'I'll speak to her.'

The next day at six o'clock it was getting dark and Ned was out buying ink powder. Ella was on her own in the kitchen, grating suet on to a plate ready for tomorrow's steak and kidney pudding. She was alarmed by her brother's nerviness and loss of weight and had decided that more red meat might counteract the overwork and the acid fumes. Every night, shut into her rectangle of darkness, she fell asleep to the creaking of his printing press. Sometimes she woke as the first grey light was coming in through the crack between the doors and heard him still moving about next door. He was getting through their supplies at an unprecedented rate. Every morning the stacks of dampened paper were used up, the linseed oil bottle empty, the floor scattered with bits of ink-stained muslin. Every morning Ella tidied up, refilled bottles, damped more paper. The stacks of finished prints under weights on the drying bench

223

were twice as high as usual. She thought about it as white flakes of suet piled into a pyramid, and imagined their saints being seen and possessed from Land's End to the Hebrides or even further afield, going with the missionaries along the steaming rivers of Africa or across the plains of China. Then the kitchen door opened and Trillow walked in, pouring blood.

Most of it came from a torn ear, though she didn't realise that at the time. She saw the odd way he was walking, hunched forward with his head sunk into his shoulders and a hand clapped over his left ear. Blood was seeping through his fingers, running down inside his coat sleeve and soaking the cuff of his shirt. He came lurching across the room and, without speaking, leaned his elbows on the table where she'd been working, his head down. She gasped and dropped the grater, scattering suet. It mingled with the drops of blood coming through his fingers on to the table. He asked in a terrible flat voice where Ned was. She gasped, 'Out.'

'Water. In a bowl.'

Shaking, she filled a soup tureen with water from the bucket in the corner, slopping it over the floor. He pulled a chair up to the table, grabbed the pudding cloth, soaked it in the water and held it to his ear. When she took a proper look at his face she gave a little scream. His left eye was closed, the flesh around it swollen and purple-red. His lip was split and a line of congealed blood ran down his chin. The pudding cloth was already turning red.

'More cloth.'

She ran into her brother's printing room and came back with a roll of muslin, used the kitchen knife to hack pieces off it. She passed piece after piece to him. As each one was soaked he let it drop to the floor and grabbed another. Gradually the flood slowed until the pieces were only stained pink. He took a long shuddering breath.

'Brandy. Down in the studio.'

It took her a long time to find it. When she got back he took the bottle and drank from it, shivering as the brandy went down. His ear had stopped bleeding but the swollen eye looked worse.

'Should I put some steak on it?'

He nodded. She went to the meat safe and took out the sliver of rump steak on its chipped plate, feeling a pang of regret for her brother's dinner, but mostly relief that she had anything to offer Trillow. He scooped it off the plate and clapped it over his eye.

'What . . . what happened?'

She hardly dared ask and thought for a long time he wasn't going to answer. Then he said, wincing from the split lip, 'There was a ruffian mistreating a woman.'

'Oh.' She felt as if somebody had punched her in the chest. 'You fought him?'

'What else could I do?'

'Wasn't there anybody else there? Nobody to help?'

He started shaking his head, then stopped because it was dislodging the steak.

'Nobody. Just me.'

'And she?'

'She's alright.'

Ella stood looking at him, so full of love that she thought it would burst her whole body apart. Love and envy, because she knew that she'd have given or done anything, suffered any of the torments the saints did before they triumphed, if she could have been the woman he'd rescued.

Much later, with Ella upstairs, Ned and Trillow talked in low voices in the studio. Trillow was on the *chaise-longue*, Ned hunched on the floor beside it.

'Her young man, that's what Kate called him. Protector's what she means.'

'Did you hit him back?'

'If you think you can stop a fourteen-stone costermonger with a slug of lead in his fist, you go and discuss it with them next time.'

'Next time?'

'They won't go away, Ned. She's decided she wants a quarter share and she says she's going to get it. She's coming here tomorrow and wants an answer.'

'Here?'

'To pose as usual, damn her. She says now she's going to be a shareholder she wants to be sure the profits keep up.'

When Ella went into Ned's workroom at breakfast time she expected to find him asleep as usual, on his camp bed beside the printing press. Instead there was a note on the table in his handwriting saying he'd gone out and wouldn't be back till the afternoon. Later, Trillow came up for his tea and toast, fully dressed with his working smock over his shirt. In spite of the steak his eye was still half closed and the bruise around it was glowing greenish-purple, like a puffed-out pigeon's breast. He hardly seemed to notice Ella, beyond saying that Catherine would be coming at ten and he'd let her in himself.

Ella stayed in the kitchen, tidying up and ironing. She heard the knock on the door just after ten, one pair of feet going downstairs, two pairs coming up to the landing below and the studio door closing. The house was quiet, apart from the occasional cart rumbling past. Then, when she was on the last of Ned's shirts, there was an interruption. Quick feet came tapping up the stairs from the floor below and a woman's voice outside the door called, 'Anybody there?' She opened the door and there was Catherine in the long green wrap that Trillow

225

kept for his models, yellow hair cascading over her shoulders and down to her waist. Ella stood with the shirt over her arm, dumbfounded. She was always uneasy in the presence of the saints, awed by whatever quality it was that they possessed and she didn't. None of them had come up to her kitchen before.

'Got a glass, ducky? 'E's gone and broken the one downstairs.'

She ran to the cupboard, took out one of their thick drinking tumblers and handed it over. Then, still tongue-tied, she shut the door and heard the feet going back downstairs. Only a few minutes after that the scream came ripping up through the floorboards, a terrible bubbling scream like a curlew's cry only longer and louder, feet pounding upstairs and Trillow's discoloured face at the door, saying something she didn't understand until he grabbed her by the shoulder and said it again. She must run to the doctor round the corner and tell him to come at once, because Catherine had drunk acid.

She had to tell the coroner about it, and the ten men on the jury who sat staring at her in a way that made her feel she'd done something wrong. She told them how quickly she'd run, not even stopping to put on hat or coat. It wasn't her fault that the doctor was away on a confinement and she had had to run again to a house three streets away, dodging carts and carriages, slipping in gutters. It wasn't her fault that by the time she'd got back, with the doctor running alongside, Catherine was beyond speaking, almost beyond breathing, beyond anything except terrible harsh yelping noises that Ella heard through the closed door out on the landing, with the landlady and the other tenants crowding round, whispering, staring. Then Ned had arrived.

It turned out, much later, that he'd been out looking for other lodgings for himself and Ella. He'd collapsed there on the landing and had to be carried upstairs. The coroner wanted to know about Ella's last sight of Catherine. Had she appeared distressed or agitated? Ella shook her head and had to be reminded to speak up. No. Had Ella seen or heard her go into the workroom next to the kitchen where the bottle of nitric acid was kept? No. She'd been back in the kitchen, door closed. When Ella was allowed to step down, Trillow followed her into the witness box, tall and grave in his black top hat. It was the first time Ella had seen him since the day Catherine died. He'd left the house that same evening, after a conversation with Ned that she didn't hear. She'd asked Ned where he was lodging but he'd said he didn't know.

Now, as he gave his evidence, her eyes didn't stray from his face. She noticed that his lip was healed and there was only a faint yellow tinge round his eye. He answered the questions put to him in a calm and grave voice. Catherine Bell was an artist's model and had sat for him many times for religious pictures. She suffered from moods in which she would make threats against both herself and other people

226

for bringing her to her low state in life. Yes sir, she had on occasions spoken of wishing to end it all. How he wished he could have guessed that on that occasion she really meant it. Yes, he'd believed it was gin she had in the glass. Yes sir, Miss Bell was accustomed to drink gin in the mornings.

The verdict was suicide, without the rider 'while of unsound mind'. When the three of them met on the steps outside, Trillow raised his hat to Ella, stared Ned blankly in the face and walked away.

Ned and Ella went home in silence to pack. They were moving out of London, down to the coast. The next morning a cart would come for the printing press, the plates and bottles, their few household goods. Ned thought there might be a market for seaside pictures, piers and so on.

'Peers?' Ella had questioned, her distraught mind picturing men in ermine and coronets on the sands.

'Piers and promenades. Not too many people, except in the middle distance with sunshades.'

As long as he didn't have to do detailed figures, he could manage both drawing and engraving himself. They'd live. Still in silence they wrapped unused copper plates in bits of clean sheet, stowed inks, instruments and bottles in baskets. As the orange light of the setting sun was coming through the window they knelt on the bare floor, cording up the last package. With her finger on the half-made knot to hold it while her brother tightened the string, Ella spoke at last.

'He killed her, didn't he?'

The string went slack. She glanced sideways and saw Ned kneeling, head down.

'How did you know?'

'The bottle. It was empty when I looked in the morning, before she came upstairs. I know because I thought how quickly it was going.'

His head went lower. She knew she was hurting him, but there were things that must be said and she could only say them in this gap, when the old life had finished and a new one not yet started.

'And now I know why he killed her. I understood this morning at the inquest – what sort of woman she was.'

'Ella, it's not right for you . . .'

'No, listen. It's because of what you and Trillow were doing.'

He groaned 'I never wanted to. I swear on our mother's grave I never wanted to.'

'The saints. Your lovely saints, and everybody all over the world seeing them. They were so beautiful, especially Catherine. He'd made her a saint and then, somehow, he found out that she wasn't worthy of it and . . .'

Ned was trembling and crying, great drops falling and spreading over the wooden floorboards.

'Ned, don't judge him harshly. I know it was wicked of him but he

227

was so pure . . . so pure, you see.' She was crying now too. She felt Ned's shaking arm round her shoulders. 'I'm right, aren't I, that's why he did it? Because she wasn't worthy'.

'Yes, yes. Don't cry now. Oh, don't cry.'

Later, packing up the things in the kitchen when Ned was downstairs, she found an engraved copper plate under the mattress in her bed cupboard. She knew it must have slipped out from the parcel that Trillow had given her the night the police came. Curious, she took it over to the lamplight and looked at the grooves in the bright copper. She'd learned to see the picture on a plate as clearly as if it were printed on paper. It was one of the saints, an ecstatic smile on her face and long hair flowing, spreadeagled and ready for a kind of martyrdom that she couldn't imagine and was clearly too terrible to be in any of the books. She stared at it for a while but when she heard her brother coming upstairs she pushed it back into the bed cupboard, where it would stay when they left so that there was nothing to remind him.

When I came to the final paragraph of Ellis Peters' first historical mystery, *A Morbid Taste for Bones*, I felt that not only had I enjoyed a riveting mystery, but also that I had been transported back in time to a new world, the world of Cadfael and his Brothers in medieval Shrewsbury. Now hooked, I sought out further tales of Brother Cadfael, looking forward eagerly to the publication of each new story that Ellis Peters produced.

Historical mystery, as the name suggests, combines two very absorbing genres. History itself is a mystery to many of us. We are fascinated by the differences between our own lives and the lives of those who lived long ago; by the attitudes, the often colourful superstitions and customs of the past. We are also fascinated by the similarities; by the way that human nature does not change, the way that the emotions of love, hate, revenge and fear are universal and apply as much to ourselves as to any who lived in times gone by.

I feel I owe a great debt to Ellis Peters for pioneering and popularising the genre of historical crime which I not only enjoy reading but also writing.

Kate Ellis

The Virgin's Circlet

Kate Ellis

Cecily knew from experience that the man who lay before her had been dead for several days. She had seen many such bodies. It had been part of her duties at the convent to prepare the dead for burial. She knelt down, her skirts protecting her knees from the hard stone of the church floor, and touched the rough stubble of the dead man's cheek. The flesh was hard and cold as stone.

She looked around, shading her eyes from the bright shafts of sunlight that streamed through the skeletal rafters of the vast roof. The lead had been stripped from the building the week before and the place already had the look and smell of dereliction; of being abandoned by God and man. His most gracious Majesty King Henry, the eighth of that name, had given orders and men had obeyed. The consequences of disobedience were too fearful to contemplate . . . even in a town like Liverpool, far from the King's formidable presence.

She heard a scurrying sound from the far end of the Priory church. She turned her head and saw a man hurrying towards the abandoned cloisters. He was small with fair hair that bore the marks of an overgrown monk's tonsure. She had seen him in the town: he had visited her brother.

She called out. 'Brother Richard . . . please help me. A man is dead . . . please.' But before the words had left her mouth he had gone.

A fortnight before she would have known what to do. The body lay within the precincts of Birkenhead Priory. The brothers would have taken charge of it and given it a Christian burial. But the brothers were gone. Two weeks ago they had each been given forty shillings and a new gown, then thrust out into the world to fend for themselves. She looked at the body, wondering what to do. The dead of Birkenhead, having no parish church, were now taken over the wide swelling waters of the River Mersey to receive burial at the church where her brother, James, was priest: the church of Our Lady and St Nicholas that stood above Liverpool strand overlooking the waterfront.

The only sound Cecily could hear was the singing of the birds in the

231

deserted priory. The tiny creatures were happily unaware of the events that had taken place there so recently; events that had changed the lives of men and women for ever. She assessed her situation: she was alone with a corpse for company. She toyed with the idea of chasing after Brother Richard . . . but he had been moving fast and would be far away by now. She forced herself to look at the dead man again and saw something she had missed during her first cursory observations: a dark stain on the man's rough brown jerkin . . . a patch of dried, crusted blood.

She sprang up and backed away, pausing only to pick up her empty basket, then she turned and ran down the steep and well-trodden path that led down to the ferry. When she reached the shore she stood, panting, catching her breath after the unaccustomed exercise.

'You've not been long, Mistress. Did you visit Mother Watkin? How does she fare?'

Cecily, still breathless, swung round to face the man who addressed her. He was a year or two younger than she was, not yet reached twenty, with curly dark hair and an open smile. He wore a leather tunic for protection against the biting river breeze. Last time she had seen him he had been wearing the coarse black habit of a Benedictine monk. Brother Bartholomew was continuing his work as a ferryman, Priory or no Priory.

'What is it, Sister? Is something wrong?'

When one has lost one's place in the world, small reminders of more secure times, like Bartholomew's use of the title 'Sister', provide some small comfort. Twelve weeks before, when the Convent of St Mary in nearby Chester had been closed by the King's commissioners, Cecily had returned to Liverpool, the town of her childhood. At the time of her eviction she had feared the future . . . now she resolved to let nothing frighten her . . . not even death.

'I found a man dead in the Priory church . . . by the look of him, I fear his death was no accident.'

Bartholomew said nothing. He made sure his boat was moored securely then hurried up the steep path towards the church, his face anxious. Cecily followed behind, determined to keep up with his long strides. When they reached the church he knelt on the ground by the corpse.

He turned to Cecily. 'I know him. His name's Randle Melkin. He was steward of our Priory.' He paused and looked at the dead man with distaste. 'Our Prior was . . . is an unworldly man . . . one who'd trust the devil himself. Melkin was a lecher and a thief. Brother Cellarer told the Prior that things were missing but Father Prior, in his goodness, said that we had no proof. Of course when the commissioners arrived Melkin showed his true nature. He helped them strip the Priory of valuables . . . no doubt pocketing some for himself. He even threw the brothers

232

from the house . . . handled them roughly, even the aged. It seems now that he has paid for his wrongdoings. His is one death that will not be mourned by many.'

'Had he a wife . . . children?'

Bartholomew shook his head and touched the body gingerly with his toe. 'What woman would have such a man? He spent many a night over in Liverpool . . . there are plenty of whores in the taverns there who will not refuse a coin for their services . . . whoever the man might be.'

Cecily smiled. 'Do you speak from experience, Brother?'

This had the desired effect of making Bartholomew blush. 'Indeed not, Sister. Unlike some, I keep to my vows . . . even now.' Finding the subject embarrassing, he changed it. 'We must take his body to lie in your brother's church. I know of no kin.'

Bartholomew lifted the limp remains of Randle Melkin. His arms were strong from rowing against the currents of the river. He carried his burden to the ferry with ease.

The crossing was smooth and the boat's progress was swift; a pleasant breeze cooled the heat of the sunlight which set the water sparkling. When they reached the Liverpool shore, Cecily stepped from the boat on to the wooden jetty then walked along the busy strand towards the church. She held her nose against the stench of the fish piled against the red sandstone walls of the Tower, Lord Stanley's house, which dominated the waterfront and was well fortified against enemies and the elements. Damp red sand penetrated her shoes, slowing her steps as Bartholomew walked behind with his gruesome burden. Fishermen, mending their nets, crossed themselves when they saw the body, and foreign sailors, loitering on the shore, made signs to ward off evil.

Cecily opened the great wooden doors of the church of Our Lady and St Nicholas, and walked slowly up the centre aisle in front of Bartholomew. Halfway up the aisle she stopped, cursing herself that she had forgotten. Today was the funeral of Jinny Wright, a young mother who had died falling from the cliffs near the abandoned Priory of Birkenhead. The cliffs were treacherous and Jinny, being new to the district, hadn't been raised with a knowledge of their dangers.

In front of her was Jinny's small, roughly hewn coffin, standing on trestles before the high altar. Cecily's brother, Father James, looked up from his prayers and signalled by his expression that their entry had come at an inappropriate time. Cecily touched Bartholomew's arm and whispered that they should seek refuge in one of the side chapels. Bartholomew laid the body of Randle Melkin on the floor of the chantry chapel of St John, where a carved oak screen hid it from the sight of the tiny congregation. They waited silently.

Cecily watched through the screen, observing Jinny Wright's bereaved husband, Matthew. He had come to Birkenhead in the early spring to work as a cartwright on the Priory estates, bringing his pretty young wife

233

and their baby to share his small cottage. Jinny's death three days ago had grieved all who heard of it: a tragic accident that had left a baby motherless just as its father's livelihood was threatened by the Priory closure. Cecily had been forced out into the world from the sanctuary of her convent to keep house for her brother, but Matthew Wright's troubles made her own seem trivial. She resolved to visit Matthew, to offer any help she could . . . and to pray for him.

When the service was over, the tiny procession snaked out into the churchyard which overlooked the strand. As the passing bell tolled, Jinny Wright was laid to rest in the sandy ground while sailors and fishermen, going about their business on the strand, paused to make the sign of the cross and reflect on the briefness of mortal existence.

Bartholomew and Cecily stayed back in the enclosed chapel, keeping their vigil over Randle Melkin's stinking earthly remains. Cecily held her breath and touched the dark crusted patch on the front of the dead man's jerkin. 'It's blood,' she said, matter of fact. Her fingers came into contact with a small slash in the cloth, a thin opening about an inch long. 'He was stabbed.'

Bartholomew nodded. He had come to the same conclusion. 'He was a man who made enemies more readily than friends. There were many with a reason to take his life.'

'Do you suspect any in particular?'

Bartholomew shrugged. 'Any brother of our house who had so endured his provocation that he forgot his duty to God . . . any tenant or worker badly treated . . . any whore he'd abused or cheated of her due reward. It is a long list. The constable must be told of his death.'

Cecily looked at her companion, worried. 'When I found the body I saw Brother Richard. He was there in the Priory church. I called to him but . . .' She hesitated. She had no wish to throw suspicion on a man who might be innocent.

Bartholomew said nothing but left to find the constable. He knew where Liverpool's guardian of law and order would be found – at the Mermaid Tavern, sampling the delights of the ale and the young women who plied their trade there. Bartholomew was loath to enter such a place, but it was his duty as an honest citizen.

Cecily was alone in the church with Melkin's body. The heat was oppressive as the candles sucked in the air that kept them alive and the heaviness of the incense mixed with the odours of putrefying flesh. Cecily felt slightly faint. She needed air.

As she walked back down the long central aisle she noticed a shaft of jewelled sunlight, filtered through a stained glass window, illuminating a cluster of small circlets hanging on the stone wall. Cecily knew what they represented. Each small wreath of flowers hung there in remembrance of a virgin – an unmarried girl of the parish who had died in the tenderness of her youth. Cecily hated them; they spoke of lives cut short by disease or misadventure; lives full of promise; lives like Cecily's own. It had been a good six weeks since such a maiden had breathed her last in Liverpool: young Mary Wills had died of a fever which no herbs or medicines could abate. Her fading wreath of brown crisped flowers hung there. But next to Mary's memorial hung a new circlet of fresh blooms: white roses, poppies and cornflowers; the bright colours of nature luminous against the dark stone wall.

Cecily wondered about this new wreath. It could hardly have been placed there in memory of Jinny Wright . . . a mother of a young child was no unmarried virgin. Somewhere in the town of Liverpool a young woman had died and, as was the custom, her circlet had been placed for all to see on the church wall. But who was she? And how had she died?

James would know. As parish priest, Cecily's older brother knew everything that happened in the town. He had probably given the unfortunate girl the last rites himself. However, when she saw her brother later that day he assured her that no young unmarried woman had died in the town since the unfortunate Mary Wills. He had no explanation for the circlet on the wall.

Cecily tried to put the matter from her mind but that night it kept returning, preventing sleep. She awoke the next morning, dressed and said her prayers. James broke his fast with a lump of bread and a small tankard of weak ale and soon left to attend to his duties in the church.

Cecily planned her day. There was work to be done in the cottage she shared with her brother . . . and the fair to visit. Liverpool would be bustling for the next three days as the whole district descended on the town: traders, country folk, jugglers, mummers, rogues, cut-purses, acrobats; they would all be there . . . and others besides. After the tranquillity of her convent years, Cecily anticipated the fair with suppressed excitement. If she went to the High Cross now to buy bread then she would see the fair folk arriving, see the stalls and booths being set up; she might even hear the latest news of events in faraway London, of the goings on at the King's court. There was many a travelling pedlar glad to dispense the latest court gossip for the price of a length of ribbon.

With a willow basket suspended from her arm, Cecily walked up Chapel Street towards the centre of the town. Tomorrow was the feast day of St James and the fair would begin, but now the dusty, rubbish-strewn streets around the High Cross buzzed with chatter and anticipation. Voices were raised as shopkeepers argued with the newcomers who, for three days, would filch their trade. Dogs roamed amongst the carts and the half-built stalls, on the lookout for any tasty morsel to steal. Thieves of the human kind, watchful and crafty-faced, kept a sharp eye on the proceedings. It would be the next day, however, when the fair began that their talents at picking pockets and cutting purses would be practised in earnest. Cecily looked down at the purse that hung from her waist; it was still there. She put her free hand on it, just in case.

When Brother Richard hurtled into her, she nearly fell on to the offal-strewn earth but somehow managed to keep her balance and dignity intact. The young man stopped a few yards from her, his desperate eyes looking this way and that, seeking escape. He was a little older than Cecily, short and fair. He wore a gown that, if not of the finest quality, was new and unworn; each brother had been given such a gown when he left the confines of Birkenhead Priory. Cecily was about to remonstrate with Brother Richard for his clumsiness when another man, a large grizzled creature with beery breath and a belly to match, pushed past her and stood face to face with the young man.

'Richard Belton, as constable of the town I do arrest you for the murder of Randle Melkin.'

Cecily had a sudden, sick feeling that it had been her testimony that had brought Brother Richard to this. Richard Belton pulled himself up to his full height and looked the constable boldly in the eye.

'I claim the sanctuary of the fair,' he said with loud confidence. 'You cannot lay hands on me.'

The constable looked as though he'd been struck. What Richard said was true. For ten days before and after the fair anyone who placed themselves within the bounds of the two sanctuary stones set into the ground to mark the fair's limits, was immune from arrest. The constable stood back; he had played this waiting game before. All he had to do was to ensure that the wanted man was arrested lawfully when the time came. If he stepped outside the protection of the sanctuary stones in the meantime, the Justice of the Peace and the hangman would be waiting.

Some of the crowd began to applaud, shouting encouragement to the sanctuary seeker. Cecily guessed that some of the fair folk had dark deeds in their own pasts that made them more sympathetic to the wrongdoer than the average upright citizen would be. But most of Richard's supporters were local people. Perhaps they had known Randle Melkin and considered that his killer had done the town a service.

Cecily felt a hand on her shoulder. She dug her elbow back sharply; former nun or no former nun, she would not let any man relieve her of her purse.

An agonised cry from behind made her swing round. Bartholomew stood there, bent slightly, his hand clutching his side, his face a grimace of agony. Cecily realised what she had done. 'I'm sorry,' she said anxiously, 'I thought you a cutpurse.'

He recovered his breath. 'I would not dare cut your purse, lady.' He managed a smile. 'Even if I were inclined to.'

236

'Did you see Brother Richard claim sanctuary? Did you tell the constable that I saw . . .'

'No, I swear. I merely informed the man of Melkin's death. It seems others saw Richard at the Priory church around the time Melkin must have died . . . and they spoke of a quarrel between the two men. It seems certain that he killed Melkin.'

'A brother . . . guilty of murder? Surely he cannot have forgotten his vows so soon.'

'If he is guilty he must have been sorely provoked. We all knew Melkin and he was much skilled in provocation.' Bartholomew spoke with bitter sincerity. 'I spoke with Brother Richard this morning and he denies all knowledge of Melkin's death. He says they quarrelled over Melkin's treatment of a sick and ageing brother who stays in a cottage near the Priory. He says he passed by the church on the way back from visiting that brother. He claims he saw nobody.'

'Do you believe him?' She looked into Bartholomew's eyes.

He looked back at her earnestly. 'Yes. I lived with him at the Priory for six years. I have never known him tell an untruth.'

'Desperate times make men desperate. I myself have done many things since I left my convent that I would not have contemplated as a docile sister.'

Bartholomew raised his dark eyebrows but made no comment. 'I fear it is only a matter of time before Brother Richard is taken. The sanctuary of the fair lasts but ten days.'

'Unless he escapes. I see the constable has set some of his men to watch over him.' She indicated a pair of sour-faced men lingering in a tavern doorway, their eyes fixed on the wanted man.

'Or he is proved innocent,' Bartholomew said softly, not really believing this was a possibility.

The prospect of the fair had lost its excitement. Cecily wandered back to the small whitewashed house set in a corner of the churchyard that had been her home for three long months since she had ceased to be a sister of the order of St Benedict.

Work . . . she needed something useful to occupy her; serving God or others. The cottage was empty when she returned. James, she knew, would be saying mass over at the church. She emptied her basket of the things she had bought: bread, cheese, a salmon fished from the Mersey that very morning. The thick stew she had made yesterday still stood in a cauldron near the hearth. She took a jug, filled it with stew and broke off half the fresh loaf. It was a fine, calm day and the river was smooth as a village pond, so if she was careful to keep the jug upright, the stew wouldn't spill out on her journey.

She met Bartholomew on the strand, busy with sailors and folk from over the river bringing their produce to sell at the fair. The ferry was full and sat low in the water. Bartholomew hoisted the single sail and

237

a summer breeze aided their passage. They dodged between huge wooden merchant ships at anchor, silent and emptied of their crews who were ashore seeking out the delights of Liverpool's taverns.

Cecily sat next to the ferryman. Bartholomew knew the river so well that little concentration was needed on such a tranquil day.

'I'm taking these victuals to Matthew Wright,' she told him.

'A man with no wife and a little one to feed will not turn away good stew and bread.'

'Your thoughts match my own, Brother. Have you heard how he copes with his loss?' Bartholomew knew all the gossip of both sides of the river. People talked to the ferryman.

'He says little to his neighbours,' Bartholomew said thoughtfully. 'He is a man who does not seek help . . . and often rejects it when it is offered.'

Cecily hoped this wouldn't apply to her stew, but her fears were groundless. When she arrived at Matthew Wright's cottage, set in a small hamlet that accommodated Birkenhead Priory's workers, he recognised her as the priest's sister and greeted her with a sad, respectful quietness. The child, he explained was asleep and was well.

When she offered the bread and stew, he hesitated before he took them from her. He was a good-looking young man of middling height, with brown hair and a clear complexion that did not bear the familiar scars of smallpox that afflicted so many people of every class and condition. He took the food with a nervous half-smile and his hand touched Cecily's rather longer than was necessary.

She blushed. But she must have been mistaken. Only a rogue would regard another woman in that way with his wife not yet cold in her grave, and Matthew Wright was no rogue; his face was honest and open, and there was admiration rather than lechery in his eyes.

Cecily looked downwards; the habit of modesty, learned from her years in the convent, had not left her. The room was poor but neat. The only hint of disorder was a small pile of soiled clothes pushed into one corner, waiting to be laundered. The rushes on the floor were fairly fresh and Cecily, her eyes still downcast, noticed a few petals scattered on the floor which stood out against the dull brown of the earth and rushes like jewels: petals of poppies, cornflowers and white roses. She had seen such a combination before, woven together in a circle and hanging on the church wall. She looked up at Matthew. Looking a man who was not a close relative in the eyes was a new experience for one who had recently been ejected from the shelter of the cloister, but times were changing. Cecily looked into Matthew Wright's blue eyes and asked her question. 'Did you put the virgin's circlet on the church wall yesterday?'

He averted his gaze. She repeated her question. After a few moments' thought he nodded.

'Why?' Cecily spoke gently, softly. If this man was to confide in her, he must first trust her.

'Jinny was a maid . . . she died a virgin.'

At first Cecily didn't understand. She thought of the baby. Then the truth began to emerge from the confusion like a shape from a fog. 'She wasn't your wife, was she?'

He shook his head. 'My wife died giving birth to the little one. Jinny is . . . was my sister, and a sweeter, gentler maid never walked this earth,' he added with conviction.

'Why did you lie?'

He thought for a moment before beginning his explanation. 'We came here from Runcorn. Our village had been visited by the sweating sickness and we feared for the health of the little one. I met with a chapman who told me that the brothers of Birkenhead were in need of a cartwright and I had heard that the brothers were good to their workers. When we came here I had not thought to lie about Jinny. I intended to tell all that she was my sister, but the steward of the Priory . . . he made . . . suggestions to her when she found herself alone with him on the day we arrived. I found him with her, saw she was afraid, and I told him not to touch my wife. Once the lie was out we had to keep to it. We put it about that we were man and wife, not brother and sister. The babe is too young to say different.'

There was a whimper from the rough-hewn wooden cradle near the hearth and Matthew looked round, suddenly anxious. He went to the cradle and bent over his son, his face gentle and loving.

Cecily took the opportunity to study the cottage's single room and her eyes were again drawn to the heap of dirty clothes in the corner. She edged towards the pile and touched it with her foot. A piece of off white linen came into view as the clothes shifted. It was stained with dots of rusty brown. Matthew Wright was still bending over the cradle, rocking it with his foot, comforting the babe whose cries were increasing in volume. Cecily, watching him, bent down and fingered the discarded shirt. As she touched the pile she felt something metallic and unyielding. Her hand explored further and, breath held, she made out the shape of a dagger amongst the clothes.

It was so clear now. Randle Melkin had made unwanted advances to young Jinny, and when things had gone too far, when even the lies about her being a married woman no longer discouraged the lecherous rogue, Jinny's devoted brother had defended his sister's honour with a dagger. She stood up and looked at the man who was rocking his baby back to its innocent sleep.

'Did you kill Randle Melkin?'

He swung round, astonished. He started to walk slowly towards her and she wondered if she had cause to be afraid. She was alone with a man who had killed. She cursed herself for her naiveté; life as a sister hadn't prepared her for the evils and passions of the world. Matthew Wright continued to come towards her, his eyes fixed on the heap of clothes.

Cecily backed away, her heart beating like a trapped bird's. She bent and grabbed at the clothes, fumbling amongst their folds for the dagger. But Matthew was too quick for her. As soon as her fingers had closed on the dagger's hilt, she felt her wrist being held tightly. Her strength left her as he tried to force the dagger, rusty and bloodstained, from her grasp. With her free hand she grabbed at the bloodstained shirt. If she could cover his eyes for a second she could free herself and make her escape. She would run back to the ferry, return to Liverpool and inform the constable of the true identity of Randle Melkin's killer. Brother Richard would be free.

She took hold of the shirt and yanked it from the pile. But it didn't free itself from the other clothes . . . it was too long. It wasn't a man's shirt – it was a woman's shift.

She let the dagger drop to the floor as Matthew loosened his grip. She looked at him with sudden understanding. 'It was Jinny – she killed him.'

Matthew stood back, tears in his eyes. 'My sister was a virtuous maid. That man . . . he would not leave her be. Three days ago she came to me in great distress. He had met her on the cliff path and tried to . . .' He paused. The memory was still painful. 'Since he helped the commissioners expel the brothers who had employed him from their Priory, he had thought himself as mighty as the King himself.' He shook his head.

'Go on,' she prompted. 'What happened?'

'I made her carry my dagger for her own protection. I knew what danger she was in from that man. My ruse had not worked. Either he had guessed the truth that we were not man and wife or he did not care a jot whether she was married or not. When he met her alone and tried to— She defended herself as I had told her she must. She ran back here, her gown covered in his blood. Nobody saw her. I . . . I . . .' Cecily noted his distress. The tale wasn't yet over. 'I had to move the body,' he continued. 'The cliff path is near this house and questions might have been asked of us. I started to drag the body away; Jinny followed, watching to make certain that we were not observed. Then she . . . she lost her footing and fell down the cliff. There was nothing I could do to save her. When I reached the foot of the cliff she was dead.'

By now his eyes were glassy with tears. Cecily touched his hand and then put her arms around him. He held her close, trying to put the image of his sweet, dead sister from his mind. Cecily stood, statue still, breathing in the warmth of his strong body. Her fingers touched the rough linen of his shirt. She had never been this close to a man before. The experience was unnerving . . . yet thrilling.

240

'There is something you must do,' she whispered.

'What?' Matthew reached out his hand and pushed an untamed strand of fair hair away from her face.

'There is a young man in Liverpool, a brother of Birkenhead, who will hang for Melkin's murder if you do not tell the truth. He claims the sanctuary of the fair but in ten days . . .'

'Then I have no choice. I cannot let an innocent man hang. And nothing can harm my sister now.'

Cecily leaned towards him and kissed him on the cheek.

'I must put this matter behind me,' he said softly. 'For the sake of my little one, I must begin a new life.'

'As must we all,' said Cecily with feeling.

As Matthew Wright kissed her, Cecily gave thanks for the deliverance of Brother Richard . . . and said a quick prayer for Jinny Wright's soul.

One of the strengths of Ellis Peters' Brother Cadfael books was that she knew – and loved – the Shropshire setting which she evoked with such skill. Research, to her, was a pleasure rather than a duty, and in a magazine interview she once said, 'I could happily spend every moment buried among books in the archives.' I felt much the same way when I decided to write this story. It is set in Balliol, the Oxford college where I spent three happy years as a student. I had been toying with the idea of creating a sort of proto-Sherlockian cerebral detective, and one day I wondered if Benjamin Jowett, the legendary Master of Balliol, might be a suitable candidate.

When I started to read up about Jowett, I realised how skimpy my knowledge of his career had been. The more I learned about this extraordinary man, the more fascinated I became by the parallels between him and Holmes. It seemed to me that the Jowler was just the sort of person who, confronted by a locked room mystery or 'impossible crime', might indulge in a bit of armchair sleuthing. It was fun, too, to learn about what Oxford was like in Victorian times. Soon I had gathered enough background material for a full-length novel; however the plot I had in mind suited a short story better. So here is the first detective adventure of Benjamin Jowett. All being well, it will not be the last.

Martin Edwards

The Mind of the Master

Martin Edwards

T he joyful cry of murder drowned the clatter of the cab-horses as I stepped from the Law Courts and into the Strand. The newsboys' raucous message made the crowd thronging the street hum with excitement: '*Mysterious slaying in Oxford! Man found strangled by invisible foe!*'

Hastily, I searched the pockets of my frock-coat for a penny. I must confess that I am a murder addict and my appetite for sensation was whetted by the prospect of a bizarre crime occurring in the city I knew so well. During my years at the university, Benjamin Jowett often teased me about my fondness for penny dreadfuls and *The Newgate Calendar*. He once claimed that if I devoted as much time to absorbing the precepts of the common law of England as I did to devouring tales of mayhem, I would surely become Lord Chancellor. I replied with a sly grin that I hoped patronage and family connections would assure me of an honoured place in the legal establishment, but that if I were to realise my private ambition to become a detective, I saw no alternative to diligent study of my subject. At that, the eyes of the Master of Balliol twinkled. He was famed as a theologian and philosopher, but perhaps it was because of those passions, rather than in spite of them, that he too found it impossible to resist a mystery.

In the gathering gloom of a December afternoon, I paused under a gas-lamp at the corner of Bell Yard to scan the report of the killing. Suddenly I froze. I could take in nothing of the details of the murder, nor of the guarded comments of the police inspector in charge of the case. I had eyes for only one thing – the name of the victim. It was George Wansborough, my oldest friend from student days.

Risking my neck as I dodged between the horses, I hurried back to my chambers in Stone Buildings. I wired Jowett at once and announced to Grayson, my clerk, that I intended to leave for Oxford by the first train.

'But Mr Castellain, your conference with Sir Fitzroy . . .'

It was my habit to wave his objections aside with a smile, but on this occasion I surprised myself with the vehemence of my reply. 'A friend

245

of mine has been strangled. Nothing else matters. Sir Fitzroy will have to wait. Get a message to his estate manager, will you?'

Barristers' clerks are nothing if not realists, and recognising that I was in no mood to brook argument, Grayson did as he was told. By midnight, I was back in my old college, warming my hands in front of the fire in the Master's Lodgings as I took advantage once again of Jowett's inimitable hospitality.

The Master shared my grief at the dreadful news. George Wansborough had been a bluff uncomplicated fellow, who had perhaps owed his place at Balliol more to intensive efforts at the best crammer school that money could buy than to particular acuity of intellect. One might have supposed that Jowett would have had little time for him; the two had little in common. Yet the Master had a genius for friendship and he relished George's amiable good humour. The death of his former pupil came as a considerable blow.

George and I had met in the Buttery on our first day as students, and were inseparable from then on, until I began my pupillage and he sailed for the sub-continent. The Wansboroughs had their roots firmly planted in the soil of Yorkshire, but they had made their fortune far from the county of broad acres. Their tea business had been founded by George's great-grandfather in the seventeenth century and had prospered from that time on. Queen Victoria herself was said to insist that Wansborough's Darjeeling was served at Windsor to honoured guests.

George and I shared a love of cricket, and although his technique was too rustic for him ever to have contemplated playing for a county eleven, he had often come to cheer me on in an important match. Our last meeting had occurred in the early weeks of the past season when I had captained the Gentlemen against the Players at Lord's. On that occasion George had been back in England, albeit briefly, for the first time in six months, but he had confided in me that he had had his fill of India for the time being. It was time for his younger brother Henry to take over the reins abroad while George managed the London office. He intended to sail back to England later in the year and hoped that he would then be able to persuade Miss Camilla Hargrave to become his wife. This was the same Camilla Hargrave who, according to the Press, had been questioned closely and at length by the detectives investigating the death of the man she loved.

Oxford, Jowett told me, was alive with rumour. Few details of the murder had been made public by the police, but it was widely believed that the method of strangulation resembled that practised by the Thugs of India. One story suggested that during the course of his business activities overseas, George had made sinister enemies. A rival theory held that the killing was not the work of mortal man, for according to a witness of impeccable character, it was impossible for an assassin to have penetrated the room where George had met his end.

246

The Master stroked his chin. 'It is an extraordinary case. And yet its very extraordinariness makes me wonder.'

He lapsed into a reverie. The only sounds in the room were the crackling of the logs on the fire and the sedate ticking of his brass lantern clock. Whilst he mused, I considered him. Jowett was a slightly built, fragile-looking man whose cherubic features gave few clues to the legendary sharpness of his mind. He was at this time at the height of his powers and had transformed the college into the leading academic institution of the British Empire. His house was the focus of the city and more than once I had heard him say that his ambition was to inoculate England with alumni of Balliol. I was one of many who had benefited from his generosity. On one occasion my antics with a young lady from the town would have caused me to be sent down had not Jowett intervened on my behalf. I was proud nowadays to call him a friend. For all that, I always found it impossible to read his thoughts. Although, as a disciple of Socrates, he valued speech more highly than any other gift, he had no interest whatsoever in small talk and never spoke idly. I had learned to pay close heed to everything he said. Even then, he revealed precisely as much as he wished to reveal and no more.

'I don't understand,' I said at length.

He shook his head, as if dissatisfied with his own speculations. 'Perhaps it is no more than an idle fancy on my part. Like you, I find it difficult to absorb such a tragedy.'

'What do you make of the journalists' suggestion of murder by supernatural means, though? It's like something out of the pages of Sheridan Le Fanu!'

'Le Fanu was another trained barrister who preferred romantic intrigue to the sober reality of legal practice, was he not?' Jowett inquired drily. 'As you know, I have in the past myself been persecuted for supposed heresy, but the idea of murder by poltergeist hardly accords with my own prejudices.'

'But the housekeeper, Mrs Foxall! According to her testimony, she saw nothing and no one enter the room after George said goodbye to Camilla. After locking the front door, George went upstairs to work on a set of papers in preparation for the tea company's annual general meeting. The window of the room was barred. So were the windows of the other rooms up there. Mrs Foxall never left the front room, where she was cleaning silver. With its door open, the papers say, that room commands an unimpeded view of the foot of the stairs. Although it is years since I last visited the house, that accords with my own recollection. She claims that no living creature – even if in possession of a key – could have entered the house, climbed to the first floor and murdered George without her becoming aware of it.'

'Yet that is exactly what happened,' Jowett pointed out. 'I would be the first to admit to you that there are many things in life beyond the wit of

247

man to explain. Yet murder, I believe, is unlikely to be one of them. Blow away the cloud of mystery and one beholds the basest human motives: envy, greed, revenge.'

'I have met Mrs Foxall more than once,' I said. 'She has looked after the house in Summertown ever since George bought it.' That had been shortly after his graduation. He was so fond of Oxford and its environs that on his periods of leave from India he preferred to spend time at his pied-à-terre rather than in London or at the family home in Yorkshire. 'She is a trustworthy soul, hard-working and reliable. As for the house, it is pleasant, but compact in size. If she says that no one could have broken in without her knowing of it, I would take her at her word.'

'Mrs Foxall claims, according to the reports, that a heated quarrel took place between George and Camilla. Camilla called on him at ten o'clock and shortly thereafter the housekeeper heard raised voices. The sound of their argument distressed her because she claims she was as fond of the girl as she was of George.'

'Again, I feel bound to treat her as an honest witness. She is a simple soul. I do not believe she would lie in order to cast even the faintest suspicion on Camilla Hargrave. As for Camilla; the very idea that she might do George harm would be laughable if it were not so serious. The police must have overlooked something.' I paused and said softly, 'George's murderer must be found, Master. We must do all we can to help.'

'You have always been a man of action, Castellain,' he said, poking the fire. 'I content myself with the academic life, theorising from my armchair.'

'But together,' I urged, 'we would make an unbeatable detective team.'

Against his better judgement, Jowett found himself accompanying me to Camilla Hargrave's lodgings off St Aldate's the next morning. It was a typically damp and grey Oxford day and the Master had encased himself in heavy coat and muffler to guard against catching a chill. His hypochondria had always amused me; it is comforting to detect the flaws of common humanity in a man of eminence. I was touched as well as relieved that he had consented to join me in my enterprise.

'You told me that you have finally managed to get Thucydides off your hands,' I teased him over breakfast.

'And I should be hard at work on Aristotle's *Politics* this morning,' he insisted.

'You ought to thank me for offering you a chance to escape. I think I would find even the Rule against Perpetuities a more colourful subject for study.'

'You forget,' he said severely, 'that I take pleasure in that which others regard as hard work.'

248

Yet finally I had convinced him that he owed it to George to humour me in my actions. My motives in seeking his help were more selfish than I was ready to admit, however. Stunned by George's murder and desperate to take steps to solve it, I recognised that my own sense of urgency needed to be complemented by his cool logic and dedication to the truth.

I had first met Camilla after she became close to George. She was then a pretty eighteen-year-old with long dark hair and an unforgettable figure who hoped to make her name as an actress. The couple's courtship had not followed a conventional path, for Camilla's delightful appearance and manner concealed a burning ambition to reach the peak of her chosen profession, and she had made it clear that becoming a wife was far from being her highest priority. For his part, George had spent most of his time since leaving Oxford in the sub-continent. Yet it had always seemed to me that they were ideally suited and I had been sure that she would accept his long-postponed proposal.

She was dressed from head to toe in black. I could tell that she had been weeping and her voice was husky with barely suppressed emotion when she greeted us. I have never seen such utter desolation in any face as when I commiserated with her on her tragic loss.

'The last twenty-four hours have been a nightmare,' she said. 'I have lost the only man I ever loved – and what haunts me is that we parted for the last time on the most acrimonious terms. Believe me, Richard, that causes me far more pain than this absurd notion that I might be a murderess. You know I would gladly die myself than cause George the slightest injury.'

As I took her small hands in mine, Jowett said, 'Could you tell us the reason for your quarrel with George?'

Two bright spots of colour came to her white cheeks. 'He had received an anonymous letter. It made wicked insinuations about my relationship with Arthur Fairhead.'

'Arthur?' I was astonished. 'But I have heard nothing of him for years. Didn't he go abroad?'

'Yes, he returned to this country only a short time ago. As you may recall, I owe him a great deal. It was Arthur who first introduced me to George.'

I nodded. Arthur Fairhead had been a contemporary of ours. He and George had been at Winchester together and they had kept in touch throughout their student days, even though Arthur's college was Exeter rather than Balliol. His great enthusiasm was for drama, and he knew many of the actors and actresses who performed professionally in the city. Thus he had become acquainted with Camilla. When, through Arthur, she met George, the attraction was instant, mutual and intense. After university, Arthur had left England to travel abroad. He was an accomplished linguist and there was enough money in the family for him

249

to have no particular need to work for a living. His father was rather more understanding than my own.

'I lost touch with him,' I said. 'I had no idea that he was back in England.'

'A week ago, shortly before George was due back here, Arthur sent me a note explaining that he had taken a suite in the Randolph for a fortnight. He had a couple of tickets for a touring music hall show and, following a tiff with the young lady he had originally invited, he wondered if I would care to accompany him. I was happy to accept. After all, he and I have long been acquainted and his manners are impeccable.'

Her tone was unmistakably defensive. I said carefully, 'And Arthur's behaviour towards you was, I trust, quite proper?'

'Entirely,' she said with emphasis. 'He has behaved splendidly from the time I first made him aware of my feelings for George. Indeed, I was delighted to see him again. He is an attentive companion and his years of wandering around the Continent have provided him with a fund of amusing anecdotes. We enjoyed ourselves hugely. The show proved entertaining enough, although one of the principal performers was absent due to sickness. Afterwards, Arthur escorted me back here and we parted outside the front door.'

She cleared her throat and then added, 'Richard, I swear to you that there was not a hint of impropriety on either my part or his. He did not even venture a farewell peck on the cheek.'

Naturally I accepted her word. I cannot deny that it crossed my mind for an instant that she was an accomplished stage performer, accustomed to playing a part, but I banished the unworthy thought at once. I could not doubt the depth of her devotion to my dead friend. Yet I had to pursue the question of the anonymous missive.

'I never saw it,' she said. 'George told me that he had thrown the foul thing on the fire as soon as he had read it. If only he had been able to brush aside the accusation with comparable ease. He should have known me well enough to realise the insane untruthfulness of the allegations concerning my conduct with Arthur Fairhead. Yet it was obvious to me that they had begun to gnaw at him.'

'Jealousy is a corrosive emotion,' Jowett said softly. I recalled that in his own field he had been a victim of envious, lesser men. 'I hope you were able to set his mind at rest?'

She chewed at her lower lip. 'I regret with all my heart that I could not do so. I was unwise, you see. The suggestion that Arthur and I had . . . no, I cannot even speak of it. Yet what inflamed my temper was that George should put even the smallest degree of credence in anonymous tittle-tattle with no foundation whatsoever.'

'Do you have any idea who may have been responsible for the letter?' I asked. 'Is there a person who might have cause to wish you ill?'

'I have racked my brains,' she said earnestly, 'but I can think of no one.'

'None of us cares for the idea that we may have enemies,' I persisted. 'Could there be an envious colleague, perhaps, or a person who might have taken deep offence at a casual remark of yours and be tempted to seek a perverted form of revenge?'

Her bewilderment was pitiful to see. 'I simply cannot say.'

Jowett coughed. 'You were unable, then, to heal this rift with George before you left the house in Summertown yesterday?'

'I am afraid so. I had called on him expecting that we would discuss in more detail the arrangements for our wedding. Instead I found myself called upon to respond to baseless lies put about by a coward unwilling to disclose his – or her – own name. It was more than I could bear and I must confess to you that anger conquered common sense. I told him that if he were reluctant to accept my word against that of an unsigned note, there was no future for the two of us together. With that, I burst into tears and rushed out of the drawing room, past Mrs Foxall and out of the house. A little way down the street, I glanced back over my shoulder. George was standing in the doorway, calling out an apology. I took no notice, telling myself that he needed to be taught a lesson. Finally I heard him bang the door shut. Little did I realise that I would never see him alive again.'

Once again she began to sob. I glanced at Jowett. He was studying her intently. 'It seems from the newspapers,' he said at length, 'that Mrs Foxall claims she was occupying the perfect place for observing anyone come and go in the hall or on the stairs. Is that correct?'

'Oh yes, she is telling the truth. I could not imagine her doing otherwise. As Richard here is well aware, she is a decent woman and in her own way she worshipped George. After I left, it seems that he went up to his study to work on business matters – and that is where he met his end.'

'Yet that is what makes the whole appalling business such a mystery,' I said. 'Someone must have entered the house and killed George. If the newspapers are right in claiming that the first floor of the house was wholly inaccessible except via the stairs, because of the bars on the windows, then the only route to the murder scene was by the staircase. One is forced to conclude that Mrs Foxall must be in error. Perhaps she left her chair for a few moments and thus allowed the malefactor to slip in and up the stairs unobserved. The incident may have passed completely from her mind, with the result that she is prepared to swear the truth of something that cannot possibly be right.'

'No other explanation has occurred to me,' she said, 'and yet it is surely a theory which underestimates Mrs Foxall. She is as straight as a die. Indeed, I owe her a debt. The policeman, McCoist, disapproves of my profession. He has tried to persuade her that I might have slipped back into the house to kill George, but she has sworn that he locked the door after I left.' She sighed. 'If she maintains that she never moved once, I would believe her. In any event, the murderer only had a short time in which to strike. Half an hour after I left the place, she called up to George to see if he would like a drink. Receiving no answer, she went up and knocked at his door. After a few moments she stepped inside and found him lying there next to his own desk.'

'The method of murder was unusual,' Jowett remarked. 'I understand – forgive me, I do not wish to add to your suffering – that it bore a resemblance to the garrotting technique associated with a band of assassins known as the Thugs of India. Have you ever heard George speak of any experience in the sub-continent which might have brought him into contact with surviving members of that murderous fraternity?'

She shook her head. 'It is all a mystery to me.'

Jowett looked thoughtful. 'I gather that the police questioned you in detail?'

'As I said, I would not be free now were it not for Mrs Foxall's testimony,' she said, so wretchedly that my heart went out to her. 'I pointed out, of course, that George was six feet tall and weighed fifteen stones. No one in his senses would regard me as physically capable of strangling him – even had I not loved him more than life itself.'

'The Thugs did not rely on brute force alone,' Jowett said softly, 'but rather on catching their victims unawares.'

He was leafing through some papers and magazines on an occasional table as he spoke and he failed to catch my glance of reproof. I considered his remark deeply unhelpful. It was self-evident that this sweet, forlorn creature could no more have harmed George Wansborough than she could have flown. Jowett had crushed her into silence and I had the awkward feeling that soon her tears would flow again.

Suddenly Jowett uttered a low exclamation and held up a theatre programme that he had found. 'I take it this came from the show that you attended with Arthur Fairhead?'

'Yes, but . . .'

'You may wish to consider it, Castellain.'

He handed me the programme and I glanced down the diverse cast-list. 'The Amazing Alphonse, a prestidigitator from Perpignan; a troupe of dancers who rejoice in the name of The Gladsome Girls; a mesmerist called El Gran Rubio; the comedian, Will Tasker; Lily Metcalfe, a singer of sentimental ballads; and, finally, a band of jugglers from Hyderabad in India!'

We took our leave of Camilla a few minutes later and I promised to keep in close touch. She thanked me, saying that Arthur and I had both been very kind. It was clear that she felt Jowett's manner had been more equivocal.

I challenged him about this as we made our way to the house in Summertown. 'Surely you cannot conceive that poor Camilla is

252

implicated in any way in this crime? What of the Indian connection? It seems remarkable to me. George worked there, he was killed by a cruel method indigenous to the country, and his fiancée had recently attended a variety performance which featured a group of performers from the self-same place.'

'A connection is suggested, certainly,' said Jowett. 'And yet . . .'

He lapsed into the meditative silence with which I was familiar. To accompany him when he was in taciturn mood could be an uncomfortable experience, particularly for those who were unaccustomed to his behaviour. On one celebrated occasion, he and a pupil had taken a lengthy walk together and he had not uttered a word. When they arrived at their destination, he had advised his hapless companion to cultivate the art of conversation. I knew better than to disturb him and kept my counsel until we arrived at the scene of the crime.

Mrs Foxall opened the door to us. She was a stout woman in her fifties, dressed in heavy mourning. The suspicious expression on her face suggested that she was expecting to be troubled again by newspaper reporters, but once she recognised me it was replaced by a look of surprise and welcome. It was plain from the redness around her honest hazel eyes and the lines on her brow that the shocking death of her master had affected her deeply.

'Mr Richard! It must be five years since you were last here!'

'Hello, Martha. Yes, glad as I am to see you again, I bitterly regret the circumstances.'

She blinked several times and I sensed that she needed to summon all her fortitude to resist tears. 'Come in, please,' she murmured. 'Mr Henry is in the front room.'

Before I could protest that Jowett and I had come particularly to see her, she ushered us into the presence of a tall pale man in a black frock coat. Henry Wansborough was seven years George's junior. I had met him several times, but had never particularly cared for him in his younger days. He was as tall as George, but thin and pale and he lacked his brother's amiable temperament. His lip had a natural curl and he could never resist an opportunity for sarcasm. George had often complained to me that Henry did not take his proper share of responsibility for the family business, preferring a flutter at the races to the demands of running a company from day to day. George's return from India would not only have given him the chance to marry, but also the opportunity to make a man out of his brother.

'Castellain! What brings you here?'

'In view of the terrible events of yesterday, Henry, I felt I must come here to express my condolences in person. May I introduce my companion? Benjamin Jowett, the Master of Balliol.'

Henry's eyebrows rose. 'The Jowler, eh? I have heard my brother speak of you, sir, though I must confess that I never understood what such a

253

legendary thinker could have seen in a ruffian of the rugby field. Ah well, *de mortuis* and all that. It is a bad business, especially since the police are demonstrating more than their customary ineptitude. That damn fool McCoist is nowhere near to making an arrest.'

'It appears to have been an impossible crime,' I said judiciously. 'Mrs Foxall has stated . . .'

He waved Mrs Foxall's statement away with an impatient gesture. 'Please, Castellain. This is no time for legal caution. The woman is willing enough, but she is naive. Depend upon it, there is a rational explanation for this so-called mystery.'

'Which is?'

'When the Hargrave woman took her leave of George, the door must have been left on the latch. She returned within minutes, wishing to take the quarrel further. Mrs Foxall was busy with her work and missed her stealthy arrival. The argument continued upstairs and . . .'

'You surely can't believe that!' I cried. 'She is incapable of such a crime. I would stake my life on it.'

'Then you will never make a gambling man. She's as guilty as sin, take my word for it. I tell you, she lulled George into a false sense of security, caught him unawares and strangled him.'

'So you think it is a straightforward crime?' asked Jowett.

'I certainly do.'

'In some particulars, I might be inclined to agree with you. And yet, you know, it strikes me as fascinating. I believe our murderer is daring as well as ingenious.'

Henry gave a dismissive grunt. 'I am aware, sir, that your forte is mental philosophy. The detection of crime is, I suggest, a very different matter. My complaint is that the police have yet to master it.'

By this time I could barely contain my anger. 'At least it is an ill wind, Henry.'

'What do you mean?'

'When I last spoke to George, he told me that he wanted you to take a turn out in India. I presume that is no longer likely to happen.'

He flushed. 'It was a foolish idea. I am no more an Indian tea trader than the Jowler here is a first-class cricketer. And now, gentlemen, if you will excuse me? It is good of you to come here today, but George's untimely death has left much to be done.'

As Mrs Foxall showed us out, I took the opportunity to put a few whispered questions to her. She was still in a state of extreme distress. 'Yes, the door was locked after Miss Camilla left. I would swear to it.' A couple of tears ran down her cheek. 'I only wish they had not parted so bitterly. You know yourself that Mr George could be fearsome on the odd occasion when he did lose his temper, but there was never any harm in him. I'm sure that within a couple of hours he would have admitted to himself that a visit to the music hall with an old friend is a perfectly innocent way of passing the time. I have seen the show myself and I found it most absorbing.'

'So you like the music hall?' Jowett asked.

'It's years since I last went to a performance,' she said, 'but the other day I had a stroke of real luck. I was sent two tickets with the compliments of the management, so I invited my sister Agnes to accompany me.'

Jowett frowned. 'Do you know what prompted such an act of generosity?'

'Lord, sir, I can't say I do. I presumed they wished to make the excellence of the show as widely known to local folk as possible. Certainly, Agnes and I have told all our friends about it.'

'I gather that when Miss Hargrave attended the performance, the cast was incomplete due to sickness,' said Jowett. 'I trust you were more fortunate?'

She nodded happily and Jowett gave me an enigmatic smile, as if her answer confirmed a subtle theory. I was bewildered and a little put out. What did it all mean? The Master was clearly not yet prepared to give me a clue. I decided that, for the time being at least, I would resist temptation and not give him the satisfaction of trying to pick his brains.

Our next call was on Arthur Fairhead in the elegant surroundings of the Randolph Hotel. He was a slightly built man, reserved and quietly spoken. I had not known him particularly well during our student days, although my impression had always been that he was an agreeable sort of fellow. George had liked him, but had always teased him for his shyness, and I could imagine how angry the malicious letter would have made him. George would not have relished the idea of Arthur suddenly becoming a rival for Camilla. If only he had thought through the slur, he would have realised how unthinkable it was for little Arthur to supplant him in Camilla's affections.

After having exchanged the usual words of shock and sorrow, we sat around a table in his sitting room, drinking tea and discussing the mystery which surrounded the murder in Summertown.

'I had planned to leave Oxford tomorrow,' Arthur said, 'but in the circumstances, of course I will stay on. I have no pressing commitments elsewhere; indeed, I was proposing to take a holiday up in the Lake District for a week or two. But that can wait. Although it is probably foolish, I feel that if I am at least on hand, then I may be doing something for George. And those he left behind. In particular, you have already seen Camilla. She has taken it all very badly, as one would expect. At present she undoubtedly needs a shoulder to lean on.'

I nodded. 'It is bad enough to lose the man one expects to marry, but the added burden of suspicion that the police seem to have placed upon her must be quite unbearable.'

'You have heard about the anonymous letter?' He fiddled absently with a gold ring on his forefinger. 'A vile piece of work and, I need scarcely add, devoid of even a shred of truth. Perhaps, on reflection, it was naive of me to take Camilla out, but I must confess that I gave the matter little thought. As you may recall, I knew her before George did and I have always cherished her friendship. George was a lucky man.'

Until yesterday, I reflected sombrely.

'It is a most peculiar business,' said Jowett. 'Have you formed any theory which might explain it?'

Arthur gave a helpless shrug. 'I must confess that I am almost inclined to believe that supernatural forces were at work.'

'So you do not share Henry's view that Camilla Hargrave is the culprit?'

Arthur coloured. 'Frankly, the suggestion is beneath contempt. For my part, I would defend her innocence to the death. No, if you must rule out the supernatural, I believe that the key to the puzzle will be found in India. The murder has all the hallmarks of a Thuggee assassination.'

'One thing has been troubling me about the link with India,' I said. 'I'd been under the impression that the Thugs were rooted out long ago, although I have to say I know very little about them.'

'For more than three centuries,' Jowett lectured me, 'the Thugs terrorised India, travelling across the country in gangs and seeking out innocents to murder and rob. They would win the confidence of a chosen victim and then, having disarmed him, throw a noose around his neck and pull it tight. Bentinck, who was Governor-General during the thirties, did indeed crack down on them and little has been heard of the cult in recent years. Those who were not hanged were jailed or transported. Yet it would be optimistic to assume that a sophisticated confederacy which wreaked havoc for so long could altogether be eradicated, even by the most vigorous upholders of law and order.'

Arthur nodded in enthusiastic agreement. 'I might have expected that the Master of Balliol would have an encyclopaedic knowledge of the subject. Perhaps, sir, you share my belief that George has fallen prey to a sinister conspiracy hatched in the East?'

Jowett simply smiled and said, 'My aim in this matter, as in any scholarly piece of work, is not to support any individual theory, but rather to establish the truth.'

'It is a terrible mystery,' I remarked, after we had regained the welcome warmth of Jowett's sitting room. A heavy rain was now falling and we had been drenched while making the short trip from the hotel to the college.

'I think not,' he said quietly.

I stared at him. 'I am sorry, I do not think I quite . . .'

'Terrible, yes. A mystery? By no means.'

I stared at him. 'So you *do* have an idea as to who might have murdered Wansborough?'

'It has been clear to me since our visit to Miss Camilla Hargrave,' said Jowett. 'Once I have explained the matter to you, we will need to speak to the police. I would rather that you did the talking. After all, you have been proved right in your belief that this tragic case offered the chance for amateur detective work. I am only glad that soon the perpetrator will be brought to book.'

'If this is a joke . . .' I began stiffly.

'Oh no, Castellain,' he said in a sad and gentle tone. 'This crime is far too serious for levity.'

I still believed he must be teasing me. 'What on earth are you suggesting?'

'Think of the problem in this case. Mrs Foxall says she saw no one enter or leave the house between the moment when Camilla Hargrave left and the time when she discovered George's body. There has been no hint that she has any motive for lying. Yet we know, do we not, that she was mistaken? I accept she would not lie intentionally. It is my belief, however, that she was persuaded to mislead the police and thus to establish a problem that no one could solve.'

'How could such a thing have been done?'

Jowett said simply, 'She was mesmerised.'

I swore. 'There was a hypnotist in the show at the music hall!'

'A show which Mrs Foxall saw,' he reminded me. 'If I were a gambling man, I would wager that she was one of the members of the audience whom El Gran Rubio put in a trance. He had, after all, carefully arranged for her to attend by sending the anonymous ticket so that he could establish that she was a suitable subject for hypnotism. The police will be able to verify as much by speaking to her sister. I fancy that, perhaps drawing on his classical education, the man used a ring both during the performance and on the day of the murder to impose his will upon the helpless woman. He commanded her to wipe the memory of his visit to Summertown from her mind and she obeyed.' He smiled mischievously. 'I hope that you will forgive my pointing out that my researches, which have afforded you such wry amusement over the years, gave me a distinct advantage when it came to making my deductions.'

'Please explain,' I said.

He reached up to a shelf and pulled down a volume of Plato. 'Do you know the story of Gyges, by any chance? No? A pity you never took a closer interest in the *Republic*. Gyges was a shepherd who found a ring that made him invisible. He used it to slay the King and seduce the Queen. Do you see the parallel?'

I was incredulous. 'You do not mean that the murderer is Arthur Fairhead?'

'I am afraid so. During the course of our enquiries, I have tried to piece together a theory which explains his actions. My supposition is that he lost his heart to Camilla when he was a student. He introduced her to

257

George and then found he had lost her. One can imagine the resentment he nourished over the years. Probably he spent several years on the Continent indulging his interest in theatricals, no doubt learning the art of mesmerism along the way. By the time he returned to this country, he was an established artiste, perfectly placed to act when he learned that George too was coming home and would at long last tie the knot with Camilla.'

'Why draw attention to himself by way of the anonymous letter?'

'It was a risky stroke, but clever too. He must have been desperate to renew his acquaintance with Camilla, and inviting her to accompany him to the music hall enabled him to do so. Of course, on that night, El Gran Rubio was indisposed. Fairhead behaved as the perfect gentleman. Any impartial judge would accept that the allegations in the anonymous letter were plainly false, yet they served to sow discord between the two lovers. With George dead, what more natural than that her loyal and chivalrous old friend Arthur should offer Camilla a shoulder to cry on? Especially when he had contrived matters so that a cloud of suspicion hung over her; although he sought to complicate the whole affair with a rather contrived attempt to suggest a Thuggee killing. Even in their hey-day, I do not think that members of the cult were inclined to come to England to seek out their victims. But for those, like the odious Henry, who were unimpressed by that piece of nonsense and the hint of murder by supernatural forces, Camilla was a credible suspect. For all your stout advocacy of her innocence, Fairhead was the one man who knew that she had not committed a crime of passion.'

I shook my head, still struggling to take it all in. 'One more thing. You said that you knew the truth before we left Camilla.'

He nodded. 'As soon as I saw the theatre programme, the principal elements of the scheme were clear to me. I am afraid that Fairhead made a fatal mistake in his choice of stage name. He must have settled upon it before deciding to exploit his theatrical persona for murderous purposes. A successful detective should, I fancy, hoard every scrap of information that ever comes into his possession. I have only a smattering of Spanish, but I can at least translate *El Gran Rubio*.'

'Which I cannot.'

Jowett bowed and said with a flourish, '*The Great Fairhead*.'

As I exclaimed with amazement, not unmixed with admiration, a rhyme from one of the college masques ran through my head:

> *Here come I, my name is Jowett*
> *There's no knowledge, but I know it,*
> *I am the Master of this college,*
> *What I know not isn't knowledge.*

I knew the late, great Ellis Peters for many years. I truly liked and admired her, still do in fact. (Here, I would normally have added, 'on and off', but she had too wry a sense of apt witticism for me to take liberties of that kind.) To follow is an anecdote about her; I am certain she wouldn't have minded.

Some years since, an acquaintance – call him Arn – called on me, having just interviewed Edith. He normally wrote, of all things, about the performance of motor cycles and analyses of computer programmes, so this was quite a departure. He had brought me an inscribed copy of her latest book, since he lived in a town nearby. Pleased, I asked how he'd got on, knowing the lady to be the best and gentlest of conversationalists.

'I only wish I'd realised that you knew her beforehand,' he said with feeling. 'You could have warned me how difficult she is!'

I was astonished. Edith Pargeter, *difficult*? Impossible! Arn recounted his sorry tale. The interview had gone something like this:

Arn (notepad at the ready): 'Now, what sort of things did they eat in the Middle Ages?'
  EP: 'Oh, all sorts of things.'
  Arn: 'Er, well what did they *wear* in the Middle Ages?'
  EP: 'Oh, all sorts of things.'
  Arn (losing steam): 'Oh. What were they interested in . . . ?'

And so on. After what seemed hours he was reduced to a grease spot and finally slid out, exhausted, vowing never to interview another writer. I expressed sympathy, but couldn't really believe his account. The following year, I made a detour on the way back to the north to see her. She brought up the matter of the interview, which I'd forgotten about until then. Ah, yes, the bloke Edith had sent with her book. Had he been an ordeal?

'Not at all,' she said, with that gentle grin.' However, I've always thought that a writer has a right to expect a certain level of non-ignorance

259

from interviewers, and readers too where possible . . .' I have since taken that to heart, and silently make that admonition to weak interviewers myself on occasion.

Edith was right. In fact, she was right about virtually everything. She was right, for instance, to claim her trilogy *The Heaven Tree* the best she'd ever written. She was, however, never pushy enough to claim that she had the right to expect that all her pre-Cadfael works should be continually in print, so I make that claim for her here.

Jonathan Gash

The Choosing of Barabbas

Jonathan Gash

To the Dean of Medicine,
The London Hospital,
Whitechapel, E1

Stratford-upon-Avon,
Warwickshire

Dear Dean,
I am an elderly doctor who trained at your famed establishment, if I may say, long before you were born. I knew your father! I graduated in 1855. You will realise by the end of this letter why it is imperative that I write. I beg you, Dean, to see my point of view.

Selecting someone truly famous to murder was my greatest ethical problem. As – modesty permitting – a highly esteemed doctor, when in practice I was confronted by many difficulties, but only in the mundanities of our exalted profession. These took the usual form of which urgent case to visit first in my brougham, clopping about the congested streets of London. Or, worse, which hospital to attend, to give desperate assistance in the horrid surgical wards, so messy, so pain-filled. In short, diagnoses, therapies, prognostications, getting the hang of this new germ theory and exploring its almost infinite possibilities, I have faced them all with aplomb.

Choosing an august pillar of society to murder was, however, a far more stupendous task. I shall explain.

Initially, my plan was to canvass a select group of colleagues who might form a kind of judicial assembly to discuss in proper parliamentary fashion whom I should murder. I, of course, would perform the execution, for execution is what it would ethically be. I have never been one to shirk responsibility. Indeed, I can honestly state that very few modern doctors show anything like my adherence to decent behavioural standards. Was I too shy, though? I found it painfully hard to chat about the problem. Times out of number I attempted to converse with fellow surgeons in the Royal Colleges about how to get started on this enterprise, only to stutter to a halt.

So I resolved to complete the murder unaided.

It is a testimony to the rigorous training of medicine, all six years of it, and a lifetime's hard practice, that I came through the ordeal with flying colours. I kept my sanity, thank goodness. And made, I am certain, the right choice. I am happy to record herein that I managed the murder rather well when eventually I got down to it. Naturally, I relied heavily on my long medical experience to achieve perfection. Now I am old, so I leave this testament for those who have equal loyalty to our great nation to follow. I shall give details of the formula for my flawless murder technique, including the ingredients. It is undetectable.

Use it sparingly, please, if ever you are called upon to act similarly.

In years to come – perhaps as far ahead as 1930 – I honestly do believe that folk will regard these halcyon days as quite extraordinary. Look at the transformations that occurred during the reign of our beloved Queen Empress, and soon after: steam trains of ever greater refinement; the electric telegraphic device; rifles are now, heaven save us, *self-loading*! Who would believe that flying machines now land in an aerodrome erected, God's sake, in Croydon? The abomination of the horseless carriage has come to plague us – I do not possess one of these infernal devices. Yet our onward progress is beautiful. In other ways, it is terrible. Once, the world simply knew that the Englishman was working out God's plan, defining what was right for everyone, and making sure the bounders stuck to it even in the darkest corners of Creation. As I say, halcyon.

Now? Now, some of us have lived long enough to see that progress isn't as halcyon as all that.

Among those, I number myself.

It was early in my career, emerging as a young doctor from the London Hospital in Whitechapel, that I recognised my need to select a murder victim. Partly it was by way of recompense for my labours, but partly it was from loyalty. And I do mean patriotism, the stand-by-your-gun heroism shown by our brave redoubtables who recently saved the guns at Colenso, and those gallant lads who withstood the *impi* onslaughts at Rourke's Drift Mission Station.

As I worked in the Whitechapel slums I began to see my responsibilities with a dreadful clarity. Of course I cannot truly say if the evil antics of the killer who called himself Saucy Jack served as an examplar ('Jack the Ripper' as our yellow press now names him). I think not, for I recall planning my choice of victim very early in my career. In fact I drew up a list of candidates. They included Gladstone, Tennyson, Dickens, that Frenchie Louis Pasteur, sundry generals of the Great War, the Kaiser, Freud, Arthur Conan Doyle, Florence Nightingale, and many other deserving notables. Over the years, no fewer than thirty worthy candidates presented themselves.

You will be interested to learn how I eventually restricted my choice to only one deserving victim. (And she died beautifully, I think you'll agree.)

Strangely, the possibles ranked themselves. The final one – odious little woman she was – nominated herself. It was fascinating. Murder always is.

Mr Gladstone, our 'Grand Old Man' of politics, I honestly considered my very best candidate. In fact, for quite a few years he was top of my list. He possesses several qualities ideally fitting him for murder. His origin (Liverpool), education (Eton, Oxford) and politics (Liberal, of all things) all argued that I murder him and spare the others. It would have been easy, for he took lonely walks through lantern-lit London – his reasons I need not go into. A gentleman must leave some things unsaid. I let him off, however, on account of his Home Rule rhetoric and the Third Reform Act. Spark of decency in the man somewhere, I suppose.

Tennyson's murder would have gained the publicity I needed for my achievement. He was a natural choice, for generally speaking poets don't do much except wring their hands, forever on about being woefully neglected. (I except our late colleague Doctor John Keats, *requiscat in pace*, of course.) But Tennyson's sorrow for Hallam – a perfectly manly sentiment, incidentally – and his patriotism, forgave the poet. Some say he wrote decent stuff. Believe it when you see it, I say.

Curiously, though, Dickens, who was one of my main contenders for quite a while, escaped by a fluke. He moved me to tears at one of his famed public readings, which I attended solely to inspect him as a possible victim. Listening to him thundering away at the lectern – he always used one – I had almost made up my mind to go ahead when, typically, my medical training asserted itself. I happened to be seated in the third row of a crowded hall, and detected by astute observation definite signs of already high blood pressure in the man. I sought him out afterwards among the throng, and passed him a note stating my diagnosis, for which he thanked me several days afterwards by means of a most courteous letter. In this oblique manner Charles Dickens became my patient, however transitorily. One cannot murder a patient, can one? The Hippocratic Oath and all that. Like I said, fluke.

Louis Pasteur I grudgingly allowed to live, but it wasn't without a deal of regret. The frightful nerve of the man, though, still rankles. A bloody *chemist*, if you please, not a real doctor, experimenting to cure *human* disease? It makes more than *this* doctor apoplectic, I can tell you! What saved him was that Pasteur was challenged to a duel by a decent French MD (so there *are* such!) over this self-same matter. Pasteur turned out to be a frightful coward. The bounder refused to show up and fight like a gentleman. 'Nuff said, eh?

Florence Nightingale came next. I have hated that woman ever since I met her. I was still working in Whitechapel when she came parading through as the Great Benefactress she *supposed* herself to be. Her sister,

Parthenope, a hard-working lady whose judgement I trust, is right to say, 'Florence? She was a *dreadful* nurse!' But a most accomplished liar, I might add. Yes, Florence Nightingale's continual lying, cheating, the jubilation with which she extolled the endless untruths put about by herself, an indefatigable, domineering, incompetent female, her entire personality I found utterly sickening. Still do. Nowadays, when word has finally got about, everybody sees her for the fraud she is, thank goodness. Even children sing street songs about the toad. And just you ask any of our brave lads returned from the Crimea who it was *really* nursed them. Not a single one will utter Miss Nightingale's name, though many lately have begun to subscribe to the myth she's invented about herself, so great is the power of persuasion.

'Angel of Scutari', indeed! 'Lady With The Lamp', indeed! Absentee landlady, more like! Anyone who lies abed for entire decades pretending she is ailing – her perennial deception, though the wretched woman will undoubtedly outlive us all, for 'creaking doors hang longest', as the proverb has it – and yet who manages to convince society that she deserves to be honoured, is worse than any King's Cross prostitute. At least street nightgowners have the merit of a pitiable honesty and the unavoidable spur of deprivation. Miss Nightingale herself saves me the bother, concocting lies about her nursing 'achievements' so blatantly based on falsity that no sane society could do other than revile the corrupt creature. It will be a sorry day when her reputation rises above the decadence she has managed to achieve. Thankfully, modern society will adhere to the truth about her. Good riddance when she finally soars – descends? – to her eternal reward, and may the Almighty prove merciful to the contemptible vixen. Am I too spiteful to mention that her very name is false? It was changed for the sake of sordid monetary gain. Actions speak loudest, Miss Nightingale! Her fiddling those accounts in that medical establishment still rankles with me, and that 'epidemic' she supposedly controlled single-handed (when she merely *saw* one case, and that from a great distance) burns yet in my mind. Falsehood will out. Thank heavens she was never associated with our great hospital!

The Kaiser deserved my next consideration. Was ever a man more hated? Yet the dolt did hold Queen Victoria's hand as she passed away, which fact alone counts in his favour. I have no real regret letting him off the hook, for he will I am sure be assassinated sooner or later by his own dreadful Prussian oafs. Continentals mostly do that to their royalty, just as American colonials dispense with their presidents. Some sort of fashion going round, I suppose. There is also another, more practical, reason that I permit the Kaiser his life. I recently heard from the man at Cook's travel bureau that the present fare to Berlin is extortionate. I would have to reside in the Kaiser's vicinity to accomplish the deed, since no other method than poison is practicable. I had fixed on the Adlon Hotel, or some other sombre establishment in the Unter den

Linden, but was glad to forget Kaiser Bill on the grounds of expense. Did you know that Berlin hotels charge you extra for a bath, and five Reichsmarks to sojourn there a *single night*? That's Prussian mentality for you.

Dr Sigmund Freud I crossed off my list of putatives not because he was of our profession, but from kindness on learning that he was a drug addict. Fearfully sick, o'course. No wonder he turns out such deranged tracts. Blighter ought to pull himself together and learn to behave. Austrians lack backbone. Inbred, I shouldn't wonder.

And now to Dr Doyle, presently a famous author of claptrap that gets more barmy each passing day. He fitted the murder bill marginally better than the Kaiser. He now wants to be known in full as 'Dr Arthur Conan Doyle'. Is it not strange how Scotch folk always collect a series of forenames, quite as if they're trying to prove who the hell they are all the damned time? Can't understand it myself. Eager to do the thing properly, I made the mistake of going into Doyle's background. Got to know him pretty well, in fact. His father died in a lunatic asylum, somebody told me, which exercised my pity. Doyle himself did excellent medical work on the south coast before he became an idle scribbler, doing nothing but waste his life away. Thus I allow him to live on, in hope that he may return to his senses and get back to doing some proper work instead of all this spiritualism guff. It'll get him nowhere. I told him so, too, last meeting at the Physicians. We still correspond, the odd friendly letter.

It was while delivering the tenth infant of one of the Houlihan families in Bethnal Green's slums that I realised how my patients could actually do my selection for me, save me all this agonising. All unknowing, *they* rather than a coterie of my colleagues could choose my murder victim! The tactic would be wholly appropriate. Hadn't I just expended nine hours of exhausting obstetric work for the sum of one shilling and eightpence that I would probably never even see? This solution would also absolve me of all my moral problems, and would recompense me for the often harrowing disappointments of my medical labours. The Houlihans – nowadays generally called 'hooligans', for the appellation has entered the language, after the recent music hall song about the inebriated street scoundrels in our Whitechapel-Aldgate area – were a violent mob of indigents who oddly began to acquire a new religious fervour of a most extreme kind. From swinish dissolute Papists (you've met their sort) they converted to Salvationists. It was such a family I was attending that day for a confinement.

'It is a boy,' I pronounced, worn out.

It had been a particularly strenuous delivery, I remember. The placenta proved difficult to extract, threatened retention for quite two hours, but I succeeded after a deal of sweaty exertion on my knees. The poor woman had no bed, and had sold the layette provided by charity ladies of the London Hospital. There was no place to wash, of course, except a bucket on the landing for ordure and uncollected night soil. I pronounced the babe whole, the mother hale, and was instantly astonished when the father, who unusually in those rough dwellings had managed to remain sober, fell to his knees and prayed for 'deliverance'. I felt a twinge of exasperation, for had not I been the one who had done the task? However, *Nihil a me alienum puto,* as we of the London proudly say. The mother too had remained sober and compliant throughout, a further astonishment in this particular clan. I took note. Within a day I'd identified my candidate for murder. I asked about among the populace, obtained several religious tracts and pamplets, heard plenty about these zealous new religionists and their hysterias.

General Booth, founder of the Salvation Army.

Ideal!

His murder would achieve maximum publicity, and so prove a stern correction to the idiocies sweeping our great capital city. Did he deserve execution? Nobody more! He is an infamous self-aggrandiser, a repellent traitor who sneers at industry, and who prays against all that makes mankind great. Specifically, General William Booth has set himself up to be the sole arbiter of morality. His aim? To undermine the moral strength of our nation. In short, his demise was long overdue. Examining his biography, I almost forgave him, for the poor witless fellow has suffered all his life from having been born in Nottingham, but we all have our crosses to bear, do we not? Why, I know a man who was schooled in Harrow yet who grew up respectable, and found decent employment in New York or some other colony. No, really. Absolutely true. So people *can* surmount misfortune, if they've a mind to.

Yes, 'General' Booth must come first! It was a relief to come to a decision at last, and by the agency of my patients. I must mention here that Booth is no more a real 'General' than Springheeled Jack. I actually went to see the pompous duckegg, making a special journey by hackney coach. Ineffably bored, I stood waiting among the demented crowds, thousands of people wailing hymns. Eventually he appeared to a roll of drums, applause from the witless throng, and oompahs galore. The tent flaps curled back to reveal the miniature moron seated there in full fig (pantomime uniform, of course, made up by fawning Salvationist needlewomen). For two hours he spoke in his squeaky tremolo, or so I heard next day; he'd only uttered three sentences when I stalked off to my club, made better use of my time.

What I would have given for my murder plan to succeed! Shut the boring little squirt up once and for all, him and his peace-with-equality yap, his 'Let us all be generous to one another'. Never heard such poppycock in my life. He'd shackle our great industries to eliminate the poor. Ever heard such drivel? Traitors come in many a guise, they say.

My plan misfired. Perhaps it was too simple. Even today I have my doubts.

This was my method: I baked a cake, injecting it with a mixture of herbal extracts – one-and-a-half drachms (initial) of each concoction per quarter pound of final crumbage. (You know that one drachm apothecaries' weight is exactly one quarter of an ounce avoirdupois.) Before the poison, it tasted splendid. I did not taste it afterwards! Wearing a coachman's cloak, I delivered it to the General's house one dark night, asking the serf who answered the door to make sure the General himself enjoyed it. In vain I watched the newspapers. The only news item of note was that General Booth's scullery maid died of the gripe and two housemaids simultaneously suffered a colicky illness but recovered. Nobody associated the cake with the death, thank goodness, or evidently bothered to investigate, for mortality and morbidity have always been the lot of the poorer classes. At the risk of appearing unduly or cynically witty, might I suggest that perhaps there is something in this tambourine-banging religion after all? Please forget that remark. I never could make a joke.

Disappointed by my attempt on General Booth, I made a rather desultory series of other sallies. I tried to murder various military dignitaries, including four British generals and one Field Marshal (Haig, incidentally), but they were all failures. I shall omit descriptions of those dismal events, save to make mention of the regrettable fact that one sad unfortunate – a batman serving a member of the General Staff – died suddenly, immediately after I'd had delivered to the General Officers' Mess in Aldershot a bottle of Grant's malt whisky with the note that it was a gift 'From a fellow officer of the Highland Regiments', in which I expressed profound admiration for the recipient officers' military capabilities, may heaven forgive me. Sad about the batman, as I say, but of course a batman's job is to defend his officers by laying down his life if necessary, which is what actually transpired, however inadvertent the process. If the servant died of natural causes, then I must presume that though our military men are the dimmest brains on Planet Earth yet they possess the constitutions of oxen. In a spirit of decency, I sent a sum of ten guineas anonymously to the batman's widow in Stepney Green. This accident made me change my stratagem, for I couldn't go on paying out such vast sums every time a slight hitch occurred. I would be bankrupt in short order.

So, finally, to my one success.

I murdered 'the world's greatest novelist'. Or so she called herself.

It is my most outstanding achievement. I deserve the accolade, so at the close of my long and distinguished medical career I hereby register my claim. In passing, I must mention that I murdered her with delight. Hardly a day now passes but what I relish the triumph. I shall be blessed by generations to come for the kindness I have done to literature, to the arts, to the written word. By killing her, single-handedly I rescued the world of learning.

267

*   *   *

Some modest medical successes have come my way in the past, but this murder was my ultimate triumph. As my days begin to number themselves, what is more natural than that I want the praise that is due?

You will know – everyone does – the writer I shall name. At the end, incidentally, I did feel a twinge or two of compassion for the poor creature. A doctor's sympathies are always to the fore in his character. It is, after all, compassion that drives him to take up his arduous duties in the first place, and suffering is always shared whosoever first feels it. Is not that what even these wretched humanists teach? Why, even Spurgeonites, Reform Methodists and other madmen occasionally include this sentiment among their babbled inanities.

Well aware of my responsibilities, I shelved my natural kindness in order to rid the world of the dreadful woman. And I did it beautifully, used every medical art I possess to achieve a truly great murder. Her death had every feature of the ideal. When playing out the final moment I was sensible of the honesty of my devotion, and felt an almost true exaltation.

Please try to guess to whom I refer. Here are a few clues:

She out-sold Tennyson (might I proudly invite you to note that past tense?). Her books were fought for, more than anything Charles Dickens ever penned. She was admired by Gladstone (!), who grovelled to be granted a few moments of her company. Her atrocious books were admired by our great Queen Empress herself, Queen Victoria. She abused publishers – not entirely a deplorable trait – and pushed Thackeray, Trollope, George Eliot, Rudyard Kipling, and the Brontës down among the also-rans.

Name?

Marie Corelli. Yes, I murdered her.

Here, a brief word of account. I know that not everyone is a natural-born reader, and that some few might not recognise her. All literates, however, will know the name as well as their own, for she truly did rule the world of publishing for the best part of half a century. At once the most mysterious, the most exotic, and the most wondrous best-seller of the age, Marie Corelli was admired, loved, adored, nay *worshipped* in every part of the world by millions upon millions. Some delusioned adherents are still about.

It now falls to me to recount my reasons, though motive is the poorest of explanations for human behaviour.

She presented a wondrous public face to her swooning fanatics. To them, she was sweet, perennially youthful, and she was spoken of as elegant, tall, dazzlingly attired, a brilliant beauty. Her lineage was of the most noble European stock, for she was the daughter of the oldest Venetian family, descendant of the Doges. Her father was a Venetian nobleman who lived in a palazzo on the Grand Canal. She was fluent,

268

she averred firmly, in numerous languages, including Hebrew, Greek (ancient and modern), Latin, Italian, and heaven knows what else. She was the greatest of all scientists, the world expert on nuclear physics. She was in short an exquisite polymathic genius, and she said so to anyone who would listen. Nobody like Marie Corelli, the world's greatest ever noveliste.

It was all lies.

These myths and fibs I forgave. In fact I quite ignored her, until I began to find her books everywhere. Some patients even declined to attend surgery on time, or were unavoidably absent from home when I called, even though they themselves had begged me to visit, claiming to be suffering a grievous decline. It always transpired that a new volume was about to be published that self-same day, and the patients had rushed off to buy it. The novel was always Marie Corelli's latest. Her echolalic piffle invariably sold out their massive printings in a matter of days. Worse, I got quoted at, patients forever citing her balderdash as revolutionary medical fact. Lunatic theories of, if you please, 'atomic survival', of soulful urges, and fanciful recoveries caused by spiritual thoughts alone were suddenly all the rage. It was as if a monstrous emotionalism gripped the nation, caused by La Corelli's incoherent tripe.

Partly moved by notions of preserving my sanity and partly wishing to defend my professional position, I obtained her book *Wormwood*, that Mr Bentley's firm recently published in 1890. (Bentley, the silly old trout, used to call her 'Thelma', in fawning endearment. He learned of her duplicity in the worst way possible, and serves him right. His son, Richard, who now runs the firm, is less of an easy touch.) *Wormwood* was utter tosh, of course. I read her drivel from cover to cover in disbelief. Dismayed and thoroughly let down in my expectations, I sought out the reviews. Mercifully they proved to my relief that somewhere standards still operate. They lambasted the book as rubbish. However others – sometimes whole nations – were swept along by her tide of awfulness. The French, for instance, debased even their culture by issuing laws controlling absinthe, and the Swiss stupidly allowed La Corelli's denunciations to sway them into enacting stringent laws against alcohol. The more fool they! In our own sensible press, the kindest word for Marie Corelli was 'tedious'. I shall not reproduce the more offensive comments, for propriety's sake. Her novel *Barabbas* was even sillier – Judith Iscariot, sister of Judas, if you please! I'd found my victim, and this time would make absolutely certain. I had the best means available, my undetectable poison, provided for me by nature. I had a clear duty.

One final yet grave moral issue lay before me as I set to work plotting the contents of my poisonous draught. In murdering this vile novelist, was I not in fact *censoring* the woman? Grinding the substances in my pestle and mortar, I remembered a dispute in Ealing Public Library when *Barabbas* was first published (a new upstart firm called Methuen perpetrated *that* particular crime). The Ealing Library custodians so far forgot themselves as to ban the book and all of Marie Corelli's novels for her pernicious cheap sensationalism. I thought this an infernal insolence, for I have always opposed censorship of any stripe. I was pleased, therefore, to learn that the Chairman at Ealing had had the moral backbone to resign in protest at such a deplorable step. Fine chap, that.

Yet how on earth could I murder my victim, thus executing the most complete form of censorship of all? Was I not acting against my very own principles? This anxiety exercised me for several weeks, until I hit on proper reasoning. It went thus: Miss Corelli's scrawls might once have been classifiable as literary works. In the end, though, her recent publications did nothing but bring disrepute and opprobium on writers everywhere.

It was admirable logic, as anyone with sensitivity must agree. Her final insolence proved beyond a shadow of doubt that I was perhaps even overdue in taking this lethal step, for she made Shakespeare's name an absolute joke in his home town of Stratford-upon-Avon. She had to go. Have I not said, *Nihil a me alienum puto*? Duty, stern duty, called. I responded to its call with a joyous heart. I would have to get close to the wretched female, eventually perhaps move myself to Stratford, where she lived. 'I think nothing human alien to me'!

Now, to the poison.

Inexperienced murderers will rush to the Aconite plant simply because they learned as children not to go near it. True, a mere one-tenth of a grain (minced dried root) will end a rabbit in three or four minutes, but speed is not everything. An extract of fresh leaves, mistakenly used to dress a wounded hand, will cause awesome muscular pains generally, with syncope, fainting, a sense of asphyxia. I've seen country people so affected, having foolishly mistaken the leaves for shredded Knitbone. Yes, the choice of potion is vitally important. I cannot emphasise this strongly enough.

During my career, I have observed many poisonings, some successfully achieved, others merely attempted. The achievers were often caught, sometimes by the simplest of faults. For instance, one would-be murderer used arsenic, unnecessarily giving the chemist spurious motives (killing vermin always figures largely in these) and thereby foolishly ensuring that the purchaser-murderer remains indelibly in the shopkeeper's memory. Others attempted to be more sophisticated. I recall one instance in Hackney, where a wife tried to poison her husband by disguising her prussic acid elixir with an extract of Heartsease! This alerted her suspicious spouse, for Heartsease when compounded with other plants invariably gives off a strong yet false scent of . . . *prussic acid*! She lingers still in gaol, and rightly so.

Yes, you can be undone by being *too* clever. Having been long fascinated by the art of poisoning, I was occasionally consulted by young Arthur Doyle, and well remember his interest when I gave him some examples of decent poisons, to bolster up his tiresome detective tales. I read one or two of these stories in manuscript, at his insistence. Poor fellow. I hope for his sake they catch on. Stranger things happen.

But the very best poison I kept for my own triumph. I give you the prescription herewith.

There is, I assure you, Dean, nothing to equal the Hog's Bean, that grows wild among old buildings and by the roadside. Why, country children sometimes mistakenly ingest the capsules for filberts. If fortunate, they merely sleep a day or two and recover from profound slumbers unscathed. There is nothing new in this, for did not Dioscorides in the first century tell of its medicinal uses? I combined it with an extract of Indian Hemp, the *Cannabis indica*, though this drug lately has attracted animosity for its spreading usage. Fortunately, our bold London merchants import it in quantity, calling it 'gua-zza'. It is a most important commodity. For instance, a varnish obtained from pressed Cannabis seeds is much prized among cabinet makers. I myself approve of Cannabis twigs – a smallish bundle distributed about a mattress speedily eliminates *Cimex lectularius*, the common bedbug, a serious nuisance when one is attending a difficult delivery or trying to perform an urgent tracheotomy for childhood diphtheria in our city slums. And its elixir (and even its tincture) is most beneficial, when sparingly employed, to moderate the spasmic contractures experienced by deformed cripples. Oh, yes indeed! Legislators are careless to ignore the inestimable benefits of the products they desire to control!

To these, I next add the Melampode, that old folk still call Christ's Herb for its Christmas flowering. This for no other purpose than to simulate a kind of toxic food poisoning. One must beware, and not let it touch the skin, incidentally, for it is a profound irritant.

Wishing to ameliorate such harsh symptomatology, I then add something so commonly available that I remember Arthur Doyle's disbelieving laughter when I explained the plant's uses. (He, being an Edinburgh trained man, was bound to be weak in pharmacognosy, so we had a high old argument over this plant.) It is *Lactuca virosa*, the common Wild Lettuce. Allow it to 'go over' as gardeners say, meaning when plants run to seed, and its tops swiftly become bitter. Scoundrels in Aldgate nowadays adulterate batches of opium, ubiquitously sold in our corner shops, with powdered *Lactuca*. To regular opium smokers the adulteration is undetectable. This is how scallywags save money. So common is this evil practice nowadays that my friends at Westminster complain that they can no longer buy pure opium for a decent smoke. No smoker myself, yet I have sympathy. I honestly believe the government should do something about this pernicious trick. Things were not like so in the days of the Old Queen, I assure you! Tradesmen were honest back then. Two penn'orth of tincture of opium once meant a good two penn'orth, as every working mother knew. How times have changed!

The best *lactucarium* extract, I discovered, is got by cutting the stem and collecting the juice. It hardens and browns in air. I always dry it, then pestle it to a powder. It takes hours to do, but is worth it, especially when one's aims provide the spur. The French use the boiled leaves as a cataplasm, but they would, knowing no better. We, being more discerning, use a quarter drachm. As one last suggestion, I would keep away from *Kalmia latifolia*, in spite of its undoubtedly fast poisonous action. I cannot logically explain my dislike of this beautiful woody shrub, except to note that I have always disliked evergreens. Also, it doesn't really look properly English to me, if you know what I mean. Some idiot in Kew is growing one 'for botanical interest' and at government expense! I have written to my Member of Parliament in protest.

Poison being what it is, of course I had never tried the whole concoction out except in the instances I mentioned earlier. One can't experiment, can one? I had, however, no doubts about its efficacy, and it would be undetectable in food or with a sound elixir or syrup. Ready!

A note to state my case.

Marie Corelli was an abomination. I was not alone in thinking so. Had not famous actresses declared loudly, 'I cannot possibly act in this!' when her exotic novel *The Sorrows of Satan* was recently dramatised for the Shaftesbury Theatre in 1897? And had not the audience rocked with laughter and jeered the atrocity in that terrible January? For all this, her sales stormed on, the public hungry for her novels, however purple the silly prose, however much she moralised and tub-thumped her way through her empty plots.

She had her successes, certainly. And her tribulations.

Her successes were in public relations – another term for falsehood. It is incredible to relate, now that I've finally settled her hash, but she was adored by not only the millions, as I have said, but by royalty. Leaving aside Gladstone, who admired her enormously, and Oscar Wilde, who praised her beyond all sense, she was even received at court. Queen Victoria sent a message approving the sentiments of Corelli's book, *The Romance of Two Worlds*. Her Majesty's wish was to receive all future books written by Marie Corelli, to be read aloud to her by Princess Beatrice. La Corelli's fame soared even higher when she was summoned to Windsor Castle to meet the Queen herself, and the Empress Frederick to boot. Newspapers, hinting that Her Majesty slept with the first copy of *The Soul of Lilith* beneath her pillow, growled in ungentlemanly fashion, 'Could there be a better soporific?'

Lord Randolph Churchill, Lord Salisbury our Prime Minister, she dined with them all. I tried, honestly I tried, to warn Miss Corelli that someone (I did not refer to myself in the first person, as a wise precaution) had threats against her life in mind, but it misfired. I warned her quite obliquely, as the decent and proper thing to do, for a gentleman does not lightly envisage murdering an unattached lady without examining conscience. I began my approach by going out of my way to meet the doctor who was her GP. This of course was when she still lived at 47, Longridge Road. With him I discussed the need to send patients abroad more, for the air. He took the notion as his own, advising Miss Corelli and her sickeningly repellent brother Eric, a profligate prostitute-addicted drunkard, to go to Homburg. There she encountered the Prince of Wales, no less, and was even publicly entertained by His Highness to dinner. It was, I think, the pinnacle of her fame. And all based on my clumsy advice to my colleague to send her out of the country for a rest cure! It was to have shut her up. Instead, by a chance meeting with the Prince, it raised her pinchbeck scrawls to even giddier heights of popularity.

You see how Dame Fortune forced my hand?

She even learned that a Corelli City was to be named after her, in a place called Colorado, which I believe is some sort of emerging conurbation in the United States of America. I sincerely hope that Colorado has sufficient available free space for such an enterprise. And all this, based on gibberish that panders to the lowest possible taste among the dull masses.

Listing her achievements, her fame, her fawning on titles, her desperate desire to be 'accepted' in society, nothing I had yet heard of the woman was enough to select her as my victim. Of course, she was a ranter against anyone, on no grounds at all. The French she called 'dirty little pygmies', and was worse to the Jews. If somebody Hebraic appears in her novels, he is a fat spider with 'swine-like eyes', et silly cetera. Christians of every chalk came off even worse, for those she dealt with more savagely still. In short, she alone had a personal relationship with the Almighty, so everybody else on earth had better watch out! Disagree with La Corelli and you were for it.

Not long after she moved to Stratford-upon-Avon, there to commune with Shakespeare's immortal soul, she began wafting along the River Avon in a gondola that she had imported from Venice. Complete with a (genuine!) costumed gondolier poling ridiculously through the town, she queened it for quite a time until she alienated the entire populace in ways that I will not bother repeating. I did the literary world a favour at this time (a sort of temporary deposit, on the larger benefit to follow) when I visited my former colleague Dr Murray (nice fellow, though only from St Bart's Hospital, so is ineffably weak on anatomy) who resides in that town, actually staying with him for a brief sojourn. The reason? He was her GP,

One day, during my stay, he had to deliver a prescription at Marie Corelli's house in Stratford. I accompanied him there, and while waiting in her hall all unobserved I stole a manuscript from an occasional table. It turned out to be the first three chapters of her novel *Hamnet*, about Shakespeare's son. That same evening I burned it in my hotel's parlour fire, and so saved English literature further insult. She never wrote it. *Jubilate!*

That was my last true encounter, until the day I killed her.

On my retirement from a lifetime of devoted medical labours, I sold up and moved to Stratford-upon-Avon. I was pretty pleased at the place. Barely 10,000 of a populace, still it is busy of a summer when travellers arrive to gaze at Trinity Church and Shakespeare's tomb. I renewed my acquaintanceship with Dr Murray, of course, and enjoyed the occasional sketching perambulation of the riverside with him.

Naturally interested in botany as I am, one of my passing times is making summer fruit concoctions with my friendly little companion, a young nurse I took with me from London, whom I shall call Delicia. She was properly trained, and came to live with me ostensibly as my housekeeper. Naturally we made merry, but in a way not to give rise to scandal, and certainly not so as to raise the fury of Miss Corelli at Mason Croft. La Corelli and her inveterate lifelong companion, Bertha Vyver, maintained an almost pathological vigilance against photographers, wayward visitors, and frolic. To act out my plan I needed to grovel somewhat in the occasional enounters with my victim, who lived in the very next street. I doffed my beaver every time I saw her go by in that miniature donkey cart of hers.

Delicia – named for the purpose after one of Miss Corelli's own characters – was to take produce from my garden as a gift to Miss Corelli. I started this ingratiation early (for all writers seem to accept worshippers as allies) sending round Delicia with a note to say how honoured I was to live in close proximity to so famous a personage, etc. For a while I kept up this codswallop, giving back excuses of medical business when she wrote extending me an invitation to tea. Cleverly, I wanted not the slightest hint of blame upon myself when the deed was done. It could safely fall on Delicia, for she was to be kept in the dark. It would be an accident. This, I seriously urge you to consider, is the very best kind of murder procedure to adopt should you, dear Dean, be moved to consider this solemn duty. Other schemes might work as quickly, but very few provide the same degree of security for the murderer.

So it was that I helped Delicia to prepare a batch of pickled walnuts the very first autumn. I felt a slight degree of haste, for friendships with La Corelli, however tenuous, tended to end in a blaze of venomous hatred before long. That was her lifelong pattern: friendship based on admiration of a sort, then some imagined slight would cause her to erupt in a savage vendetta. I needed her to accept my gifts.

They started, these regular presents, with a jar of my special preserves. It was the purest marmalade ever made, Sevile oranges that Delicia and I prepared together. My bonny companion is so witty, so vibrant and vivacious. Some might allege that she is after my wealth, influenced more by my relative affluence than my elderly, sophisticated charm. Fair enough, I always say. She may not stay long. I quite understand all that. And La Corelli's famous gondolier, forever drunk at the Black Swan tavern, proves quite an attraction to admiring servant girls, though he is too inebriated these days to guide the noveliste down the Avon, having been replaced by a local gardener. So I have no illusions about Delicia's permanence. She will be my twenty-third Delicia in residence. They come and go. Does anyone feel prudish about this sort of thing these days?

'Why do you admire Miss Corelli so, dear?' my sweet innocent asked me once, when we were tying up a small bouquet of freesias, long my favourites with perhaps the russet wallflower.

'Because she insists that she is the one true inheritor of Shakespeare,' I replied, suppressing my rage. 'For this reason I must try to please her until her dying day.'

'Aren't you a kind old thing?' she simpered.

The bonny darling thought no more about it.

My chance came unexpectedly, in early April.

A servant came round hot afoot bearing a message from Dr Murray. Our sketching perambulation, planned for that afternoon, would have to be postponed for, it seemed, the great noveliste had been taken unwell with a slight ague. I chatted to the servant while penning a reply of acknowledgement in my hall, and she garrulously gave me all the details my plan required. Then off she flew.

In my note I had offered my housekeeper's services to help, so friendly was I known to be towards dear Marie Corelli by now. It all happened with astonishing speed after that, and before the end of the afternoon my attractive Delicia was installed as Miss Corelli's special nurse.

It was at my suggestion that Delicia immediately banished Bertha from the sickroom. I accompanied her when she went to take up her new duties and actually witnessed Miss Corelli there, the closest I had ever been. Squat, sour of face, no longer the teenage curly-haired sweet charmer that she liked to project to her admirers, she sat glowering as the door closed on her world. As Delicia took over the arrangements, it was easy for me to add a drachm of my own concoction to the draught left by Dr Murray, whereupon I left. Later I sent some flowers, then wisely stayed away.

That evening I went to the Black Swan, conversing with acquaintances about the state of our Indian Empire where famine was again proving a problem and the nefarious sect called Thuggees had been exposed at last. It was converse not devoid of interest, and many drinkers there would be sure to remember it. You notice the extent of my caution? No one could then accuse me of being at the house when the end came.

Marie Corelli passed away that night, some three hours after having partaken of the draught prescribed for her by Dr Murray. My woman Delicia kept Bertha Vyver from the room, at my veiled suggestion of course. She remained unaware of the depth of sentiment between La Corelli and her half-sister, but sadly I could not have warned Delicia about this or she might have been suspicious.

Ever the stalwart, Marie Corelli seemingly rebuked my nurse when checking the time. 'If it pleases the Almighty,' she whispered feebly, 'to take me tonight, Nurse, please record the hour in God's measure, and not by Greenwich Mean Time.' For the great noveliste hated Daylight Saving, as contrary to God's Law. And who knew His divine edicts better than Marie Corelli, obit. quarter past seven o'clock, twentieth of April? I honestly felt an enormous relief, quite as if I had had the entire populace from which to select a murder victim, and by careful detailed thought managed rightly to choose Barabbas!

There is little left to say, except perhaps my reason for writing this extensive letter so soon – three weeks – after my murderous act. It is this: lately, I have observed that Delicia has formed some kind of strong emotional attachment to that wretchedly drunken Venetian gondolier. She now tends to do a great many unnecessary shopping expeditions, and has begun attending church in the midweek as well as Sundays. I doubt her new-found religious devotion.

Lately, too, she has started to take a deal of interest in my medical journals, of which there are many. Several times I have found her poring by candlelight over my botanical and herbal notes, wherein I keep details of my studies on poisons.

She has visited, I know for a fact, the seed merchants in Stratford town on numerous occasions, and twice has returned home of an evening slightly intoxicated. As she prepares all our meals – we sup and dine together – I have started to worry lest some slight *accident* might befall the soups, the mutton, or the tartlets. At these last, I might add, she excels. And for the life of me I could not lay hands on the remainder of the batch of poison I compounded to kill Miss Marie Corelli. Ever sweetly innocent, my pretty housekeeper says that she simply discarded it when washing up my pestle and mortar, my glass jars and vials. It is a perfectly feasible explanation. Logic suggests others.

Therefore I address this note to you with all its frank details. Making a clean breast of things, you might say. I shall hand it in the morning to my solicitor, with the instructions that, should fatality or sudden illness take me, he is to send it soon as may be to you, for submission to your new police station in Leman Street, Whitechapel.

My name you will find, Dean, listed in the London Hospital register of medical students who graduated in 1855. I am – or must I say *was*? – on the register of the Royal Colleges.

Yours in the noblest of professions,

Doctor No. 16 of the Class of 1855

F or me, there are only two games in town – murder and history. As a six-year-old, I was taken by my parents to the Majestic Cinema in Macclesfield to see Laurence Oliver's *Richard III*. That was 1955 p.c. (or rather un-p.c.), when film categories were confused or the lady on the ticket counter was woefully short-sighted. God knows what damage that film did to me, but in all other respects it made me the neurotic, obsessive psychopath that I am today and I thank Larry (oh, and Will) for making this so.

I sat in that darkened cinema mesmerised as Larry hobbled around the set with his pointed witch's nose and sleek, black hair. He had a gammy leg and a gammy heart, black as his wig, and he was obviously (stranger to Jacobean-speak though I was) up to no good. My hair stood on end when one of his little nephews made fun of his crooked back and he spun to face *me* (of all people) as if I'd said it. And I hope I was wearing my brown trousers that night as I watched the murderous monarch hacked to pieces at Bosworth by the hooded men of Cheshire, his body convulsing in the glade where they killed him.

This was history – of a sort – and I loved it. This was murder – and I loved that too. The man, according to Larry and Will, killed umpteen opponents, a few friends, his nephews, even his wife. That monster image has, one way and another, stayed with me ever since.

I don't know what impelled Edith Pargeter to write her Cadfael series, but the fact that she set it in the Middle Ages doesn't surprise me at all. I have never set fiction in that era – partially because it's damned difficult to do – but all the ingredients of the modern whodunnit abound. We have murders aplenty; it was an age infinitely more violent than our own and life was a lot cheaper. The motives for murder – greed, ambition, jealousy, lust – improperly understood and rarely discussed, were always present. There were powerful princes and a neurotic church obsessed with sin. Women were harlots; even ladies' long-cuffed sleeves were known as the 'windows of Hell'. Unmentionable ethnic groups such as the Jews routinely ate babies, it was believed. Above all, Death and the Devil were constantly on the road. In the thinly disguised Summoner and Pardoner characters in Chaucer's *Canterbury Tales*, they ride on pilgrimage with that whole, wonderful, colourful cross-section on the route to Canterbury, 'the holy, blissful martyr for to seek.'

They were the worst of times, they were the best of times, but setting tales of murder and mayhem in the past is not only enormous fun to do, it will soon, I fear, become a necessity. Dear old Francis Galton started the rot with fingerprints. The Holmes computer and DNA have continued to cramp our style. I predict with confidence that by the year 2049 (when I receive my telegram from King Charles II, who will be 102) the crime mystery book (or CrimRom as it will be known) will be exactly three pages long. Forensic science is already becoming so scarily good that there is no mystery. In three pages, we will know whodunnit, how he dunnit and why he dunnit. And everybody who has contributed to this book will be out of a job.

So, why do I write in the historical mystery genre? Survival, pure and simple; but I set my books in the nineteenth century – a *lot* safer than the Middle Ages!

M. J. Trow

Miss Nightingale Sang in Berkeley Square

M. J. Trow

It muffled all sound, the fog. Wreathing the river where the lighters floated like ghosts, it curled north over the sleeping city, through the bars of Traitors' Gate and west along the Cheap, crawling to meet yet more at Ludgate Circus. The great wagons lumbering with the morning milk waded through it, the iron hoofs deadened on the damp cobbles. Barely awake boys with bundles plodded along Fleet Street, colliding with tobacconists sliding back their grilles and skirting the great silent dray-horses as their barrel-loads thundered and rumbled into cellars.

Day came to the Strand as clerks in their crisp white collars tumbled out of the trains and scurried through the mist of Westminster Bridge like ants foraging in some grey-green jungle.

Sergeant Walter Dew was on the second floor at Scotland Yard, arranging his paperwork for that grey day. He'd timed it badly.

'That's what I hate about the fog,' he heard a familiar voice call from the outer office, 'you can't hear the kettle boiling.'

Dew was on his feet. 'Benson! Hedges! It's the guv'nor.'

One hiss from Sergeant Dew was the same as a wink to a blind horse and the constables fell over each other to leap into action. The kettle was on, the cups were out, the packet of Peak Freans was placed on the plate Benson had half-inched from Special Branch. Through the frosted glass, Dew saw the donegal and bowler wobble into view – the shade of Lestrade.

'Morning, guv'nor,' Benson and Hedges chorused.

'Well, well,' the Inspector hauled off his scarf. 'Ten out of ten for observation, lads. What have we got, Walter?' and he hung his donegal, still steaming, on the rack.

'Bishop of Bath and Wells's been at it again, sir.' The sergeant was reading the telegrams.

'There ought to be a law,' Hedges muttered.

'There *is*,' Lestrade told him. 'The question is, which one? Do we really want to bring in the RSPCA at this stage? Anything else?'

'Er . . . Flat Henry, making his usual threats against the Commissioner, guv.'

'Oh, good,' Lestrade warmed his hands by the open fire. 'I'll hold his coat. What's the news with you, Benson, dare I ask?'

'Robert Louis Stevenson's dead, sir.'

'Really?' Lestrade cocked a professional eyebrow, 'Anything suspicious?'

'Natural causes I believe, sir,' Benson told him. 'Samoa.'

'Well,' Lestrade sighed. 'We've all got to go of something. To be honest I never trusted him. Anybody whose dad invents a railway network with a gauge of four foot eight-and-a-half inches can't really be playing with a full deck, can he? Ah, char.'

He cupped his throbbing hands around the teacup Hedges had given him; the one for Inspectors and above, the one that had a handle.

'Oh, there is this one, guv,' Dew passed the paper to him. 'Came in during the night from C Division. Quite a nasty one in Berkeley Square.'

'Pi Whackett,' Lestrade read. 'That name sounds familiar. Who's on it?'

'Mr Menteith, sir.'

'Oh, Christ!' Lestrade was on his feet. 'Come on Benson, Hedges. Time you learned from a master.' He snatched up his coat and hat again. 'Keep the pot hot, Walter. Fog permitting, I'll be back.'

Berkeley Square isn't normally difficult to find. Big thing; lots of opulent houses and plane trees. But that December day was an exception and it was nearly lunch-time before the growler dropped the dauntless three outside the Greek portico of Number Eighty-Five. A quite ancient retainer, who didn't look unlike Gladstone, opened the door and showed them into a bleak hall with the appropriate Dutch flooring and flying aspidistra. One of Lord Leighton's rather large women loomed over them from a Roman canvas, somewhere south of Brindisium.

'Inspector Lestrade, Scotland Yard,' Lestrade said. 'Is Inspector Menteith here?'

'Sholto!' A thick-set, sandy-haired man was hurrying down the stairs.

'Alex.' Lestrade was a little less enthusiastic.

'Good of you to come. Er . . . you've met Hillyard?'

'Hillyer, sir,' the quite ancient retainer corrected him.

'Yes, quite,' Menteith was relatively new to all this. His daddy was something quite enormous in the Home Office and he'd clawed his way up from Constable to Inspector with frightening rapidity. 'Er . . .'

'The body?' Lestrade prompted him. 'It is usual in murder cases to have one.'

'Ah,' Benson saw his moment of glory. 'Not in the case of Regina versus Plunkett, sir, where . . .'

'Yes, thank you, Constable,' Lestrade held up his hand. 'We'll stroll down felony lane another time, shall we?'

'Up here.' Menteith led the way. 'In the master bedroom.'

The master bedroom was a charnel house. There were blood smears on the walls, spatters across the bedposts. The carpet had been rucked up as though by a terrible struggle and an upturned chamber pot had emptied its contents over the bottom of the velvet curtains. The stain had soaked nearly two feet from the floor. What was left of the deceased lay across the four-poster bed, diagonally, and a pillow was lying across his body.

'This was Joseph Whackett,' Menteith said. Lestrade was surprised the Johnnie-Come-Lately had the stomach for all this. Benson and Hedges had turned the colour of the fog. 'Not very pretty, is it?'

It wasn't. What seemed once to have been an old man was sprawled on his back, his eyes staring at the ceiling, bruised and purple with the beating he'd taken. His face was a mask of blood, dried dark brown and his nightshirt was saturated.

'Give me that,' Lestrade pointed to a towel on a rail. Benson wet it from the jug on the washstand and the Inspector went to work. He placed his bowler on the bedside table, whisked the end of his scarf out of the way and dabbed at the dead man's face.

'Axe,' he muttered. 'Two blows to the front of the head . . .' He trailed the towel down. '. . . One more to the throat. How old was he?'

'Er . . .' Menteith checked his notebook. 'Sixty-four.'

Lestrade nodded. He was only forty yet any one of these blows would have killed him. 'Has anyone found a weapon?'

'Er . . . oh, Lord.' Menteith flipped pointlessly through his book. 'That's rule one, isn't it?'

'No,' Lestrade straightened, wiping the blood from his hands. 'That's rule two. Rule one is – don't panic. He put up quite a struggle.' The Inspector began to wander the room. He checked the window. The sash was locked. There had been a fire in the chimney, now cold ashes in the grate. There were two doors, the one he'd come in by and another.

'What's through there?' he asked Menteith.

'Er . . . ah. Rule three, I suppose,' and the Inspector of C Division opened it. The Deluge Water Closet Company's contraption stared back at him in the dim light. 'Usual offices,' he said.

'It began here,' Lestrade told the waiting policemen, 'near the door. The first blow missed,' he bent down, 'and took off the arm of this rather revolting chair.'

'That's one of Charles Rennie Mackintosh's,' Benson offered.

'Well,' Lestrade let the arm go with a clatter, 'I don't suppose he'll want it back now. It's my guess the old man fell backwards over the carpet and collapsed on the bed. There are bad bruises on his arms. That's where he held them up to protect his head. The shaft of the axe caught him a couple of times, but he'd lost his balance by then. Which of these blows was the first I wouldn't like to say. He'd have lost consciousness from either of those to the head.'

'Absolutely,' Menteith agreed. 'Well, thanks for all that, Sholto. It merely confirms my suspicions. I'll be off, then. Reports, eh?' and he clicked his tongue.

'Are you passing this case over to me?' Lestrade asked.

'To you?' Menteith frowned, pausing at the door. 'Good heavens, no. I just wanted confirmation of the *modus operandi*, that's all. No, I've got my woman.'

'Woman?' three of the four policemen chorused.

'Yes.' Menteith smiled. 'Didn't I tell you? Mrs Flora Whackett, the wife. Got her banged up in stir this very minute, as I believe our working-class brethren say. 'Bye, Sholto. I'll see myself out.'

'A woman,' Lestrade snorted, clattering down the corridor with Matron McGillivray in tow.

'Don't you denigrate the fair sex, Mr Lestrade,' the Matron was matching him stride for stride through the gloom of the prison's A wing, 'If you breathed today, thank a woman.'

'I do, madam,' he answered her, 'on a regular basis. I just can't believe a woman would hack her husband to death with an axe.'

She gripped his arm and spun him round. There was fire in her cold, grey eyes. 'Before I left my native Kirkcudbrightshire to take up the divine calling of prison nursing, I was four times arm-wrestling champion of Palnackie.'

'I don't doubt it, Mrs McGillivray.' Lestrade still had the guts to pat her bicep tentatively. 'But could you use those highly commendable and womanly skills to decapitate your husband?'

Matron McGillivray laughed her tinkling falsetto until her lace cap wobbled along with her multifarious chins. 'If I wished to decapitate au'd Reekie, there'd be no "try" about it.'

'Au'd Reekie?' Lestrade was confused.

'Mr McGillivray,' the Matron slid back the bolts in the heavy metal door behind her. 'He used to work in a sheep-dip factory before I introduced him to the benison of Snitterton's soap – and only tuppence a bar. Here she is, the murdering besom.'

Lestrade waited for the iron door to clang behind him. He heard the bolts slide and turned to wave and smile cheerily as the Matron checked that all was well in the nine-by-thirteen cell.

'Murdering besom?' Lestrade cocked an eyebrow at the woman

in front of him. Her eyes were red with crying and she'd screwed her grey fustian prison skirt into a knot around her anguished fingers.

'Mr Lestrade? Is it really you?'

The Inspector took her hands and sat her down gently on the mattress where the ticking made no sound and the fleas were glad of the company.

'Mrs Whackett – Flora. I'm sorry. I didn't connect the name until I saw the photographs a moment ago.'

'Not my best side,' she sniffed. 'It's difficult to be photogenic with a wooden frame around your neck.'

'How are you?' It was not one of the most intelligent questions Lestrade had ever asked. He had not seen Flora Whackett for two years, not since the engagement party of Harry and Letitia Bandicoot, his dearest friends. She'd seemed more radiant then, more devil-may-care. But then she had not been stripped and locked in a Holloway cell. Then she had not been charged with murder.

'I was allowed one telegram,' she told him. 'I sent it to Harry and Letitia. They're my dearest friends – and I didn't know where else to turn.'

'What happened?' Lestrade asked. It was not the first or last time she'd hear that question and she gently released her hands, took a deep breath and began.

'Right, Walter,' Lestrade stirred his cocoa with a less-than-runcible spoon. 'Take me through it, step by step, twist by twist.'

The sergeant cleared his throat. He'd been on duty now for nearly twelve hours. Hadn't they introduced an eight-hour day some time ago? And stopped shoving little kids up chimneys? And abolished slavery? Ah well, clearly, none of that applied to policemen.

'The deceased was one Joseph Adolphus Whackett, retired. Formerly Regius Professor of Mathematics at Oxford. Because of his mathematical bent, known as "Pi" after the Greek . . .'

'Yes, yes, all right. Skip that bit.'

'Clubs – the Reform, the Athenaeum and the Differential Calculus. Hobbies – addition, subtraction, multiplication, division. Bit of a bore, really.'

'Family?'

'One son. Lives next door.'

'Next door?'

'Number Eighty-Four, Berkeley Square.'

'Has he been interviewed?'

'No, sir, at least, not by us.'

'And not by Alex Menteith, because he's got his woman, so to speak. What else do we know about the late Whackett?'

Dew flicked through his notebook. 'Something of a recluse, sir. Kept himself to himself.'

'Thank you, Dew,' Lestrade caught his upper lip a nasty one on the hot cocoa skin. 'I do know the meaning of the word.'

'The servants say there was some tension there, between Mr and Mrs, I mean.'

'Hmmm,' Lestrade mused, patting his scalded lip with a Peak Frean. 'What was there, thirty odd years between them?'

'Thirty-four, guv. She's thirty.'

'Hmm.'

'Match made in hell, sir, d'you think?' Dew ventured. An axe wasn't your typical woman's weapon, but if she'd been driven beyond her tether . . .

'I don't know, Walter,' Lestrade leaned back in his chair, his ankles crossed on the desk, 'but I know a man and woman who might.'

He met them at Paddington the next day. The swirling fog had dispersed to leave an icy city, the pavements silver with frost in the mid-morning. Letitia was gorgeous as ever in the locomotive smoke, swathed in furs and feathers. Harry was huge and laughing, despite the gloom that hung over them both. It would be their second married Christmas and the awful news about Pi Whackett threatened to spoil it.

'What is this place, Sholto?' Harry asked as he slid the chair back for Letitia in the tearoom the growler had dropped them at.

'Number One-Hundred-and-Twenty-Three Piccadilly, Harry,' the Inspector told him. 'New tearooms I've discovered. They do a divine Gentleman's Relish.'

An obsequious flunkey hovered at his elbow. 'Er . . . pot of tea for three please,' Lestrade ordered. 'And two Gentleman's and one Lady's Relish. Easy on the chutney.'

'Very good, sir.'

'Now, to business.' Lestrade leaned forward, 'Flora.'

'Sholto, I still can't believe her telegram,' Letitia was peeling off her gloves. 'The poor darling must be distraught. Can we see her?'

'I'm afraid not.' He shook his head. 'Tell me about the marriage . . .'

Letitia looked at Harry.

'Well . . .' the old Etonian ex-copper began.

'This is no time to be an old Etonian, Harry,' Letitia scolded him. 'Remember you used to be a policeman.'

'You're right,' he said.

'Three teas, two Gentleman's, one Lady's Relish.' The flunkey had returned in double-quick time.

'Thank you.' Lestrade waited until he had gone, apron flying, to accost his next customer.

'The fact is, Sholto,' Harry was being as *sotto* as his *voce* would allow, elbow to elbow with Christmas shoppers as he was, 'we did find it a little odd.'

'Well, not really, did we?' Letitia was being mother. Unbeknownst to any of them around that table, the twins who would be Rupert and Ivo were curled up, snuggling in Letitia's womb. For now, she just poured the tea. 'The thing was, she was his student at Brasenose – the first woman they'd allowed. He rather took a shine to her and she to him. Even so, we had our misgivings, didn't we, darling?'

'Well, Sholto,' Harry flustered, spraying relish in all directions, 'it's a little delicate . . .'

'Sex, Sholto,' Letitia said, quite loudly, and the whole throbbing restaurant seemed to turn into one huge ear. She plummeted towards her teacake and whispered as loudly as she dared, 'Flora wasn't very specific – her father was a rural dean – but I don't think they shared a room. He was too set in his ways. His first wife died years ago.'

'And there was only one issue,' Harry said.

'Bless you,' said Lestrade.

'Have you met David?' Letitia asked.

'Pi's son,' Harry explained. 'He lives next door.'

Lestrade shook his head. 'I haven't had the pleasure yet,' he said.

'I don't think you'll like him,' Letitia volunteered.

'Now, Letitia.' Harry raised a disapproving eyebrow.

'Oh, I know, I know,' she said. 'Call it woman's intuition if you like, but something's not right there.'

'What exactly happened, Sholto?' Harry asked.

'Somebody took an axe to the old professor.' Lestrade leaned back, wiping the relish from his chin. 'Flora found him night before last. She was covered in blood, of course.'

'Oh, how dreadful!' Letitia shuddered.

'Not very likely is it, Sholto?' Harry asked. 'I mean, I know I wasn't at the Yard for long but . . . do women do that sort of thing? This side of the Rockies, I mean?'

'They don't usually do it any side of the Rockies, Harry. That's my problem.'

'Is everything all right, sir?' The be-aproned flunkey was back.

'Excellent fare, thank you,' Lestrade told him. 'But . . . just one thing. These premises . . .'

The flunkey straightened. 'This *is* Piccadilly, sir,' he said.

'Yes, quite, quite. But I couldn't help noticing a lot for sale a couple of hundred yards in that direction, by the Circus between Piccadilly and Whitehall. That would give you the clientele of *both* streets, wouldn't it? Why not move to the corner, Mr Lyons?'

And the flunkey left them, deep in thought.

'You've talked to Flora, Sholto,' Letitia said. 'What does she say? Who does she say did it?'

An odd light came into Lestrade's eyes. 'The ghost,' he said. 'That's who.'

'Didn't somebody call in that medium bloke in the Ripper case? Name of Lees?' Walter Dew didn't actually like remembering the Ripper case. That was where he'd first met the guv'nor, standing over what was left of Mary Jane Kelly in her dingy little room in Miller's Court.

'Somebody did, Walter,' Lestrade nodded. 'What's your point?'

'Well, this ghost thing, guv. Maybe if we . . .' But he didn't care for the look on his guv'nor's face and let the matter drop.

'"Footsteps" Flora said.' Lestrade was talking to himself, really. 'She'd heard footsteps several times, overhead, in the library, in the master bedroom itself.'

'At odd times of the night,' Hedges confirmed. He had sat in on the guv'nor's second interview with Flora Whackett. 'When the entire household was asleep.'

'You've got a view, Benson, of course?' Lestrade had been afraid to ask.

'Well, guv,' the constable was a little taken aback at first, 'the Square is old of course. It was named after John, Lord Berkeley of Stratton, an officer in the Cavalier army of the late King Charles the First. It was laid out in 1698 and among its residents have been the Poet Laureate Alexander Pope, the diarist Horace Walpole, the actor and dramatist Colley Cibber . . .'

'Will this take long?' Lestrade yawned, looking at his watch, 'Only, I shall have to put in for my retirement, soon.'

'The most interesting bit is Number Forty-Five, sir,' Benson was in full flow. 'Robert, Lord Clive committed suicide there in 1774. There's your ghost.'

'Robert, Lord Clive?'

'Clive of India, sir.'

'Yes, yes,' Lestrade dimly remembered old Taylor's history lessons at Mr Poulson's Academy for the Sons of Nearly Respectable Gentlefolk. 'How did he do it?'

'Pistol, sir. Flintlock. Probably French.'

'Well, there you are. He didn't use an axe – in fact, I'd have been very surprised if he had – and he did it forty houses away from the Whacketts'. Stop wasting my time, Benson.'

'What if it walks again, sir?' the constable was nothing if not persistent.

Lestrade scanned the apprehensive faces ahead of him. 'Walter, there's an aged sister living in the house, isn't there?'

'Yes, guv,' Dew nodded. 'Name of Agatha.'

'Hmm,' Lestrade nodded. 'Now there's a spinsterish name if ever I heard one. Talk to her. See what she knows. Benson, Hedges, you talk to the staff. Who've we got, Dew?'

'Er . . . the butler is Arthur Hillyer, sir, faithful flunkey etcetera, etcetera. The cook is a Mrs Boyle, taken to her bed with upsetness. There are two new footmen – Ned Bailey and Josiah Spencer – and a couple of tweenies, I believe.'

'Right, get on to it, then.'

'Er . . . guv?'

'Yes, Sergeant?' Lestrade knew that wheedling tone of old. 'What is it, Walter, me old detective?'

'Well, it's just that . . . I thought this was Inspector Menteith's case, sir.'

Lestrade chuckled. 'It's all right, Walter. We all thought Mr Gladstone had retired as Prime Minister, didn't we? But it didn't stop the senile old bugger coming back three times more. If anybody wants me, I'll be at Berkeley Square, next door to you three. Tell you what – in this age of cutting costs and counting the coppers and so on, we'll share a cab. Walter, it's your shout.'

David Whackett broke insurances for a living and Lestrade had never *quite* understood what that meant. He was a man in his mid thirties with hard eyes and a slim moustache.

'I'd offer you a drink, Inspector,' he was saying, 'but I don't believe you chappies do, do you, not on duty?'

'Indeed not, sir,' Lestrade assured him. 'Tell me, when did you last see your father?'

'Ah. Let me think. Monday. No, Sunday. He was going to church.'

'You went with him?'

'Good Lord, no,' the younger Whackett squirted soda into his glass of Scotch. 'No, I haven't been to church since my confirmation. Only did that to please the old man.'

'Were you close?' Lestrade asked.

'Just next door . . . oh, I see what you mean. Well, as much as most sons and fathers, I suppose. Look here, Inspector,' Whackett sat down on his *chaise-longue*. 'Why all these questions? Surely you have your murderess?'

'Mrs Whackett, sir?' Lestrade smiled, shaking his head. 'No, I don't think so.'

Whackett's face darkened and he put down his glass in one fluid movement. 'Inspector, I won't mince words. One doesn't like to speak ill of the soon-to-be-dead, but it will have to come out at the trial.'

'What will, sir?'

'Inspector, have you talked to my stepmother?'

'I have,' Lestrade nodded.

'Well, then, you must see it,' Whackett laughed incredulously. 'She's a Jezebel, Lestrade, to put it bluntly. Anything in trousers. I sensed it the moment we met. Tell me, did she take your hand?'

'I took hers, sir, as a matter of fact.'

'What?'

'I know Mrs Whackett, not intimately, of course.'

'Really?' Whackett sneered. 'You're the only man south of Finsbury Park who doesn't.'

'Are you implying . . . ?'

'I am implying,' Whackett whirled to face the window, 'that Flora Giles married my father for his money. He was a silly old fart, Inspector, if you'll forgive the vernacular, and she wound him round her little finger – with which, I understand, she is very adept. I don't know what he can have been thinking of . . . well, I can, of course, I'm a man of the world, but to *marry* her! It nearly killed Aunt Agatha.'

'Aunt Agatha who lives next door?'

'The same. Avaricious old bat, and hasn't I fear got all her horses in harness, but blood is thicker than . . . well, you know the saying.'

Lestrade did. 'Tell me, sir, who stands to inherit from your father's will?'

Whackett turned to face the Yard man and he didn't like what he saw. That parchment yellow face, those sad, dark eyes. The man looked like an undertaker. He put his glass down on the table. 'My father was a very rich man, Inspector. Of private means. Family money. His salary from Oxford merely kept him in cigars. I was given an allowance from the age of twenty-one. I understand that the bulk of my father's estate goes to Flora.'

'Unless she is found guilty of your father's murder?'

Whackett's scowl said it all. 'Are you telling me there's some doubt of that, Inspector?'

'Oh, Mr Whackett, when you've spent as much time as I have around courts of law, there's doubt about anything, believe me.'

Walter Dew had never seen anything quite so homely since he was at school, struggling with the complexities of Greek legends. Some woman with hair of coiling snakes and deadly eyes that turned all she looked upon to stone. Went by the unlikely name of Gordon.

'As a young woman I danced with Lord Melbourne,' Agatha Whackett confided as they sat in her airy upstairs drawing room.

'Fancy!' said Dew, always one to be impressed by the Australian aristocracy. 'Now, about your late brother . . .'

'No, no,' Agatha shook her tortoiseshell lorgnette at him. 'He never danced with Lord Melbourne. Melbourne never asked him, y'see. Nothing funny about dear old Melly, dear me, no. Had a member like Nelson's column, I understand. *And* I can remember when they put that up.'

'Yes,' Dew eased his collar that was suddenly too tight, too starched, 'yes, madam, quite. Now, tell me, can you think of anyone who would want to take your brother's life?'

'Pi?' she frowned. 'Certainly not. Oh dear, I can't quite grasp it still. The poor dear boy. He was so young. So very young.'

'Well, er . . . yes, I suppose . . . sixty – four – yes, it's no age, is it, really? No age at all.'

Agatha looked at him scornfully. 'Don't be absurd, young man. Sixty-four is positively decrepit. But I was talking about By. Lord Byron. I can't have been more than six, but I remember him vividly. Clumping around with that gammy leg of his, spouting his gibberish. But oh, my, he was so handsome. Who wanted him dead, you ask. Several thousand Turks, I understand – and not a few of our very own aristocracy. Melly was one of them.'

'I was talking about your *brother*, Miss Whackett. Joseph Adolphus.'

'Fatuous name. I told Papa at the time. Apparently, Papa's favourite king of Sweden was Gustavus Adolphus, hence Joseph's name. Tell me, young man, who is *your* favourite king of Sweden?'

'Did he have any enemies?' Dew tried again, feeling the perspiration trickling down his neck.

'Gustavus Adolphus? Several thousand Catholics I understand, mostly in what I believe is now Germany. Wait a minute; I don't want to tell you your job or anything, but shouldn't you be asking questions about my brother?'

'Indeed, madam,' Dew squirmed on the hardwood stool she'd sat him on. 'How can I have been so neglectful?'

'Well, take more care,' she tapped him playfully with her lorgnette, 'or I'll have a word with that nice Sir Robert Peel about you.'

'Did your brother appear to have any worries, Miss Whackett?' the sergeant asked.

'No more than the rest of us.' She shrugged and rang a little bell by her side. 'His arches had fallen lower than Babylon's, I believe, and he took tablets for every ailment under the sun.'

'He was a hypochondriac?'

'Church of England. Ah, gel. At last.'

The door had creaked open and a pretty tweenie stood there, just the right side of Mr Labouchere's new age of consent.

'Tea,' the old lady croaked. 'And is the Prince Consort without?'

'He is, ma'am,' the girl curtsyed.

'Well, show him in, show him in. A man can catch typhus fever being kept waiting in dank corridors.'

'Very good, mum,' she bobbed again and made to go.

291

Walter Dew saw his exit. 'I'll help you,' he said. 'Thank you, Miss Whackett, you've been very . . .' and he slammed the door behind them both.

'Thanks,' he said, pacing along the passage with the girl. 'I'm Detective Sergeant Dew.'

'Charmed.' The girl's dimples seemed to have vanished in the dimmer light of the landing. 'Got a fag?'

'Er . . . no,' Dew confessed. 'Look, er . . . ?'

'Maisie.'

'Have my men seen you yet? Asked you any questions?'

'Nah. Look, mister, my plates are killin' me. I've been on 'em now for bleedin' hours. Come in 'ere for a bit.'

Dew's eyes widened. 'I beg your pardon?'

She swiped him with a dishcloth. 'Cor, you fancy yourself, doncha? You must be knocking thirty. 'Ere we are,' she swung a panel in the wall and beckoned Dew inside. It was cosy enough – a broom cupboard made into a tiny sitting room. Maisie plonked herself down and hauled off her boots. Catching sight of Dew's gaze, she pulled down the hem of her skirt. 'Ere, I've heard about men like you,' she said. 'That'll be a tanner if you want another look.'

'This is nifty,' Dew changed the subject, looking around the maid's bolt-hole.

'House is full of 'em,' Maisie said, 'passageways and corridors going every which way. They say you can get to Number Forty-Five from the kitchen.'

'Number Forty-Five?' Like his guv'nor, Dew was all ears.

'Yeah, you know, comes before forty-six and after forty-four.'

'Tell me,' Dew ventured, trying to find somewhere to put his bowler, 'about Miss Agatha . . .'

'Mad as a parrot, that one.'

'And the Prince Consort?'

'Oh, I'll show him up later.' She lit a lucifer in the half-light and took several grateful puffs from her Camel. She chuckled at the look on Dew's face. 'Only joking, sarge,' she kicked his leg playfully. 'There ain't *really* a Prince Consort or any of the uvver buggers she used to know as a kid. But . . . well, she's harmless. Might as well leave 'er 'ere in the West wing as have her put away. She has regular conversations with old Gladeye too.'

'Mr Gladstone?' But he isn't dead . . . is he?'

'Maybe not,' Maisie blew elegant smoke rings to the ceiling, 'but then, 'e don't come to visit Miss Agatha neiver. You sure you won't have a ciggie?'

'Yes, thanks.' Dew was. 'Tell me some more about these secret passages, Maisie.'

*　　*　　*

'Secret passages, sor?' Bridget's eyes were huge grey pools of terror. 'No, sor. We don't have any of dose, sor. No.'

Detective Constable Benson caught the rising tide of panic in the girl's voice and left it there.

'Tell us about Mr Whackett, Bridget,' Hedges said, sipping the tea she'd made them both.

'Would that be Mr Whackett senior, or Mr Whackett junior, sor?'

'Mr Whackett senior, Bridget,' Hedges was patience itself. 'What sort of man was he?'

The clock ticked in the kitchen to the beat of Bridget's heart. 'He was a darlin' man, sor,' she suddenly sobbed. 'Salt o' the earth, he was, sor. A saint, to be sure.'

'He 'ad 'ands,' Maisie was just answering the same question in her little hidey-hole upstairs, ''ands like a bloody octopus. Used to 'ave little Bridget over the kitchen table.'

Bridget suddenly removed her hands from the kitchen table. 'He was like a grandfather to me, sor,' she smiled.

'I don't know 'ow she stood it,' Maisie lit a second cigarette from the first, 'all that pawin' and gropin'. Fair turned me up, it did. I got old 'Illyer to 'ave a word wiv 'im.'

'Old 'Illyer?'

'The butler. The head of the household. He's a pompous old sod, but 'is heart's in the right place – and 'is hands.'

'Oh, she was spiteful to 'im, sor, that Maisie,' Bridget said, her huge eyes narrow slits of hatred now. 'Kept himself waiting, so she did. Never around when he needed her. Old Hillyer had to talk to her about it.'

'But Mr Whackett didn't fire her?' Benson asked, between slurps.

'I don't like to speak ill of anyone, sor,' Bridget told him, 'but he should have done. He should have thrown her out, the idle little trollop.'

''Course,' Maisie confided to Dew, 'she was asking for it, all the time. Well, they're all the same, ain't they, these bog Irish? That Mr Parnell and that Kitty O'Shea. Oh, yes. I can read, you know. I read the papers. They're all at it. She led him on.'

'Mrs O'Shea?'

'Nah. *Listen*, will you? That Bridget. She led the master on. Know what I'm saying?'

'What about the mistress?' Dew asked.

Maisie scowled, stubbing out a butt in an ashtray and fanning the air. 'She done for 'im, didn't she?' she said. 'Now, come on,' she pulled

293

an iron lever and the wall swung wide, 'I've got to make the tea for the Dowager Empress of China in there. The Prince Consort's come callin'.'

'Ghosts, sor?' Bridget's eyes were wide, her voice barely audible.

Benson looked at Hedges, 'Yes, Bridget.' His voice was calm, soothing. 'Do you believe in ghosts?'

She crossed herself quickly, 'I believe in the Lord God Almighty, in His Son, the Lord Jesus Christ . . .'

'Yes, yes, of course,' Benson took the girl's hands. They were cold as ice. 'But what about ghosts? Have you seen anything? Heard anything? Felt anything?' Each question was answered by a violent shake, not just of the tweenie's head, but her whole body.

'Bridget!' a powerful voice made them all look up.

'Oh, Mr Hillyer,' she ran to him, sobbing, and he cradled her in his arms.

'Gentlemen,' he said, 'I think that's enough for one day, don't you?' Benson and Hedges nodded.

The butler took out his handkerchief and gave it to the girl. 'Now, big blow.' Bridget sounded like the Cork ferry. 'That's my girl. Now, off with you and let the men talk.' He slid back a chair, lit a taper from the fire and put it in the bowl of his pipe. 'You mustn't be too hard on her,' he rumbled. 'She's from County Mayo. They're all a bit O'Looney down there.'

'And where are you from, Hillyer?' Hedges asked.

The butler blew his pipe smoke into the lad's face. 'Walthamstow, son,' he said. 'And that's *Mr* Hillyer, if it's all the same to you.'

'Er . . . yes, of course,' Hedges coughed. 'You've been with old Mr Whackett, how long?'

'Fifteen years, man and boy.'

'You knew him pretty well, then?' Benson threw in.

'How well can one man know another? He was the master, I was the servant. We weren't friends.'

'But you were devoted to him?'

'If you mean would I stand by and see someone stove in his head, no I wouldn't. Is that what you mean?'

Benson nodded. It would do for now.

'What about *Mrs* Whackett?' Hedges asked, leaning forward among the great copper pans. 'Were they close?'

'It's not for me to say,' Hillyer said, his face an eerie orange in the pipe's glow. 'She was very young, of course.'

'Tell me, Mr Hillyer,' Benson said, 'On the night in question, was the house locked as usual?'

'It was. Bailey locked up at eleven. I checked the keys and bolts myself. All was in order.'

'And what time did you retire?'

'Ha,' Hillyer scoffed. 'I'm never going to retire. They'll carry me to my grave, but I'll still be upright, still buttling, still polishing the silver. Only it'll be the silver handles, then, won't it? If you mean what time did I go to bed, it was near enough midnight.'

'Midnight,' nodded Benson ruefully. 'The witching hour. Tell me, Mr Hillyer, do you believe in things that go bump in the night?'

The butler looked at the green young coppers in front of him. 'Something did *that* night,' he said slowly, his voice rumbling up from the depths of hell. 'Something was walking abroad *then*, all right.'

Cook wasn't receiving visitors that day, not even the police. Devlin, the family doctor, had put her to bed with a sleeping draught that would have felled a rhinoceros and positively refused admission to anyone of a detective persuasion. No amount of cajoling on the part of Lestrade that Walter Dew didn't count as a detective would work. The old girl snored resolutely through the whole of that night and well into the next day. The household was on cold collations.

Time and the hour had run through the roughest of days for everybody, and as the rookies wrote up their reports in triplicate, Superintendents and above for the reading of, Harry and Letitia Bandicoot went to see *The Mikado* at the Lyceum, to take their minds off executions. Flora Whackett, meanwhile, lay in the inky blackness of her cell, counting the seconds that crawled by like years.

Only Lestrade was awake, sitting in the narrow space between the bed and the sideboard. It was nearly midnight and a fitful winter moon ducked behind clouds across Berkeley Square. The Inspector glanced through the nets of the open curtains where a solitary bobby clattered past at the time-honoured two-and-a-half miles an hour, the breath snaking out on the chill air under his helmet.

He heard the clock of St George's in Hanover Square toll the hour. The passing of another day. Not that Lestrade would ever admit it, least of all to Detective Constable Benson, but he'd spent the early evening in the Yard library, mugging up on Clive of India. The general had been a squat man with piggy eyes and no mouth to speak of, and Lestrade could fancy he saw the tormented hero hurrying home through the silent square, the linklights flickering at the door of Number 45, the door Lestrade could see through the window across the frost of the West End night. He saw him, in his mind's eye, pause at the door while a flunkey took his hat and his cape. Then the lights came on in the upper storey as a candle lit him to his room. Beyond the pale blinds he saw the general's shadow raise the horse-pistol to his temple, click back the serpentine and fire.

The crash made him jump. But when his heart descended again, it wasn't a gunshot he'd heard. It was the click of Pi Whackett's closet door opening. It swung inward, scraping softly on the carpet as the hairs rose on the back of Lestrade's neck. He tightened his grip on the brass knuckles in his pocket and his grip on reality. A shadow slid across the bed, a hunched figure in a long, dark cape, followed by another. Like ghouls they hovered over the mattress, still stained from Pi Whackett's blood, dipping and snooping, as though searching for something in the lost recesses of the haunted night.

Lestrade's finger hit the light switch at the same time as he hit his head on one of the bedposts. Swimming though his vision was, he stood his ground. 'Police,' he said. 'Stay where you are.'

The two men in overcoats and derbies did as they were told. 'Who are you?' Lestrade barked.

'Bailey and Spencer, sir,' the taller of the two shot back in clipped Cockney. 'We work here.'

'Ah, yes, the footmen,' Lestrade remembered from Benson and Hedges' notes. 'Doing a spot of moonlighting, eh?'

'Well . . . er . . .'

'You see, gentlemen,' the Inspector edged his way around the bed, wondering which of them could be the first to make a break, 'there's a rather silly idea in sleuthing, which I've never really believed by the way, that criminals always return to the scene of the crime. What had you left behind, I wonder?'

'Our reputations, I should think,' the tall man said, the Cockney suddenly gone. 'You're Lestrade, aren't you? Lestrade of the Yard?'

'That's right,' Lestrade said, 'and if you're a footman, I'll eat my warrant card.'

'Here,' the tall man whipped something small from his pocket, 'try mine.'

Lestrade read the calling card, 'Grand of the Strand?' he said. 'You? Here?'

'It would seem so.'

'Then you must be . . .'

'Batchelor,' the shorter man nodded. 'The other half of the private investigation team.' They all shook hands.

'Odd our paths have never crossed before,' Lestrade smiled. 'Odder still of Dr Conan Doyle to chronicle the doings of Holmes and Watson rather than you two. Well,' Lestrade perched on the end of Pi Whackett's bed, 'to quote the good doctor "What's afoot?" Or, in your case, "Footmen"?'

Grand threw himself into the chair, unwrapping his scarf and peeling off his gloves. 'We were engaged by Mr Whackett junior a month ago. The old man was convinced someone was trying to kill him.'

'Who?'

'That was just it. Neither of them knew. Although Mr Whackett junior seemed to eye Mrs Whackett with something akin to suspicion. Oh, it was little things at first – a runaway bull at Smithfield, a rather strange tang to the raspberry conserve. Then this . . .' Grand hauled a woodman's axe from the deep pocket of his poacher's coat.

'The murder weapon?' Lestrade's eyes narrowed.

'No. It came by post last week. Together with a card that said "Beware the ghost. This might come in handy".'

'The ghost?'

'There's supposed to be one,' Batchelor lit a cigar. 'Everybody in the house has heard something. Bridget, the Irish girl's terrified.'

'What did old Mr Whackett think of all this?' Lestrade asked.

'He couldn't fathom it at all. We'd keep an eye on him when we could. Had a rota going, day and night. Unfortunately . . .'

'Well, we have to sleep sometime,' Batchelor apologised for his friend.

'I'll be the first to admit,' Grand said, 'we did rather fall down on the job.'

'Not as far as Pi Whackett,' Lestrade observed. 'So, you're still on the case, then?'

'We feel a bit rotten, actually,' Batchelor told him. 'We've waived our fees now the old boy's dead. We nipped in here tonight in the hope of finding something, *anything* that your boys had overlooked.'

Lestrade sighed. The end of his tether was in sight. He knew of old that if you didn't crack a case wide open in the first twenty-four hours, chances were it wouldn't crack at all. 'I may be right,' he said, 'I may be wrong, but I'm practically willing to swear!'

'We know how you feel,' Grand and Batchelor chorused.

'Well, gentlemen,' Lestrade paced the murder room while the others watched him. 'It's not common knowledge that, contrary to what Dr Conan Doyle would have you believe, I have never asked for the help of a private detective in my life. But this once,' he looked at them both, 'how would you like to play a little game with me?'

It took a lot of wangling, but Lestrade, after all, had something on the Home Secretary. The deal was that as long as Matron McGillivray was handcuffed *at all times* to the prisoner, then Flora Whackett could be released for a total of four hours from Holloway gaol. After that, all bets were off and Lestrade could tell the *Sun*'s editor any damned story he liked.

They all sat in the drawing room on that bitter winter's day at Number 85 Berkeley Square. Bridget had made up the roaring log fire, but no one was in the mood to celebrate the Yuletide season, so soon to be upon them. Lestrade roasted his chestnuts while the various guests assembled, and while Sergeant Dew made notes, Constables Benson and Hedges flanked the door.

'Thank you,' Lestrade said, 'for agreeing to give up your valuable time.'

'I won't pretend it isn't a nuisance, Lestrade,' Mr Whackett junior said, helping himself to some of his late father's Scotch, 'but if it serves to prove that bitch guilty, fine.'

'How dare you, David?' Flora was on her feet. So, by definition and the short chain-link of the handcuffs, was Matron McGillivray. 'You can't seriously think that I'd kill poor Pi . . .' she disintegrated and the Matron sank beside her. 'I loved him.'

'Did you, Flora?' Lestrade had crossed the floor to her. 'She, beautiful, vivacious, likes socialising; he . . .' the Inspector looked up to the oil portrait of the late Whackett over the fireplace, 'over the hill, reclusive, never happier than when calculating his differences.'

'That's not how it was . . . at first, Mr Lestrade,' she said, not looking anyone in the eyes. 'He . . . he got old, I suppose. When I first knew him at Oxford he was charming, witty, always ready with some light-hearted mathematical quip.'

'Always ready with his wallet,' David Whackett hissed.

Lestrade held up his hand as the woman began to sob, her face buried in her hands, Matron McGillivray's moving with hers.

'Blow!' she commanded, whipping out a handkerchief, and it wasn't until Bridget, Benson and Hedges had all done so, that they realised she'd been talking to Flora.

'Wonderful fire, Bridget,' Lestrade stood beside the girl.

'Thank you, sor,' she bobbed.

'Make it up every day, do you?'

'In winter, sor,' she told him. 'As the master orders . . . er . . . ordered.'

'And the kindling, do you chop it yourself?'

'Yes, sor, I . . .'

'With what do you chop it, dear Bridget?'

The girl stared silently at her shoes.

'Dear Bridget? With what do you chop it, dear Bridget? With what?'

'With an axe, sor,' she whispered.

'Bailey,' Lestrade turned to Grand, 'where do you keep the axe that Bridget uses for the kindling?'

'In the yard, sir,' Grand told him, maintaining his Cockney Sparrer pretty well.

'And is it there now?'

'No, sir. It's gone missin'.'

'Has it now? And who, apart from you and Bridget, have access to the axe?'

'Er . . . Spencer 'ere, sir.'

'Spencer,' Lestrade spun round to face Batchelor. 'How long have you been employed in this house?'

'One monf, sir,' Batchelor told him, straightening his cravat with some pride.

'And who employed you?'

'Mr Whackett, sir,' Batchelor replied.

'Would that be Mr Whackett senior, or Mr Whackett junior?'

Batchelor frowned. This wasn't what he and Lestrade had rehearsed. 'Junior, sir.'

'What?' Flora asked, lifting her and Matron McGillivray's hands.

'I employed them, Flora,' David Whackett said. 'What of it?'

'Why?' she wanted to know. 'Why should you employ servants in a house that wasn't yours? I assumed that Pi . . .'

'*Wasn't* is the operative word there, you Jezebel,' David spat. 'It damned well will be soon.'

'You!' A falsetto shriek made them all turn. 'Yes! You!' Aunt Agatha Whackett sat quivering in a corner, pointing her lorgnette at Lestrade. 'Who are you?'

'I am Inspector Lestrade, madam, from Scotland Yard.'

'Ah, a Peeler, eh?'

'Er . . . yes, indeed.' Lestrade tried to smile.

'Well, when are you going to stop that woman from singing?'

'Woman, madam?' Lestrade felt he spoke for the whole company. 'Singing?'

'Yes, that confounded Nightingale woman, that nurse. She was out there again last night, out there in the Square, singing. I thought I'd put a stop to that once.'

'There, there, Aunt,' Flora and Matron McGillivray scuttled over to her.

'Don't fuss, don't fuss,' Agatha insisted. 'It's just that I can't bear noise, you know that. Who's this revolting creature?'

'I am Matron McGillivray,' the prison wardress pulled herself up to her full height, threatening to lift Flora off the ground.

'Hillyer,' the old girl fixed the butler with a fierce scowl, 'there's a strange woman in the house.'

'Ah, but there's more than one of those, Maisie, isn't there?' Lestrade appeared at the tweenie's shoulder.

'I'm sure I don't know, sir,' she said, smiling sweetly at Aunt Agatha.

Lestrade chuckled. 'Oh, there are lots of things you know, Maisie. Like, for example, who killed old Mr Whackett and where your father hid the axe that did it.'

A chorus of 'whats' filled the room. In the silence that followed, a piece of coal fell from the fire to roll glowing on the hearth. No one moved.

'What do you mean, Mr Lestrade?' Flora asked at last.

The Inspector had crossed to Benson and Hedges by the door. He smiled at them both. 'Let me explain,' he said. 'These two might make halfway decent coppers in ten or fifteen years, but they missed a couple of things yesterday. But then,' he turned back to the assembled group, 'I missed a couple of things myself. My first thought – and please forgive me, Flora – is that Inspector Menteith got lucky first time out. In general, he's right of course. When a wife is murdered, the husband is often guilty and vice versa. But not in this case. That's what Mr Whackett junior would have me believe,' he crossed to him. 'And he tried just a *little* too hard to convince me of the avariciousness and infidelity of his stepmother.'

'Thank you, Mr Lestrade,' Flora said, snatching his hand. Matron McGillivray snatched it too.

'So naturally,' the Inspector was in full flight, 'I next turned my suspicious old gaze on you, Mr Whackett.'

'Me?' The insurance broker was outraged, gulping on his Scotch.

'You – the wronged son, the insurance broker turned out in the cold. You who stood to lose a fortune if your father left everything – as indeed he had, I checked – to his pretty new wife. But,' he raised a finger before Whackett could protest, 'with that pretty new wife mouldering in lime at Wandsworth, it would all revert to you, wouldn't it? The house, the fortune, all of it?'

'That's a lie,' Whackett insisted.

'Is it? Walter?'

Sergeant Dew looked up from his note-taking and brandished a piece of paper.

'What's that?' Whackett asked.

'It's a receipt, sir,' Dew told him. 'For an axe, purchased from Harrods' Ironmongery department the week before last.'

'Where did you get that?'

'From your desk drawer, sir,' Lestrade told him.

'What? You've been through my house? Ransacked my drawers? That's not legal.'

'Neither is sending threatening weapons through the post,' Lestrade said. 'Mr Hartingwell of Harrods' Ironmongery has a phenomenal memory. As soon as we showed him your photograph in the Insurance Brokers' Who's Who, he identified you as the man who bought an axe. You sent it to your father to frighten him. What did you hope it would do? Give him a heart attack?'

'All right,' Whackett snapped. 'All right. I sent the axe. And I wandered about the house at night, opening and closing doors. I drew the line at clanking chains. The stupid old swine had changed his will. I wouldn't get a penny. Oh, I wanted to kill him all right. But if I had,' he growled at Flora, 'he wouldn't have been the only one.'

'Rash of you, then, to employ Grand and Batchelor, the famous detectives.'

'Who?' old Hillyer asked.

Lestrade emerged between the footmen. 'Allow me to present Messrs Bailey and Spencer, undercover.'

The footmen bowed.

'Useless!' snorted Whackett. 'I employed them so that they could swear away the life of that besom. Dear daddy had a heart condition all right and a few more shocks like the axe and the hauntings would finish him off. They were there as honest observers, to report on the clues I left, mostly in darling Flora's room: hobnailed boots; muslin dipped in phosphorus that would pass for ectoplasm. Unfortunately, the dolts missed them all.'

'Contemptible,' hissed Flora, shaking her head.

'But not as contemptible as the behaviour of Mr Whackett senior, eh, Bridget?' Lestrade moved towards the Irish tweenie.

She jumped at his approach. 'He was a saint, sor,' she wailed, her eyes brimming with tears.

'What?' Lestrade's own eyes widened. 'Didn't he have hands like an octopus?'

'No, sor!' The girl was appalled.

'Didn't he have you over the kitchen table?'

Gasps all round.

'No, sor!' Bridget insisted.

'No,' Lestrade nodded. 'It was you he had over the kitchen table, wasn't it, Maisie? And so we come at last to your father and the axe.'

The girl breathed in to scream.

'Shut up, gel,' Hillyer was alongside her. 'Can't you see, he's trying to trick yer.'

'Oh, there's no trick, Mr Hillyer. Except on your part. Why didn't you tell old Mr Whackett that Maisie was your daughter?'

'He wouldn't have employed her,' the butler growled. 'Tight-fisted old skinflint. When he employed me fifteen years ago, it was on the condition I was a single man. Well, I was a widower. But I had a daughter, my Maisie. I told the old bastard I'd farmed her out, whereas in fact I'd kept her all the time.' He put a loving arm around Maisie. 'She was desperate, my girl. Lost her job at her last place and no references. Some talk of stealing – oh, it was nonsense, of course – but he wouldn't've listened. We invented a new name for her, a new identity. And the old bastard took her on.'

'And the old bastard took a shine to your Maisie, didn't he, Hillyer?' Lestrade looked his man in the eye. 'And she unwittingly told my lads about it. Oh, she said it was Bridget who was the object of the old man's attentions, but she also said she'd had a word with you about it. Awkward thing for a butler to do, tackle his employer about sexual indiscretions. But when the person who he'd been indiscreet with is your own daughter, well . . . tell me, Mr Hillyer, where was the axe?'

'In my cupboard,' the butler muttered.

More gasps all round.

'Dad!' Maisie was sobbing. 'No! No!'

'It's all right, gel. I'd have killed him all right, Mr Lestrade. Intended to. Went to have it out with him, man to man. Putting his filthy hands on my girl. I wasn't having that. By the time I got here, he was already dead. God, the blood . . . I thought . . . I thought you'd done it, Maisie. What else could I do?'

Lestrade looked around the shaken little group while father and daughter held each other. Then he turned to his man, 'Reginald John Hillyer, I am arresting you for the murder of Joseph Whackett at Eighty-Five Berkeley Square on Wednesday last. You are not obliged to say anything, but anything you do say will be taken down and given in evidence. Benson, Hedges, the bracelets if you please.'

The constables obliged and Hedges held Maisie at arm's length while her father was taken, shambling, away.

'Mr Lestrade,' Flora and Matron McGillivray crossed to him, 'I can't thank you enough.'

'We aren't out of the woods yet, Flora,' the Inspector said. 'The paperwork alone . . .'

'Funny he denied it,' Matron McGillivray commented. 'The murdering bastard.'

'You won't be going very far, will you, Mr Whackett?' Lestrade said to the insurance broker. 'We have a little unfinished business.'

He turned to the others. 'Shall we?' he said.

Walter Dew picked up his notepad. The tweenies had left, both sobbing. Benson and Hedges had gone with old Hillyer. Flora had rattled back, albeit temporarily, to Holloway with Matron McGillivray. David Whackett had gone to make urgent contact with his solicitor. Only Aunt Agatha sat in her chair, looking quizzically at Dew.

In the hallway outside, Grand and Batchelor hauled off their postilions' livery, ready to take a cab back to the Strand.

'Funny, that,' Grand commented.

'Funny, what?' Batchelor asked.

'Well, I thought Lestrade was right in that ploy he set up last night – that old Hillyer would do a bolt into the secret passage, you know, the one that led up to the old boy's room and then into next door, via the water closet.'

'Yes,' said Batchelor. 'So did I. Not much point our sealing up the panel was there, really?'

'Not a lot,' Grand agreed. 'No, I expect Hillyer's the sort who'll go on protesting his innocence until they give him the drop.'

'I shouldn't be at all surprised,' Batchelor agreed.

'Arthur?'

'Yes, George?'

'Who *did* you have your money on, honestly, I mean?'

'Well, actually, I . . .' and Batchelor's words turned into a chuckle. 'No, it's too silly. I *do* have a reputation, you know.'

In the drawing room, Walter Dew was gathering up his bits and pieces.

'Young man,' Aunt Agatha tottered to her feet. 'Are you going, too?'

'I am, madam. It's all over now.'

'Oh, good,' and the old lady lifted her long, many-layered skirts and hauled out an axe, its once-gleaming head dark with blood. She hobbled across to the far wall and placed her right hand on one of the panels, pushing gently at first, then harder.

'Damnation, it's stuck,' she muttered.

'Madam?' Dew had watched her with a dreadful fascination. 'Where did you get that axe?'

'From the cupboard of that idiot, Hillyer,' she told him. 'One never knows when one will need one, does one? This is the quickest way to my brother's room, Sergeant,' she said. 'Fewer stairs for my tired old legs. He's gone now, you know, dear Pi. Do you know?' she turned to Dew with the axe over her shoulder and a weird look in her eyes, 'There was a man in Pi's room the other night. A total stranger. I can't abide noise – that dreadful Nightingale woman out in the Square – and I can't abide strangers. He must have been a thief, I suppose. Anyway,' she smiled and patted the axe shaft, 'he's not there any more, is he? The stranger's gone now.' The smile vanished as quickly as it had appeared. 'Who are you, by the way?' she snapped suddenly. 'Have we met?'

'Er . . . guv,' Dew whispered, wondering how many paces it was to the door. 'Can I have a word with you about this case? Guv?'

As is true, I suspect, of most writers in this collection, I had been a reader of the Ellis Peters' novels long before I thought of writing an historical mystery myself. What drew me to them was their authenticity, the accuracy and vividness with which the author evoked the medieval era. Unless a writer can recreate a past time period with such accuracy, he or she will fail in that most delicate of manoeuvres – persuading a reader to suspend disbelief for the duration of the story. In the Brother Cadfael novels, the author deftly interweaves the details of everyday life in a medieval village or abbey with her mystery, never stopping the story to dwell needlessly on historic minutiae, always making her historical details part of the fabric of the plot, characters and setting. This ability to enmesh artefact and story to create a believable fictional world is the hallmark of a truly accomplished historical novelist.

To this I must add an ability to create characters whose motivations and values belong not to the current century but to that in which the story takes place. This ability to abandon one's values, one's cultural prejudices, for those of a time long past, is the most difficult and essential skill a historical novelist must acquire. Indeed, it is the white water concealing treacherous rocks upon which the fragile fictional canoe often breaks itself. Thus, for her skill in creating characters who possess a medieval mindset, as well as for her adroit recreation of the everyday medieval world, Ellis Peters remains the standard by which other historical mysteries are judged.

Lynda S. Robinson

Disease-Demon

Lynda S. Robinson

Year Five of the Reign of the Pharaoh Tutankhamun

O ne of the requirements of a nobleman and Friend of the King was the ability to stand in one place for hours at a time, enduring the speeches of foreign ambassadors, recitations of Pharaoh's praises, and stultifying boredom. At the moment Lord Meren, Eyes and Ears of Pharaoh and the King's confidential inquiry agent, was enduring such a test of his loyalty to the boy king. He stood beside Pharaoh's chief minister, Ay, in the great reception hall of the palace and watched the approach of a vassal prince bearing tribute.

Although his surroundings were as familiar as his sandals, Meren tried to view them as the vassal prince might. Long rows of papyrus-bundle columns soared above his head, and around him brilliant painted frescos depicted Pharaoh conquering his enemies, returning home in triumph and receiving the approval of the king of the gods, Amun.

The enormous gold-covered doors swung shut with a boom behind the vassal prince, who followed the overseer of the audience hall down the long avenue of courtiers. The journey rarely failed to intimidate a novice ambassador, either because of the richness of the jewelled trappings on the nobles or because of the vastness of the hall itself. The ceiling was so high that the capitals of the columns almost vanished in darkness despite the dozens of lamps and torches. And few who came to court had witnessed so opulent a display of gold, electrum, lapis lazuli, jasper and malachite.

Egypt was the land of gold, and Pharaoh, her living god, controlled it all. That was why this particular vassal prince was here today. He wanted some of it. Meren listened without much interest to the recital of the prince's needs. It was a typical plea, the essence of which was that the prince needed the gold to finance his army and maintain control of his city in the face of a rival claimant. The prince emphasised a point with a sweep of his arm, bowed low before the dais and lifted his gaze slowly to the face of Pharaoh for the first time.

Meren smiled at the barely concealed surprise that resulted. The

Lord of the Two Lands was barely fourteen, but his youth only served to emphasise the air of grave dignity that surrounded Tutankhamun. Lithe, with brooding, heavy-lidded dark eyes and the gently rounded face of youth, Pharaoh sat on his gold and ebony throne and stared over the head of the vassal prince. He wore a white, gold and blue headcloth secured by a gold headband bearing the royal uraeus serpent. A gold and lapis lazuli broad collar hung from his shoulders while more gold encircled his wrists and ankles and decorated the royal sceptres.

Meren's eye caught a quick movement beside the throne. A sleek black tail lashed back and forth. It was attached to the King's black leopard, Sa, the guardian. It amused Meren that most people only noticed Sa after they'd recovered from beholding the face of the living god. Sa yawned, exposing ivory fangs and a rose-coloured tongue, then lowered his head to his paws and stared at the vassal prince. Finally, the cat closed his eyes. Meren felt his own lids grow heavy.

He'd endured countless such receptions over the years, and their content seldom varied. Perhaps he was so bored because his position required that he hunt traitors and murderers for the King. These duties often placed him in danger and pitted him against evil ones. Their menace required Meren to be constantly alert for violence. His gaze wandered past the bent figure of his mentor, Ay, touched the rough countenance of General Horemheb, and slid beyond him to a young man.

Meren wouldn't have noticed him had the courtier not been staring back. The younger man's gaze moved, and Meren realised he hadn't been staring at all, simply lost in thought. Who was that? Ah, yes, Ro-an, the son of Pentu, chief of physicians of the Lord of the Two Lands.

He was still thinking about Ro-an when a stir among the courtiers brought him out of his reverie. Trumpets sounded, echoing off the walls and out of the palace. Pharaoh rose, and with a small gesture of his hand sent all but his innermost circle of ministers retreating through the golden doors. Meren smiled to himself, knowing what would happen next.

The moment the doors closed the boy jumped up and thrust his sceptres into the hands of the overseer of the audience hall. Then Tutankhamun, living god of Egypt, dropped to his knees and began pulling the ears of his pet leopard. He laughed when Sa licked his face.

At the foot of the dais Ay stood in the midst of a group that included the treasurer Maya, Pentu, his son and Pentu's nephew Ineni, along with Bay, the overseer of the granaries of Upper and Lower Egypt. General Horemheb joined Meren, who was rubbing a scar beneath the thick gold bracelet on his wrist as he leaned against a column and waited for Ay to call a meeting of councillors. Meren would have liked to cast aside his finely pleated robe sewn with electrum roundels, the heavy black wig and gold headband, and especially the jewel-studded electrum broad collar that weighed on his shoulders. Unfortunately, his duties would keep him from home for most of the day.

'If you keep leaning against that column you really will fall asleep,' Horemheb said. He clasped his hands behind his back, rocked on his heels and watched Meren rub his wrist.

'You detest the tedium of court functions as much as I, old friend.'

Horemheb grunted. 'Rubbing it won't make the sun disc go away.'

Meren shoved the wide wristband down over the scar. The King's older brother, the heretic Pharaoh Akhenaten, had ordered him branded for his defiance and because his father had refused to join Akhenaten's attempt to banish all the old gods of Egypt. Akhenaten was dead, but his legacy of hatred lived on in powerful factions at court. Meren's scar was only a visible sign of those he carried in his ka, his soul.

'Don't think about it,' Horemheb said. 'The heretic is dead. Think of something pleasant.'

Meren had to smile. Horemheb had little use for contemplations, musings, or regrets of the past. Meren's smile turned pensive as he watched the group around Ay. 'Have you ever noticed Ro-an?'

'Who? Oh, the physician. I try not to notice doctors.'

'You should. We have the finest in the world,' Meren said. 'The kings of Babylon and Assyria and the Hittite emperor all beg Pharaoh to send a physician to their court. But that's not what I mean. I was just thinking about Ro-an and how diffidence can interfere with a man's path in life.'

'What are you babbling about?'

Meren glanced at his friend. Horemheb had leathery skin, the legacy of countless military campaigns, and the expression of an intelligent thoroughbred. 'It's simple. Ro-an might have been popular at court, especially with the ladies. He has even features and an athletic build, but his nature is diffident. It shows in the way he holds his arms close to his body and how his shoulders slump. Look at the golden one. When Pharaoh enters a room he commands it, though he barely has fourteen years. When Ro-an, a man double the King's age, enters a room he might as well be a dust mote for all anyone notices.'

'Don't you think it's unfair to compare poor Ro-an to a living god?'

Before Meren could answer he was interrupted by the sudden eruption of loud voices from the group around Ay.

Pentu the royal physician pounded his staff on the painted floor. 'You're making a dust storm out of nothing!'

'It's not nothing,' Ro-an replied, his face red.

'It can do no harm,' soothed Ineni.

Bay's voice rose over Ineni's: 'Are you trying to hide something, Pentu?'

At this Pentu turned vermilion and burst into a tirade. Ro-an protested, Ineni denied, and the argument raged while Ay's scimitar-like gaze darted from one to the other. Meren saw the King rise. He

309

shoved away from the column and met the King as the boy reached the quarrelling courtiers.

'What is this noise?' Tutankhamun demanded in his strong young voice.

The noise ceased abruptly, and the men all bowed low.

'Speak, Pentu,' Tutankhamun said.

'A paltry matter unworthy of thy notice, golden one.'

Bay's outraged tones intervened. 'My father's death is hardly a paltry matter, Physician.'

'He had the best of care.'

'You say that because Ro-an is your son.'

The two glared at each other. Tutankhamun looked at Ay, who continued smoothly, 'All know the skill of Ro-an. Soon he will become his father's staff of old age and serve as thy majesty's chief royal physician. It's a testament to his skill that Ro-an seeks to bring the matter of his patient's sudden death to the attention of the Eyes and Ears of Pharaoh.'

Suddenly alert, Meren looked at Ro-an. It was rare for a courtier to require his services, and those who did usually gained his attention involuntarily. Yet this physician thought the death of a patient worth his attention. Bay's father had been elderly but healthy except for a painful swelling of the joints and a few bad teeth. Old Amunwa had been the former overseer of the granaries of the Two Lands before his son, as well as the governor of several important towns and a distant relative of the King.

'Is that what you wish, Ro-an?' the King asked. His dark eyes, sad even when he was at his merriest, rested on the physician.

Ro-an inclined his head. 'I beg leave to ask it, Majesty. Lord Amunwa has died in his sleep early this morning.'

'My Majesty doesn't see how Lord Meren can be more adept than you at understanding why Amunwa died.'

Ineni spoke up in cloud-soft tones. 'Thy Majesty is wise. Ro-an merely wishes to be conscientious in his duty. No doubt the gods called Amunwa to the netherworld at his appointed time.'

'He wasn't sick,' snapped Bay. 'His joints ached.'

Tutankhamun's severe gaze fastened on the man. 'Then you should welcome the attentions of my Eyes, Lord Bay.'

'Oh.'

Meren smiled sweetly at Bay and watched the dawning of uncertainty.

'Oh, er, of course, Divine One.' Bay cast an uneasy look at Meren before hurrying on. 'Thy Majesty is generous in his care of his unworthy subjects.'

'We'll see if you still feel the same way in a few days.' Tutankhamun said. Without another word he turned and left by a door behind the dais, followed by his Nubian bodyguards.

Bay and Ineni began walking toward the doors as soon as the King was gone, but Meren's summons halted them.

'Wait. I assume it's too soon for you to have taken your father's body to the priests of Anubis for embalming.' Bay nodded. 'Good. Then I will accompany you home.'

'There's no need for haste,' Bay said.

'If you felt that way,' Meren replied, 'you should never have brought this matter to Pharaoh's attention. You forget he's of age now. I have been commanded to investigate. And what Pharaoh commands is done.'

Bay narrowed his eyes but said nothing. He walked ahead with Ineni and Ro-an. As Meren followed them he felt a dry, cool touch and found Pentu's claw-like hand on his arm.

'A word before you go, Meren.'

'I am always fair in my investigations, Pentu.'

'I know that, boy.'

Meren almost smiled. He was thirty-four, the father of three daughters and an adopted son of eighteen years, yet to the aged Pentu he was a youth.

'You don't know my son well,' Pentu continued, 'but Ro-an is too conscientious and makes a great fuss over nothing. A disease-demon had attacked Amunwa's joints, and he was aged. By the gods, he was older than I am, and ailing.'

'That isn't what your son said. According to him there was no reason to fear for Amunwa's life.' Meren glanced at the others who had paused in the doorway to wait for him.

Pentu pursed his lips. 'If there was mischief, it was probably done by that family of his.'

Meren turned his gaze back on the great physician. 'Amunwa was greatly beloved. He was an indulgent father and a generous man to all.'

'Exactly.' Pentu curled his hands around his staff and beamed at him.

'What are you hinting at?'

Pentu was eyeing the group at the door. 'Let it not be said that I made accusations against an innocent. Everyone knows your reputation, Meren. You'll decipher my meaning if it's necessary.'

Pentu left him with a speed surprising in one of his age and vanished behind the royal dais. Meren watched him go and wondered at the endless currents and crosscurrents that flowed through the court. In the space of a few moments he'd been thrown into a scorpion's nest of intrigue between several powerful members of Pharaoh's court. Amunwa's family was ambitious and anxious for a greater role in governing the Two Lands, especially Bay.

Lord Bay seemed to blame Ro-an for his father's sudden death, yet it was Bay who requested that Ro-an care for Amunwa. Ro-an had sought to bring the matter to Pharaoh's attention, either to protect himself from Bay or to avoid suspicion himself. Pentu was trying to protect Ro-an, and Pentu had the ear of the King. Unfortunately for all involved, Pharaoh had learned long ago to avoid taking sides. Meren had taught him that, and now Meren would have to find the truth and bring it back to the King.

Several hours later Meren was in the dead man's bedchamber with Ro-an. He'd sent for those who usually assisted him – his son, his personal physician and several royal charioteers. All were busy investigating throughout the house.

Amunwa's room was similar to Meren's own, with a low bed of polished cedar surrounded by a frame from which hung sheer curtains. The walls had been brightened with paintings of river scenes, and the floor was blue with a pond scene in which fish swam beneath water lilies.

Amunwa lay on his bed, his arms and legs twisted in a sheet. His headrest had been knocked to the floor and lay on its side. Meren's physician, Nebamun, had finished a cursory examination and agreed with Ro-an that the old man's contorted features and limbs might mean that he had been poisoned.

'But all that you gave him last night was this?' Meren pointed to a bottle of Egyptian blue faience with ribbons of bright yellow zigzagging through the blue. It rested on the bed in a wooden box of medicines that contained a dozen small bottles and jars of various sizes.

'Yes,' Ro-an said. 'You can see the label clearly.'

Attached to the neck of the bottle by twine, the wooden label read 'preparation for the lord Amunwa to be taken in beer or wine'. Meren pulled the clay plug from the bottle and tipped out a small amount of brown powder.

'What's in it?'

Ro-an was at a table sorting through the contents of a second box. 'Several herbs – mountain celery, birthwort, hemp, along with dried dates.'

'So if I gave this to a dog?'

'Your dog would go to sleep,' Ro-an said. 'But you needn't do that. I'll take some right now.' Ro-an took the bottle from Meren, but as he did so he sniffed, then paused and sniffed again. 'That's not right.' He touched his finger to the mixture that was still in Meren's hand and put it to his tongue. His gaze lifted to Meren's as the colour faded from his cheeks. 'This can't be.'

Meren lifted a brow. 'Poison.'

'Star flower, but I never keep the dangerous herbs in this box.'

Meren thrust the box into Ro-an's hands and went to the table. He plucked a bottle from the box there, one identical to the bottle containing Amunwa's preparation. It was labeled 'star flower'. Meren opened it and sniffed a pungent odour in which he detected the scent of dates.

312

'This must be the preparation.' He gave the bottle to Ro-an, who held it to his nose. The physician swallowed hard and nodded.

Meren clapped his hands. Immediately a charioteer, one of the company assigned to him, appeared. Meren gave him both bottles and whispered a message to be given to his son, Kysen, who was questioning the household. As the man left, Ro-an began pacing.

'I don't understand. I always keep the dangerous herbs separate. That's why I have two medicine boxes. All physicians are taught to do so. Such a mistake is impossible.'

'I agree,' Meren said, and Ro-an looked relieved until he went on. 'A mistake is impossible. Therefore it was deliberate. A simple task, to switch labels on two bottles so similar in appearance.'

'This can't be.' Ro-an was pacing again. 'I haven't touched the star flower in months. It has its uses. It speeds up the voice of the heart. But I would never give it to so aged a patient.' Ro-an began to look desperate. He hurried to Meren. 'You must believe me. Lord Meren, you know little of me, but you must believe me. I am well versed in medicine. I studied with the priests of Sekhmet and have assisted my father for many years. You know I cured Pharaoh of that terrible cough last year, and I—'

'Only a fool would have called this death to the attention of Pharaoh if he'd been the guilty one,' Meren said.

Ro-an sighed his relief.

'Or an extremely clever murderer.'

'What?'

'One who knew the crime would be discovered and who sought to allay my suspicions by pointing it out himself.'

'But I didn't kill him.'

'More important than your protests is the fact that I can see no gain for you in Amunwa's death.'

'That's true! I gain nothing.'

'Nothing that I can see at the moment.'

'Oh.'

'You said you came to this house last night and gave Amunwa the medicine, which he was to take before he went to bed because his joints had swelled and he couldn't sleep. You brought your medicine boxes. Were they out of your sight for any length of time?'

'No. That is, not for long. I took wine with the family and left them in the antechamber outside the reception hall, but I'm sure I would have noticed if anyone had interfered with them.' Ro-an's voice faded as he realised the implications of what he'd said.

Meren relented. 'Take heart, Ro-an. You may be a talented physician—'

'I am. I'm to be my father's staff of old age.'

'Indeed?'

A staff of old age was the successor to a man in his profession. Usually

313

the successor was a man's son, the one who had trained from childhood to take his father's place. Ro-an father held the powerful and lucrative position of chief of physicians of the Lord of the Two Lands. Now Ro-an would serve as co-chief until his father finally relinquished his position altogether.

'As I was saying,' Meren began. He never finished, for a woman entered the room, causing both men to turn and bow.

Meren straightened and said, 'Lady Hekat, you shouldn't be here.'

Tall, lean, with the bearing of a regal falcon, Hekat waved a hand at him and seated herself in Amunwa's ebony and ivory chair. 'My husband is dead, and I demand to know how he died, young Meren.'

'I see that you've yet to rend your clothing and throw ashes upon yourself in expression of your grief, lady.'

Hekat leaned forward and gripped the arms of the chair. 'Don't insinuate at me, you insolent colt. I was there when your mother gave birth to you, and you were a squalling little red face. I'll mourn my husband in my own way, and not when a passel of charioteers is roaming the house and you're skulking about sticking your nose into my private affairs.'

'Forgive me, lady.'

'Hmm. Why has my husband died?'

Ro-an threw up his hands and began to speak, but Meren cut him off. 'I fear that age wasn't the cause of Amunwa's death.'

'Then what was?' Hekat asked.

'Who was in the house last night when Ro-an came to see your husband?'

'Everyone who should have been and no one who shouldn't.'

Meren lifted a brow, and Hekat gave him a world-weary smile.

'You're not the only one who can give answerless answers.'

'But I'm the only one who must report to Pharaoh, may he live forever.'

Hekat scowled at him. 'I was here, of course, and Bay. My daughter Edjo and her husband left yesterday afternoon for an overnight desert hunt. They should be back later today. My youngest daughter Tia was also here.'

'And the servants?' Meren asked.

'What about them? They're always here, but none of them could have had reason to harm Amunwa. My husband was a generous man, Meren, you know that. He tolerated that lazy body servant Geb who sleeps more than he works. I gave up trying to convince my husband to get rid of him many years ago. The same with other unsatisfactory servants. That's why we have to have twice as many as most people to accomplish the same tasks.'

Ro-an nodded. 'Amunwa was indulgent and kind of heart.'

'Amunwa was a fool,' Hekat said with a sniff. 'I can say this because

I said it to him, often. Did you know he was going to loan one of our richest estates to a distant relative because the man had got himself into debt to the temple of Amun? He came here with some tale of woe and misfortune, and Amunwa believed it.'

'So you're saying none of the servants would have wanted to harm their master,' Meren said.

'Ha! They're all moaning and wailing at this moment. I'm surprised you haven't heard them. Likely they're upset because they know I'm going to reduce their wages. No more double portions of bread and beer. And after Amunwa is put in his house of eternity, Geb will have to find another post. If anyone will have him.'

Meren glanced through the sheers at the body on the bed. 'Then I assume you'll inherit the usual one-third of Amunwa's estate.'

'True.' Hekat narrowed her eyes. 'Are you suggesting I killed my own husband for my share of his wealth? I have my own lands, you presumptuous puppy.'

'I suggest nothing,' Meren said.

Ro-an looked scandalised. 'No one would believe such a thing.'

'It's in Meren's character to suspect evil of everyone,' Hekat retorted.

Meren didn't bother to protest. His good opinion was seldom bestowed, it was true.

'Mother.' Bay entered and took his mother's hand. 'The priests of Anubis are here to take Father.' He gave Meren an inquiring glance.

'Lady Hekat, can you tell me if anything looks amiss in this room?'

The old woman's glance surveyed the bedchamber slowly. 'All seems as it should be.'

'Then I shall leave and allow you to attend to this painful duty.'

Once out of the death chamber Meren hurried toward the kitchen at the back of the house. Pentu had hinted at what Meren now realised – someone might be tempted to hasten his death rather than stand by and watch a gullible and ingenuous elder drain his inheritance. He was crossing the long reception hall when Ro-an caught up with him.

'A moment, Lord Meren, please.'

Meren stopped and waited. Ro-an hovered in front of him, his chin and forehead damp with sweat, his medicine boxes clutched in his arms. He licked his lips.

'I knew something was wrong the moment they sent for me this morning. Last night I gave Amunwa that preparation with instructions to take it in beer or wine, only it wasn't my preparation. It was star flower. I don't understand how the two bottles could have gotten mixed up.'

'We've been over this,' Meren said.

'I know, I know.' Ro-an glanced around the empty reception hall and drew closer to Meren. He wet his lips again. 'Star flower is not the correct treatment for swelling and pain in the joints.'

'I should have thought that obvious.'

'No, you don't understand. If it is proven that I gave a treatment other than the one written in the books of medicine, the books of wisdom handed down by our ancestors since the days of the pyramid builders . . .'

'Ah.'

Meren had been so wrapped up in unravelling the snarls and knots of this mystery he'd forgotten that a physician who dispenses a treatment not found in the books of medicine is subject to court judgement. Should the patient die of the treatment, the physician would suffer the penalty of death.

Watching the hapless Ro-an, Meren noted the way his bony fingers gripped the medicine boxes until the knuckles turned white. 'Are you in the habit of dispensing treatments not set forth in the books?'

'What makes you ask that?' Ro-an swallowed and lowered his voice as Meren regarded him in silence and waited for an answer. 'Only to slaves. Sometimes I have ideas, speculations about the use of certain herbs and mixtures. How else am I to discover if they work?'

'Was giving star flower to Amunwa such a case of speculation?'

'No!' Ro-an started at the sound of his voice booming in the hall. 'No. I swear by Amun-Ra, king of the gods. I didn't give him star flower on purpose. I'm telling you the truth.'

'Then you have nothing to fear,' Meren said. He left Ro-an in the hall.

Outside, the solar boat of Ra had reached the zenith of its journey. Silver paths of reflected light cut swaths across the reflection pool that dominated the pleasure garden that lay behind the house. As Meren passed rows of incense trees in special tubs he glimpsed Lord Bay hurrying along the loggia at the back of the house.

Bay met a young woman Meren recognised as his sister Tia, and the two engaged in an animated exchange. Tia threw up her hands in exasperation. Bay shook a finger at her, which provoked Tia. The girl knocked it aside. Slipping along the row of incense trees, Meren drew closer so that he could hear the two unobserved.

'It won't be for much longer, sister.'

'Make them leave now,' Tia said. 'They're poking into all my private things, reading my letters, sniffing my cosmetics.'

'I can't throw Lord Meren out of my house, curse it. No one throws Meren out.'

'Then I'll tell him to leave.'

'You will not! I don't want him here either. There's no telling what he'll find out, but trying to convince him to leave before he's ready will only make him suspicious of us.'

Tia whirled around and marched away, hurling a last remark over her shoulder. 'Make him leave, Bay, or we'll all regret it.'

When Tia and Bay were gone, Meren went to the gate in the wall surrounding the garden and into the area reserved for service buildings and servants' quarters. He would have to talk to Kysen about those two. People always had secrets they didn't want exposed. Tia's and Bay's argument could have been about such secrets, or about a more sinister need for concealment.

In the kitchen yard several women squatted around an oven, one pounding on dough, another flattening it and a third shoving loaves into the oven. Inside the kitchen a slave was plucking the feathers of a duck and casting fearful glances at Ineni and Nebamun, Meren's personal physician.

'That's the lot,' Ineni was saying. He saw Meren and gave him a slight bow.

Nebamun set down a pot of dried herbs. 'Nothing harmful in here, Lord. Physician Ineni was kind enough to help or the task of inspection would have taken much longer.' Nebamun gestured, indicating the dozens of jars, bottles and baskets set on shelves around the kitchen. Beyond Nebamun lay a storeroom packed with more provisions.

'My thanks,' Meren said. 'Bay said you were a friend.'

Ineni smiled. 'We were at the same temple school.'

'And you're Ro-an's cousin.' Meren picked up an open jar of coriander and examined its contents. 'Were you here when he visited Amunwa last night?'

'I was invited to dine.'

'But Edjo and her husband were gone by then,' Meren said.

'Yes.'

'Tell me, Ineni. Can you think of anyone who would wish to harm Amunwa?'

'No. Lord Meren, are you saying that Amunwa was murdered?'

'I'm saying he didn't die of old age.'

Ineni frowned and drew closer. 'You were with Ro-an for a long time. Surely you don't think he killed his own patient?'

'Amunwa was a generous man, was he not?'

'Yes. Too generous. Were I to speak plainly . . .'

Meren put down the jar and faced Ineni. 'Do so.'

'Some of Amunwa's recent plans might have threatened the prosperity of his family.'

'The debt-ridden relative,' Meren said.

Ineni widened his eyes. 'You know about that? Of course you do. The Eyes and Ears of Pharaoh know many secrets, I'm sure. Well, Bay has grown more and more frustrated. Amunwa seemed prey to any importunate pleader, and he insisted upon receiving all who sought an audience. His expenditures in this regard were a great drain on the family resources.' Ineni suddenly flushed. 'Don't misunderstand me. Amunwa was beloved by all – his family, his friends, his servants. Such a gentle, kindly man could have no enemies.'

317

Meren didn't challenge this statement. He plucked a fig from a ceramic bowl and bit into it. 'Last night someone killed Amunwa. Unless you'd have me believe he did it himself.'

'Why would he?'

'Why weren't you Amunwa's physician?'

Ineni grinned, then laughed. 'That was Lady Hekat's idea. She liked having the next chief royal physician as the family attendant.'

'Nebamun, if you wish to make any further examinations of Amunwa, you should do it quickly now that the priests of Anubis have arrived.'

Once his physician was gone, Meren asked Ineni to accompany him to the garden. The trees here were carefully irrigated – acacias, sycamores, which were the abode of the goddess Hathor, date palms and sacred persea trees. Meren sought shelter from the sun beneath the branches of an ancient fig tree. Ineni stood beside him gazing at the reflection pool. Meren couldn't help but compare him to his cousin. Both men had slightly rounded faces and short noses, but Ineni's manner was confident, his speech devoid of hesitation.

'Would you say that Lady Hekat's decision to entrust her family's care to Ro-an was wise?'

'Of course, Lord.'

'At the palace I saw you talking with Bay. You seemed to be trying to dissuade him from appealing for help in this matter of Amunwa's death.'

Ineni turned away and plucked a fig from a branch over his head. 'Ro-an is an excellent physician. I felt that my cousin had alarmed the family needlessly. There was no reason to suspect – there was no reason to believe Amunwa's death was unnatural.'

'No reason to suspect what?'

Ineni toyed with the fig stem, avoiding Meren's gaze.

'No reason to suspect Ro-an of using a treatment not set forth in the books of medicine?'

Ineni's head shot up, and his alarm was all the answer Meren needed.

'I see. Very well, Ineni, you may go.'

'That's not what I meant,' the physician protested. 'All I meant was there was no reason to suspect anything was wrong.'

'You were here last night too,' Meren said.

'Yes, but nothing out of the ordinary happened. Amunwa ate well at dinner. He had two helpings of roasted oryx as well as pomegranates, plums and olive bread.'

'And at bedtime Ro-an's medicine mixed in his wine.'

Ineni's chin jutted out. 'Yes.'

'Thank you.'

Meren's tone left no doubt that Ineni was dismissed. The physician might have pressed on with his defence, but Kysen was walking toward them from the house. Ineni left while Meren joined his son inside a painted wooden pavilion at the far end of the garden.

Meren glanced around at the stools and couches in the pavilion. 'We're far enough away from the house. What have you found?'

'It's unlikely that a servant switched the labels on the medicine bottles.' Kysen settled on a couch with a frame carved in the image of a lion. 'Most can't read, and anyway, they were content having so generous a master as Amunwa. Now their fortunes are bound to be more limited.'

Meren nodded. 'But the family?'

'Another matter,' Kysen said. 'Lady Hekat and her children chafed at Amunwa's lack of prudence and his gullibility. Bay, Hekat and the sisters were furious over his latest plan to loan his richest estate to some relative.'

'Yes. They had to have feared he'd leave nothing for them to inherit.'

'That's true of Bay, Edjo and Tia, but not Lady Hekat.'

'Kysen, if Hekat is accustomed to living the life of a great lady, she may have resented having to do without accustomed luxuries. Poverty means something quite different to those born as high as she was. And she certainly had little respect for Amunwa.'

'Perhaps, but any of them could have switched the bottles last night. Ro-an arrived after the evening meal and took wine with the family. Everyone was in and out of the hall and garden, including the physician Ineni.'

'Who seems to be the only one here last night without a reason to harm Amunwa.'

'And Ro-an.' Kysen got up and leaned on a post that supported the roof of the pavilion. 'Ro-an had no reason to kill Amunwa.'

'No? If he did it, he switched the labels by accident or because he was trying a forbidden treatment and was naive enough to think he could pretend it was a mistake should anything go wrong.'

Kysen shook his head. 'It's more likely that someone in his family got rid of Amunwa before he ruined them.'

'I agree,' Meren replied, 'but the most likely explanation isn't always the true one. I overheard Bay and Tia arguing just now. They're afraid we're going to discover something they want kept secret.'

Kysen snorted. 'They're trying to arrange an advantageous marriage for Tia with one of the King's cousins, Prince Amunhotep.'

'Without the King's knowledge.' Meren sighed. 'A plan to ally oneself with royal blood. Dangerous, and typical of Bay and his family, who have been busy climbing the ranks and court like green monkeys. If Tia marries the prince without Pharaoh's consent, his majesty will suspect an attempt to acquire a claim to the throne.'

'What if Amunwa tried to stop them?' Kysen asked.

'Perhaps Tia and the prince are already betrothed,' Meren said. 'If Amunwa discovered the alliance and tried to destroy it . . .'

Kysen said, 'But would they kill him to preserve their plan?'

319

'I don't know,' Meren replied. 'I've seen people commit all manner of evil acts for a chance to grasp the throne of Egypt. If this marriage is the beginning of such an attempt . . .'

They remained silent for a moment. Then Kysen said, 'Ro-an is miserable. He said Ineni is going to take him to a beer tavern tonight. To distract him.'

'Perhaps that's wise,' Meren said as he rose and went down the pavilion steps. Kysen joined him at the bottom. 'I'm going back to the palace to talk to the other royal physicians. Remain here and send charioteers to find Amunwa's daughter and her husband. All the children will share in the inheritance, and those two could have stolen into the city last night and switched the medicine labels.'

At the palace Meren was walking by one of the smaller reception chambers when its door crashed open and a hoard of priests rushed out, nearly knocking him aside in their haste.

From the chamber came Pharaoh's voice raised in fury. 'Out! All of you.'

Meren watched the bobbing retreat of shaved heads, then his mouth almost fell open when he recognised the pointed dome of the high priest of Amun.

'Damnation,' Meren muttered.

'Indeed.'

'Ay, what's happened?'

'The high priest of Amun was fool enough to try to subject the golden one to a harangue regarding the heresies of the dead king.'

During the heresy, Akhenaten had disestablished the temples of Amun and the other old gods in favour of his own deity, the sun disc called the Aten. The young king lived with the turmoil that resulted from this heresy. The priests of Amun nursed a virulent hatred of Akhenaten, and they had bestowed this antipathy upon Tutankhamun as well.

From the reception hall came the royal voice: 'Meren, is that you? Come at once.'

Meren shook his head as he walked past Ay.

'Take heart,' Ay said. 'He values your advice, and he'll listen to you when he's angry, for which I thank the gods.'

It took Meren several hours to convince Pharaoh not to have the high priest of Amun thrown into a scorpion pit or fed to crocodiles. By the time he left the King it was dusk. He made his way to the rear of the palace complex hoping that the royal physicians hadn't yet left for their homes. He entered the small building in which the medical attendants occupied several rooms, and found two of them still there – Surero, the physician of the King's eyes, and Maherpa, who specialised in ailments of internal organs.

The two men were seated side-by-side on stools with papyri spread around them on the floor. More documents and whole books took up much of the room. They lay stacked in shelves and stored in leather document cases and chests. A tray of scalpels lay on a work table along with a pile of clean bandages and several boxes of medical instruments. Through an alcove Meren saw a room packed with medicines in all sorts of containers. Herbs hung from the roof beams and lay strewn on drying racks.

'We heard about Amunwa,' Surero said as he pretended to survey a medical text.

'Did you?' Meren replied. Surero was about Meren's age, and his air of epicene fussiness was irritating after such a hard day.

'One would think the word of a royal physician sufficient in regard to a death, and that the services of the Eyes of Pharaoh would be superfluous.'

Maherpa snorted. He was many years older than the other two and had served the King's father, Amunhotep the Magnificent.

'One would think you'd have heard the truth by now,' Meren said. 'Evil tidings usually sprout the wings of a hawk at court. Amunwa didn't die of old age.'

Surero and Maherpa exchanged hooded glances and set aside their papyri.

'What do you want, young one?' Maherpa asked.

'I want to know about Ro-an.'

Surero responded, his manner suddenly reserved. 'Ro-an is a royal physician, as skilled as any since the great Imhotep of the pyramid time. His whole family is like that. If Ineni had been Pentu's son, he would have made an excellent chief physician as well.'

Looking from Surero to Maherpa, Meren sighed. 'I know that. Listen to me, Surero. My day has been long, and much of it was spent in a place where great evil was done. I've no patience left. Pharaoh will not appreciate you holding your physicians' brotherhood higher than your duty to him.'

'Don't lecture us, boy.' Maherpa held out his hand, and Surero helped him rise. 'If you want to know something, ask us instead of dancing around the subject like some Babylonian strumpet.'

There was no point in losing his temper. Maherpa had been at court too long to hold Meren in awe. He'd served three kings and many queens, and he treated everyone except Ay and Pharaoh with scant courtesy. Only his amazing skill as a physician had saved him from ruin at court.

'Very well,' Meren said. 'Is it true that Ro-an is in the habit of testing new remedies, potions and treatments and such?'

'Only on slaves,' Surero snapped, fanning himself with a papyrus roll. 'He has had great success in curing rashes and—'

'Where are these new treatments?'

Maherpa jerked his head in the direction of the alcove and preceded

Meren using a crab-like walk. The old man pointed to a corner where a table sat bearing jars and bottles similar to those he'd seen in Ro-an's medicine box, along with a small mortar and pestle and a stack of bowls.

Meren looked at the physicians. 'Have you witnessed him applying these new treatments?'

Both men nodded.

'How do you know they're new?'

Surero rolled his eyes and stopped fanning himself. Unrolling the papyrus in his hands, he held it so that Meren could see. 'Look at this. It's a copy of the text found under the feet of the statue of Anubis at Letopolis and has been passed down since the first dynasty. In such books one usually finds the symptoms set out, then the possible cause, and after that instructions for treatment. It's all quite precise.'

'So it would be a simple matter to determine if a treatment were set out in one of your books,' Meren said to himself. He turned to Maherpa. 'Do you know if Ro-an had any reason to hate Amunwa?'

'He liked Amunwa,' Maherpa said. 'Everyone did.'

'Amunwa was easy to persuade. Do you think Ro-an might have asked him to try a new treatment?'

The physicians exchanged glances again, and said nothing.

'So it's possible.'

Maherpa turned his back on Meren and left the alcove. 'We didn't say that.'

Following the old man, Meren was rubbing his temple. Surero brushed past him and began stuffing papyri in a document case with abrupt, angry movements. Meren's mood grew dark as he contemplated the possibility that Ro-an had caused Amunwa's death by accident and was engaged in a clumsy attempt to avert blame. Pentu's son might have an intelligent heart in medical matters, but his dealings with the rest of the world were marked by clumsiness.

Ro-an felt more comfortable talking to his herbs, potions and medical texts than to people. Indeed, the physician seemed quite timid when forced into a situation in which he had to function outside his medical realm. Such fearfulness plus the knowledge of the extreme penalty for his actions might account for the blunders in attempting to cover up his mistake.

Looking over his shoulder at the herbs hanging from the roof, Meren said, 'Tell me what you know of star flower.'

Surero's hands stilled in their task while Maherpa lowered himself into a chair without speaking.

'I can ask Nebamun, but since I'm here . . .' Meren strolled over to the table and picked up a papyrus.

'Star flower is used in minute amounts to combat some demons of disease,' Maherpa said.

322

Surero took a book from a shelf and unrolled it. 'The plant has flowers in the shape of white stars that grow on a stem without leaves. Any of it – stem, flower, bulb – is poisonous.'

The physician showed Meren a passage in the book, an herbal. Scanning the cursive hieroglyphs, Meren read of the speed with which the herb acted upon its victim. Taking it in wine, Amunwa would have had little warning before his breath of life grew short, then ceased altogether. Someone had chosen well, which meant that the evil one must have known something about herbs.

Who knew about herbs? Physicians, gardeners, most women in their capacity as mistress of a house, perfumers. There were others – magician priests, scribes, almost any learned person might obtain such knowledge by reading. Which meant Amunwa's family could not be ruled out by lack of knowledge.

'Amunwa suffered from swollen joints,' Meren said. 'Ro-an was treating him with some concoction of mountain celery, birthwort, hemp, and dates.'

Maherpa nodded. 'The correct treatment for one suffering from the persecution of a water demon. The joints swell and become painful. If not corrected the disease can immobilise a sufferer.'

'I see.' Meren started to leave, but the younger physician's plaintive voice stopped him.

'This is another example of the lack of respect for our calling,' Surero said. 'Not a word of thanks for our trouble. You warriors think that just because we don't fight we aren't worthy of respect. I could have been a warrior, a charioteer who slaughters Pharaoh's enemies, but my father was a physician. Ro-an's father is a physician, and we all follow that path of our fathers.'

Having heard this complaint from Surero before, Meren had little patience with it. 'Neither of you has cause to complain. Ro-an is well aware of the august rank to which he'll succeed as chief of royal physicians. There is no higher position for a doctor, not even high priest of Sekhmet.'

Meren glanced up at the high, narrow windows and realised darkness had come. He would go home. Kysen would be there by now, and perhaps he'd discovered proof against someone other than Ro-an. Meren hoped so, for if Ro-an was guilty, as the King's physician he would be judged by Pharaoh. Having to condemn to death someone so close to him was an experience he longed to spare the King for as long as possible. The golden one had already endured much unhappiness in his short life, especially the loss of his brother's wife, Queen Nefertiti, upon whom he looked as a mother. It had been Nefertiti who entrusted Tutankhamun's safety to Meren.

He left the physicians, sent word that his chariot and driver should go home, and slipped out of the palace complex by a guarded rear gate.

323

He needed time to think, and a walk would provide it. At home he was surrounded by servants, family, and his charioteers who were quartered in a barracks on the grounds, as well as slaves.

Circling around the palace wall Meren walked to the royal quay, accepting the salutes of guards until he left the palace precinct. He kept to the path that ran between the fields of cultivation and the riverbank and was careful not to stray too near the water. Crocodiles had a nasty habit of resting among the reeds, looking like small mud hills, and snapping up unwary travellers. He could easily be dragged under water by those powerful jaws. Once there the crocodile would hold him while it rolled, twisting over and over until he drowned.

As Meren walked something began to bother him. Something had happened. He wasn't sure what, but he realised now that a small, irritating little dagger was pricking his memory.

He'd missed something important. Apprehension burned in his chest, a steady fire stoked by frustration as he searched for that small piece of information he'd overlooked – an unwary look, something heard during Bay's argument with Tia, a phrase in one of those medical texts, something someone said, a sign left in Amunwa's bedchamber that he'd ignored. What was it?

The north breeze stirred the wheat stalks to Meren's left, and the moon's shimmering veil trailed across the waters of the Nile. Meren stopped, lost in reviewing the events of the day, and gazed out at the ink-black water. He smelled river air, that combination of fresh water, reeds, decaying plant matter and soil that called to every Egyptian. Well, perhaps not to men like Surero or Ro-an, whose noses seemed perpetually stuck in medicine pots or ancient writings.

Poor Ro-an. Meren had great difficulty in imagining him as an evildoer capable of deliberately harming Amunwa. He had no difficulty believing him capable of getting himself into trouble and bungling an attempt to escape. The fate of his birth had placed him in a position to which he was well suited in one way, and yet in another completely unsuitable.

The breeze picked up and whipped around Meren, moulding the folds of his kilt to his body. He lifted his face to the coolness and closed his eyes. They flew open.

'His birth,' Meren remembered. 'By the altar of Isis!'

He burst into a run, speeding along a canal that carried water to the fields. His warrior's training allowed him to maintain a fast pace, but the lack of light still slowed him. Each breath seemed to take hours, and Meren raced into the palace courtyard in a state of near frenzy. Barking orders at the guards on duty he paced in front of the pylons that protected the King's residence while he waited for a chariot. The moment a groom rode into view he raced for the vehicle. Without waiting for it to stop he mounted and thrust the attendant out.

Meren cracked a whip over the heads of his team and hurtled through the streets of Memphis to his villa. He took barely a moment to confer with Kysen. His son jumped into the chariot with him, and they barrelled down a wide avenue, past the temple of Ptah and into a district of artisans. Here the houses were dark. Most people rose before light and went to bed with the sun. Meren hauled back on the reins before a three-storey building alight with torches and oil lamps.

Two drunken Syrian merchants stumbled over the doorsill and laughed their way down the street. Leaving his chariot unattended, Meren entered the building with Kysen right behind him. Before them lay a room that took up most of the bottom floor. At one end stood tables laden with jars, stacks of ceramic cups and goblets, and strainers. Groups of men and women sat on floor cushions or stools in various parts of the room. A serving girl clad in a shift and lotus blossoms bowed to them.

'Welcome good masters.' She drew closer and was able to see Meren's finely pleated kilt, the gold and lapis lazuli bracelets on his arms, the whip in his hand. The servant bowed again. 'What is thy wish, great one?'

'I seek the physician Ro-an. He was to be here tonight.'

The girl didn't know Ro-an, but her master did.

'Yes, great Lord. That one can't hold his beer. He broke a strainer trying to pour his ninth cup a while ago. I think he's in one of the rooms upstairs.'

Barely waiting for the tavern owner to finish, Meren charged upstairs with Kysen at his heels. The door to the first room was open, revealing two men and a woman. Kysen hurried ahead and pushed aside the next door. It banged against the wall, and he jerked his head at Meren.

'Here, Father.'

Meren walked into the room. A sputtering lamp revealed Ro-an lying on the floor, a shattered cup nearby. Kysen touched his fingertip to a puddle of beer and tasted the liquid.

'I can taste nothing.'

Meren tapped his palm with the whip, lifted his gaze to the shadows beyond Ro-an and said quietly, 'You're fortunate we interrupted. Come out of the darkness.'

'How did you know?' asked one of the shadows.

'I wasn't certain until I saw you.'

'But how—'

'It was more likely that someone with a knowledge of herbs killed Amunwa. Of all the people at his house last night, the physicians and the women are the most skilled in that area. But I had no suspicion of you until I realised that the key to the mystery wasn't who benefited from Amunwa's death, but who benefited from Ro-an's, should he be put to death for using an unsanctioned treatment.'

Kysen moved to Meren's side, eyeing the shadows.

'Ro-an was about to become his father's staff of old age,' Meren said. 'If he succeeded Pentu, you would be condemned to a secondary position for life. You, who are everything Ro-an is not – polished of manner, a skilled navigator of the dangerous political currents at court. But by virtue of your birth, you had no claim to a position in which you could have made yourself a great power in the land. Not unless Ro-an vanished. Come out of the shadows, Ineni.'

The physician moved into the light holding an obsidian bottle. He was smiling bitterly. 'I never expected him to go to court with his suspicions. I thought I'd have to work through Bay and Hekat to create suspicion of him.'

'I think the disease-demon that attacked Amunwa settled in your heart,' Meren said.

Ineni's smile disappeared, and he hissed, 'May Sekhmet curse you, Eyes of Pharaoh.'

The physician hurled the obsidian bottle at Meren's head. Meren dodged the missile as Ineni sprang past him, knocking Kysen against a wall. They raced after him, but Ineni was already halfway downstairs. As Meren and Kysen came after him he grabbed a woman on her way upstairs and shoved her into his pursuers. They stumbled and fell in a tangle, allowing Ineni to escape the tavern before they got to their feet again.

'The chariot,' Meren cried as he pulled Kysen upright.

He charged outside to find Ineni barrelling down the street in the vehicle. Meren whistled – three loud notes – and the pair of thoroughbreds slowed, then began to rear in protest when Ineni slapped the reins. In desperation the physician grabbed a bow from the case fitted to the side of the chariot and beat the backs of the horses.

Running toward the chariot, Meren made a final leap, swung his whip and lashed Ineni's hand. The physician yelped and dropped the bow. Kysen grabbed the neck of the man's robe and hauled him out of the chariot. Ineni stumbled, fell to his knees. He would have jumped up again had Kysen not drawn his dagger and placed the edge of the blade on the physician's neck.

Meren looked over his horses before stepping down from the chariot. 'Ineni, this is Kysen.' Meren's gaze rested on the furious physician held at bay by Kysen's dagger. 'As you can see, like Pentu I'm blessed with a son who will make an excellent staff of old age.'

Like Conan Doyle with Sherlock Holmes, Ellis Peters is now becoming locked in public memory as simply the author of Brother Cadfael mysteries. The fact that, prior to the emergence of Cadfael in 1977, she had written some fifteen Ellis Peters thrillers plus the corpus of novels under her real name, Edith Pargeter, is overlooked. While one cannot gainsay the tremendous impact the Cadfael stories have had in raising the standards and bringing into public (and critical) focus the genre of historical mystery writing, I do feel a sympathetic sadness for Ellis Peters/Edith Pargeter the 'complete' writer.

Even when we wax lyrical over Cadfael and his creator, I cannot help thinking how Edith, the professional, would view things. Would she be asking: how is it that Edith Pargeter did not become as popular as Ellis Peters? Or: why is it that the first fifteen Ellis Peters books are now forgotten?

Life is fickle, and the life of a writer is definitely a capricious one. No wonder my father, who used to describe himself as an old Fleet Street 'hack' and was a popular magazine writer of the 1920s and 1930s, tried to dissuade me from following his example. Yet there is no escaping our fate. *Fata obstant*, as Brother Cadfael might observe, quoting Virgil. Or, as Sister Fidelma from the Irish sages might express it, *tá lán mara eile ins an fhairge* – there is another tide in the sea.

My experience is rather like Edith's. Before Sister Fidelma came along, I had written a score of novels as Peter Tremayne, and, like Edith, I had also published a large body of historical works under my real name. Yet, these days, most of my mail and invitations to give talks concern Fidelma. The good Sister has firmly moved into our house and taken over. Will all other work, as in Edith's case, tend to be overlooked? Even now Sister Fidelma is tapping me on the shoulder and uttering another of her proverbs. *Fearr amhail ná dóith*. Better 'it is' than 'it may be so'!

Peter Tremayne

Those That Trespass
A Sister Fidelma Mystery

Peter Tremayne

'The matter is clear to me. I cannot understand why the Abbot should be bothered to send you here.'

Father Febal was irritable and clearly displeased at the presence of the advocate in his small church, especially an advocate in the person of the attractive, red-haired religieuse who sat before him in the stuffy vestry. In contrast to her relaxed, almost gentle attitude, he exuded an attitude of restlessness and suspicion. He was a short, swarthy man with pale, almost cadaverous features; the stubble of his beard, though shaven, was blue on his chin and cheeks and his hair was dark like the colour of a raven's wing. His eyes were deep-set but dark and penetrating. When he expressed his irritability his whole body showed his aggravation.

'Perhaps it is because the matter is as unclear to the Abbot as it appears clear to you,' Sister Fidelma replied in an innocent tone. She was unperturbed by the aggressive attitude of the priest.

Father Febal frowned; his narrowed eyes scanned her face rapidly, seeking out some hidden message in her features. However, Fidelma's face remained a mask of unaffected candour. He compressed his lips sourly.

'Then you can return to the Abbot and report to him that he has no need for concern.'

Fidelma smiled gently. There was a hint of a shrug in the position of her shoulders.

'The Abbot takes his position as father of his flock very seriously. He would want to know more details of this tragedy before he could be assured that he need not concern himself in the matter. As the matter is so clear to you, perhaps you will explain it to me?'

Father Febal gazed at the religieuse, hearing for the first time the note of cold determination in her soft tones.

He was aware that Sister Fidelma was not merely a religieuse but a qualified advocate of the Brehon law courts of the five kingdoms. Furthermore, he knew that she was the young sister of King Colgú of Cashel himself, otherwise he might have been more brusque in his responses to the young woman. He hesitated a moment or two and then shrugged indifferently.

'The facts are simple. My assistant, Father Ibor, a young and indolent man, went missing the day before yesterday. I had known for some time that there had been something troubling him, something distracting him from his priestly duties. I tried to talk to him about it but he refused to be guided by me. I came to the church that morning and found that the golden crucifix from our altar and the silver chalice, with which we dispense the communion wine, were both missing. Once I found that Father Ibor had also vanished from our small community here, it needed no great legal mind to connect the two events. He had obviously stolen the sacred objects and fled.'

Sister Fidelma inclined her head slowly. 'Having come to this conclusion, what did you do then?'

'I immediately organised a search. Our little church here is attended by Brother Finnlug and Brother Adag. I called upon them to help me. Before entering the order, Finnlug was master huntsman to the Lord of Maine, an excellent tracker and huntsman. We picked up the trail of Ibor and followed it to the woods nearby. We were only a short distance into the woods when we came across his body. He was hanging from the branch of a tree with the cord of his habit as a noose.'

Sister Fidelma was thoughtful. 'And how did you interpret this sight?' she asked quietly.

Father Febal was puzzled. 'How should I interpret this sight?' he demanded.

Fidelma's expression did not change.

'You tell me that you believed that Father Ibor had stolen the crucifix and chalice from the church and run off.'

'That is so.'

'Then you say that you came across him hanging on a tree.'

'True again.'

'Having stolen these value items and run off, why would he hang himself? There seems some illogic in this action.'

Father Febal did not even attempt to suppress a sneer.

'It should be as obvious to you as it was to me.'

'I would like to hear what you thought,' Fidelma did not rise to his derisive tone.

Father Febal smiled thinly.

'Why, Father Ibor was overcome with remorse. Knowing that we would track him down, realising how heinous his crime against the Church was, he gave up to despair and pronounced his own punishment. He therefore hanged himself. In fact, so great was his fear that we would find him still alive, he even stabbed himself as he was suffocating in the noose, the knife entering his heart.'

330

'He must have bled a lot from such a wound. Was there much blood on the ground?'

'Not as I recall.' There was distaste in the priest's voice, as if he felt the religieuse was unduly occupied with gory detail. 'Anyway, the knife lay on the ground below the body where it had fallen from his hand.'

Fidelma did not say anything for a long while. She remained gazing thoughtfully at the priest. Father Febal glared back defiantly, but it was he who dropped his eyes first.

'Was Father Ibor such a weak young man?' Fidelma mused softly.

'Of course. What else but weakness would have caused him to act in this manner?' demanded the priest.

'So, you recovered both the crucifix and chalice from his person, then?'

A frown crossed Father Febal's features as he hesitated a moment. He made a curiously negative gesture with one hand.

Fidelma's eyes widened and she bent forward.

'You mean that you did not recover the missing items?' she pressed sharply.

'No,' admitted the priest.

'Then this matter is not at all clear,' she observed grimly. 'Surely, you cannot expect the Abbot to rest easy in his mind when these items have not been recovered? How can you be so sure that it was Father Ibor who stole them?'

Fidelma waited for an explanation but none was forthcoming.

'Perhaps you had better tell me how you deem this matter is clear then?' Her voice was acerbic. 'If I am to explain this clarity to the Abbot, I must also be clear in my own mind. If Father Ibor felt that his apprehension was inevitable and he felt constrained to inflict the punishment of death on himself when he realised the nearness of your approach, what did he do with the items he had apparently stolen?'

'There is one logical answer,' muttered Father Febal without conviction.

'Which is?'

'Having hanged himself, some wandering thief happened by and took the items with him before we arrived.'

'And there is evidence of that occurrence?'

The priest shook his head reluctantly.

'So that is just your supposition?' Now there was just a hint of derision in Fidelma's voice.

'What other explanation is there?' demanded Father Febal in annoyance.

Fidelma cast a scornful glance at him.

'Would you have me report this to the Abbot? that a valuable crucifix and a chalice have been stolen from one of his churches and a priest has been found hanged but there is no need to worry?'

Father Febal's features grew tight.

'I am satisfied that Father Ibor stole the items and took his own life in a fit of remorse. I am satisfied that someone then stole the items after Ibor committed suicide.'

'But I am not,' replied Fidelma bitingly. 'Send Brother Finnlug to me.'

Father Febal had risen automatically in response to the commanding tone in her voice. Now he hesitated at the vestry door.

'I am not used . . .' he began harshly.

'I am not used to being kept waiting,' Fidelma's tone was icy as she cut in, turning her head away from him in dismissal. Father Febal blinked and then banged the door shut behind him in anger.

Brother Finnlug was a wiry-looking individual; his sinewy body, tanned by sun and wind, proclaimed him to be more a man used to being out in all sorts of weather than sheltering in the cloisters of some abbey. Fidelma greeted him as he entered the vestry.

'I am Fidelma of . . .'

Brother Finnlug interrupted her with a quick, friendly grin. 'I know well who you are, lady,' he replied. 'I saw you and your brother, Colgú the King, many times hunting in the company of my Lord of Maine.'

'Then you know that I am also an advocate of the courts and that you are duty bound to tell me the truth?'

'I know that much. You are here to inquire about the tragic death of Father Ibor.' Brother Finnlug was straightforward and friendly in contrast to his superior.

'Why do you call it a tragic death?'

'Is not all death tragic?'

'Did you know Father Ibor well?'

The former huntsman shook his head. 'I knew little of him. He was a young man, newly ordained and very unsure of himself. He was only here about a month.'

'But Father Febal has been here for some years?'

'Father Febal has been priest here for seven years. I came here a year ago and Brother Adag has been here a little more than that.'

'I presume that the members of your little community were on good terms with one another?'

Brother Finnlug frowned slightly and did not reply.

'I mean, I presume that there was no animosity between the four of you?' explained Fidelma.

Finnlug's features wrinkled in an expression which Fidelma was not able to interpret.

'To be truthful, Father Febal liked to emphasise his seniority over us. I believe he entered the Church from some noble family and does not forget it.'

'Was that attitude resented?'

'Not by me. I was in service to the Lord of Maine. I am used to being given orders and to obeying them. I know my place.'

Was there a slight note of bitterness there? Fidelma wondered.

'If I recall rightly, the Lord of Maine was a generous man and those in his service were well looked after. It must have been a wrench for you to leave such an employer to enter religious life?'

Brother Finnlug grimaced.

'Spiritual rewards are often richer than temporal ones. But, as I say, I have been used to service. The same may be said for Brother Adag, who was once a servant to another lord. But he is somewhat of a simpleton.' The monk touched his forehead. 'They say such people are blessed of God.'

'Did Father Ibor get on well with Father Febal?'

'Ah, that I can't say. He was a quiet young man. Kept himself to himself. I do not think he liked Father Febal. I have seen resentment in his eyes.'

'Why would he be resentful? Father Febal was the senior of your community. Father Ibor should have recognised his authority without question.'

The monk shrugged.

'All I can say is that he was hostile to Father Febal's authority.'

'Why do you think he stole the items from the church?' Fidelma asked the question sharply.

Brother Finnlug's expression did not alter. He simply spread his arms.

'Who can say what motivates a person to such actions? Who can know the deep secrets of men's hearts?'

'That is what I am here to discover,' Fidelma replied drily. 'Surely, you must have an idea? Even to hazard a guess?'

'What does Father Febal say?'

'Does it matter what he says?'

'I would have thought that he was closer to Father Ibor than either Brother Adag or myself.'

'Closer? Yet you said there was hostility between them.'

'I did not mean close in the manner of friends. But they were priests together. Of similar social backgrounds, unlike Adag and I. As brothers of this community, our task was more like servants in this church rather than the equals of Fathers Febal and Ibor.'

'I see.' Fidelma frowned thoughtfully. 'I am sure the Abbot will be distressed to learn that this is the way your community is governed. We are all servants of God and all one under His Supreme Power.'

'That is not exactly the Faith which Father Febal espouses.' There was clearly bitterness in his voice.

'So you do not know why Ibor might have stolen the items?'

'They were items of great value. They would never be poor on the proceeds of that wealth.'

'*They?*'

'I mean, whoever stole the items.'

'You have a doubt that Father Ibor stole them, then?'

'You are sharp, Sister. Alas, I do not have the precise way with words that you do.'

'Why do you think Father Ibor hanged himself having fled with these valuable items?'

'To avoid capture?'

'Your reply is in the form of a question. You mean that you are not sure of this fact either?'

Brother Finnlug shrugged. 'It is difficult for me to say. I cannot understand why a priest should take his life in any event. Surely no priest would commit such a sin?'

'Would you say that you cannot be sure that Father Ibor took his life?'

Brother Finnlug was startled. 'Did I say that?'

'You implied it. Tell me, in your own words, what happened during the last two days. Had there been any tension between Ibor and Febal or any one else?'

Finnlug set his jaw firmly and stared at her for a moment.

'I did hear Father Ibor arguing the night before he disappeared.'

Fidelma leant forward encouragingly.

'Arguing? With Father Febal?'

Brother Finnlug shook his head.

'I cannot be sure. I passed his cell and heard his voice raised. The other voice was quiet and muffled. It was as if Father Ibor had lost his temper but the person he was arguing with was in control.'

'You have no idea who this other person was?'

'None.'

'And you heard nothing of the substance of the argument?'

'I caught only a few words here and there.'

'And what were these words?'

'Nothing that makes sense. Ibor said: "it is the only way". Then he paused, and after the other person said something, he replied: "No, no, no. If it has to end, I shall not be the one to end it." That was all I heard.'

Fidelma was quiet as she considered the matter.

'Did you interpret anything from these words, especially in the light of what subsequently happened?'

Brother Finnlug shook his head.

The door of the vestry suddenly opened and Father Febal stood on the threshold; his features wore a peculiar look of satisfaction. He was clearly a man who had heard some news which pleased him.

'We have found the thief who took the crucifix and chalice from Father Ibor,' he announced.

Brother Finnlug rose swiftly to his feet. His eyes flickered from Father Febal to Sister Fidelma. Fidelma saw something in his eyes and could not quite interpret the expression. Was it fear?

'Bring the thief forth,' she instructed calmly, remaining seated.

Father Febal shook his head. 'That would be impossible.'

'Impossible?' asked Fidelma with a dangerous note to her voice.

'The thief is dead.'

'You'd best explain,' Fidelma invited. 'In detail. Does this thief have a name?'

Father Febal nodded. 'Téite was her name.'

There was a deep intake of breath from Brother Finnlug.

'I take it that you knew her, Brother Finnlug?' Fidelma turned her head inquiringly.

'We all did,' replied Father Febal shortly.

'Who was she?'

'A young girl who lived not far from our community in the forest. She was a seamstress. She sewed garments for our community. She also laundered clothes for us.'

'Where was she found and how was she identified as the thief?'

'Her cabin is within a short distance of where we found Father Ibor,' explained the priest. 'I understand from Brother Adag that she had picked up some garments from the community, and when she did not return with them this morning, as she had arranged, Brother Adag went to her cabin and found her . . .'

Fidelma raised a hand to silence him.

'Let Brother Adag come forth and tell me his story in his own words. It is proper that I hear this matter at first hand. You and Brother Finnlug may wait outside.'

Father Febal looked uncomfortable.

'I think that you had better be warned, Sister.'

'Warned?' Fidelma's head came up quickly to stare at the priest.

'Brother Adag is slightly simple in nature. In many ways his mind has not matured into adulthood. His role in our community is to do simple manual tasks. He . . . how shall I explain it? . . . has a child's mind.'

'It might be refreshing to speak with one who has remained a child and not developed the contrived attitudes of an adult,' Fidelma smiled thinly. 'Bring him hither.'

Brother Adag was a handsome youth, but clearly one who was used to taking orders rather than thinking for himself. His eyes were rounded and seemed to hold an expression of permanent innocence; of inoffensive naiveté. His hands were calloused and showed that he was also a man used to manual work.

'You found the body of the woman, Téite, in her cabin, so I am told?'

The young man drew his brows together as if giving earnest consideration to the question before answering.

'Yes, Sister. When she did not arrive here at mid-day, with some garments which she had collected the day before and promised to deliver, Father Febal sent me to fetch them. I went to her cabin and she was lying stretched on the floor. There was blood on her clothing. She had been stabbed several times.'

'Ah? So Father Febal sent you to her cabin?'

The youth nodded slowly.

'How old was this woman, Téite? Did you know her?'

'Everyone knew her, Sister, and she was eighteen years and three months of age.'

'You are very exact.' Fidelma smiled at his meticulous diction, as if he considered each word almost before he uttered it.

'Téite told me her age and, as you ask me for it, I told you.' It was a simple statement of fact.

'Was she pretty?'

The youth blushed a little. He dropped his eyes.

'Very pretty, Sister.'

'You liked her?' pressed Fidelma.

The young man seemed agitated. 'No. No, I didn't.' He protested. His face was now crimson.

'Why ever not?'

'It is the Father's rule.'

'Father Febal's rule?'

Brother Adag hung his head and did not reply.

'Rule or not, you still liked her. You may tell me.'

'She was kind to me. She did not make fun like the others.'

'So, what persuaded you that she had stolen the crucifix and chalice from Father Ibor?'

The young brother turned an ingenuous look upon her. 'Why, the chalice was lying by the side of her body in the cabin.'

Fidelma hid her surprise.

'The chalice only?' She swallowed hard. 'Why would someone enter her cottage, kill her and leave such a valuable item by the body?'

Brother Adag clearly did not understand the point she was making. He said nothing.

'What did you do after you found the body?' she continued after a pause.

'Why, I came to tell Father Febal.'

'And left the chalice there?'

Brother Adag sniffed disparagingly.

'I am not stupid. No, I brought it with me. Father Febal has been searching for it these last two days. I brought it back to Father Febal for safe-keeping. I even searched for the crucifix but could not find it there.'

'That is all, Adag. Send Father Febal in to me,' Fidelma instructed the youth.

The priest entered a moment later and sat down before Fidelma without waiting to be asked.

'A sad tale,' he muttered. 'But at least the matter should be cleared up to your satisfaction now. You may return to give your report to the Abbot.'

'How well did you know this woman, Téite?' asked Fidelma, without commenting.

Father Febal raised his eyebrows a moment and then sighed.

'I have known her since she was a small girl. I went to administer the last rites when her mother died. Téite had barely reached the age of choice then. However, she had a talent with a needle and therefore was able to make a good living. She has lived within the forest these last four years to my knowledge and often repaired or made garments for our community.'

'Did Father Ibor know her?'

Febal hesitated and then gave an odd dismissive gesture with his hand.

'He was a young man. Young men are often attracted to young women.'

Fidelma glanced at the priest curiously.

'So Father Ibor was attracted to the girl?' she asked with emphasis.

'He was in her company more than I found to be usual. I had occasion to reprimand him.'

'Reprimand him? That sounds serious.'

'I felt that he was neglecting his duties to be with the girl.'

'Are you telling me that there was a relationship between Father Ibor and this girl?'

'I am not one to judge such a matter. I know only that they were frequently in one another's company during the past few weeks, almost since the time he arrived at our little community. I felt that he was ignoring his obligation to his community. That is all.'

'Did he resent your admonition?'

'I really have no idea whether he resented my telling him or not. That was not my concern. My concern was to bring him to an awareness of what was expected of him in this community.'

'You did not have an argument about it?'

'An argument? I am . . . I *was* his superior, and when I told him of my concern that should have been an end to the matter.'

'Clearly it was not an end to it,' observed Fidelma.

Father Febal gave her an angry look. 'I do not know what you mean.'

'The events that have unfolded since you told Father Ibor that he was spending too much time with Téite have demonstrated that it was not

337

an end to the matter,' Fidelma pointed out coldly. 'Or do you have some other interpretation of these events?'

Father Febal hesitated. 'You are right. You are implying that the two of them were in the plot to steal the artefacts from the church and, having done so, Father Ibor was overcome with remorse and killed himself . . .' The priest's eyes suddenly widened. 'Having killed the girl first,' he added.

Fidelma reflectively stroked the side of her nose with a forefinger.

'It is an explanation,' she conceded. 'But it is not one that I particularly favour.'

'Why not?' demanded the priest.

'The hypothesis would be that the young priest was so enamoured of the girl that they decided to run away, stealing the valuable objects as a means of securing themselves from want and poverty. We would also have to conclude that, having reached as far as the girl's cabin, the young priest is overcome with remorse. He quarrels with the girl and stabs her to death. Then, leaving the precious chalice by her body, yet curiously hiding the crucifix, he wanders into the forest and, after travelling some distance, he decides he is so distressed that he hangs himself. Furthermore, while hanging, suffocating to death, he is able to take out a knife and stab himself through the heart.'

'What is wrong with that surmise?'

Fidelma smiled thinly. 'Let us have Brother Adag back here again. You may stay, Father Febal.'

The ingenuous young monk stood looking from Fidelma to Father Febal with unstudied innocence.

'I am told that it was you who saw Téite when she came to the community yesterday?'

The boy was thoughtful.

'Yes. It is my task to gather the clothes that need washing or mending and prepare a bundle for Téite.'

'And this you did yesterday morning?'

'Yes.'

'Téite collected them? These were garments for sewing?'

'And two habits for washing. Father Febal and Brother Finnlug had given me . . . They had been torn and one bloodied in the search for Father Ibor.'

'Let me be sure of this,' interrupted Fidelma. 'Téite collected them yesterday morning?'

Brother Adag looked across at Father Febal, dropped his eyes, and shifted his weight from one foot to another.

'Yes, yesterday morning.'

'You are sure that she collected them after the search had been made for Father Ibor then?'

'Yes; Father Ibor was found on the day before.'

338

'Think carefully,' snapped Father Febal irritated. 'Think again.'

The young monk flushed and shrugged helplessly.

Father Febal sniffed in annoyance.

'There you are, Sister, you see that little credit may be placed on this simpleton's memory. The clothes must have been taken before we found Father Ibor.'

The young monk whirled around. For a moment Fidelma thought that he was going to attack Father Febal for both hands came up, balled into clenched fists. But he kept them tight against his chest, in a defensive attitude. His face was red and there was anger in his eye.

'Simple I may be but at least I cared for Téite.' There was a sob in his voice.

Father Febal took an involuntary step backwards.

'Who did not care for Téite?' Fidelma prompted gently. 'Father Ibor?'

'Of course he did not care. But she cared for him. She loved him. Not like . . .'

The youth was suddenly silent.

'I would take no notice of this boy's foolishness, Sister,' Father Febal interposed blandly. 'We all know what happened.'

'Do we? Since we are talking of people being attracted to this young girl, was Brother Finnlug attracted to her?'

'Finnlug?' Brother Adag grimaced dismissively. 'He has no time for women.'

Father Febal looked pained. 'Brother Finnlug has several faults. Women were certainly not one of them.'

'Faults?' pressed Fidelma with interest. 'What faults does he have then?'

'Alas, if only he had the gift of spirituality we would be compensated. He is of use to us only in his ability to hunt and gather food for our table. He is not suited for this religious life. Now, I think we have spoken enough. Let us call a halt to this unhappy affair before things are said that may be regretted.'

'We will end it only when we discover the truth of the matter,' replied Fidelma firmly. 'Truth is never to be regretted.' She turned to the youth. 'I know you liked the girl, Téite. Yet now she is dead and has been murdered. Father Febal's rule does not apply now. You owe it to your feelings for her to tell us the truth.'

The boy stuck out his chin. 'I am telling the truth.'

'Of course you are. You say that Father Ibor did not like Téite?'

'He did not love her as I did.'

'And how did Téite feel to Ibor?'

'She was blinded by Father Ibor's cleverness. She thought that she loved him. I overheard them. He told her to stop . . . stop pestering, that was his word . . . stop pestering him. She thought that she loved him just as Father Febal thought that he loved her.'

The priest rose angrily. 'What are you saying, boy?' he thundered. 'You are crazy!'

'You cannot deny that you told her that you loved her,' Brother Adag replied, not intimidated by the priest's anger. 'I overheard you arguing with her on the day before Father Ibor died.'

Father Febal's eyes narrowed.

'Ah, now you are not so stupid that you forget times and places and events. The boy cannot be trusted, Sister. I would discount his evidence.'

'I loved Téite and can be trusted!' cried Brother Adag.

'I did not love her . . .' Father Febal insisted. 'I do not love anyone.'

'A priest should love all his flock,' smiled Fidelma in gentle rebuke.

'I refer to the licentious love of women. I merely looked after Téite when her mother died. Without me she would not have survived.'

'But you felt, perhaps, that she owed you something?'

Father Febal scowled at her.

'We are not here to speak of Téite but the crime of Father Ibor.'

'Crime? No, I think that we are here to speak of a crime committed against him rather than by him.'

Father Febal paled. 'What do you mean?'

'Téite was murdered. But she was not murdered by Father Ibor. Nor was she responsible for stealing the crucifix nor chalice, which was found so conveniently by her body.'

'How have you worked this out?'

'Send for Brother Finnlug. Then we may all discuss the resolution of this matter.'

They set in the small vestry facing her: Father Febal, Brother Finnlug and Brother Adag. Their faces all wore expressions of curiosity.

'I grant that people behave curiously,' began Fidelma. 'Even at the best of times their behaviour can be strange, but I doubt that they would behave in the manner that is presented to me.'

She smiled, turning to each of them in turn.

'What is your solution to this matter?' sneered the priest.

'Certainly it would not be one where the murder victim appears alive and well after the murderer has hanged himself.'

Father Febal blinked. 'Adag must be mistaken.'

'No. Father Ibor and the artefacts vanished the day before yesterday. You immediately raised the alarm. Brother Finnlug tracked Ibor through the forest and you found him hanging from a tree. Isn't that right?'

'Quite right.'

'Had he killed Téite, as is now being suggested, before he hanged himself, she could not have come to the community yesterday noon to pick up the garments that needed sewing.'

'Why do you discount the fact that Adag might be confused about the day?'

'Because he gave Téite two habits that had been torn and bloodied in the search for Father Ibor, those worn by you and Finnlung when you found him hanging on the tree. Doubtless they will be found in her cabin to prove the point.' Fidelma paused. 'Am I to presume that no one thought to tell the girl that Ibor had just been discovered having hanged himself? She did think she was in love with him?'

'I did not see the girl,' Father Febal replied quickly. 'Brother Adag did.'

'And Brother Adag admits that he loved Téite,' added Brother Finnlug cynically.

The young man raised his head defiantly.

'I do not deny it. But she didn't return my love, she loved Father Ibor who rejected her.'

'And that made you angry?' asked Fidelma.

'Yes. Very angry!' replied Brother Adag vehemently.

Brother Finnlug turned to gaze at his companion in suspicion. 'Angry enough to kill them both?' he whispered.

'No,' Fidelma replied before Brother Adag could put in his denial. 'Ibor and Téite were not killed in anger, but in cold blood. Weren't they, Brother Finnlug?'

Brother Finnlug turned sharply to her, his eyes suddenly dead. 'Why would I know that, Sister Fidelma?'

'Because you killed them both,' she said quietly.

'That's nonsense! Why would I do that?' exploded the monk, after a moment's shocked silence.

'Because when you stole the crucifix and chalice from the church, you were discovered by Father Ibor. You had to kill him. You stabbed him in the heart and then took the body to the forest where you concocted a suicide by hanging. Then you realised the knife wound could not be hidden and so you left the knife lying by his body. As if anyone, hanging by a cord from a tree, would be able to take out a knife and stab themselves in the heart. How, incidentally, was the poor man able to climb to the branch to hang himself? No one has reported to me any means whereby he could have climbed up. Think of the effort involved. The body was placed there by someone else.'

She gazed at Father Febal who was deep in thought. He shook his head, denying he could offer an explanation.

Fidelma returned her gaze to Brother Finnlug. 'You concocted an elaborate plan to deceive everyone as to what had truly happened.'

There was a tension in the vestry now.

'You are insane,' muttered Brother Finnlug.

Fidelma smiled gently.

'You were huntsman to the Lord of Maine. We have already discussed what a generous man he was to those in his service. None went in want, not even when the harvest was bad. When I asked you what reason you had to leave such a gainful employer, you said it was because of your spiritual convictions. Do you maintain that? That you rejected the temporal life for the spiritual life?'

Father Febal was gazing at Brother Finnlug in bemusement. The monk was silent.

'You also revealed to me, unwittingly perhaps, your resentment at the structure of this community. If it was a spiritual life you wanted, this was surely not it, was it?'

Father Febal intervened softly. 'The truth was that Finnlug was dismissed by the Lord of Maine for stealing and we took him in here.'

'What does that prove?' demanded Finnlug.

'I am not trying to prove anything. I will tell you what you did. You had initially hoped to get away with the robbery. The motive was simple, as you told me; the sale of those precious artefacts would make you rich for life. That would appease your resentment that others had power and riches but you did not. As I have said, Ibor discovered you and you stabbed him and took his body to the forest. When you returned, you realised that you had his blood on your clothing.

'The theft was now discovered and Father Febal sought your help. The blood was not noticed. Maybe you put on a cloak to disguise it. You, naturally, led him to Father Ibor's body. Everything was going as you planned. Father Ibor had been blamed for the theft. Now Father Febal was led to believe that Ibor must have killed himself in a fit of remorse. Even the fact that Ibor had been stabbed was explained. The fact that there was little blood on the ground did not cause any questions. You could pretend that the bloodstains were received in the search for Ibor. Perhaps you, Finnlug, came up with the idea that the missing crucifix and chalice had been taken by some robber.

'The following day Téite, unaware, came to collect the sewing and washing. Adag had gathered the washing as usual, including your habit, the bloodstained one. You had not meant the girl to have it. You hurried to her cottage to make sure she did not suspect. Perhaps you had made your plan even before you went there? You killed her and placed the chalice by her side. After all, the crucifix was such as would still give you wealth and property. It was known that Téite and Ibor had some relationship. Everyone would think the worst. All you had to do was return and bide your time until you could leave the community without arousing suspicion.'

Brother Finnlug's face was white.

'You can't prove it,' he whispered without conviction.

'Do I need to? Shall we go to search for the crucifix? Will you tell us where it is . . . or shall I tell you?' She stood up decisively as if to leave the room.

Brother Finnlug groaned, raising his hands to his head.

'All right, all right. It is true. You know it is still hidden in my cell. It was my chance to escape . . . to have some wealth, a good life.'

Father Febal walked slowly with Fidelma to the gate of the complex of buildings which formed the community.

'How did you know where Brother Finnlug had hidden the crucifix?' he asked.

Sister Fidelma glanced at the grave-looking priest and suddenly allowed a swift mischievous grin to flit across her features.

'I didn't,' she confessed.

Father Febal frowned. 'How did you know then . . . ? Know it was Finnlug and what he had done?' he demanded.

'It was only an instinct. Certainly it was a deduction based on the facts, such as they were. But had Brother Finnlug demanded that I prove my accusation, I do not think I would have been able to under the strictures of the proceedings of a court of law. Sometimes, in this business of obtaining proof, more depends on what the guilty person thinks you know and believes that you can prove than what you are actually able to prove. Had Brother Finnlug not confessed, I might not have been able to clear up this business at all.'

Father Febal was still staring at her aghast as she raised her hand in farewell and began to stride along the road in the direction of Cashel.

The historical mystery is too often cosy and tidy; horrible crimes have taken place, admittedly, but in a remote past, idealised through nostalgia or colourful historical detail. Of course, the game is to project a modern mystery sensibility into the past, to turn someone into an avatar of the twentieth-century figure of the official or private detective – hence, those mostly asinine efforts in which Jesus Christ, Jane Austen or Benjamin Franklin crack cases. In the future, will we see 'historical mysteries' about Adolf Hitler, Madonna or Tony Blair? But crime and history wind around each other in a far more interesting manner than this suggests, as writers as diverse as Charles Dickens, Wilkie Collins, Ross MacDonald and James Ellroy understand only too well. In this story, I'm obviously evoking one of the major mystery writers (if unappreciated as such) of the nineteenth century. The stories are so well known now that it's easy to forget that *Treasure Island* and *Strange Case of Dr Jekyll and Mr Hyde* are mysteries, that their first readers didn't know what the Black Spot meant, whether or not Long John Silver was the villain (that's still open for debate) and that . . . gasp! . . . Dr Jekyll *was* Mr Hyde. Like Jim Rockford, a detective from one of my favourite historical periods (the 1970s), I prefer to work on closed cases, and no case in literary history would seem to be more closed than that of the Good Doctor and the Mad Mister. But, perhaps . . .

Kim Newman

Further Developments in the Strange Case of Dr Jekyll and Mr Hyde

Kim Newman

1: Story of the Photograph

Through the lawyer Mr Utterson, who placed the documents before the public, all the world knew the facts in the strange case of Dr Jekyll and Mr Hyde. The slaying of the Member of Parliament Sir Danvers Carew was laid at the door of Edward Hyde, whose self-poisoned corpse was discovered by Utterson in Jekyll's private laboratory. With the publication of the posthumous accounts known as 'Doctor Lanyon's Narrative' and 'Henry Jekyll's Full Statement of the Case', attempts to search for the missing Jekyll were abandoned and his obituary published in *The Times*. Initial scepticism evaporated to be replaced by a species of affrighted credulousness. Though much of the affair remained as murky as the brown fog that clung to London during the months when the murderer was at large, one thing was agreed upon: Jekyll was Hyde, and Hyde Jekyll.

Of all the wonders and horrors of a wondrous and horrid age, the transformation of Jekyll into Hyde was the most wonderful and the most horrible. The sensation-seeking press sponsored attempts to repeat the experiment; to again compound that drug which enabled the respected, middle-aged scientist Jekyll to become the young brute in human form, Hyde. Thus far, as Jekyll himself found, it had proved mercifully impossible to duplicate the impurity of a vital salt which seemed the key to his tragic success. The term 'a Jekyll-and-Hyde character' entered common parlance to denote a duality of personality inherent to some extent in all souls. The doctor's sad example epitomised a struggle between higher and base instincts that makes battlefields of all hearts, and was used to explain the cruelties of archbishops and the kindnesses of thieves.

It was Utterson's intent in publishing the statements of Hastie Lanyon and Henry Jekyll to end the storm of speculation surrounding the death of Hyde and the disappearance of Jekyll. Once the solution was known to the public, he assumed the mystery would cease to be of interest. He

347

would no longer be beleaguered by newspaper reporters or Scotland Yard investigators. He soon realised the assumption was unworldly: in this case, the solution was more fascinating than the mystery, and interest increased tenfold.

Never a clubbable man, Utterson withdrew even from his few involvements in society, to escape the confounded questions that accompanied him everywhere. It seemed a boom time for his practice, but fully nine-tenths of those who secured appointments were revealed as busybodies. Dramatists wished to present the strange case as a blood and thunder production for the stage – with a woman or two written in, of course, to spice the pudding. Clergymen were eager to save each and every divided soul by securing an endorsement for some species of new apostasy. And alienists wanted to claim Jekyll for their own, naming a new-discovered strain of lunacy for him.

Utterson was forced to disengage almost entirely from his practice but could not shuck off the burdensome task of managing Jekyll's estate. The chore was complicated by successive and discredited wills that left the bulk of Jekyll's substantial fortune 'in the event of my death or disappearance' to Hyde or to Utterson himself. Distant relatives of the doctor put in claims against the estate, as did a horde of low people with real or imagined cases for compensation against debts of dissolution run up by Edward Hyde. The lawyer had first heard of Hyde in connection with the trampling in the street of a little girl, an incident witnessed by his cousin Richard Enfield and settled by a sizeable cheque to the child's family drawn on Jekyll's account at Coutt's. Now it seemed every urchin in London had been under Hyde's loose-fitting boots, and their families were righteously determined to make Jekyll's estate pay through the nose for the injury.

His house became his prison, Utterson lamented. While the shut-up mansion of Jekyll was shunned by the superstitious, the lawyer's less impressive town castle was besieged. Even on Sunday nights, when he was wont to divide his attention between a book of divinity and a bottle of gin, he was not unmolested, though now there was a moment of peace. For perhaps the first time in eight months, he was not thinking exclusively of Jekyll and Hyde but of that most English of all concerns, the weather. Tonight the fog was again thick, a gaseous sea eddying through the city. Rising up above the hats of the unwary pedestrian and freezing the knees of the huddled cabbie, fog made reefs of the meaner dwellings and archipelagoes of the streets of detached houses. Fog was a curse, to be sure, a numbing thing that crept through cracks and wisped even in gaslit and coal-warmed homes, but it could be a mercy, a blanket upon the mind and heart, a killing of pain. The book of sermons was closed and the bottle of gin unopened. Utterson heard the ticking of the long case clock in his study and the beating of his own heart. All else was fog.

An urgent knocking came at the door. A hand of dread closed upon Utterson's heart: it would be Jekyll and Hyde again. A new claimant or some fresh crank. One madman, having allegedly duplicated Jekyll's formula, had drunk a bubbling phial of it on Utterson's doorstep; his convulsions climaxed not with physical transformation but extensive dyspepsia.

Utterson's instinct was to shout 'Away to the Devil with you!' and have done with it. The knocking shut off and was not renewed. Yet he had not shouted out. No sooner did he wish not to be bothered than fog swallowed up his botherer. He would have thanked providence and allowed himself a rare smile but experience taught him to be wary of answered prayers.

He stirred himself from his armchair and ventured out into the hallway. A packet lay upon the mat by the door. His caller had made a delivery. Again, this was not unusual. For every blockhead who assailed him in person, another half-dozen put inane proposals or wild theories in writing.

Bending down to pick up the packet, he felt his age in his back and limbs. Some pains were heightened not dulled by the fog. He carried the prize back into his study – his name was printed in an ill-formed hand on the label, misspelled 'Uterson' – and used his penknife to sever the pink string and break the sealing wax. Within brown paper, he found a rough oblong of wood with a sepia-tone photograph pasted to it. The wood was planed as a mount. He recognised a cheap, home-made species of framing. A child might fashion such a thing to preserve a favourite picture from the illustrated press. Yet the photograph was a studio-posed family portrait.

At first, he could see nothing extraordinary in the picture. A man in a sergeant's uniform stood erect by a seated woman in a wicker chair. She was gathering a boy in a sailor suit to her lap while an older girl knelt at her feet. The father's moustache was waxed to points and his eyes were fixed. The boy's hands were blurred because he had not kept them still throughout the exposure. The mother and daughter had identical, rather sad expressions.

From the style of the ladies' dress and the unfashionable stiffness of the pose, Utterson judged the portrait to be about fifteen or twenty years old. He turned the block over and found nothing of interest. There was no note of explanation in the packet and no photographer's card to indicate the studio in which the picture was taken. He was puzzled, though something nagged at him, nastily.

He looked again at the photograph, wondering what message was being sent to him. He did not know this family.

The fog lifted and terror rushed in. One face was familiar, horribly so.

The boy, who seemed eight or nine, was a monkeyish lad, his cap twisted off-centre. There was nothing truly misshapen about the face or the limbs, but he gave an impression of irregularity, even deformity. His young face already reflected a malformation of his soul.

The boy in the picture was Edward Hyde. Mr Hyde as a child. But Jekyll was Hyde. There had never been a boy Hyde. And yet here he was.

2: E.H.

Two days after the arrival of the photograph, Utterson received in the morning post a note in the same hand – and with the same misspelling – as the address on the packet. It announced that the sender would call on the lawyer that afternoon and was signed with the initials 'E.H.'

His caller was a small woman of perhaps thirty-five. He admitted her into his home and saw her in his study. She was obviously not entirely of the gentle classes, but neither was there anything in her dress or manner to suggest complete degradation. Her clothes were not new but were neat.

'My name is Ellen Hyde,' she announced.

Utterson looked at her face and saw the resemblance. He had once confronted Edward Hyde and tried to warn him away from his friend, Jekyll. Ellen Hyde had the same eyes and the same undefinable cast to her features. She was not unattractive but there was something about her face, her very posture, that was hostile, sly, repulsive. Yet he could not but pity her.

'I am the girl in the photograph,' she said.

'And the boy . . . ?'

'. . . is my brother Ned.'

He had thought himself prepared for this but his knees gave him gyp. He had to sit down.

'Edward Hyde,' she underlined.

The woman stood over him, merciless. She was barely five feet tall, but there was a wiry strength to her. Her hands were habitually knotted into fists.

He felt obliged to explain himself.

'Attempts were made to uncover Hyde's past,' he insisted, 'by Inspector Newcomen of Scotland Yard and later by myself. We made every effort to trace any family.'

'I am all that's left of us. And I made every effort not to be found, Mr Utterson. You know what it means to be associated with Mr Hyde. Imagine what it means to bear his name. Not that it's the one he was born with. He took it from me, the devil. From my husband, rather. Then he took my husband. He was like that as a boy. If I had a toy, it had to be his to break. If I had a pet, it was for his pleasure to torment. My husband, the real Mr Hyde, is dead now. Just like Ned.'

He imagined the lad in the photograph breaking a doll or throttling a cat, building a sand-castle or whipping a spinning top. Even before reading Henry Jekyll's statement, Utterson had never considered what Edward Hyde might have been like as a child. Since the fantastic story had come out, he had believed Hyde to be a creature without a childhood. New-born in Jekyll's laboratory, instilled from his first consciousness with a singular and malign intellect, he had not grown and developed like others.

'And your parents?' he prompted.

Utterson handed her the photograph, which she looked at and slipped into a pocket.

'Father died months after this was taken,' she said. 'In India, of some disease. Mother was never the same. It wasn't as if he'd been killed in a war. Then there'd have been medals and a pension. Some disgraceful thing caught from a native girl fetched him away. Or maybe something he had all along, that he bequeathed to us all. Mother . . . well, I needn't say how it took her, or where Ned and me were left. I sometimes think it might have been best to be born in the depths rather than descend to them. We always had the memory, you see, of how things had been, and knew there was a better life than the one we were reduced to.'

'You have my deepest sympathy, Mrs Hyde.'

The woman grimaced as if to laugh bitterly, then accepted his sentiment.

'It's no use blaming anyone or anything, Mr Utterson. We have all made of ourselves what we would. Plenty have gone down Ned's road with the encouragement of a father and the love of a mother. It doesn't matter whether it was in his nature or he was driven to it. It was always a toss-up as to whether he would end up on the gallows for some other poor devil, or whether the other poor devil would end up on the gallows for him.'

Utterson was puzzled, almost beyond enduring. A pain in his head joined those in his limbs.

'Mrs Hyde, I can't put this all together. You must appreciate how difficult this has been for me, to learn of my good friend Henry Jekyll that he was involved in such a bizarre affair, that he was *transformed* somehow into this Hyde. And now, you come forward, with the revelation that there was an *original* Mr Hyde, an individual independent from Dr Jekyll. Are you suggesting your brother was the model for what Jekyll became? Did Jekyll's Hyde apprentice himself to your Ned, perhaps murder and replace him?'

'I read what that man Lanyon wrote and the confession Jekyll left. I can't account for what either of those *gentlemen*' – she bit down on the word – 'might have meant. But there was only one Ned I know of, and the world is well quit of him. His very name has justly become a byword for the beast in man. The illustrated papers always depict him as a monster, as a fanged human ape in fancy clothes that don't fit. He was a monster all right, just not the sort you read about in penny dreadfuls. Somehow, people like it when a person is all good or all bad. They don't want to hear about reasons. Jekyll-and-Hyde mixes all that up but still doesn't make it any clearer. If *anyone* was all bad, it was Ned. But he had a hard life and he was always afraid. He wasn't just the fiend in the fog. He was a frightened man, a *little* man. He hurt people because he had been hurt. He was weak and without power, so he looked for those weaker than himself to be master over. If he hadn't done the things he did, you'd be sorry for him.'

Utterson recalled Enfield's description of Hyde after the trampling of the child, a small man seized by an angry mob, 'with a kind of black, sneering coolness – frightened, too, I could see that – but carrying it off, sir, really like Satan.' Utterson had found Hyde pale and dwarfish, giving the impression of deformity without any nameable malformation, with a displeasing smile and a bearing that was a sort of murderous mixture of timidity and boldness. In retrospect, the worst of Hyde was his insignificance; he seemed a man without even the courage of his vices, the sort of small boy who acts the bully and then hides behind tears. Only when he bludgeoned a Member of Parliament did anyone really take notice of him.

'But I'm not sorry for him,' Ellen Hyde continued. 'And I'm not sorry for myself either.'

Utterson saw the woman's determination, and recognised in it a sibling to Hyde's fixed nature. He had no conception of Ellen Hyde's morals or behaviour, no idea whether she earned her keep as the worst harlot in Soho or the most angelic nurse in a charity hospital. Yet he discerned a reflection of her brother in the eyes, in the set of the shoulders, the unconscious darting of her tongue, the movements of her large hands. Elements of the likeness was evident even in the photograph, not only in the children but in the parents.

'You will forgive me my puzzlement and must allow that you have further muddied waters which were far from clear in the beginning. Of the many things I do not understand, the most paramount is not to do with Mr Hyde but with yourself. Mrs Hyde, what service might I perform for you?'

She smiled and for a moment the evil of Edward Hyde burned fully in her eyes. Except it wasn't evil, really. Just slyness.

'Now we come to it,' she said. 'You are the executor of Dr Jekyll's estate. I know what that means because I have taken pains to find out.'

'Indeed. There are many things not yet settled.'

'It is my understanding that Dr Jekyll left everything to my brother. What was the phrase, "in the event . . . "?'

'". . . of my death or disappearance or unexplained absence". It is an unusual clause.'

Ellen Hyde extended a bony finger, making a point.

'My brother was found dead in Jekyll's laboratory, *after Dr Jekyll's disappearance*. I am my brother's only living relative. When he died, he should have inherited Jekyll's fortune. Now that money is due to me.'

Utterson could not have been more surprised if Ellen Hyde had kissed him. In an instant, he wondered why he had not seen this coming. The case had always been so wrapped up with the weird he had quite forgotten that, at bottom, it was about money.

Without mirth, he barked laughter.

Ellen Hyde glared death at him.

'And what do you find so amusing, Mr Utterson?'

'It is time I retired,' he said, shutting off his laughter as if it were a flowing tap. 'That I could have been so taken in. In the case of Jekyll and Hyde, we are so desperate for an *explanation*. Not just a solution, but an explanation. It was so hard to accept the truth when it came out that you were able to open it all up again, to unpick all the answers and throw me back to all the questions. And yet, in the end, you overplayed your hand. You are quite the most entertaining of the many claimants, Mrs Hyde. Is that indeed your name? I rather think it might be. Your story has touched my flinty old heart and darts in and out of the established facts so cunningly that I admit I am shaken by it, but its conclusion undoes all the good work. You ask for money.'

'Only what is legally mine.'

'Not necessarily. Even if you are who you say you are and bear the relationship to Edward Hyde that you claim, then your entitlement to the Jekyll estate is moot. Quite apart from the existence of a later though equally disputable will in which I am myself the sole legatee, the fortune was to go to Hyde only if Jekyll's disappearance exceeded three calendar months. Jekyll was seen only days before the time of Hyde's death. Hyde was dead long before he might have inherited the estate and with him died any claim you might have made.'

'Another lawyer might disagree with you.'

'Perhaps. But most judges would not.'

Ellen Hyde left Utterson's house. Only now did he allow himself a glass of gin. He wished fervently never again to hear the names of Jekyll or Hyde, but knew that was in vain. Whether or not he was ever bothered by the woman again, she had reopened the case. It would have to be raked over and with each new examination the business became more painful.

3: *The Broken Key*

One of the sadnesses brought into Utterson's life by the case of Jekyll and Hyde was the curtailment of the weekly rambles he had been wont to take with his cousin, the man-about-town Enfield. Neither had called a halt to their meetings but both were jarred out of their orbits by their parts in the now-famous story. He felt Enfield rather resented being roped into the tale: as a witness to Hyde's first recorded crime, the trampling of the girl. As an indication of a connection between the good doctor and the disreputable villain, Enfield's testimony was the beginning of the thread that had led to the revelation that they were one and the same.

Since publication of the truth, Enfield had been travelling abroad. Utterson knew his cousin had lately returned from the South Seas and reopened his London house. He had intended to make overtures towards the resumption of their association as soon as he was himself free of the entanglements of Jekyll and Hyde. Ellen Hyde having forced his hand, he found himself on Enfield's front steps. A footman opened the door and admitted him into a warm, well-lit hallway.

'Why, it's Gabriel Utterson,' declared Enfield, from the landing above. 'Good old Utterson, come to call. This is a cause for celebration.'

Enfield's reception was warm and sincere and made Utterson sorry he had stayed away. His cousin clapped him around the shoulders and dragged him into a comfortably appointed den. The walls were liberally decorated with exotic fetishes and other souvenirs of Enfield's voyages.

Wine was poured and toasts drunk.

'I see at once that something troubles you, Utterson,' said Enfield. 'It is Jekyll and Hyde again, isn't it. Curse their memory. Or should it be his memory?'

'I can keep nothing from you, Enfield.'

Utterson told his cousin of his meeting with Ellen Hyde and of her claim to a prior relationship with Edward Hyde.

'There was a photograph, you say? I've heard tell they can play some tricks with plates and exposures.'

It was not Utterson's impression that the family portrait was manufactured from whole cloth, but it was reassuring to hear Enfield's opinion that it might have been.

'The rummest thing is that your caller posed as Hyde's sister. If she'd presented herself as his wife, then she could have made her claim without asking you to discredit everything we've learned of Jekyll's double life. Then again, who'd have married Hyde? I knew at once he was a fellow with no use for women. You come across chaps like that from time to time. In the islands, all sorts of degenerates and outcasts gather. They pester the native youths.'

Utterson was disturbed by Enfield's line of thinking. It was, apart from its distastefulness, a distraction.

'I no longer know what to think,' Utterson confided. 'When I read what Lanyon and Jekyll wrote, I didn't believe it. Who *could* believe something like that? I'm not a scientist, but it seemed impossible that a drug could change one man into another, twist his soul from the good to the bad. Then, with the evidence before me, I was forced to believe. All questions, every aspect of the mystery, was answered. If Jekyll was Hyde, it made sense. Now if Jekyll and Hyde were two separate people, mystery returns like the tide crashing over a pebble beach.'

Enfield refilled Utterson's glass and lit a long pipe with a coal from the fire.

'You're a good lawyer, Utterson. Look to the evidence, argue the case, pick it apart. Consider the clues: what proof do you have to support Jekyll's confession?'

'Many minor matters and one very great one. To state the obvious, no one has come forward to testify that they saw Henry Jekyll and Edward Hyde at the same time. The first clue that was presented was that Jekyll showed me a letter which purported to be from Hyde. Questioning Poole, the butler, I later discovered this could not, as Jekyll had told me, have been delivered to him by special messenger. Furthermore, Mr Guest, my head clerk and an expert in these matters, believed the letter to be the work of Jekyll himself, disguising his hand.'

'So we think Jekyll wrote a letter, purporting to be Hyde,' Enfield said, puffing on his pipe. 'At the time, your assumption was that Henry Jekyll was forging for a murderer, trying to throw the police off the track by making it seem as if Hyde had fled the country. That might still be the case, if there was some other tie between them – blackmail, as I at first assumed – without needing to involve fabulous potions or miraculous transformations.'

'Indeed,' Utterson said. 'Other circumstances like that could be open to similar explanation. The evidence for the transformation comes to us in Jekyll's statement, which is at least partially corroborated by a log-book of his experiments. The book certainly concerns a series of trials with a drug of his own devising, and of the desperate attempts later made to reduplicate the impurity that led to his first successes. The most convincing corroboration, however, is the statement left by Dr Lanyon.'

'Ah yes, the fellow who *saw* Hyde turn into Jekyll.'

'That is correct. Lanyon was Jekyll's old mentor, before breaking with him after a quarrel which, as Lanyon had it, "would have estranged Damon and Pythias". Hyde, wanted for murder, barged into Lanyon's house with a note from Jekyll, demanding Lanyon secure from Jekyll's laboratory the ingredients for a potion. Hyde mixed up the solution in Lanyon's presence and drank it. Lanyon says Hyde turned into Jekyll before his eyes and swore him to silence. Lanyon left a memoir of this incident, but never spoke of it. Three weeks later, he was dead of shock.'

'I suppose Jekyll or Hyde couldn't have forged Lanyon's narrative?'

Utterson considered the suggestion. 'The document, marked for my attention alone and to be read only after the death or disappearance of

Dr Jekyll, was included with other papers in Lanyon's hand and passed to me upon his death. The same Mr Guest who adjudged Hyde's letter to be the work of Jekyll cast an eye over the narrative and declared it to be in the hand of Hastie Lanyon. Besides, it was entrusted to me – though not of course opened – before I came into possession of the Jekyll statement which corroborates its account of that incident and enlarges upon its circumstances, giving a full explanation not only of Hyde's fatal visit to Lanyon but of the whole course of experimentation that led Jekyll to compound his drug and become addicted to its effects.'

Enfield was thoughtful. 'Even so,' he rejoindered, 'you've only the word of two dead men. They can't go into a court and be cross-examined. Could Lanyon and Jekyll have cooked the whole thing up between them?'

'It is my judgement that the estrangement between them was genuine. It was, as you know, awkward for me to be so close professionally and personally to them both during the period of their virulent quarrel. I always had the sense of being excluded on the grounds that they were explorers in a country I could never visit. Their conversations were full of queer leaps and ellipses a layman like myself could never follow. They were like a father and son or an old married couple who have their own private history and language. This mystery also was something that seemed settled by the revelation of Jekyll's experiments. I had thought that at last I understood what it was they could never quite discuss when I was there, what secret passions they shared. The root of their quarrel was Lanyon's inflexibility in the face of Jekyll's unwise daring, his devotion to scientific truth, to the demonstrable. It would have been completely out of character for him to collaborate in a hoax, no matter what the reason for it.'

'Don't you see, Utterson: all you've proved is that Lanyon believed what you came to believe when you read Jekyll's statement, what we've all come to believe. Damn it man, forget belief; give me evidence. What makes *you* so sure Jekyll was Hyde.'

The comfortable warmth of Enfield's den receded as a fog of memory drifted in, dimming the gaslight, throwing into relief the hideous faces of carved idols that snarled like Edward Hyde. Sharks' teeth eyes glittered like those of Ellen Hyde. Utterson was taken back to the end of it all, when it seemed Jekyll was held hostage within his laboratory by Hyde. With Poole, the butler, and Bradshaw, the footman, Utterson had broached the door and found Hyde still twitching but dead, apparently poisoned by his own hand, shrouded in Jekyll's clothes, leaving behind Jekyll's confession.

'Before I read that document, my fear was that Hyde had murdered Jekyll before ending his own life,' Utterson said. 'We searched for a body or a grave but found neither. Then, hoping that Jekyll had escaped his tormentor and lived still, we tried to find another way out.

As you know, we found none. Not only was the only other door to the laboratory locked, but it was curtained over with cobwebs. There was undisturbed dust and filth everywhere, around the windows, covering every possible place of concealment. Then, I read Jekyll's statement, and all seemed clear.'

'Hyde could not have killed Jekyll and concealed his body, or thrown him out of the laboratory?'

Utterson shook his head. 'The most important item of evidence was the broken key. By his own account, Jekyll tried to banish Hyde from his life. He broke the key to the backdoor – through which Hyde was wont to come and go – shutting his other half out of his house. This symbolic rejection did not keep Hyde down for long, but it did in the end serve to trap him in the laboratory. At the conclusion of his statement, Jekyll asks "will Hyde die upon the scaffold, or will he find courage to release himself at the last moment"? My assumption is that Jekyll carried the thought of suicide through the transformation. Hyde took Jekyll's last advice and poisoned himself.'

'Did the doctor leave the poison out for his other self? Like the cat's milk?'

Utterson thought of it, imagined the final metamorphosis. Hyde must have been desperate again, the little man trapped but with his protector gone. Was it courage or cowardice that drove him to the poison?

'It is definite that Jekyll went into his laboratory and that Hyde was found dead there,' said Utterson, repressing the chill. 'If Jekyll was not Hyde, the question would remain: where is he, alive or dead? The only solution to this, which we must consider a "locked-room mystery", is that Jekyll and Hyde were one. Jekyll's statement confirms this.'

'And so your mystery is solved again?' asked Enfield.

'In my mind, yes,' said Utterson. 'But this affair goes beyond the reach of my mind. In the light of day, we know Jekyll was Hyde, but in the dark of night, with the fog rising around everything, the mystery stands.'

'Talk is all very well, Utterson, but we need action. We must visit the scene of the crime. You still have the keys to Jekyll's house?'

It was what he had been expecting, and dreading. His cousin was right. They would have to go back to the place where Jekyll had lived and Hyde died.

4: The House of Dr Jekyll

Utterson and Enfield walked again, not with the aimlessness of their former rambles but with purpose. Their course took them through the by-street where Enfield had first encountered Edward Hyde. The infamous back door was nailed shut: Utterson had commissioned the job himself, to keep the curious and the morbid from breaking in. A fearful obscenity was chalked upon the door, but a single red rose had been laid on the step as if on a grave. Those were the tributes rightfully earned by the odious Mr Hyde and the sainted Dr Jekyll. Or was the rose intended – by Ellen perhaps – for the monster and the oath for the good doctor?

'You recall the last time we passed this way?' prompted Utterson. 'Not when you told me the story of the child, but later.'

Enfield nodded. He took a draught of whiskey from a flask, cursorily offering it to Utterson for his refusal.

'We saw Jekyll at his window,' Enfield said. 'He was on the point of inviting us in when something struck him and he withdrew suddenly.'

Utterson, stepping out of character, took the flask and – to his cousin's surprise – indulged in a healthy swallow. The liquor was a fire in his throat, but didn't serve to keep out the chill of the fog.

'I've often dwelled upon that moment. It was the last time I saw the face of Henry Jekyll. It seems we narrowly avoided witnessing one of his transformations. The seizure which made him bar us from his house was the beginnings of the frightful metamorphosis.'

Enfield took the flask back. The two men emerged from the side-street and stood before the impressive frontage of Dr Jekyll's mansion. Beside the door was a shining brass plate, announcing 'Dr Henry Jekyll, M.D, D.C.L., LL.D., F.R.S., etc.' Some of the upper windows were broken. The place had stood empty since the disbanding of Jekyll's household. Faithful Poole was retired on the small legacy left by his master and the others gone to fresh situations.

Utterson took out the ring of keys. As executor, it was his duty to take care of the house until the estate was settled. He had already arranged for the repair of one set of windows, and was now irritated that more had been broken. This must be the district's haunted house, he thought, the lair of the monster. It would be a place of fascination and horror for children, and not a few who should be more sensible.

'Are we going in?' ventured Enfield, not quite managing to sound intrepid.

Utterson found the long key to the front door and turned it in the lock. The gas was shut off, so it was necessary to hunt around by the light of a lucifer match for a candle left in the hallway. He had himself placed the candle there, having once before been required to be in the house after dark to pay the glazier. The candle was not where he had thought it would be, but Enfield discovered it and touched a flame to the wick.

'That's odd,' Enfield said, looking down at the doormat.

'What?'

'When I opened up my house after returning from abroad, I had to wade through the sea of circulars and letters piled up in the hall-way.'

Utterson proceeded down the hallway. If answer there was to the case, it would be found here.

The two men passed through the house and, unlocking new doors, crossed the dismal courtyard to the building at the rear of the mansion that had served Jekyll as a laboratory and Hyde as a last redoubt. The door hung slightly ajar, its lock burst the night Hyde died. Utterson pushed the door open, and they stepped into the laboratory.

Enfield whistled. Utterson realised his cousin had never been there before.

Candlelight was reflected in dozens of glass surfaces. Cases of instruments lined the walls, complex arrangements of retorts and tubes stood on the benches and a full-length cheval glass was erected in a frame in the middle of the large room. Utterson remembered Hyde, dead but writhing at the foot of the long mirror. His position on the floor was still clearly marked by a stained rug that had been disturbed by his death throes. Here, the monster had turned upon himself. Here, Utterson had thought, the monster was born.

Enfield was taken with the cheval glass, which was angled so anyone laid out on a divan could study his own reflection. He held up the candle and looked at himself. Shadows moved on his face, lending his features strange expressions.

'When he changed, he observed the process?' Enfield ventured.

'That's what we assumed,' Utterson agreed. 'Poole said the glass "had seen some strange things".'

'Maybe Jekyll liked looking at himself. He had more than a touch of vanity, wouldn't you say? D'you remember that string of degrees trailed after his name on the plate outside? Even on his calling cards? That "et cetera" tells a lot. And Hyde was full of himself too. That sort always is. Like a woman, obsessed with looks, and not averse to a spot of paint and powder.'

They came at last to Jekyll's desk, where his full statement had been left for Utterson, along with a will cutting out Edward Hyde and making Utterson himself beneficiary of the estate. It had not proved valid and Utterson could not say he was sorry; he had no need of a fortune, and the temporary custodianship of this house was burden enough without the strain of actual ownership.

'This is where you found it? Jekyll's story?'

'Indeed.'

Enfield held the light over the desk. Everything was neat and tidy. There wasn't even any dust. Utterson had arranged for the house to be cleaned, but neglected the laboratory. Madame Tussaud's had made an offer for the contents, which he had rejected out of hand.

Utterson had a crawling feeling. Someone must have been here.

'Supposing your lady caller' – Utterson blushed at Enfield's allusion to Ellen Hyde – 'to be telling the truth, then previous searches of this place have missed something. Either Jekyll is still here, or there is some way of escape. The doctor is dead or fled.'

359

'We made an extensive search. Every inch was gone over, looking for loose flagstones, or a grave.'

'Could Hyde have killed Jekyll and disposed of him completely? Dissolved the corpse in acid, perhaps?'

'No acid was found. And no evidence of such butchery.'

'You considered the floor? What about the ceiling?'

'The attic cabinet above the laboratory is windowless. There is no way of egress through it.'

'Not the roof, the ceiling. I scent an old tiger hunter's trick. You don't need an escape hatch to pull off a locked-room mystery if you can contrive a place of perfect concealment. If Jekyll is dead, he might be there still. If he is fled, he would merely have had to *hide* and emerge later when you had all departed.'

Enfield raised the candle. The laboratory was a high-ceilinged space. A network of pipes and gas-jets had lit it from above. These cast a grid-like shadow on the painted ceiling. It was not hard to imagine Hyde swinging from the pipes like a monkey, as a servant had described him.

'Take the candle a moment,' Enfield said.

Utterson did so.

'Now leave the laboratory and come back.'

Irritated by his cousin's frivolity, which betokened a childish streak he had often found as irksome as it was endearing, Utterson complied with Enfield's request. He stepped out into the courtyard, where thick fog pooled waist-deep and misty strands spiralled upwards in some draught, and closed the laboratory door behind him. After a few moments, he turned around and opened the door again, crossing the threshold.

Enfield was gone. Utterson felt no panic, no terror. His cousin had seen through the trick and duplicated it. He would bound back in again soon, having slipped out somehow to the street. Utterson turned, expecting Enfield to make his way around the house and in through the front door.

He looked up at the ceiling. That was where Enfield had found the clue.

A minute or so passed. Enfield did not return. Utterson had a pricking of irritation. His cousin was showing off more than was seemly, prolonging the moment of his triumph.

Utterson peered again up beyond the network of gas-jets. The shadows on the ceiling were strange, swelling like the fog. There was a straining sound.

The ceiling cracked open and a heavy, loose bundle fell on to him. The candle-flame was snuffed and complete darkness obtained within the laboratory.

Utterson lay under the dead-weight of a man.

There were quick footsteps and a boot trod on one of his hands. He heard the door open. Fog and the faintest traces of light crept in.

He threw off the weight of the warm body and found his lucifers. He struck a match; a flare showed him the red, swollen face of Richard Enfield.

He felt his cousin's neck and found a pulse. Enfield had been throttled to unconsciousness but still lived.

Hyde was back, to plague the memory of Henry Jekyll.

Utterson found the candle and lit it again. His shoulders were shaking but he forced his hands to be steady. He knew another had been in the laboratory, concealed in the bolt-hole Enfield found. When Enfield clambered up to the ceiling and discovered the trap-door – which Utterson now saw was hanging down like an idiot's tongue – the interloper assaulted him and kept him close. Only their shared weight exploded the hiding-place.

Along with footsteps, Utterson had heard a rustle of skirts. He knew who had been in the dark with them, who had trodden on his hand.

It always came back to Hyde. This time, it was the sister.

Enfield coughed and spluttered out of his swoon. He tried to sit up.

'Some devil was in wait,' he got out. 'Some long-fingered devil.'

'You've had a near thing,' Utterson said. 'I was afraid you'd gone the way of Sir Danvers Carew.'

He set the candle down on Jekyll's desk and a talon scraped his spine. In the exact same spot where he had once found the envelope containing Dr Jekyll's Full Statement of the Case lay an identical packet. On it, in a familiar hand, was written his own name.

The last envelope had promised a solution but left only more mystification. What would this contain? Utterson turned it over in his hands. Would it be best to touch its corner to the candle-flame and let its contents burn unread? He knew he could never take that measure.

Whatever was within, he must know.

5: *Henry Jekyll's Further Statement of the Case*

I ask you to consider again the opening words of my original statement:

'I was born in the year 18 – to a large fortune, endowed besides with excellent parts, inclined by nature to industry, fond of the respect of the wise and the good among my fellow men, and thus, as might have been supposed, with every guarantee of an honourable and distinguished future. And indeed the worst of my faults was a certain impatient gaiety of disposition, such as has made the happiness of many, but such as I found it hard to reconcile with my imperious desire to carry my head high, and wear a more than commonly grave countenance before the public. Hence it came about that I concealed my pleasures; and that when I reached years of reflection, and began to look around me and take stock of my progress and position in the world, I stood already committed to a profound duplicity of life. Many a man would have even blazoned such irregularities as I was guilty of, but from the high views that I had set before me, I regarded and hid them with an almost morbid sense of shame. It was thus rather the exacting nature of my aspirations than any particular degradation in my faults that made me what I was, and with even a deeper trench than in the majority of men, severed in me those provinces of good and ill which divide and compound man's dual nature.'

Further, let me draw your attention to the phrase 'a certain gaiety of disposition'. Men like myself often wink at their audiences, flirting with revelation but stopping just short of the outright declaration of our nature. It is a harmless trait, even endearing. However, the time for such flirtation is ended, and I wish in this statement finally to set the record straight. I am well aware that what I have to say of my life – though far less outlandish than the improbable fiction I was forced in haste to compose – will not be publishable. Many will accuse me of hypocrisy in the life I have led and the actions I have taken, but ask yourselves: what manner of society is it that will concede the possibility of one man transforming entirely into another through the agency of a magic potion, but shuts minds to the actuality of love, in the fullest senses of the word, between one man and another?

I loved Edward Hyde. I love him still.

I have never had any use for women. For many years, I was forced to compound the duality of my life with a further duality. While I was for many years friend and companion to my old mentor Hastie Lanyon, physical intimacies between us were unsatisfactory to my tastes. Lanyon introduced me to my nature, opened for me the book of uranian desires, but was a timid explorer of his own potential. From an early age, as I suggested in the statement quoted above, I have searched elsewhere for a form of love that can be purchased in any city in the world. There are houses in London, districts even, that cater to the tastes of men like myself.

It is not my purpose to justify my predilections, but experience has taught me that they are shared by many: Members of Parliament, Ministers of Religion, Captains of Industry, Officers of the Armed Forces. Our secret history is written between the chapters of the lives of the great and the good. Even monarchs have not been immune to the lusts that sparked – and spark still – in my heart.

When I first met Hyde, singling him out from a knot of gay loiterers in Piccadilly and exchanging a few paltry coins for his favours, I was well past youth. I stood towards the end of the middle of my life having experienced a variety of physical forms of love, but my heart was essentially untouched. I had once thought I could love Lanyon, but my mentor's crankiness, his periods of desperate clinging, had become as irksome to me as the nagging of many a cold wife is to her husband.

Hyde did not return to his fellows. Having first bought him – cheaply

– I kept him. He was the first of his kind I allowed into my home, though I kept him closeted in the cabinet above my laboratory out of sight of the servants. Later I gave instructions to my butler, Poole, that my friend and benefactor was in my absence to be obeyed as if he were myself. Hyde took a delight in bossing my servants; their bitter resentment of taking orders from so low a person accounts for descriptions they have left of him as less than human and worse than a brute. It was a quirk of our relationship that we took care never to be seen in each other's company – Hyde even establishing an address in Soho separate from my own house – and excluded the whole world from our intimacies.

How could I love Hyde? Reports of his person and character suggest him to be a creature beyond the reach of gentle emotion. I concede that what the world knows of Edward Hyde is not distorted. He was cruel, twisted inside, capricious, petty, dishonest, common. Yet, from the first I caught his glittering eye and selected him from a cluster of far prettier fellows, he was inside my heart like a worm in an apple. Gentle emotion could not contain him, but our love was not gentle: it was a violent need, a storm of possession, a fervid hunger that would not be satisfied.

For his part, Hyde returned my love. How could he not, to be taken from the streets and set up in a flat, to be coddled and dressed like a doll, to be a part of the life of the great Dr Henry Jekyll? He loved to wear my clothes, not minding how loose they were on him, just as he loved to bark orders at my servants or gamble and drink away my money.

Lanyon, of course, quarreled with me over Hyde and shut me out of his life, babbling of Damon and Pythias. He blustered that I would be hurt by Hyde as he had been hurt by me, and that I would crawl back into his house a ruin. Hyde and I laughed when I reported the old fool's words. Others would never understand.

In love, it is impossible to tell master from slave. I was vulnerable, for I had much to lose from exposure; throughout everything, my position was of almost paramount importance to me. Yet Hyde too was on perilous ground; he had in the distant past suffered a fall from grace and, having found security in my person as much as my fortune, was terrified of its loss.

We were both cruel. Hyde would threaten to leave me. I would threaten to throw him out. Then our quarrels – which often extended to exchanges of blows – would become caresses, and we would redouble our love, our conjoined search for physical expression of what was in our hearts.

There were periods of remorse. I would turn to books of religion or good works as a way of assuaging not guilt over my nature or my love, but of filling the void where I had been taught – by Lanyon, for instance – that guilt should be. The paradox was that I was ashamed of not being ashamed. At these times, Hyde would abandon me for his Soho rooms and try to excite my jealousy by affecting an interest in others.

363

Hyde was used to bad treatment. His body was marked with the scars of the lash. His peculiar gait, which witnesses have remarked upon, was the result of bones broken and ill-set by a band of drunken sailors who once abducted him and used him for rough pleasures over the space of three days. He bore rope-burns on his wrists from this ordeal, which varied in its titillating particulars with each retelling.

The worst I could do to Hyde was laugh at him. I discovered this early in our association and was unable to refrain from the joy of this especial torment. Was he not, after all, ridiculous? With my fine clothes flopping over his hands and boots, he looked like an organ grinder's monkey dressed up. His ignorance could not but be amusing to one with my education; each mispronounced word tickled my humour, each defence of something he mistakenly understood to be true – that Asia was in Egypt, Scotland over the sea, the bumblebee a small bird – was a prompt to cruel hilarity. When I laughed at him, he became stone-faced, indignant, and stuck by his doomed position, until I would end the game with a hungry kiss.

The walls of our world were the walls of the laboratory. I gave Hyde a key to the back door, an expression he found apt, and he would always return. The world knows of the night he barged in, terrified, and demanded money to settle an account with the family of some street drab he had knocked over. He told me the child had offered to lift her skirts for him for a penny and that he had trampled her in instinctive disgust. I do not necessarily believe that, nor does the girl's character excuse her treatment. It is my belief that Hyde was vicious, in this instance, because he saw in the girl his own face, saw the wretchedness from which he had so lately come and to which he could so easily be forced to return.

There was never an idyll for us. Our love was not an oasis but a jungle. Together we explored, deliberately throwing ourselves into the lairs of dangerous beasts. The slowness that had come over me in my middle years fell away, and I was as enthusiastic as my young adventurer. He was physically smaller than I, and I could always wrestle him to the mat. I came to adore his sobs of pain and joy as he thrust his face against the pillow, tearing the cover with his stubby teeth, while I was his master and lover and tormentor.

Yet my years weighed me down. After our exertions, Hyde was frisky and flushed, eager to take to the streets, while I was drained and exhausted, heart pounding like a hammer against an anvil. Once or twice, I was physically incapable of the basic necessity of the act of love. Hyde would seize mercilessly on my failure, pawing and jeering at my limpness, grinning like a baboon.

Other men, like Lanyon, might have accepted. But I am a medical doctor, a researcher, a chemist. I knew there were drugs which could help me, would help us. In my position, I had access to many substances unknown even in the opium dens of Limehouse. We experimented with compounds of many different elements. More than once, we were almost poisoned and spent a night in each other's arms, retching. But still we persisted, delighted with our successes.

Finally, we found our perfect potion.

We shared it. I would take a mouthful, swallow a little, and pass it into Hyde's mouth through a deep kiss. Under the influence of this tonic, we were invincible and tireless, free of all physical and moral restraints. The effects were as much mental as physical, inducing first a dreamlike period of hallucination then a sudden vivid clarity of the senses accompanied by overpowering urges and the ability to act upon them. I installed a large looking-glass in the laboratory, so we could look upon our reflections as we became one two-faced creature. It seemed to me that in the act of love, we became a single being, a giant pulsating heart.

Our exertions were acrobatic and cacophonous enough on one occasion to wake the household. In my delirium, I discerned Poole's tapping at the laboratory door. We had smashed glasses and given vent to screams of passion. As my servant pestered us, we were naked together, hanging like copulating apes from the gas-pipes. I do not remember which of us ordered the fool away but his interruption was a gnat-bite soon forgotten.

Of course, we became slaves to this drug of my devising. A shared need is a terrible thing. Each was affected in his own way and would recover at a different time. To come to and find Hyde still under the influence was to feel cast out from Eden and to be possessed by a desire to return. And returning was a simple matter of a little mixing and heating. At times, Hyde pleaded with me to make up a new batch of our delight – for it was beyond his talents to do so – and I would withhold acceding to his needs until he had abased himself. At others, I would snap out of a daze filled with panic that he had died of the effects of the drug, and he would titter at me like a girl, gnawing at my nerves. In a rare moment of mutual clarity, he forced me to show him exactly how to mix up the potion, and I tutored him in its making. For an instant, I saw the native intelligence in him that had been dulled by the life he had led, and a new strain of love, sentiment tinged with pity, joined the rapturous addiction that gripped my brain.

In this period, when we were equals, I wrote Hyde into my will. On occasion, he showed himself to my servants. My acquaintances Enfield and Utterson encountered him, and Utterson warned me against him. I listened to reason, for I was never so blind as to think my monster any species of angel, but could not break free of my need. Hyde became more devoted, more clinging, more of a pest. I tried to ration our sessions with the drug, but vows of abstinence never lasted, as one or other of us would break down.

Once, Hyde tried without my assistance to mix the potion. He nearly died, but did not learn his lesson.

The laboratory that had been our world became our prison. In trances or crazes, we only had each other. Eventually, one night in October, one or other of us suggested we venture out into the city to see the metropolis with new eyes. The fog was very beautiful and in it all things were possible.

A maidservant was witness to the unfortunate event. That she did not see my part in it was due to the fact that I was leaning in a daze against the wall directly below her window, a spectator though in some sense also a director.

We found ourselves in a spot Hyde knew from his previous life, and to the spot came a man he knew well, Sir Danvers Carew, MP. You recall the maid's description of Carew as 'an aged and beautiful gentleman with white hair', and may be interested to know that Carew's beauty was not altogether the gift of nature but had been augmented by feminine tricks.

Our shared indulgence in the drug was not an excuse for our actions. As I said in my earlier statement, the drug set free what was always inside us, let loose a part of our nature. Carew approached us and ventured a proposition. It strikes me as horribly funny that the servant, who admitted to being 'romantically given', described his face as he spoke words she could not hear as seeming 'to breathe such an innocent and old-world kindness of disposition, yet with something high, too, as of a well-founded self-content.' Hyde and I were of course beyond moral disgust at Carew's suggestion, but he was an intruder into our haze. Suddenly his presence seemed the spur for a final test of Hyde's devotion.

I told Hyde to kill Carew. As the maid said, 'the old gentleman took a step back, with the air of one very much surprised and a trifle hurt, and at that Mr Hyde broke out of all bounds and clubbed him to the earth. And next moment, with ape-like fury, he was trampling his victim under foot and hailing down a storm of blows, under which the bones were audibly shattered and the body jumped upon the roadway.' Then, unknown to us, the maid – our audience – fainted dead away. She did not see Hyde hand me my own stick to finish the job. It was my blows which snapped the stout cane and caved in the old queen's skull. We were exultant in our shared adventure and returned to my laboratory, heedless of all consequence, to renew our caresses. Sticky with Carew's blood, we rutted until insensibility came over us.

As we slept, the body was discovered and the identity of the murderer became generally known. The maid recognised Hyde as an occasional visitor to the house in which she was in service; which calls into question the nature of the house in which she was employed and perhaps clarifies precisely what she meant by 'romantically given'. Just as we had no idea there had been a witness to our exploit, it was no contrivance of mine that Hyde should take the blame for our shared crime. When I learned of the circumstances and communicated them, Hyde – who seemed peculiarly to be suffering spasms of remorse to which I was myself immune – immediately informed me he had no intention of hanging alone and would, if cornered, do his best to rope me in on the gallows.

'Who would believe you?' I asked him.

He was struck silent and terrified. It might have been the after-effects of the drug, but suddenly he was pathetic again, nagged by a realisation that he alone of all the world was sufficiently wretched to suffer for his crimes while one as respected as I would naturally be allowed free. If the maid had actually seen me take my cane to Carew's head, she would not have believed it. Everyone so wanted Jekyll to be a saint and Hyde to be a monster that any evidence to the contrary would simply not be credited.

He became almost comatose with panic.

When Utterson came to my doorstep, I was forced to fob him off with a letter of my own writing – in a disguised hand – that purported to be from my 'friend and benefactor' Hyde, claiming to have fled the country. It was not the first time I had written something for him. At the time we met, he was almost a complete illiterate though he had a surprising talent for sketching. To amuse myself, I had taught him the alphabet but the only words he was disposed to set down were the obscenities he was wont, in the throes of a drug-fit, to scrawl in my books of theology.

Hyde then became my charge and prisoner. Having broken his key to the back door, it was a simple matter to secrete him in the cabinet above my laboratory. At this time, we collaborated on the construction of a priest hole to be used in the event of a thorough search. A false section of ceiling was put up, creating a space in which a small body could be crammed – when it came to be used, my longer limbs were confined uncomfortably – for an hour or two.

Months passed. I concluded the programme of experiments and shut the book on our drug. There was no more to be learned from it. Hyde squealed and protested but I locked away the ingredients. He far more than I felt the murderous tug of need as we withdrew from the addiction. Yet he was terrified, far more than I, of the monster the drug had made of him.

I endeavoured to order my life. It seemed that as I no longer needed the drug, I no longer needed Hyde. It was not that I cared any the less for him, but the first burning of our love had run its course. Were he not an obligation, I might have cut him loose.

He was a thorny problem. In concealment, he became clinging. As the only soul he saw, I became his master and keeper. He desired me in a way I no longer desired him. He made himself available to me with the sickening devotion of a small dog. He wheedled desperately, trying always to keep on my right side. That in him which had been defiant and cruel and needling was stifled. With this change, I found he became as repulsive to me as to the rest of the world.

When he conceived his project, I misunderstood it entirely. I thought it an indulgence to pass the time, a desperate reversion to some long-forgotten need to better himself. He implored me to help him again learn how to read and write. The letter I had forged from him was his inspiration. It became an obsession with him, and in two months of study – to which he applied himself with sweaty tenacity – he was capable of producing his own letters. It is an irony that his hand became an approximate match for the altered script I had used on his letter, but that should have alerted me to his purpose. To him, this was not an end in itself but part of a trick, a need to simulate.

I was lulled.

In January, I had cause to be away from town for some days. This, I decided, was the time for Hyde to go. To my surprise, he agreed entirely. I gave him money for a cheap lodging room and a ticket for the boat train the next day, assuring him that the search had died down and that he should be able to make his escape from the country. There was more grief on my side and less on his than I had expected, but this would be a clean break and a conclusion to my involvement with Hyde.

From hence forth, there would only be the good Dr Jekyll.

Upon my return, satisfied that Hyde was out of my life but also aware of a certain hollowness, I swept through my house to the laboratory and found the door hung open. Also forced by a locksmith was the safe in which my most dangerous chemicals were kept.

My head spun. Hyde had played a trick, I knew.

At the lodging I had arranged for him, I found imperfectly burned papers, successive drafts of two letters – one to Poole, and one to Lanyon. The hand was a fair forgery of my own. This was what Hyde had been learning. I remembered his knack for sketching, and realised what a good eye he had. Once he was beyond earning a living with his body, he would have the trade of forgery to fall back on.

He had presented himself to Lanyon as my messenger and had Lanyon's man despatched to my own house, where Poole was under orders he supposed to be from me to break into my laboratory and secure the ingredients for our drug.

For months, Hyde had been planning this. And all to secure a supply of the potion to which he was addicted.

Some of this I was able to deduce as I made my way to Lanyon's house, some I learned later. I entered Lanyon's house not by the front door but through French windows at the rear, and came upon the scene just as Hyde had prepared a dose of the drug and was raising it to his lips.

Catching sight of me over Lanyon's shoulder, Hyde was exultant with triumph. He had tricked me at last and become the master. At this moment, he chose to demonstrate his mastery with a gesture of extreme cruelty.

'Lanyon,' he sneered, addressing myself as much as the old man, 'you who have so long been bound to the most narrow and material views, you who have denied the virtue of transcendental medicine, you who have derided your superiors – behold!'

He took a swig of the potion and embraced Lanyon, squirting the drug into his mouth. I stepped forward to protest, but my old friend was seized by the effects of the potion. Well I remembered the burning of the brain, the strange hallucinations, the burst of clarity, the unfettering of desires.

Hyde laughed and held out the bubbling retort to me.

Lanyon was clearly thunderstruck. Had Hyde again mixed a lethal, impure dosage? At that moment, I cared not. The mere whiff of the drug reawakened in me an overpowering need, just as Hyde had known it would.

I took some of the liquid and surrendered to the spell.

Hyde and I tore off our clothes, and Lanyon's. Hyde and I spent our lusts in every way upon my old tutor, forcing him to the indulgence of every pricking desire suppressed over the years. He was maddened, I know, and resisted us, but there was a part of him that joined willingly in our debauch, that was at last freed from the shackles he had placed upon himself.

Exultant, we left Lanyon a wreck. I smuggled Hyde back into my laboratory and slept. When I awoke, I needed more than anything to take another draught of my drug. As I mixed and stirred in a frenzy, Hyde laughed like the Devil. When I threatened to withhold from him the blessed potion, he went down on his knees and begged.

We were chained to each other and to the drug.

The full horror of our situation was soon brought home to us. Supply of vital elements ran low, and I endeavoured to replenish my stock of a certain ingredient. As I have said, 'my provision of the salt, which had never been renewed since the date of the first experiment, began to run low. I sent out for a fresh supply, and mixed the draught: the ebullition followed, and the first change of colour, not the second. I drank it and it was without efficiency. You will learn from Poole how I have had London ransacked; it was in vain; and I am now persuaded that my first supply was impure, and that it was that unknown impurity which lent efficacy to the draught.'

Then, truly, Hyde became the monster he is believed to be. He raged and raved, venting his destructive urges on my person and anything to hand. His plan to ensnare me had succeeded, but had further trapped him as well. As each new experiment failed to produce results and our supplies of the original drug – doled out like water in the desert – dwindled, Hyde took to blaming me for his misfortunes.

If we had been thinking rationally, we should have worried about Lanyon. A message came to me from him and I assumed we were about to be exposed to the world. Though it meant shameful revelations about himself and what he had suffered under us, he would tell the truth.

Those familiar with Lanyon's account of Hyde's visit to his home and of the effects of the potion can imagine my puzzlement upon first reading it. Hyde and I read and re-read Lanyon's demented fantasy, in which Hyde transformed into Jekyll. We were both familiar with the hallucinations that came with the first rush of the drug and of the strange liberation that followed, and I remembered again my theory that many people – especially self-deluded prigs like Lanyon – will strain to believe all manner of incredible things rather than face the truth about themselves or any other outwardly respectable person.

It is plain that Lanyon believed what he wrote: 'He put the glass to his lips, and drank at one gulp. A cry followed; he reeled, staggered, clutched at the table, and held on, staring with injected eyes, gasping with open mouth; and, as I looked, there came, I thought, a change; he seemed to swell; his face became suddenly black, and the features seemed to melt and alter – and the next moment I had sprung to my feet and leaped back against the wall, my arm raised to shield me from that prodigy, my mind submerged in terror. "Oh, God!" I screamed, and "Oh, God!" again and again; for there before my eyes – pale and shaken, and half-fainting, and groping before him with his hands, like a man restored from death – there stood Henry Jekyll!'

The key phrase is 'my mind submerged in terror'. From his experience with the drug and his participation in what followed, he had mixed up Jekyll and Hyde, imposing one upon the other, refusing to admit his own part in our union. The world owes much to Hastie Lanyon, for he is the creator of the myth of Jekyll and Hyde. His mind, affected by our potion, dreamed up the bogy tale for which we are remembered.

What Lanyon sent me was a copy of a letter to Utterson, which would not be opened by the lawyer until my death or disappearance. His narrative was the inspiration for all that followed.

Starved of the potion, I was in hell. Awful pains coursed through my abused body. Hyde was always by my side, insistent, a fellow sufferer, a merciless torturer. I knew, long before he did, that it was hopeless. The drug could never be duplicated.

I would have to be rid of Hyde, in such a way as to conceal the true nature of our relationship. It would be easy to poison him. He drank every experimental potion I handed him, draining it down with a desperate glee that turned instantly to bitter disappointment.

Soon after I heard of the death of Hastie Lanyon, his body and mind too shocked by what we had done to survive, I wrote the memoir which has become known as 'Henry Jekyll's Full Statement of the Case'. A key to my success in this fiction is how close to the truth I stayed, straying only to drag in Lanyon's fantasy of metamorphosis. My true feelings for Hyde and the drug, of the addiction I have to both, are plain for all to read. In composing the statement, I forced myself to an understanding of my own divided soul.

Then, on that last night, Hyde flew out of control. He determined I was concealing from him the last dosage of the original drug – which was true – and endeavoured to beat it out of me. Knowing this was the last of him, I surrendered at once to mercy and murder and yielded the vial of the drug, admixed with a dose of poison.

From the commotion in the courtyard, I knew my servants had at last paid attention to the sounds of violence from within the laboratory. Soon, they would breach the door.

Hyde kissed me with real love and drank the potion. He paused with the vial half-empty, and – displaying character and generosity with which I would not have credited him – offered me the remainder. I declined and he finished the draft, crushing the glass in his hand as the killing seizure took him.

As he fell, the door jarred.

I concealed myself in the priest hole and heard my servants and Utterson searching the building. I thought I might die in my lightless, airless space. However, in my confinement and in all the months of hiding that have followed, I have often wished that I had accepted Hyde's last, unwitting offer of the poisoned drug. To have departed this world in ecstasy hand-in-hand with the other half of my soul would have been a more fit conclusion to my dual life than has been this assumption of living death. Cut off from my fortune, a trespasser in the abandoned ruin of my house, bereft of even my grave (in which Hyde lies), I am become a ghost.

The world believes I died with Edward Hyde. I now think this is the truth. My mind has been permanently affected by my involvement with Hyde and with the drug we compounded for ourselves; and it seems to me that Hyde is with me still, as much a phantom as myself, and that until I rejoin him, I shall not be a complete person. Sometimes I see his smooth face, hear his high voice, transformed again, imploring me to come away from this place. Outside there is only fog.

6: In the Fog

Further search of the property uncovered evidence that a tramp or some other low person had been camping out in what had once been the laboratory of the great Dr Jekyll. However, that person was now fled and all efforts to trace him came to naught. Ellen Hyde, too, disappeared into the fog, never in person to trouble Utterson again.

It seemed Jekyll and Hyde were together again. Without his Hyde, Jekyll was an incomplete person. Had the pathetic remnant of the doctor gone willingly with his victim's sister? Or was there an element of abduction involved? Ellen Hyde remained as much a mystery as her brother. It seemed she had known all along where Dr Jekyll was to be found. It occurred to Utterson that her attempt to come into the inheritance might partly have been for the doctor's benefit, to secure funds for their escape. Yet it was impossible to decide whether 'Sister Hyde' was the rescuer or tormentor of Dr Jekyll.

Drawing on funds from the estate, Utterson commissioned a fresh headstone. Hyde had been buried under the name of Jekyll, but it was not too late to change that. The disgust he had felt for Hyde was if anything increased by what he had learned from Jekyll's second statement, but it was accompanied by a wave of pity that would not be denied. When he thought of Hyde, he remembered the snarling, strutting degenerate, but also the little boy in his mother's lap.

One morning, Utterson and Enfield paid a ritual visit to the grave. The sun was entirely unable to penetrate the gloom of the fog, and they spent some minutes searching the churchyard for the newly erected stone.

'Perhaps we should have had the grave dug up,' Enfield suggested. 'To make sure.'

'Of what?' Utterson asked.

'That there's anyone there. It occurs to me that we might have been hoodwinked again. Or perhaps for the first time. Who knows what effects that damnable drug might have had? Is it not possible Jekyll-and-Hyde only seemed to die, and that he has returned, clawed his way out of the earth. Is it not conceivable that the transformations have become more extreme, more violent, more radical. If Henry Jekyll could become Edward Hyde, could he not also become Ellen?'

In some strange way, it would be more comfortable to believe that.

When they found the headstone of Hyde, they were unsurprised to see it defaced with a blasphemy. However, below the obscene epitaph, a fresh rose was laid upon the grave.